For Casey ♥

Traced in Ash

Veronique Wallrapp

Cup of Tea Publishing
New York

For:
All the mamas of all the angel babies in heaven.
Until you meet again.

Traced in Ash is a work of fiction. Names, characters, places, and incidents either are the product of the author's imagination or are used fictitiously. Any resemblance to actual events, locales, or persons, living or dead, is entirely coincidental.

Copyright © 2025 by Veronique Wallrapp

Cover art and interior art copyright © 2025 by Veronique Wallrapp

All rights reserved.

Published in the United States by Cup of Tea Publishing, New York.

Library of Congress Control Number: 2025903273

ISBN: 979-8-9901761-2-6

eBook ISBN: 979-8-9901761-3-3

The scanning, uploading, and distribution of this book without permission is theft of the author's intellectual property. No portion of this book may be reproduced in any form without written permission from the publisher or author, except as permitted by U.S. copyright law.

Contents

Family Tree	VIII
1. Black Hole	1
2. Crows	8
3. Fairy Spells	12
4. Opium Dreams	16
5. Gods of Death	20
6. Omens	25
7. Le Bon Dieu	31
8. Kaleidoscope Misery	36
9. Machine Gun Gusto	42
10. Liar, Liar	48
11. A Self-Satisfied Glow	52
12. Flamboyant Dukes and Crysanthemums	56
13. Castle Creations	65
14. Patience is a Virtue	71
15. Le Jardin	79
16. Poppy Fields	85
17. Boar's Head	91

18.	Trust and Sinking Ships	96
19.	A Murder of Crows	102
20.	Fever Dreams and Tea with the Queen	108
21.	All that Glitters	117
22.	Three Times Three Strokes	126
23.	Amidst Rats and Refuse	138
24.	Don't Rock the Boat	149
25.	Midnight Visitors	158
26.	Inherited	166
27.	Blades of Grass	173
28.	"We are here by the will of the people and can only be made to leave by the force of bayonets." Le Comte de Mirabeau	179
29.	Corrosion and Clock Gears	185
30.	Strawberries and Cream	193
31.	Copper and Crockery	200
32.	Skip a Stone	210
33.	Street Walking	223
34.	Trampled	232
35.	Two Birds, One Stone	240
36.	Charmed	254
37.	Hairpins and Daggers	263
38.	Wedding Cake Hair	275

39.	Smoke and Pearls on the Breeze	288
40.	"I'm Just a Girl, in the World." -No Doubt	298
41.	The Gate of Hell	310
42.	Resurrection	317
43.	The Song of the Sea	328
44.	Tryst	337
45.	Comeuppance	343
46.	Reverberations	356

Rise of the Guillotine Family Tree

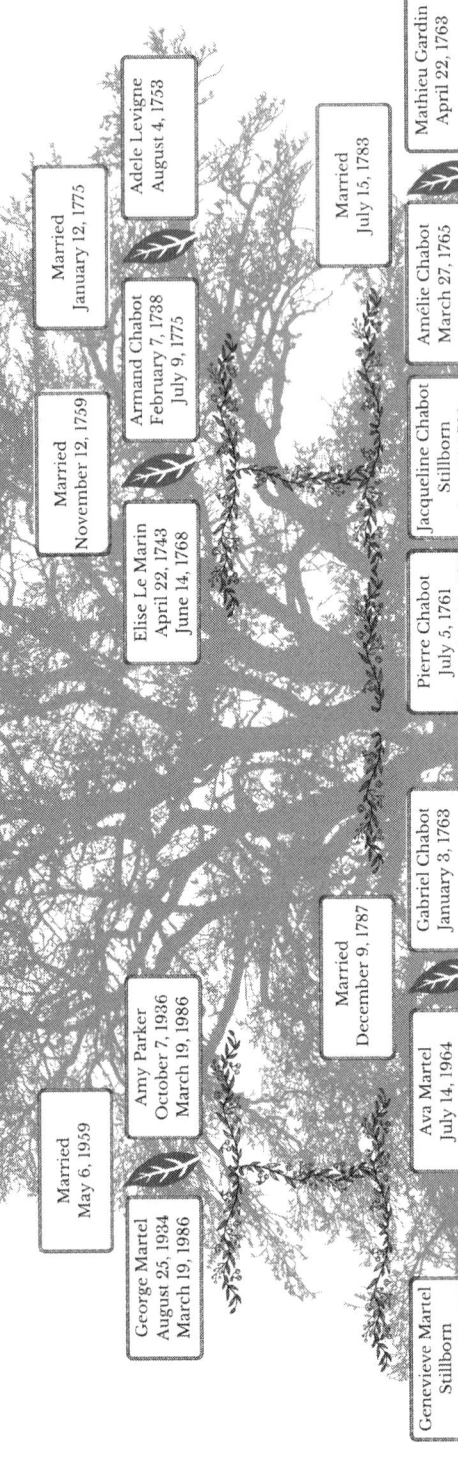

Married January 12, 1775

Adele Levigne
August 4, 1753

Armand Chabot
February 7, 1738
July 9, 1775

Married November 12, 1759

Elise Le Marin
April 22, 1743
June 14, 1768

Married July 15, 1783

Mathieu Gardin
April 22, 1763

Amélie Chabot
March 27, 1765

Jacqueline Chabot
Stillborn
June 14, 1768

Pierre Chabot
July 5, 1761
September 14, 1775

Thérèse Gardin
December 1, 1787

Étienne Gardin
March 3, 1785

Gabriel Chabot
January 3, 1763

Married December 9, 1787

Armand Chabot
October 17, 1788

Aimée Chabot
Stillborn
October 17, 1788

Ava Martel
July 14, 1964

Amy Parker
October 7, 1936
March 19, 1986

Married May 6, 1959

George Martel
August 25, 1934
March 19, 1986

Geneviève Martel
Stillborn
November 20, 1961

One
Black Hole

As I paced, I stared at the pattern in the wide, gleaming floorboards, picking out the knots and imperfections until they whirled and smudged before my eyes. The ache in my lower back was a constant, gnawing monster that grew and receded, keeping time with my endless marching. I tried to sit; picked up my book, and put it down a moment later, unable to concentrate on the words as my vision swayed and smeared.

An uneasiness lived inside me—had for months now—although I couldn't seem to verbalize my anxiety in a way that made sense. I chewed my bottom lip and noticed vaguely that my lips were chapped. I should apply some lavender balm...

A sudden spasm made me grab blindly for the bed and grip the post as I tried to breathe. White hot knives stabbed and twisted, making me double over and clutch my belly with both hands. When I could stand again, the ache remained, reverberating through my bones. *Is it time?*

I had spent the day achy and irritable, unable to get comfortable no matter what I did—although to be fair, I hadn't been comfortable for weeks. I'd never believed myself to be a nervous person, but as the pregnancy had progressed, I found myself entertaining every worst-case scenario possible. What if the baby wasn't, okay? What if something happened to me? Infant and maternal death rates were high in the eighteenth century. Would Gabriel be home when I went into labor?

The nightmares! I heard that pregnant women had vivid dreams, but these were horribly convincing. I'd awakened in a cold sweat nearly every night, my heart racing. Unable to beat back the unspeakable visions, close my eyes, and fall back asleep— my nights were spent in terror that they'd return the instant I slipped back into dreams.

But the worst by far, had been the inexorable, unnamable dread that had stalked me by day and night for the last three months. A fear that crawled up from my belly and clawed up my spine whispering incessantly and ominously. *Something is wrong. Something is wrong.*

The next contraction had me curled in the fetal position on the floor, moaning through gritted teeth.

This must be it.

It was too early, and Gabriel was not due to be home from Phillipe's for another three weeks, but none of that mattered. This baby was coming now.

When the worst of it passed, I pulled myself onto my feet and managed to ring the bell. It was the middle of the night, and I prayed someone heard and came quickly. I'd delayed calling for help, not knowing what labor felt like, and hating the thought of disturbing anyone's sleep unless it was absolutely necessary.

Another pang gripped me, a burning vise clamped on my lower back; so intense that I found myself keening. I sounded like an animal caught in the brutal metal teeth of a trap, and in some distant, remote part of myself, I was embarrassed at my inability to be stoic through the agony ripping through my body. *Oh God, oh my God, save me.*

Breathe. In through the nose, out through the mouth.

Breathe.

But I couldn't. Instead of calming, deep breaths, I was gasping; gulping down short, shallow mouthfuls of air, as panic pressed down on my chest and threatened to engulf me. *Something is wrong. Something is wrong.*

The rapid patter of footsteps echoing in the corridor brought me back to myself. My forehead was pressed against the cool, wood floor, my hair spread around me like a cloud.

I should get up, but I couldn't summon the strength.

There was a quiet knock at the door, before the heavy, oak door creaked open.

"My lady?"

I heard it all through a fog, but I still lay on the ground, huffing, sweating, and freezing by turns, speculating whether I could manage to respond.

A cool, gentle hand settled on my cheek.

"Let me help you onto the bed, Madame, and I'll summon the women. I do believe the *bébé* is coming."

I pried my eyes open and put a name to the friendly, smiling face. I should have recognized Mademoiselle Noemi's calm, soothing voice, but the alarm mounting in my chest disoriented me.

"Thank you, Mademoiselle." I grimaced as she wrapped her arm around my waist, walking me back to the four-poster bed.

I leaned back against the chilly, crisp linens, sinking into the plush mattress with a sigh. It only lasted for seconds. I could already feel the next contraction building— my stomach tightening, the muscles in my back clamping down and twisting viciously. I drew my knees up and desperately gripped the blanket in my sweaty palms, crumpling the fabric as if I could somehow transfer the agony tearing through my body to the down-filled quilt.

Noemi watched me sympathetically, a small frown between her soft, brown eyes. "All right now, Madame? I'll be back directly," she promised as soon as she could see the pain had eased.

I shook my head vehemently. "No. Please, don't leave me." Fear forced me to grab her hand as if I expected her to flee the room.

"I'll just ring the bell then, aye?" She delicately disentangled her hand from my grip at my nod.

Now that I'd acknowledged that labor had begun, the pain seemed to come in unrelenting waves, stacking on itself ruthlessly like layers of rock, compressed under immense pressure for millennia. Our bedchamber and the steady stream of women busily arranging linens, stripping the bed, plaiting my hair, and pressing cool, lavender-soaked cloths against my neck took on the shadowy quality of half-remembered dreams. The only thing that kept me from surrendering to a fuzzy unconsciousness was the fear, insidiously whispering that something was amiss.

Every time my eyes got heavy, I sensed it— weaving its way like smoke, infiltrating every corner of my body, murmuring disquieting statistics. I saw it in the exchanged glances and the falsely cheerful voices of Esme and the attendants who had gathered in my room.

Doubled over in crushing agony, the room had begun to spin and oscillate, retreating and contracting dizzily. *Gabriel should be here.*

Nausea overwhelmed me, making my skin damp and clammy. I closed my eyes and struggled to breathe as I tried to tamp down the urge to eject the contents of my stomach all over the Aubusson rug. *Something is wrong.*

Something is wrong.

The thought pushed its way into her brain, like a persistent man that couldn't take no for an answer. Aggravated for even allowing such a disloyal thought to take up residence, Esme shoved it away.

"Ava." She gently placed one hand on either side of her friend's face, forcing her to focus on what she was saying. Ava's eyes were laced with pain and fatigue. Esme knew that exhaustion was one of the most real threats a woman in travail could face.

It sapped her strength, robbing her of the ability to push when necessary. She suspected that Ava had been fighting active labor for some time, likely in a desperate bid to await Gabriel's arrival. But it was equally clear that this child was coming now, even if her mistress was not ready.

"Esme." Her voice could barely be heard over the preparations surrounding them.

"I'm going to examine you now. It's going to be uncomfortable, to put it mildly. But I need to see how close you are."

Ava gave the barest nod; her eyes were glassy and unfocused, and Esme was not entirely certain she fully understood what needed to be done. Her gaze was fixated inward as another contraction bore down on her.

Esme gently brushed a damp lock of Ava's hair off her sweaty brow as she waited for it to pass.

The moment Ava sagged back against the pillows, Esme nodded at Madame Bleuzen and Mademoiselle Noemi, who each held one of Ava's legs back. She took a deep breath, squared her shoulders, and reached in, pausing only briefly when she felt Ava's body tense at the intrusion. Closing her eyes, she concentrated on what she was feeling. There was the head, down as it should be. The smooth curve of the spine and buttocks. Her shoulders were beginning to relax, everything seemed as it should be, and she began to pull her hand out but froze. *It can't be.*

Her brows scrunched in consternation, and she hastily pasted a calm smile on her face, though not before inadvertently making eye contact with Madame Bleuzen.

A hushed, heated conversation was taking place by the fire, and although they cautiously turned their backs so I couldn't see their expressions, I could tell by their rigid postures that whatever it was, it didn't bode well for me, and the baby. The persistent anguish made everything hazy and indistinct; rather like I was observing the world from underwater; sounds were muffled and distorted, and people blurred.

Esme said something and several faces glanced back at me apprehensively. Madame Bleuzen made a short, chopping motion with her hand and Noemi threw a sympathetic smile in my direction. Something had been decided, because they all turned toward me, and Esme was approaching the bed. Nervously, I pushed myself into a more comfortable position and tried to read into the deliberately serene face Esme presented to me.

"It's time to start pushing, Ava."

"What's— What's wrong?" I gasped.

In the clutches of a contraction that felt like it was cleaving me in two, I tried to concentrate through the agony as a giant hand squeezed and released, like a bloody, crimson heart, pumping relentlessly.

"Now, Ava, bear down with all your strength."

I pushed, scrunching my face, biting my lip, clutching the hands that held mine until I felt the bones and tendons grinding against each other.

It subsided slightly and I collapsed against the cushions and headboard, panting.

"Good, Ava. Listen to me, you're squeezing with every part of your body but, you're not pushing effectively. The *bébé* is close. Push *down* on the next one."

I nodded, even though I had no idea what she meant.

The next contraction built like a black hole, expanding, and consuming everything. The torment was unbearable, but Esme's voice somehow broke through.

"Excellent, my friend. Another one like that and this *bébé* will be earthside."

I heaved with every last ounce of my strength and the world went black.

Two
Crows

"*Fils de pute.*"

"Aye." Gabriel stared into the swirling, amber liquid in his goblet and wished he had better news for Phillipe.

"First the treasury, now this. How will the poor survive the winter?" His friend was pacing before the flickering fire in the stone hearth, his footsteps dampened by the thick, blue, and gold, Turkish rug that covered the floor.

Gabriel tilted his glass meditatively, as though he might find the answer in the honey-colored cognac. He and Ava had decided that he should visit Phillipe as planned in the autumn, although she had remained in Landévennec. As her pregnancy progressed, Ava had been beset by fear for their baby's health and trepidation about what lay ahead for the country.

He had agonized over the decision to stay or go for weeks, but when news arrived in their corner of France that the royal treasury was indeed empty— exactly when Ava had predicted it would be— he'd settled on a short visit. He could not bury his head in the limestone-tinted sand and ignore the signs of oncoming war, any more than he could force the sky to offer the rain his crops so desperately needed.

The lack of precipitation followed them through the summer, intensifying as the heat ramped up and the heavens refused to shed more than a few drops of precious water. Day after day, Gabriel watched as the tender green shoots of his wheat yellowed, withering away into the hardened, dusty land.

In desperation, Ava and the women cleared a small area under the cooler, shady canopy of the nearby forest, transplanting as many of the vegetables and herbs as they could from the kitchen gardens. They tirelessly hauled buckets of water, coaxing along what survived by daily watering. Thanks to their efforts, his tenants wouldn't starve over the coming winter, but stores would be meager. Again.

He thought of the farmers north of Paris and crossed himself. The coming winter wouldn't be kind to them. Shortly after the news of the treasury reached them in Landévennec, Phillipe had written to Gabriel about decimating hailstorms that had assailed northern France in mid-July. According to the reports, the struggling crops had been destroyed, and trees were ripped limb from limb. Gabriel even heard a few accounts of deaths attributed to hail stones that had supposedly been as large as quart bottles.

"Gabriel."

He pulled himself out of his bleak thoughts and focused on Phillipe, noting the lines of worry etched on his friend's face, knowing they mirrored his own.

"Aye?"

"Necker will be there tonight, we'll speak to him. There must be more *le Roi* can do to protect against famine."

Gabriel raised his cup to his lips, but the sweet, fiery cognac tasted bitter on his tongue.

"Necker has already banned corn exports and promised to purchase seventy million *livres* of wheat."

"It's not enough, Gabriel."

"No," he murmured. "It's not. He might suspend all crop exports and purchase more grain, Phillipe. Perhaps inspect private grain stores. Open up imports and reduce taxes so the Third Estate can afford to feed their families. Necker has the soul of a reformist, but the rest of the regime does not share his enthusiasm. They must be in accord to effect change. We need to speak to the others, Berry, and Haute-Guyenne. It's time to expand our circle."

"Tonight," emphasized Phillipe.

"I imagine they'll be there. The sooner the better." He stood up, stretching his long legs, cramped after too many hours spent seated, and thoughtfully gazed out the mullioned windows at the early autumn sun that hung low over the horizon. "I'll only be here for another week. I promised Ava I would return before the *bébé's* arrival."

Phillipe moved to stand beside him, and they stared at the desolate garden that drought had reduced to shades of yellow and brown. "At least the news is not all bad, eh?"

"Aye," he agreed. Ava and the *bébé* she carried were a source of sunshine in an otherwise bleak year. He couldn't imagine how much worse it was for his friend. "I'm going to take Automne for a ride. Come with me?"

Phillipe grimaced. "I have letters to write before the ball. You go."

"Alright. I'll see you in a few hours then." Gabriel emptied his cup, set it on a nearby mahogany table inlaid with ivory, and strode toward the door, suddenly impatient to be outside.

He arrived at the stables, his feet finding Automne's stall automatically. His thoughts raced as he inhaled the comforting, familiar scent of hay, grain, sweat and manure, barely noticing the soft nickering that greeted him as he passed the other horses. From the hooks on the wall, he removed his engraved saddle and tack, quickly and efficiently saddling Automne, automatically checking and adjusting the leather straps and buckles.

As he led his stallion out into the dusky twilight, he breathed a sigh of relief. He preferred the peace of the countryside. The last few weeks had been a whirlwind of balls, socializing, wheeling, and dealing and he was honestly sick of it. He longed to be home with Ava with the roar of the crashing sea and the resinous scent of the pines drifting through the open windows of the château. Soon.

Automne whickered and pulled at the reins, anxious to run, and Gabriel ran his hand lovingly down the horse's soft muzzle.

"Aye, boy. Let's go for a ride, shall we?" He mounted in one swift, practiced motion, and gave the horse his head, leaning low over Automne's neck as his hooves thundered down the street that led to the outskirts of Paris. He needed to get out of the city for a while. He couldn't breathe.

He ambled up the cobbled road on his return. The sky was the deep violet of twilight, and both he and Automne were pleasantly winded. He paused at the intersection of the Champs-Élysées, allowing an ornate carriage pulled by a team of matched grays to pass.

Gabriel glanced to his right as a flutter in his periphery drew his attention. Shiny, ebony wings landed next to a dying rose bush. The bird tilted his head, observing Gabriel and Automne, then raised its head and emitted a shrill *caw-caw*. A shiver ran down Gabriel's spine as an answering pair of wings beat from behind him and came to rest beside the first raven. *Two*. A moment later, a third crow perched on the bush.

Gabriel waited.

Three.

Three crows.

He wasn't a superstitious man.

"*Merde.*"

He needed to get back home. Now.

Three
Fairy Spells

I stared at the swaddled bundle that Esme placed in my arms, taking in the smooth curve of his cheek, the downy, swirl of dark hair, and the tiny, puckered lips.

Two.

There had been two.

"Where is his sister?"

Esme flinched, but it barely registered. Outwardly, I appeared calm; lovingly staring at the sweet, sleeping infant nestled on my lap. Inwardly, I was a seething tornado of destructive emotion.

"Ava," she began hesitantly. "I'm not sure if—"

"Where is she? I need to see her."

She frowned and concern flared in her blue eyes, but I knew she wouldn't deny me.

"I'll be right back." She hurried from the room I'd ordered darkened—like ghouls were chasing her.

In her absence, I gazed at the baby. This perfect, rosy-cheeked little angel that Gabriel and I created. There were hints of his father in the shape of his mouth and nose. In a perfect world, seeing the resemblance would make me smile.

But this wasn't a perfect world, and I was overcome with anger; immense, overwhelming, rage, bubbling like a cauldron threatening to overflow onto the fire beneath at any moment.

I knew it wasn't warranted. Somewhere deep down, I was aware that it wasn't Gabriel's fault he wasn't here for the horror of the birth. In the end, I told him to go.

Regardless of whether or not he'd been home, it wouldn't have changed the outcome.

It wouldn't have saved our daughter.

But my grief was not a rational beast. It demanded that blame be laid at someone's doorstep. As I fought down the rising tide of despair, I laid it squarely on Gabriel.

I was so lost, that I felt nothing for this blameless little boy. Certainly, I didn't feel the rushing surge of love I expected to feel.

I recognized the quiet, returning footsteps as Esme's and turned my gaze back to the door expectantly.

She approached holding a smaller bundle than the one currently in my arms. Gently laying my live, sleeping baby in the carved, cherry wood cradle by the bed, I soundlessly held my arms out for my daughter.

My daughter.

She was tiny. Flawless. I didn't know what to expect, but it wasn't this. If it weren't for the paleness of her skin, I wouldn't believe it. She lacked the rose-tinted, golden glow of health that would have marked her as a living infant. If only I could feel her little heartbeat through her linen swaddle, I could almost imagine that she was alive. That some evil fairy had cast a spell on her.

But this was not a Disney movie, and this beautiful little princess would never open her eyes. I wondered what color they were. My mother's feline green? My husband's steely gray? I would never know, and the unfairness of it hit me so hard my throat closed, and my eyes filled. The rush of maternal love I expected to feel when I held her brother, swamped me as I gazed down into her face.

"Hello, little one."

I ran the tip of my finger down her smooth, little cheek.

It was cold.

It held none of the warmth and life that her twin's held.

"I will never get to see you grow." My voice was thick with emotion. "Who would you have been?"

Tears streamed unchecked down my cheeks. My nose ran. I licked my lips and tasted the salt of my grief on them. Undone, I bent my head over my tiny daughter who would never draw a breath.

"I love you. I love you. God, I love you so much."

I sobbed. The agony of losing her before I ever knew her crushed my lungs, squeezing the air out of them until I felt I would hyperventilate. Within seconds, my tears soaked through the white linen they'd swaddled her diminutive body in.

"Ava, please." Esme tentatively tried to sit me up and ease her away from me, but I snatched her back.

"Don't take her away!"

She backed away as if I were a feral animal; hands raised in a show of surrender.

I suddenly realized that they *would* take her away. I couldn't keep her. I would never see her again after this. It ripped an otherworldly howl from my throat.

Before I knew what I was doing, I unswaddled her, gently removing the linen cloth from her body. Reverently, I counted ten perfect little fingers, each with the tiniest fingernail I'd seen in my life— ten matching toes. I ran my hands softly across her smooth skin, feeling the bumps of her ribs and the roundness of her joints. I marveled at the dimples in her fingers and the miniature seashell whorl of her ears. My tears dripped on her constantly, but I barely noticed. I had to commit every inch of her to memory.

It was all I would have when they took her away.

Four
Opium Dreams

Afterward, I remembered little.

Disjointed, murmured words. The hurried tapping of feet. Candlelight flickering, casting shadowy angels and demons against the tapestried walls. Time became liquid, ebbing and flowing like the ocean tides.

Utterly broken in my despair, I let myself drown. I knew the household was worried— the women checked on me constantly. Esme became a fixture in my bedchamber, hovering anxiously. I had no patience for any of it. I largely ignored them.

Madame Bleuzen and Mademoiselle Ollivier sent beautiful meals laid temptingly out on trays— my favorite *cotriade*, cups of steaming *chocolat* with fresh bread and whipped, salty butter, bowls of stewed apples, fragrant with cinnamon and clove. Still, I had no appetite.

My baby—the one that lived— stirred and whimpered in the cradle by our bed. He must be hungry again— all he wanted to do was eat and sleep.

Thank God for his wet nurse— I had no desire to feed him myself. Initially, I thought I would embrace my role as a mother. I thought the custom that demanded that noble-born children have a wet nurse was ridiculous. If my sweet daughter lived, perhaps I would still feel that way.

A pang of guilt assailed me. I was lucky I still had a living child. I should be showering him in love... But I couldn't seem to find a single grain of it left within myself. Every bit of love left in my heart was hastily buried in the dusty, unforgiving ground with his sister. They didn't even let me attend the burial.

Our little boy was working himself up into a full-blown frenzy; but I couldn't even pretend that I wanted to pick him up and soothe him. *If only the noise would stop.* His plump cheeks were rosy with anger, his little eyes screwed shut. I turned away and reached to ring the bell beside my bed in irritation. *Where is that damned wet nurse anyway?*

His incessant wailing made it difficult for me to concentrate. I preferred to spend my days recalling Aimée to memory, desperate not to forget a single detail, certain that I'd wake up one morning unable to remember her perfect, petite features. *I live in fear of it happening.*

Esme's face when I told her what her name was flashed before my eyes, and it reignited my fury with them all.

"The priest must baptize and bless her. She cannot be buried until she's been baptized."

"Ava, you know that Père Bourgault will not baptize a stillborn infant."

Please." I pleaded, hot tears streaming unchecked down my cheeks. "Her name is Aimée. My mother was named Amy. It means beloved."

Esme eyes were filled with sympathy, but it was meaningless as she shook her head, denying me— denying Aimée. "It is not his choice to make Ava. You know the church's stance."

"She is my beloved, Esme. I cannot let her go. I never even knew her. It's as though she never really existed except in my mind. Now everyone is intent on *forgetting her— on moving on— on focusing their attention on her brother. She will be forgotten even by God."*

Esme perched on the edge of my bed, uninvited, hesitantly. I knew she wanted to embrace me, and I could see the uncertainty in her cerulean eyes. She was right to wonder at my reaction. I hadn't exactly welcomed affection the last two days. She settled for picking up my hand and I choose not to pull away, letting it lie limp in her warm grasp.

"I don't believe that God forgets any of his children. . . ever. Aimée is pure, blameless, and entirely without sin. She does not need Père Bourgault to baptize her."

"But—"

"Nay." She squeezed my hand. "You wish her to be baptized, and I understand why. I know you are in pain, Ava— it's wrenching to see you like this and to think of what you have lost. No one deserves such a thing. But she does not need it."

I shook my head quickly, trying to block out Esme's words. It made the room sway and blur around me dizzily, and I closed my eyes for a minute as I tried to gain my bearings.

"Ava." She said softly, bringing me back to the room; the bed with its luxurious linens, the crimson and jade tapestried walls; my hand in hers. "You will never forget Aimée, nor will I, nor Gabriel when he returns, nor anyone else that laid eyes on her precious face. But you cannot lie down and die with her, Ava. Your son needs you. Gabriel is going to need you. You did not survive a shipwreck only to give up now."

I listened to her words, but the truth was, they didn't resonate with me. Why not die now? Why not spend eternity with my innocent, precious daughter? Everyone else would figure out a way to move on without me.

The baby was still screaming.

His little mouth was open wide as he howled. Actual tears were squeezing out from beneath his teeny eyelashes— as though hunger was a legitimate reason for tears. As though his twin didn't lie in a miniature coffin in the Chabot family cemetery.

The wet nurse suddenly opened the heavy bedchamber door and nervously dropped a curtsey before she hastened to the cradle and tenderly picked up my son, hugging him to her chest. He latched on immediately and a blessed silence fell over the room.

"Where were you?" I asked testily.

"*Pardon*, my lady. I fell asleep. The poor little dear had me awake most of the night."

I turned away, uninterested.

"Please have someone move his cradle to your room, Madame. He's far too loud to stay in here."

If she was shocked, she wisely didn't say so. I didn't bother looking back to watch her leave. After all, she wouldn't dare challenge my wishes. I picked up the goblet of brandy laced with laudanum from the bedside table, took a healthy swig, snuggled down into the furs, and closed my eyes. Oblivion was the only way to escape the anguish.

Five
Gods of Death

Gabriel clicked softly to Automne as the horse picked his way carefully amongst the boulders that dotted the heavily forested countryside. He'd left Paris in a flurry of activity, barely lingering long enough to pack and express his regrets to Phillipe, leaving the problems plaguing France to his friend to work out.

Dread followed Automne's steady hoofbeats, reminding Gabriel of the relentless rat-a-tat-tat of the drums of war, as they left Paris behind and rode hell for leather toward home. He urged Automne as close to his limits as he dared— riding well after the moon rose each evening, pausing to sleep for only a few hours each night, before rising in the early morn, when the dew still clung to the ferns and scented the air with the resin of pines, and hitting the road again.

The closer they got to Landévennec the worse Gabriel felt. He was constantly short of breath, anxiety making his heart race uncomfortably— as if it could somehow arrive home faster than Automne could carry him there. The genuine fear in Ava's jade-green eyes when she told him about the nightmares she had, and her certainty that something was amiss traveled beside him every step of the way.

He never should have gone to Phillipe's.

What did the treasury matter if something had happened to Ava in his absence?

He swallowed hard, trying to force down the fist of fear that made his throat ache constantly.

Tonight, there was a new moon; making the pines and brush appear darker than ink, rendering the stones that littered the narrow path nearly invisible. He had pushed Automne mercilessly, making the ten or eleven-day journey in just seven days. They were now outside the tiny, nondescript village of Treuzeulom. Landévennec was only a couple hours away, but the moonless night conspired against him, laughing at his apprehension, drawing out the end of the journey cruelly.

He pulled back on the reins lightly, peering into the unforgiving forest. Somewhere to his right, a stream trickled musically as the water moved sluggishly over stones rounded by time. Gabriel nudged Automne with his knees and eased his head toward the refreshing sound.

Within a few minutes, Automne was slaking his thirst as Gabriel refilled his wineskin. He splashed some on his face— he felt sweaty despite the cool autumn air— and stood beside his horse, resting his forehead against his reassuring bulk. Every muscle in his body throbbed from the sleepless nights and long hours spent in the saddle. Automne turned his head and affectionately bumped Gabriel's shoulder with his muzzle. With a sigh, he ran his hand lovingly down the chestnut's face.

"We're almost home Automne. You can have anything you want when we get there," he promised. "You've earned it."

He rolled his head from side to side, trying vainly to ease the stiffness from his neck and shoulders. Mounting his horse, he leaned forward over his neck, superstitiously rubbed Automne's mane between his forefinger and thumb for luck, and murmured, "Let's go."

They trudged on through the opaque night, Automne slipping occasionally on loose gravel until the footing got so poor that Gabriel dismounted, opting to lead Automne through the thick brush and sliding stones rather than risk injury. The rustling wings of an owl swooped overhead, startling Automne and making Gabriel duck reflexively. *Hadn't he heard that owls were a bad omen?*

Unbidden, the memory of an evening spent around a campfire with Mathieu and cohorts flashed across his mind. They had just completed their first successful smuggling operation. Among their numbers, there had been a native gentleman from America that Friloux had befriended. The old seadog was constantly surrounding himself with interesting people.

A fearsomely large owl glided soundlessly down, emitting a muffled shriek from its prey as cruel claws sank in. As it flew back to its perch in a nearby elm, Friloux's companion— his name had meant *'He walks on Water,'* he remembered suddenly— explained that owls were considered messengers of the underworld and often carried warnings from the Gods of Death.

Trepidation skittered down his spine and a fresh rash of goosebumps broke out on his arms. A fitful breeze stirred a few strands of hair that had come loose from its binding, and tickled against his face and neck, irritating him.

After what felt like an eternity, they broke through the edge of the forest into what was usually a lush meadow on the outskirts of his land. Automne pulled at the reins impatiently as he recognized the briny scent of home, and Gabriel chuckled, relief at being almost there washing over him. Confident that the horse could find his way from here, Gabriel swung up on his back and gave the tired chestnut his head. He bent low over the horse's neck and let the rushing wind sweep past them both as his hooves thundered up the hill and along the long meandering drive.

The hour was late, and he expected he would have to rouse Monsieur Dubois or one of the maids. He slid off Automne and loosely tied his reins on the hitching post. He rubbed his hand lovingly down the horse's neck and turned toward the *château's* steps, stopping short when the door swung open.

A frisson of fear teased the fine hairs on the nape of his neck, making them stand at attention. He had hoped the entire way home, that he was merely being superstitious. Endlessly, he had repeated to himself that everything must be fine; he was simply overly cautious, and wouldn't Ava be surprised and excited to see him back sooner than expected? He hadn't been able to convince himself, and this— this solemn meeting at the door, well past midnight, by several fully dressed members of his household didn't bode well.

Gabriel took a moment to take stock of the situation. Monsieur Dubois, fully dressed, every gray hair on his head impeccably combed, standing at attention, as though Gabriel had been expected. Madame Pichon, face implacable, blonde hair liberally streaked with white, brushed strictly away from her aging face. Mademoiselle Noemi and Esme, both betraying their anxiety in their expressions. The fact that Esme was here surely meant that something was grievously wrong. *Where was Luc?*

He stepped toward the door and silently took in the lit candles in the entry, along the stairs, and beyond.

"Monsieur le Vicomte! I am so pleased to welcome you home," intoned Monsieur Dubois. "I will have the stable lads roused immediately."

"Thank you, Monsieur. Automne has been ridden hard the past several days. Please let them know."

"Of course, my lord."

Gabriel turned his attention to the women, one eyebrow raised in question.

"You're home early, Gabriel," murmured Esme.

"Thank God you are back, Monsieur le Vicomte!" exclaimed Mademoiselle Noemi.

"Where is Ava?" he asked brusquely, trying to keep the panic out of his voice.

"She is sleeping peacefully," answered Madame Pichon.

He closed his eyes and let relief sweep through him violently as he crossed himself.

"Dieu, merci."

He opened his eyes and carefully inspected the women's faces. Esme's eyes were tired and melancholy. Mademoiselle Noemi's bore similar strain in them. His gut tightened. Ava might be sleeping, but something was still wrong.

"Who has died?" he asked bluntly.

Mademoiselle Noemi recoiled, and Madame Pichon stepped back unconsciously before recovering her composure.

"You have a handsome, healthy, baby boy, my—"

"Your daughter, Gabriel, I am so sorry." Esme's blue eyes were miserable.

He looked back and forth, first at the stubbornly stoic expression on Madame Pichon's face, then at Esme and Noemi's distress.

"Twins... Ava had twins?"

"Oui."

Six
Omens

How could she explain to Gabriel everything that transpired during his visit with le Comte de Saint-Denis? Esme asked herself as she followed him rapidly up the curving stairs. He was taking them two at a time and she struggled to keep up in her voluminous skirts. Her mind echoed his shocked expression at the news of twins. He would be quite a bit more surprised when he discovered the state Ava was in.

She trailed behind him down the corridor, stopping short only when he arrived at his bedchamber door. Should she follow him? Warn him? Wait?

He threw a glance over his shoulder at her, naked trepidation painted in his eyes. He looked surprisingly vulnerable at that moment, and she had to hold herself back from comforting him. Once, she wouldn't have hesitated, but things weren't the same. Perhaps now that he was home, he and Ava would find solace in each other.

"Go," she heard herself say. "Ava needs you. She hasn't been the same since the birth."

It barely scratched the surface of what was wrong with Ava, but at least he wouldn't be entirely blindsided.

She watched him open the heavy, wood door, duck his head inside, and quietly close it behind him. She crossed herself and offered up a swift prayer as her shoulders slumped.

Gabriel let the solid, oak door click shut behind him and rested his back against it. His heart hammered in his ears in response to what the women had revealed. Ava lay curled on her side in their wide four poster bed, facing the door. Her body was so slight beneath the mound of blankets she was barely visible.

His pulse tripping, he walked quietly to the fire dancing in the cavernous stone fireplace and eased his boots off his sore feet, shucked the layers of coat, waistcoat, stockings and breeches all caked with a fine layer of dust and dirt, leaving them where they fell. His skin prickled from the heat of the fire and the chill of the bare floor against the soles of his feet.

He padded to Ava's side of the bed, his toes curling into the plush crimson carpet spread on the wood and stared down at his wife. Wordlessly, he took in the violet bruises beneath her eyes, hardly noticeable under the fringe of heavy lashes that lay curled against her pallid cheeks. Her mouth, usually soft and begging to be kissed, was chapped and raw, her lips cracked in places. He watched in silence as her chest rose and fell regularly, a tiny puff of breath escaping from her parted lips.

Gabriel's own breath shuddered out as he crossed himself.

"*Dieu, merci,*" he managed in a choked whisper. Thank God she was alive, and their son too. He wanted desperately to see the *bébé* for himself and assuage the fear that still coursed through his veins, but he wouldn't awaken the rest of the household in his selfish desire to see his child.

Gently, he tucked a dark, tumbled strand of hair away from Ava's face as he sank to his knees beside their bed. Hands clasped, head bowed, he prayed for the soul of the daughter he would never meet and thanked God in a broken murmur for the lives of his wife and son. When he raised his face, it was streaked with tears, but there was no one there to witness his grief, and he didn't bother wiping away the evidence of it.

Utterly spent, he crawled shivering under the quilts and reached for the comfort of Ava's warmth. His body molded itself to the contours of hers and he fell into an exhausted, dreamless slumber.

I felt his comforting, solid presence in my sleep, his body curved protectively around mine, one arm wrapped loosely over me, his breath warm and soft against my hair. It was as lovely and golden as a dream, momentarily banishing the ugly, opium nightmares I'd found myself trapped in for days. Or was it weeks?

As I came awake, my mouth painfully dry, my head throbbing, reality and remembrance crashed down on me, and I stiffened, my body pulling away from his, seeking solace in the cool bedding where we hadn't lain.

Even though I was furious with him, I was still attuned to his obvious confusion as he awoke groggily. His silver-gray eyes opened and looked sorrowfully into mine.

"Ava, *mon cœur*." His voice was husky with sleep as he reached out to me.

I scootched away, as close to the edge of the bed as I could retreat, without falling off.

Uncertainty and hurt clouded his face, but I didn't care. The only thing that mattered anymore was Aimée.

"*Dieu*, I am so sorry. I never should have left when you were expecting. I never thought—"his voice broke. "Esme told me. . . twins. . . but our daughter—"

His face crumpled and for a moment, I almost relented. His anguish was obvious, but it changed nothing, I reminded myself. He reached out one hand, imploringly. It would be so easy to move toward him, embrace him as he wept, as I sobbed for our lost child, but no.

I was not interested in empty, meaningless consolation. The only solace I would ever find again would be when I held my daughter in my arms in heaven.

I watched him impassively, for several long seconds, then I turned away and closed my eyes as I firmly shut the world out.

Silence fell heavily in our bedchamber, tainting the air I breathed with questions and expectations. I knew that Gabriel believed I would roll back toward him, to open my arms to him. As he waited, my skin began to prickle. I could feel his eyes on me, sense his hope and regret. Stubbornly, I kept my eyes shut, pushing him away, silently waiting for him to get the hint and leave.

But he didn't, and time stretched out infinitely. In the background, I was aware of the sounds of the bustling household, the tapping of feet, the rustling of skirts, the clock in the entry chiming the hour. *Why isn't there another draught of wine and laudanum on my bedside table?*

Last night's empty goblet had been removed, and it thoughtlessly hadn't been replaced. I needed it to sleep. I couldn't ignore Gabriel for much longer, his stubborn presence in our room was beginning to make me angry.

A fire burned within me, usually banked safely beneath a haze of drugs and alcohol, but his selfish expectations had thrown kindling on it, and a raging inferno was building in me. I wanted to be calm, but in another moment, I was going to lose all semblance of control.

He had the audacity to put his hand on my shoulder. I felt the warmth of his palm against the linen of my night rail a moment before the full weight of it settled on me. I stiffened further, my muscles cramped and trembling from the effort it took not to melt against him.

"Please speak to me, Ava."

I answered him in silence. A single, salty tear crept out and made its solitary way down my cheek and into my braided hair.

"I should have been here with you. As soon as I sensed something was amiss, I returned. I made the trip back in seven days."

This piqued my interest, but only marginally.

"How did you know to return?" I hadn't turned back to face him, yet. I didn't want to. We were talking around the root of my anger instead of addressing my implacable fury, but I allowed it for now.

"Ah, well..." He sounded sheepish. "Crows."

"Crows?" Surprised, I rolled over to gauge his expression. Too late, I remembered that people used to believe three crows to be the harbingers of death.

"Aye." His voice was soft.

"Well, it was an accurate omen."

"Twas," he agreed. "*Mon cœur*, I can never tell you how sorry I am that I was not here."

I turned back away.

"That doesn't bring her back." My voice was muffled against the pillow, but the acid had gone out of it. I was tired.

"Ava—"

"Please have Esme bring me a fresh draught."

Seven
Le Bon Dieu

"Has she been like this since the birth?" Gabriel's gray eyes looked tortured.

"Aye, well, since we told her there were twins and your daughter was stillborn," replied Esme, uncomfortably picking at her gown.

Although months had passed since Marguerite Cariou's death, she still felt awkward around Gabriel, and truth be told, Ava as well, though not to the same degree.

"How was she? When you told her." He had his son nestled on his lap and stared down into his face, as though he might find the answers therein instead of meeting Esme's eyes.

"As you might imagine. Heartbroken." Esme's voice cracked on the word as she recalled the anguish on her friend's face.

Gabriel looked up at her then. "'Tis a terrible thing," he said softly. "A parent should never bury a child."

"Well, that didn't help either. She wanted Aimée to be baptized."

He winced. "She knows—"

"It doesn't matter what she knows, Gabriel. She's out of her head with grief."

He bowed his head, and she watched as he ran the tip of his finger down his son's cheek. The caress was eerily similar to what Ava had done to Aimée when she'd held her.

"I never even saw her," he murmured.

Her throat closed up. "Aye, I know," she choked out.

"Was she—" he paused as though searching for the right word. "Was she. . . whole?" He grimaced at his choice.

"She was perfect, Gabriel." She shut her eyes against the telltale prickling, trying to compose herself. "When Ava is more herself, she will tell you. But there was naught wrong with her. A mite small, mayhap. Only her little heart wasn't beating."

Esme watched as his eyes filled and she looked away, studying the pattern on the Turkish rug. When she glanced back, he was staring down at the baby again.

"She hasn't chosen a name for him yet. Mayhap she will discuss it with you," she offered.

"Ava doesn't seem to be much interested in him," he observed.

"She's not," agreed Esme, bluntly.

"Poor *bébé*. 'Tis not your fault that your sister wasn't meant for this earth. You still need your *maman* and *papa*, eh?" he murmured as he bent his face close to his sleeping son, pressing a soft kiss against his forehead.

"I suppose Ava needs time to grieve." He glanced at Esme as though he wanted her affirmation.

She nodded.

"She's spent the entire time since drinking that draught and sleeping?"

"Aye." Esme looked out the window at the horsetail clouds sweeping across the sky and wished herself anywhere else.

"It's not helping her." There was a hint a impotent frustration in Gabriel's voice.

She shrugged helplessly, tearing her gaze from the outside world. "She asks for it. Nay, she demands it."

"I will speak to her. No more laudanum," he declared firmly.

"Aye. I'll let the others know."

"Thank you, Esme. And one more thing. . . Why didn't we know Ava was pregnant with twins?"

"She didn't allow any examinations, Gabriel. You know it's been challenging since Madame Cariou. . . and we haven't found a proper replacement for her." They should have known, she thought to herself.

"But could you have known, if you'd examined her?" he pressed.

"Aye. I know enough to get by. But Gabriel, I don't think foreknowledge would have changed the outcome."

His eyes narrowed and darkened as he listened to her.

"*Le bon Dieu* wanted your daughter for his own."

They say hell hath no fury like a woman scorned, but I wasn't sure that was correct. Hell, hath no fury like a woman denied, maybe. Hell, hath no fury like a mother with empty arms, perhaps.

Regardless, I was furious.

They told me I could no longer seek oblivion in the draught they were making me. After two days spent with a splintering headache, and itchy with irritation at their refusal to help me, I got out of bed on the third day and made my way shakily, but resolutely down the stairs and into the surgery, only to find that the laudanum was gone.

Now I sat on my favorite window seat in the library, resting my face against the cool glass and staring out at the dry, autumn garden. It looked downright dismal outside. Between the drought and the leaves that had preemptively dropped from the trees, *le jardin* was a sorry collection of textures ranging in color from dirt brown to mustard yellow. The cloudless azure sky did little to brighten the dead branches that stretched eerily up to the heavens.

Dead, like my baby girl in heaven.

There was a noise at the door, and I listlessly glanced over to see Esme and the wet nurse hovering uncertainly. The wet nurse looked disheveled. What was her name?

I searched my memory for it halfheartedly, but nothing came to mind. My interest lost; I gazed back outside. If they were going to follow me around the house, maybe I would go sit outside in my brown garden.

"Madame la Vicomtesse?"

Irritated, I turned my attention back to the women. Now, I realized they'd brought my son in with them, and the wet nurse held him out to me like an offering at a temple altar.

I ignored her outstretched arms. "Why are you here? I didn't summon you."

Impressively, Esme pretended I hadn't just said what might be the rudest thing she'd ever heard come out of my mouth. "Your son needs you, Ava. Madame Devereux is keeping him fed and we are all showering him in affection, but he needs his mother's love."

"Why did my daughter die, Esme?"

She winced. "Only *le bon Dieu* knows that."

"Do you suppose that he—" I nodded my head toward the infant still held in the wet nurse's arms. "Took all the nutrients and life's blood in my womb?"

A queer look crossed Esme's face. "Ava..." She hesitated like she couldn't quite believe I would ask such a question. "You're not thinking that this innocent babe is responsible for his twin's death?" Her face was strangely green as if she were going to vomit at the thought.

The wet nurse, for her part, looked impassive.

"Could he be?"

"Nay." Her reply was firm; she left no room for doubt, though my mind was filled with it.

"Very well."

I was done with the conversation and let them know by turning my gaze back toward the window.

They stood there for several uncomfortably long minutes, but then my son began to squall and wail for another feeding, and they scurried away.

I waited until they were gone, then I wept for my lost child until my throat was raw, and my eyes burned. They flaunted my son and paraded his living, breathing, perfection before me— as if this living child might replace the one that died. But there was nothing that could fill the hole in my heart.

Eight
Kaleidoscope Misery

I shivered and pulled my wool cloak tight around my shoulders, hunching them against the bitter wind that blew off the sea, and hurried toward the small chapel that stood proudly on the promontory a few hundred yards from the chateau. Since they denied me the oblivion I sought to drown myself in, I'd been forced to find other methods. When the weather allowed, I walked the meandering path down the rocky, limestone cliffs and stared into the ocean. It was often angry this time of year, a dark bluish gray in color, churned up from the relentless storms that blew in like clockwork every few days, reflecting my somber rage in its muddied, salt sprayed depths.

There was a rock I liked to perch on when the tide was out. I'd sit for hours dry-eyed; my tears evaporated; my heart numb; until my muscles ached, and my nose ran from the cold. Sometimes I contemplated hurling myself into the sea. I fantasized about filling my pockets with the smooth, many colored rocks and pebbles strewn along the beach, walking into the waves, and not looking back. Sometimes, I didn't think at all; I simply sat, my mind blessedly empty, a dull roar filling my ears until something caught my attention—a gull diving for its's dinner, or a spectacularly large swell rolling in—and I returned to myself, idly wondering how long I'd been caught in a world in-between.

Today, the sky was low and threatening, a dark steely gray that promised a full-blown storm soon. My face was pelted by sleet, stinging like a thousand, sharp, frozen needles and I pulled my hood back over my hair, ducking my head to protect my exposed skin.

Other than mass, I rarely visited the chapel. I didn't feel Aimée, or my parents or Carri in the small, whitewashed building. On days when the sun shone, the interior was bathed in scarlet, turmeric, bottle green and virgin's blue; the light streaming in through the stained glass set high in the wall above the altar, a kaleidoscope of color rioting on the plain wooden pews and flagstone floor. It was beautiful, but empty. I preferred the wide-open expanse of the outdoors, but for today, the emptiness and silence of the chapel would have to do.

The handle on the heavy oak door was frigid against my palm, even through my leather glove. I leaned back as I pulled, using my body as a counterweight against the combined forces of the buffeting wind and the door's solid construction. It eased open and I slipped through the crack, letting it close silently behind me. As my eyes adjusted to the dim light, I realized my intention for a solitary afternoon was thwarted by the bowed figure on his knees just beneath the dais.

I took a hasty step back— I had no intention of staying to make conversation with the very person I'd been actively avoiding for weeks. In a flurry of skirts and cloak, I turned and threw my weight against the door.

"Ava—"

His voice was thick with tears, and I risked a glance over my shoulder, my gaze colliding with his anguished silver eyes. I was not ready for this. I'd come for peace and solitude, maybe absolution. . . I had no interest in sharing guilt or sorrow with someone else. I could not bear the brunt of another's misery in addition to my own. Not even Gabriel's.

I shook my head and closed my eyes, denying his unspoken question and shoved with all my might, fleeing the quiet chapel as if all the demons of hell were after me.

The harvest from the plants you and your women transplanted in the forest has been better than we could have hoped for. That was truly an inspired idea *mon cœur.*"

I didn't bother looking at him.

Each day he came to me with these little tidbits, as though dangling fragments of objects and ideas that used to interest me would magically revive me now. Every evening, he came to our bedchamber and spoke to me. About our son. About the state of the country. About any and every little thing he thought might pique my interest. He even tried to talk to me about Aimée. In truth, this was generally the only matter that yielded so much as a glance in his direction.

Yesterday, he told me he was commissioning a headstone for her. *Or was it the day before?*

We spoke for a bit about what should be inscribed upon it. Poetically, he suggested *'Born in Heaven,'* which made me cry; but then, I spent most of my time crying nowadays anyway.

During that conversation, he tentatively placed his hand on mine. I immediately withdrew from him and saw the look of sadness on his face. It stabbed me with the tiniest amount of guilt, but it wasn't enough. Would it ever be enough?

"Ava."

I glanced at him. Was he still talking this entire time?

"Ava, my love. It's been a month since I got back—"

Fury rose within me, and I opened my mouth to retort, but he held up a hand to silence me.

"I would never— will never put a limit on your grief. But you cannot let life go by without you. It's all right to feel sorrow. I grieve for our daughter too—" His voice broke, and I watched mesmerized, as he swallowed convulsively. "But there is more to life than death and grief. You have a husband and a son who love and need you."

I stared down at my lap and picked at the folds in my gown.

He knelt at my feet, and I had a flashback to the last time he did, after Cifarelli accosted me. My eyes blurred as I recalled that evening, but he grabbed both my hands in his, desperately, and it snapped me back to the moment.

"Ava, please." He had my hands pressed to his mouth. Uncertainly, I looked at him. Was he begging for my attention, my affection, or both?

As I looked down at his bowed head and watched the candlelight pick up strands of crimson and gold in his hair, I felt a flicker move within me. Maybe it was the remembrance of another night like this one. Perhaps, it was the warmth of his breath against my skin.

Against my will, my hand turned over in his, and now it was cradled against the stubble on his cheek. A sensation from another life washed gently over me, like a warm, enveloping wave, another memory.

He raised his quicksilver eyes to mine; it reminded me of a hundred moments like this one. Of a thousand recollections of fire in his eyes and molten lava in my belly. But I was still irate, clinging to my anger like armor in a battle, afraid that without it I would feel too much.

He must have seen something in my expression that gave him hope, because he was standing, tugging me out of my seat, pulling me roughly against him. It took a moment for my sluggish, grieving brain to react, but when I realized what he was doing, I struggled and tried to pull away.

"Let go of me!"

"Never." His voice was shattered, but firm.

I pushed him with all my strength, all my pent-up wrath; all my fear that he would succeed in breaking down the barrier I'd built so carefully around myself.

He was immovable.

I shoved, slapped at his chest and arms, and used my elbows to try to create space between us, but I could get no reprieve. I was furious now, panic pushing its way through my chest, crushing my lungs as it expanded to fill my body. Tears and hysteria bubbled within me, threatening to drown me where I stood. I was on the cusp of losing my slender hold on my composure.

Still, he held me.

His arms were wrapped around me like steel bands, and something snapped within me. My head dropped against his chest, and it fit right where it always had.

I could hear the steady thump of his heart, and I was sobbing; weeping for our tiny daughter's heart that would never pulse like his; bawling because his body against mine felt like coming home, and despite my heartache and rage, I couldn't deny the comfort he was offering me any longer. He said he needed me, but the truth was I needed him.

"Shhh. I love you," he murmured softly. "I love you so much, Ava."

He was rubbing his hands comfortingly up and down my back as my tears soaked into his linen shirt. I lifted my head from his chest, and he steadily but tenderly pressed it back down.

"I was so mad, Gabriel," I whimpered. "I needed to blame someone. You, for not being here. Our son, for surviving when she didn't. It consumed me."

"Grief is a strange thing, *mon cœur*."

"I wanted you to go away." I sniffed.

"It takes more than that to get rid of me." His voice rumbled through his chest, reminding me how much I loved the sound and vibration.

"I've neglected our son."

"Aye, you have." There was acknowledgement, but no recrimination in his deep voice.

I lifted my head again and this time he let me.

He stared into my swollen, snotty, tear-streaked face like it was the most beautiful thing he'd ever seen and gently tucked a stray curl behind my ear.

"But he will never remember this. You have a lifetime to show him you love him."

"Gabriel."

"Oui."

"I love you."

"I know." He shot me a crooked smile. "Please don't ever shut me out like that again. I will never relinquish my love for you. Don't you forsake me."

My eyes filled with fresh tears, and he bent his head to mine, claiming my mouth. My knees buckled— in relief, in exhaustion, and desire, as an all-but-forgotten flame flickered to life deep within me.

When he carried me to bed and laid me down without taking his lips from mine, all I could think was finally.

But there was no rush or frenzy to reclaim me. He merely tucked my body firmly against his and spent forever paying homage to my lips, cheeks, and the curve of my jaw. At some point, I fell asleep, still fully clothed, cradled in his arms, and feeling safe for the first time in months.

Nine
Machine Gun Gusto

Is it silly that I'm nervous about holding my son?

Sheepishly, I asked Gabriel to have him brought to our room after we ate a simple *déjeuner* of fresh bread, apricot marmalade, and a soft, creamy goat cheese in our bedchamber this morning.

I woke up a new person, or perhaps it was just my old self. Sadness still infiltrated my every breath; I'd lost count of how many times I blinked back tears at the thought of Aimée since I woke up, but somewhere between yesterday and today, I became determined to cherish the living child I had, instead of punishing him for existing.

Too many times in my life, I'd been reminded how short it could be. The loss of Aimée broke me in a way that the others didn't, and I suspected I would feel the reverberation of the grief for the rest of my days, but as Gabriel said, *'there is more to life than death and grief.'*

I needed to pick up the pieces and focus on life.

There was a knock at the door and a moment later Esme and the wet nurse were standing before me. Esme gave me a gentle smile and it occurred to me that she must have been staying here since the birth. In my haze of sorrow, I hadn't noticed how much she's been around or questioned her constant presence. I was suddenly overwhelmed with gratitude for her unswerving friendship and beamed a tentative smile back at her. There was a hint of relief in her summer blue eyes, but I barely noticed because I was staring at my son.

Wordlessly, I held my arms out to receive him and I was surprised; both by how much bigger he was then I recalled— but also by the look of barely restrained hostility on the wet nurse's face. Confused, I glanced back at Gabriel, and he moved forward to stand behind my chair and put a hand on my shoulder. I looked back toward the wet nurse to find that her face had transformed into one of acquiescence, as she carefully placed the infant in my arms.

It was a somber, gray day outside, with dark clouds scudding across a dismal, chilly, autumn sky; but a ray of sunlight pierced through the window just then illuminating my son's perfect, little face.

Mothers always think their babies are beautiful, but this one had been blessed. Silky eyebrows arched over aquamarine eyes fringed in absurdly long, dark lashes. His cheeks were soft, plump, and rosy; his lips pursed like a cherub's. I wasn't sure how I managed to immure myself to his charms until now, but as I stared at his round, wiggly body, I found myself utterly smitten with him. He batted his little fists; waving them around and shattering the wall of ice I'd erected around my heart.

I don't know how long I sat there, gently running my hands over his body, and smiling like a loon at his coos and funny expressions, but when I glanced up, the women were gone, and Gabriel was staring at us with tears in his eyes and a smile that matched mine.

"How could I not have seen how amazing he is?" My stomach was queasy at the thought of what I'd done.

Gabriel shook his head. "Don't do that to yourself, *mon cœur*. Look ahead."

Carefully, I adjusted my hold on my son and stood before him, cradling our baby between us.

"He needs a name," I said softly, guilt eating at me despite his words.

"I've been calling him Armand when I see him, but we can name him anything you want."

"You wish to name him for your father?"

He raised a shoulder negligently. "If you like?" He was striving for nonchalance, but I knew this was important to him.

"I think it's perfect. He looks like an Armand to me. I hope he grows up as wise and kind as everyone says your papa was." I smiled up at him and he brushed his lips over mine.

"*Merci, mon amour.*"

"No. Thank you for not giving up on me."

"I told you I would never do that. I meant it." His eyes were stern and there was a frown line between his brows.

There was a telltale sound, rather like a machine gun coming from little Armand, and I looked down in surprise. His face was bright red, eyes screwed shut in concentration, and I couldn't help but emit a shocked giggle.

Suddenly, I was laughing so hard tears were streaming down my cheeks; I couldn't remember how long it had been since I last laughed. My eyes met Gabriel's silver eyes, dancing with mirth.

"Ah, yes. I forgot to mention that he presents quite a bit of er. . . gusto with his bowel movements." He was trying to keep a straight face, but he was barely holding it together. "I suggest we ring for Esme and Madame Devereux to change his diaper. Unless you wish to have a go at it yourself?"

At that moment, I was assailed by a smell so intense I nearly dropped the poor child, and Gabriel lost his hold on his control and started laughing.

"I don't believe I'm quite ready for that." I managed to say as I held my breath.

"Don't blame you a bit, *mon cœur*," he managed with a straight face.

I came awake inch by inch, fighting the sensation, but recognizing the inevitability of it. I clung to the gossamer threads of my dream, knowing it would slip through my fingers in another minute. My cheeks were wet with tears, but though I was sad; the tears were mostly happy.

I dreamt I walked through fields of wildflowers backlit by a setting, golden sun. The air was heavy and sweet with the scent of nectar, bees droned drunkenly by, and birds tweeted and trilled.

When I came to the end of the meadow, there stood my lovely mother, green eyes crinkled in a smile so beautiful, it hurt my heart. She stood beside my father, whose head was tilted back in his great, booming laugh, and Carri was there, the breeze stirring tendrils of blonde hair away from her face. My gorgeous, tiny Aimée was nestled in my mother's arms. She was gurgling and cooing happily, and it was the most exquisite sound I'd ever heard.

My eyes opened sleepily as I burrowed beneath the blankets; it'd been frigid— this first week of December— and our room was freezing in the mornings when the fire from the previous night had burned down to embers.

Gabriel's face was a few inches from mine and I studied its chiseled edges and planes in the predawn light. As if he sensed my staring, his quicksilver eyes opened, fully awake, and instantly alert in that way of his I couldn't comprehend. *Who comes fully awake in a second like that?*

But my irritation melted away as he wiped a stray tear off my cheek, his dark eyes full of concern.

"Why are you sad this morning, my love?"

I shook my head a bit and offered him a tearful smile. "I dreamt of my parents and Carri and our petite Aimée."

"How was it?" he murmured.

"Beautiful. What I imagine heaven must be like."

He brushed my plait back over my shoulder and drew me close. I nestled my head against his chest and silently took in the warmth of his body against mine. His lips moved over my hair, and I tilted my head back to look at him.

"Hmmm?" he asked, in answer to my gaze.

I ducked my head back under his chin, embarrassed and unsure how to phrase the question that had been on my mind for the last two weeks.

"Well," I began in a small voice. "I was wondering. . . that is, I was thinking—" I trailed off.

"What were you thinking?"

He rolled my body over and pulled me backward, so we were spooned together. His chest was solid against my back, his arm negligently draped over me. I was enveloped in love and safety.

Incidentally, it was also much easier to get my words out when I wasn't facing him.

"Doyounotwantmeanymore?" I asked in a rush.

I felt his surprise in the way his body momentarily stiffened, but then he chuckled, and confusion washed over me.

"Why would you think that *mon cœur*?"

"Well, you haven't tried to, er. . . you know. Since you came back," I muttered.

He tightened his hold on me, pulling me firmly against him, leaving no room to ignore what was presently poking me in the backside. His lips pressed against my collarbone; my neck and shoulder, and a wave of desire crashed over me.

"It wasn't for lack of wanting you, Ava. I don't think I go through an hour of the day without the thought crossing my mind." His voice was husky with need.

"Then why—"

"I didn't know if you were ready. . . and I didn't want to push you," he admitted.

"Oh," I replied in a tiny voice.

He rolled me onto my back and propped himself above me, gazing into my face.

"Do you want me then?" he asked, one corner of his mouth twitching up.

In answer, I wrapped my arms around his neck and pulled his mouth down to mine. He kissed me slowly and deeply; refusing to let me rush him when I tugged his hair and yanked his hips against mine.

He lifted his head a hairsbreadth from mine, and I opened my lashes dizzily, drunkenly. His eyes were opaque with desire, cloudy with need.

"It's been months, Ava. I mean to take my time with you."

Ten
Liar, Liar

Esme slowly and methodically measured the almond oil and added it to the glass suspended above the brazier. She stirred it carefully and counted out drops of marjoram oil as they dripped into the mixture. She was killing time, but the truth was that things had been awkward between Ava and herself for so long, that she struggled to navigate her way back.

Finally, she could no longer pretend she was busy and turned to face Ava.

"Luc is doing as well as one might expect. He tires easily, which frustrates him; he still suffers from bouts of stomach pain, though I think they are becoming less frequent. I hope that in time he will make a full recovery."

Ava nodded, her face looking at Esme's gravely and earnestly.

"I'm sorry I haven't asked after his health very much."

"Aye, well. You've had troubles of your own to contend with."

"Yes, but I've been a poor friend to you, Esme, and I regret it," she said softly.

Esme turned back to the brazier, carefully removed the glass, and began pouring the hot salve into jars to cool, but paused, glancing over her shoulder back at Ava.

"I've made more than my share of mistakes." She placed the empty glass cautiously on the worktable and faced Ava again. "I should have managed the situation with Marguerite differently. Maybe, if I had, things would have been normal between all of us. Perhaps we would have known you were pregnant with twins." She reached out and took both of Ava's hands in hers. "I'm sorry that things turned out the way they did."

Ava's eyes were wet, but her gaze was steady. "It wouldn't have made a difference in Aimée's death if we had known— would it have?"

"Likely not," admitted Esme, biting her bottom lip. "I imagine we will both always wonder though."

Ava squeezed her hands before letting go. "Sit with me a bit?" She took two cups from the wood shelf and a bottle of brandy and plunked them down on the table.

"I would love that," Esme managed around the lump in her throat.

"What happened with Madame Cariou?" Ava sat and poured a few fingers into each cup.

Esme sighed, took her cup, and stared into its depths like the answers to the world were within.

"When I confronted her, you mean?"

"Yes."

"I told you most of it after it happened." She tilted her cup to its side and watched as the amber liquid sloshed around. The scent released from the brandy was intoxicating and she felt slightly dizzy, even though she hadn't taken a sip yet.

"Not all of it though," answered Ava shrewdly.

"Nay. Not all of it." She lifted the brandy to her mouth and took a healthy swig, reveling in the burn as it went down her throat.

There was no response from Ava, she was merely watching Esme quietly.

"At first, she offered me tea. We sat down and I asked her about Luc. She denied it." Esme looked hard into Ava's eyes. "She's a good liar, aye? If I hadn't the proof of Luc's illness staring me in the face. . . if I didn't trust you and Gabriel as much as I do. I might have believed what she was telling me."

"Yes. She was convincing when I spoke to her about her husband. I thought her grief was genuine."

"She never grieved for him."

"I know," she said softly.

"Aye. Well anyway. I challenged her, she offered me wine, then we argued. I told you what she said about how she was trying to save me. . . I don't know what she put in the wine, but I felt odd shortly after, and then I don't recall anything else until I woke up days later."

"Wait. . . Did this all happen at her cottage?"

Esme furrowed her brows. "Well, yes. Where else?"

"But how did she get you to the Kirouac place?"

Esme's cerulean eyes met Ava's in confusion. "She didn't have a horse. . ."

"Which means someone helped her," concluded Ava grimly.

Esme's skin paled as she considered the possibilities. Her stomach clenched uncomfortably, and her hand shook as she raised her cup to her mouth and finished the brandy in one gulp. Ava silently saluted her and drank deeply from her cup.

The two women sat in silence; contemplating the repercussions of what they'd just discovered. The fire crackled, jolting Esme out of her reverie.

"What do we do now?"

Ava shook her head. "I don't know. I suppose we should tell Gabriel and Luc, but we shouldn't speak of it to anyone else. We have no idea who helped her or how involved they were."

Esme absorbed her words as she poured herself another brandy. She cocked the bottle toward Ava, wordlessly offering her another serving.

Ava held her cup out.

"Do you remember when Gabriel was hurt, and she was nowhere to be found?" she asked finally.

"She was in Argol, no?"

"*Oui*. But how did she get there?"

"You think that whoever lent her a horse then, is the same person who did when she drugged you?" There was a light in Ava's eyes that looked like excitement.

"Maybe?"

"We need to tread carefully, Esme. I don't want to risk anyone's health or life."

Esme nodded, but she wasn't listening, her mind was racing with potential accomplices.

"What about the man at her cottage the day I went to ask her if she would help teach us?"

Ava frowned, her dark brows lowering. "Did that really happen?"

She looked at her, startled. "Aye, of course. Why do you ask?"

"It's just that. . . it doesn't make sense that she would have reacted that way." Ava paused and licked her lips. "At the time, I didn't know that you knew Madame Cariou, and while her reaction to your query was strange, it was somewhat acceptable. Now that I know you had this history with her, it's much more eyebrow-raising that she behaved the way she did."

"Aye. But Ava, what if that man was who helped her?"

"But who is he?"

Esme sat back, defeated. "I don't know."

Eleven
A Self-Satisfied Glow

"Have you seen Ava?" asked Gabriel, striving for calmness. He'd spent the last twenty minutes searching the *château*, and it seemed like no one had seen her for the last hour. She hadn't been in the stables, and he'd just caught up to Luc and Esme, walking arm in arm toward home. They both shook their heads.

"I'm sorry, Gabriel. Have you checked the cemetery?" offered Esme.

He dragged a hand through his hair. *Why hadn't he thought of that?*

"Thank you, that's probably where she is." Turning away, he headed toward the small family plot, hunching his shoulders against the bitterly cold wind, and wrapping his cloak more securely around his body. Leaves that had dried and fallen due to the lack of rain long before their time, danced around his legs and crunched underfoot. Autumn had arrived with a vengeance this year, and with Christmas just days away, it was looking like it was going to be a harsh winter.

The Landévennec chapel and attached churchyard were located on a picturesque bluff, not far from the *château*. The Chabot plot was there, usually set amidst a meadow of wildflowers that undulated gently in the consistent breeze that blew off the sea. Some distant relative of his had planted an ash in its center and it stood as a graceful, silent sentinel over the family plot.

From a distance, he could see a small figure huddled with their back against the trunk of the massive tree. Ava. A rush of relief swept through him, and he lengthened his long stride, wanting to reach her as quickly as he could.

She had drawn her knees up and sat with her arms wrapped around herself, her chin resting on top as she stared at the small mound of dirt that marked Aimée's resting place. As he approached, she looked up. Her face was melancholy but serene. He didn't think she'd been crying, but it scared him how intensely she felt the loss of their daughter.

His own grief snuck up on him at the oddest times, ambushing him when he least expected it. It profoundly bothered him that he never laid eyes on this child of his, that he had never and would never know her in this life. It gripped his heart in a vise when he was alone writing letters or when he lay sleepless in bed. But what terrified him the most, was the way it had changed Ava; as if Aimée's loss had broken her in some irretrievable way.

He forced a smile and sat beside her, wrapping his cloak around both of them and drawing her close to his body. She leaned into him, resting her head on his shoulder and he relaxed slightly. Some days were bad; it seemed this wasn't one of them.

"How long have you been here, *mon cœur*?"

"Mmph. I don't know. A while I guess. Is the sun setting already?"

"*Oui*. You must be half frozen."

She rubbed her cheek against his shoulder, like an animal nuzzling its mate. "A bit. It's so peaceful here right now. . . I felt close to her."

He pressed his lips to the top of her head and inhaled the scent of roses in her hair.

"I'm sorry these last months have been so hard."

She tilted her head back, studying his unsmiling face, and laid her gloved palm against his cheek. "You promised me love and safety. You've cherished me, protected me, and refused to give up on me. But my love, you cannot shelter me from the losses life will deal us, no matter how much you may wish to."

He swallowed hard against the lump in his throat. "I hate that," he said vehemently. "I do not accept that I must stand aside and watch you be torn asunder by heartache. I want to take all your pain unto myself so you may be joyful every day of your life."

She shook her head sorrowfully. "I would do the same for you if I could. I imagine that's a true sign of love. But you have given me something far more important than an eternal lack of sadness. You've provided me with a safe place to rest, grieve, and heal. Your love and patience have been unwavering, even when I pushed you away and behaved horribly, and would have deserved it if you walked away. It told me more about the man you are than anything else that has happened so far."

He watched ruefully as she angrily swiped at her tears. He caught her fist in his and gently thumbed the moisture away from her spring-green eyes with his other hand. Cupping the back of her head, he bent his face to hers and pressed a feather-light kiss to her forehead, across her cheek, to her downturned, trembling mouth. He tasted the salt of her grief on her lips, sensed the frustration, thrumming beneath the surface of her smooth, pale skin, and reveled in the desperation and yearning that sprang to life between them as he rubbed his mouth tenderly over hers.

"I will never walk away from you, Ava. God help me. There is nothing you could ever do to change how you make me feel. I'm damned to love you for the rest of my life."

Dark lashes lifted over jade eyes cloudy with desire. Her expression shattered his control, snapping the tether on his emotions like it was no more than a fine thread of silk. He hauled her against his body, more roughly than intended, but he was unable to force himself to slow. Need made him clumsy as his hands fumbled over their clothing. In the back of his mind, he worried he would scare her with his unslakable thirst for her, but she met him beat for beat, boldly answering his bruising kisses, urging him to ever greater heights, until he was shuddering at his climax, and she was sobbing his name against his lips.

His senses came back to him in increments. Her damp, goose-fleshed skin against his. The trill of a jaybird from somewhere above. He propped himself up on an elbow and ran the tip of his index finger down the curve of her cheek.

"I'm—" He stopped. He was going to apologize for taking her so roughly, but he'd enjoyed himself far too much; and if he weren't mistaken, he rather thought she might have relished it too. Ava stretched lazily beneath him and offered him a self-satisfied smirk.

"Don't tell me you were going to say you're sorry," she teased. Her soft mouth was swollen and her normally flawless skin showed the evidence of his lovemaking.

A wave of remorse washed through him. How dare he desecrate this woman he loved more than life itself?

"*Oui*," he answered huskily. "I should have been more careful with you."

She shot him a saucy smile. "Gabriel, I needed that. I like knowing I bring you to the edge. It's a powerful feeling, and I've been feeling rather powerless of late." She grabbed both his ears and pulled his mouth down to hers for a searing kiss that made his toes curl in his boots. "Thank you." Then, she gave him a firm nudge in the ribs. "Now if you don't mind, it's getting rather cold out here."

The laugh rolled up from his gut, loosening every tense muscle along the way.

"*Dieu*, I love you, Ava. Let's go home."

Twelve

Flamboyant Dukes and Crysanthemums

Our first anniversary and second Christmas were a muted affair. There was joy, in Armand's cooing, smiling face; in the roaring fires in the hearths, and the cheerful scent of the pine boughs we brought into the *château*; in the coziness of our little family of three, safe inside while the snow accumulated into ever higher drifts outside, transforming the landscape into a glittering, snow globe. But underneath it all was a sadness I couldn't seem to shake.

My smile was often forced and there were shadows in Gabriel's eyes. What was responsible for putting them there, I couldn't say— the possibilities seemed endless. We lived under the specter of war and famine, yet we were blessed in many ways. Life in the country gave us the means to grow and store what the drought hadn't killed. There was abundant meat, and our proximity to the ocean assured us a steady supply of seafood. Gabriel's smuggling gave us access to items we would be hard-pressed to purchase otherwise, funds notwithstanding.

Gabriel was acutely aware of how dire this winter might be for his tenants, and he spent weeks planning and discussing how he could lessen the burden on the families that lived here, coordinating hunting, and fishing parties, doling out what grain we could share and visiting each family to see how we might help. We were in a unique position to help improve the odds of survival for those around us, and the importance of that was not lost on either of us.

It was the poor people living in the cities who were going to bear the brunt of this famine, and the knowledge twisted my belly in knots every time I thought about it. Underscoring the other sources of stress was the knowledge that we were no closer to discovering who Madame Cariou's mystery helper was, which weighed heavily on us all.

Gabriel and I were ensconced in his study, heads together, drafting letters to Phillipe, Necker, and others— even the king. Ever since he returned from Paris in October, he'd spent hours writing to friends, acquaintances, and influential people surrounding the throne. He and Phillipe had been tireless in their attempts to sway the nobility and those in positions of power to heed and answer the call to equality and lower taxes before the country descended into chaos.

There had been some small successes; names brought over to our side. Necker, reformist that he was, was open to many of their ideas and suggestions. The problem, of course, was convincing the rest of the nobility and the king that there would be bloodshed if a course correction was not made. Sadly, and predictably, this was likely where our mission would fail. The rich were so insulated, that they could not imagine that the fallout and repercussions of this winter might affect their comfortable lives.

I leaned back in my chair and closed my eyes. We'd been at it for the last two hours and a nasty headache was brewing behind my eyes. Gabriel scraped his chair back, and I lifted my lashes to find him standing before me, hand extended. I took it gratefully and leaned into him when he wrapped his arms around me, clasping my hands behind his waist in response. We stood together, gathering strength from each other until I reluctantly stepped away.

"It's long past time we took a break," he murmured.

"Mmm. I have a headache."

He leaned down and pressed a kiss against my forehead. "*Diner* should be ready; you need to eat."

My stomach rumbled in response and my cheeks warmed. He grinned, and the smile crinkled the corners of his eyes. It was a real smile, and I couldn't help but smile back at him as I took his arm.

The weather had been atrocious since before Christmas, but today there was finally a break in the howling winds, icy sleet, and snow. The sky was bluebird blue, the wind had disappeared, and I could hear the sweet sound of snow melting. Really.

I'd always found that my mood was affected by the weather, and as I walked the garden paths that had been cleared, drinking in the weak, winter sun; my spirits lifted, and my lips stretched in a rare smile. I linked arms with Esme, and she shot me a guarded look. There were a thousand thoughts behind her shuttered blue gaze, and I only caught a glimpse of them.

"It's a beautiful day." I heard the exuberance in my voice, but I'd never hidden my thoughts or feelings well. Why begin now?

"*Oui*."

"How is Luc?"

She shrugged elegantly. "The same. Some days he feels much better, almost like his old self. Others he struggles to get out of bed."

I stopped short and turned to face her, earnestly grabbing her freezing hands in mine. "How are you?" I asked, meaningfully.

Esme looked somewhere over my right shoulder, refusing to meet my gaze. "The same as Luc, I suppose. When he has a good day, I am filled with hope that we are turning a corner. When he has a bad day it feels like he will never be well again."

"But you see an improvement overall?" I pressed. "There are more good days and less bad ones as time passes?"

"I think so. I just—" She paused and finally looked at me, her eyes full of fear.

I squeezed her hands, silently willing her to continue.

"I wonder if we will ever have babes of our own. Do you think what Marguerite gave him damaged his ability?"

I realized with a start, that I'd been so caught up in my misery that I didn't even know Esme was thinking about children, or whether Luc would be able to now. I was so stunned; I didn't immediately reply.

"Ava?" Her brows were scrunched, and a stray breeze tugged a strand of chestnut hair out of her coiffure and whipped it across her pale face.

"I don't know. . ." I admitted, as my mind raced. "You never mentioned children before, I didn't know you wanted them."

She raised one perfectly plucked brow, disbelief plain on her face. "Why wouldn't I want them?"

"Some people don't." I offered weakly.

She snorted, skeptically. "Well, I do. Luc and I talked about it a lot when we first married, but now. . ."

"Now?" I prompted when she didn't continue.

"Now he doesn't feel well enough to err. . ." She looked at me for help and I nodded encouragingly. ". . . very often." She gestured toward her flat stomach. "And I'm not with child."

"It's early days, yet," I said soothingly. "You haven't been wed for a year and a lot has happened since last March."

"You were with child within a few months." She pointed out.

"You can't compare our situations, Esme. I'm sure that given enough time, it will happen for you and Luc. Give him a little longer to heal and give yourself some grace."

She turned back to the *château* and walked ahead of me, but not before I saw the shimmer of tears and disbelief in her eyes.

I followed her slowly, my skirt dragging on the muddy cobblestones, lost in my thoughts. *Had Luc lost his ability to father children?*

I found him in his study, head bent over Phillipe's latest letter. His jacket and cravat had been pulled off and tossed aside. His usually proud shoulders were slumped, a dead giveaway that there was more bad news. I wrapped my arms around him from behind and kissed his cheek.

"What news?" I straightened and began kneading the tight muscles in his neck and shoulders.

He didn't reply immediately, merely moving his head, first one way and then the other, giving me better access. My fingers found a knot and he hissed out a breath as I worked it loose. Finally, he reached behind him and laid his hand on mine. He tugged gently and I moved as he pushed his chair away from the desk, inviting me to sit with him. I plunked down on his lap and loosely looped my arms around his neck.

"Necker has been peddling some of our ideas to *le Roi*. Information is slow to arrive, but the king doesn't appear to be particularly interested or impressed with the bread lines and riots in Paris."

"Does he know?"

"*Oui*, of course. How could he not know? According to Phillipe, it's beginning to gain some of the other noble's attention. It's the social season and it will have been a topic of discussion at *l'Opéra* as well. I've had a letter from Berry today telling me there was an altercation between Haute-Guyenne and le Marquis de Lafayette during the New Year celebration at Versailles that ended with Louis having them both removed."

I raised my eyebrows. "What was it about? They agree with us, don't they?"

Gabriel shrugged a shoulder. "No one seems to know exactly. It may have had nothing to do with the Revolution; it could just as easily have been over some amorous affair."

I harrumphed.

He leaned his head down and gently bumped his forehead against mine. "What?"

"I don't know. I want to believe we could have influence, but it doesn't feel like we are making much headway, does it?"

"I don't know either, *mon cœur*. All we can do is try, *non*?"

"I guess." I sighed, trying not to feel defeated. "What about le Duc d'Orléans?"

"The king's cousin?" The fine lines between his brows were back.

"He thinks as we do."

"Aye, I know. But he's a bit. . ." He paused and I knew he was searching for the proper word to describe the fundamental differences between the Duke and ourselves.

"Flamboyant?" I offered.

"*Oui*. And not very careful."

I thought about how the history between the duke and his cousin the king played out and silently agreed. *Le Duc* would vote to have his cousin beheaded. Louis Phillipe d'Orléans would buy himself a few years and outlive *le Roi*, before being falsely accused of treason, and meeting his own end at the guillotine's blade. Treachery against one's family didn't seem to pay.

"I do have some better news."

"Please tell me, I need something to cheer me up." I absentmindedly rubbed the charm on my bracelet.

"First, tell me about this." He touched the chain on my wrist gently. "You never take it off."

"It was my mother's. My father gave it to her to remember my sister by."

"I thought you had no siblings?" His face looked puzzled.

"Mmm. She was stillborn. It happened a few years before my birth."

"I'm sorry." There was an odd tremor in his voice, and I looked up to see his eyes shiny with suppressed tears.

I leaned against him. "Are you thinking of Aimée?"

"Always," he admitted hoarsely.

"Me too. Although, I find this doesn't bother me."

"How did you come by it?"

I shrugged one shouldered. "I've worn it since their deaths."

"It's very finely wrought, it's a miracle it survived the wreck," he observed.

"It's the only thing I have from before. It reminds me of them, I suppose, it makes me feel close to them."

"Mmm." He was still inspecting the thin chain. "So, the flower is for your sister?" he asked, pointing to the small, intricately engraved flower that dangled from it.

I looked at the tiny chrysanthemum. "I suppose so," I murmured.

"Aye, well, I'm glad you have something to remember them by." He tucked a curl behind my ear.

"You had news?" I prompted.

"Ah *oui*, I've heard from Amélie; she wants to visit us as soon as the weather allows. Likely in March."

A genuine smile tugged at the corners of my lips at the thought of my sister-in-law and her adorable children. "That is good news. I can't wait to see how much Étienne and Thérèse have grown!"

He dropped a kiss on the end of my nose. "I miss your smiles."

I leaned my head against his shoulder and rubbed my face against his neck, inhaling his rosemary and citrus scent. The hands that were resting lightly on my lower back a moment ago, gripped my hips. He turned his face to mine and captured my mouth in a kiss that spoke of hunger gone too long unsatiated. I could taste the desperation lurking beneath the surface and a rising tide of heat swept over me, drowning me in his dark taste.

I broke off the kiss, gasping for breath against his lips, and he rubbed his mouth softly over mine, until I capitulated. Unable to help myself, I leaned into him, reclaiming his kiss, secretly thrilled when his hands fisted in my brocade skirt, crushing the soft fabric between his fingers. We'd been slow to find our way back to each other the last two months and I'd missed the passion he filled me with, subsisting on stolen crumbs when my body craved the entire damn loaf.

"Ava," he groaned against my mouth, yanking me closer to him.

I tunneled my fingers through his hair until the ribbon holding it back fell to the floor. The strands were soft and curled against my palms invitingly.

"Remember a few weeks ago when you found me under the ash?" I whispered against his mouth.

His lips trailed fire across my jaw, pausing at the soft skin beneath my ear when I let out a breathless moan. He detoured up, gently nipping my earlobe between his teeth before huskily replying.

"I remember," he growled.

My stomach clenched in anticipation. It sounded like a promise.

Thirteen
Castle Creations

"I'm so glad you're here," I admitted, enveloping Amélie in a spontaneous hug.

She stopped playing *Trois Petits Chats*, a French version of Pattycake with Thérèse, and gave me a soft smile. "I am too. I wish we could have come sooner, but with the children and the condition of the roads this winter, it just didn't seem like a good idea."

"It's all right, I understand. I wouldn't want you to put them in harm's way."

Amélie straightened and stretched after leaning over the children playing on the nursery room floor. She rested her back against the wall, grimacing at the uncomfortable position.

"I know the last months have been hard—"

I waved away her tentative foray. I wasn't interested in plumbing the depths of my soul and dredging up the grief I was just managing to hold at bay. Explaining it all to someone who hadn't experienced the loss of a child was impossible in my eyes. It was an event I wouldn't wish on anyone.

"It's alright, Amélie. Truly. I'm doing much better now. I'm still sad, of course, but it's not like before."

"You scared Gabriel." There was no reproach in her voice, but it stung regardless.

I hid my flaming face as I fiddled with Armand's linen shirt, straightening it. "I know," I said finally.

She reached across and squeezed my hand until I forced myself to look into her clear blue eyes. Her feelings of remorse and forgiveness lay naked in them. Uneasiness coiled like a serpent in my belly, and I looked away. The awkward moment stretched out while she studied my face before she finally dropped it and moved on.

"Are you having any household troubles?" she asked, lightly.

My brow scrunched and I idly ran my finger down Armand's little nose, making him giggle and grab for my hand.

"No, nothing out of the ordinary. We're still looking for a midwife, of course. Esme is considering leaving us briefly to train with Madame Simon in Trégarvan. I don't know if I mentioned that?"

She was building a tower of blocks for Étienne and paused to look at me. "Is she? What do you think about that?"

"She's well suited for it. She was interested in healing and midwifery before everything happened with Luc's health. I think she feels she has even more reason to pursue it now."

"Aye, I agree." She handed a painted block to Thérèse and sighed when she promptly lobbed it at her brother.

"Ow! *Maman!*" screeched Étienne, rubbing his arm.

"*Viens ici.*" She held her arms out as he clambered into her lap.

I waited for Étienne to settle down before continuing the conversation.

"What about you? Are you having troubles with the household then?" Something told me she didn't ask her question out of the blue; there was something she wanted to discuss.

It was her turn to fidget uncomfortably. I waited while she offered a carved train to Étienne. With a wary eye on his sister, he took the proffered toy and moved off his mother to a safe distance while Amélie smoothed nonexistent wrinkles out of her dress.

"One of our maids, she's a lovely young woman. We've had her with us since just after Mathieu and I married. . ." She paused.

"Yes?" I prompted, wiggling my fingers in front of Armand, and rewarding him with a beaming smile when he captured them.

"Well, she married herself recently, and her work has slacked off since. She arrives late, she's incredibly slow. There are days she moves like an old woman instead of a girl younger than me!"

My hackles rose as a young girl's face flashed before my eyes.

"Amélie, what is your maid's name? Is it Jeanne?"

Startled glacial eyes met mine. "How did you know?"

"It began after she wed?" I asked her urgently.

"Aye."

"Is she with child?"

She raised her shoulders in an elegant shrug. "Not that I'm aware. I suppose she might be. Why all the questions Ava?"

"Her husband beats her. Or will begin to soon."

She stopped smoothing her periwinkle skirt mid-stroke. "He abuses her? You're certain?"

"Yes."

"But, how—"

I sighed. "It's a long story. But please trust me, Amélie. We need to get her away from him."

"That's not a simple thing to do. . . the laws protect a husband's right. . ."

"I know, but that doesn't make it right. He will kill her eventually. And the babe she carries. I'm sure of it."

"*Merde.*"

I raised an eyebrow, I'd never heard Amélie curse, even mildly. "I suppose we will have to involve the men?" I asked.

"Aye. There's no way around it. Perhaps Mathieu can arrange for him to be sent away for work," she mused.

"And then what? It's only temporary. What happens when he returns?"

"Well, what if she's gone by then? Would you offer her a position here?"

"Mmm. That might work," I said slowly, rearranging the painted wooden blocks Thérèse enthusiastically knocked over. "Are we far enough away that he couldn't find her?"

She pursed her lips. "What if we said she passed?"

My hand froze in mid-air. "You propose we fake her death? How would we do such a thing? Wouldn't your tenants talk?"

"There must be a way, Ava. We say she went to visit her *maman* and fell ill." There was a touch of frustration in her voice, she looked more agitated than I'd ever seen her.

"All right," I said soothingly. "We'll figure it out." Carefully, I placed the final block on the tower. Thérèse flashed a drooling smile in my direction and immediately knocked over my creation.

I laughed and the little imp rewarded me by toddling over and wrapping her chubby arms around my neck. I leaned into her embrace, closed my eyes, and inhaled the warm, baby sweetness of her.

"Ava."

I let go of Thérèse and glanced over her curly head at Amélie. "Yes?"

"How do you know about Jeanne?"

"I had a vision of it," I answered, resigned to the inevitable.

"A vision?" Her voice was neutral, but the touch of disbelief in her eyes gave her away.

"Yes. It was over a year ago. I wondered how long it would take before it came to pass."

"I see. Have you had such visions before?" She handed a block to Étienne, who had abandoned the train and was now diligently rebuilding the castle.

"Yes." I picked Armand up off the rug and snuggled him; I hated being interrogated.

"Many times?"

I looked up at her. "No, I never had visions before the shipwreck. There have only been a few, but thus far they've all come true. Except for the one of Jeanne, but I suspect it will be true soon."

"Which ones have come true?"

I stretched my neck from side to side and adjusted my hold on Armand, bouncing him lightly on my lap. He was getting fussy; it was nearly his nap time.

"The first was about you. That little Thérèse would be a girl." I answered, with a nod toward my tow-headed niece.

"Before she was born?"

"Yes." I shifted Armand again; he was about to begin crying any minute now.

"What else?" Her gaze was rapt.

"That Luc would get ill."

She nodded. "And?"

"That's all so far."

She sighed. "Right then. I suppose Gabriel knows?"

I nodded right as Armand began to howl in earnest.

"Alright, Thérèse, Étienne. Your little cousin needs to sleep now. Give him a kiss." She stood, smoothing out her dress with one hand and scooping Thérèse up with the other. "Come along Étienne. Let's go find Margaret."

I gave them a smile and a little wave as Madame Devereux bustled into the room. I tenderly handed Armand over to her and she gave me a tight smile. She had warmed considerably toward me in the last two months, but either her natural reserve or my atrocious behavior postpartum had cast a pall over our relationship that I wasn't sure would ever be surmounted.

Armand settled down to suckle immediately; his eyes getting heavy, and I ran my palm over his soft hair. A pang of regret pierced me, that he found comfort and peace so easily in another woman's arms. It was my fault of course, and it filled me with gratitude that Madame Devereux took care of him when I was unable, but it still stung.

I dropped my hand and turned my face away, forcing myself to leave the nursery. I quietly shut the door behind me as I blinked back the prickle of tears. It had been an exhausting afternoon. I could do with a nap myself.

Fourteen
Patience is a Virtue

"We can accommodate another maid, can't we?" I asked Gabriel as I applied an even layer of creamy butter to my bread.

He raised a chestnut brow at me. "If the situation is as dire as you and Amélie believe, then yes, of course. We will find work for her here."

I swallowed my bite of breakfast, lifted my *serviette* daintily to my mouth, and beamed at him. "Thank you." I shot a wink in Amélie's direction.

"It will be complicated for Mathieu to have him sent away to work. It needs to be a well-thought-out and believable mission," he warned.

"I've been thinking about that, and I think I may have a solution," put in Mathieu. "I still need to iron out the finer details though."

Amélie placed her teacup back into its saucer with a soft clink. "You didn't tell me! What have you come up with?"

Mathieu shrugged modestly. "Jeanne's husband, Corbin is a stone mason— he's quite talented. . ." Amélie shot him a venomous look and he straightened up. "Anyway, I know he's long wished to see the standing stones at Carnac. There's a quarry nearby producing exceptional quality granite. I thought I might send him to choose a piece for the hearthstone we want to replace."

I glanced at Amélie who was nodding in approval. "How long will that keep him away for?"

"I reckon three or four weeks." He elegantly motioned for a refill of his tea.

"All right." I was thinking furiously.

"Amélie, you'll send Jeanne for a visit with her mother while he's gone?" Gabriel's steel gray eyes looked worried beneath his wrinkled brow.

"*Oui*. I think I will arrange that ahead of time. That way Corbin will know she will be away while he is gone." She looked at Mathieu. "What do you think? Or will he forbid her to see her *maman*?"

"If he's as controlling and abusive as you say, he might forbid it. Although we could always say she went anyway. Let his wrath fall on us. He will have no recourse," he mused.

"He will believe us, if we tell him she passed while he was gone, won't he?" Amélie anxiously chewed on her bottom lip.

Mathieu sent his wife a reassuring smile. "Of course, *mon chou*. What's not to believe?"

"I don't know," she said slowly. "If she's with child as Ava believes, I think it's best to say she lost the *bébé* and hemorrhaged." Her cerulean eyes looked at me guiltily, as though the mention of infant loss might send me running for the hills.

Considering that I hoped these drastic actions would save the lives of mother and child, I was okay with it.

"What about her mother? Where does she live? You will have to contact her to explain the situation to her."

"*Oui*, I thought of that. Her mother lives a few hours away by horseback. Mathieu and I will speak to her."

I sat back in my chair. Something was niggling at the back of my mind. The plan seemed simple and foolproof; were we underestimating Jeanne's husband? I bit my lip and met Gabriel's eyes.

"What are you thinking *mon cœur*?"

"What are the odds that Corbin will disbelieve Mathieu and Amélie and go searching for his wife?" My stomach churned with acid at the thought of him following her trail here.

Gabriel's mouth tightened in a grimace. "We'll deal with him if need be. Jeanne and her *bébé* will be under our protection no matter the cost."

His response did not reassure me, though I knew we could only mitigate the danger to a certain degree. Resigned, I lifted my teacup and breathed deeply of the fragrant steam, allowing it to relax me slightly.

"Everything will be fine," said Amélie soothingly.

Mathieu raised his cup in a salute. "Here's to saving lives."

7th April, 1789
Madame Esme Morvan
Care of Madame Simon
7 Rue de Rivoli
Trégarvan, France

My dear Esme,

How are your studies coming along with Madame Simon? I hope this time is as fulfilling and educational as you hoped. We will certainly be putting your new knowledge to the test when you return to Landévennec!

I am sure Luc has been writing diligently to you, he seems quite lost without you (though I confess, I feel rather lost without your presence here as well). Gabriel and I have been monitoring his health as well as we can, and I do believe his vigor and strength have improved further during your absence. He's been helping Gabriel out with collecting the quarterly rents, which as you know, can be a taxing affair.

Our new maid Jeanne has arrived from Trégoudan and seems to be settling in nicely. The poor child has been treated most atrociously by her husband, and I am so grateful we were able to get her away from him. She is extraordinarily quiet, preferring to keep to herself, and shying away from the smallest infractions, but I believe that with our dedication to showing her care and love (as well as your fabulous sense of humor), we will have her coming out of her shell in no time.

She is in fact with child, so she will be one of your first midwife customers when you return home to us! Thus far, from what I can ascertain, she and the bébé appear to be in good health. You'll be pleased to hear I've made it my mission to ensure she is eating well and resting appropriately.

You will want to know how our little Armand is doing. I can imagine the scolding I would receive from you (complete with a wagging finger) if I didn't mention the pocket-sized darling. He is beginning to sit up when Gabriel and I play with him in the nursery, and he has us both in stitches with his babbles, drooly smiles, and waving hands. When it comes to mealtimes, he is a most avid and dedicated eater, and Madame Devereux assures me that he is sleeping for longer stretches overnight. You won't believe how he's grown when you return!

Speaking of your return, when should we expect you back? I'm sure you've heard Jacques Necker has called for the Estates-General to convene at Versailles on the fifth of May. Of course, Gabriel will have to go, and I am considering accompanying him as he believes he may be called away for some time. I cannot stand the idea of being separated from Armand for what promises to be weeks, if not months, which means he will be traveling with us if I go. It will be quite the entourage, as Madame Devereux will be coming with us. I have told Gabriel that I would like Mademoiselle Noemi to come with us as well. I hope that you will be back before we have to leave. Gabriel tells me we should be going the third week in April to ensure our timely arrival.

I eagerly await your response.

Your dear friend,
Ava Chabot
Vicomtesse de Landévennec

Gabriel and Luc walked companionably out of the dazzling, spring sunshine and into the shadowy stables. His eyes slowly adjusted to the diffused light as he paused at each stall to check on its occupant. He ran his left hand along Automne's withers and picked up each hoof to inspect his horseshoes. Done with his examination, he offered the stallion a carrot and patted his neck.

"I'm taking the matched grays for the carriage, Automne for myself, and I think, Minuit for Ava, or do you think I should take Flamme?" He stepped out of Automne's stall and carefully latched the door before resuming his walk.

Luc didn't reply immediately, and Gabriel glanced at him as he lifted the bar on the next stall. Flamme greeted him with a whinny and bumped her nose against his palm, searching for the treats he always brought. "Calm down," he laughed as she lipped up the proffered apple, tickling his palm.

"Flamme is a mite young, but her spirit matches my lady's," stated Luc, thoughtfully. "Minuit is a steadier horse. If you travel to Paris after Versailles, she will manage the crowds and noises better than Flamme would."

Gabriel nodded. "*Oui*, you're right."

He shot a sideways look at Luc, silently assessing how his favorite tenant looked. His health had improved steadily, albeit slowly over the last year and although he hadn't regained his former vigor, Gabriel was pleased with his progress. "The wheat is coming in nicely this year. I would make you foreman when we leave if you are amenable to it."

A dull red stained Luc's face, but Gabriel thought he looked pleased.

"I would be honored."

"Splendid." Gabriel clapped a hand on Luc's shoulder as they turned to leave the stables. "I need someone here that I can rely on. There's no one I trust more than you."

"I—" Luc cleared his throat. "Thank you, my lord."

"As you know, the Navy has made our other endeavor rather complicated, of late." He added, referring to their smuggling operation. "But we are expecting another shipment in May. I'll need you to see to that as well. You'll have to rendezvous with Mathieu and the others."

"Consider it done."

"*Merci*, Luc. Have you had any word from Esme?" He fixed his piercing steady gaze on Luc.

"*Oui*. She is leaving Madame Simon on Sunday. God willing, she will be home before you and my lady leave for Versailles."

Gabriel flashed a heartfelt grin at the man. "Ava will be elated to hear that. She's been hoping we would see her before we left." He leaned against the corral, propping his forearms on the top rail, observing as one of the horses was put through their paces.

"Aye, I know Esme would be crushed if she missed the opportunity to say goodbye to Armand. She's grown quite attached to him." He smiled, but Gabriel noticed it didn't quite reach his eyes.

"What's wrong man?" Gabriel nudged Luc, intuition tingling between his shoulder blades.

Luc mimicked his stance; arms resting on the wood railing. He gripped his hands together tightly, looking down at the sandy, loamy earth as though he were fighting some inner demon.

Gabriel waited patiently, watching Le Gall as he skillfully swung a leg over Têtue's back. The stubborn horse's muscles bunched together, threatening to throw him. Le Gall lay low, running one hand soothingly over his charcoal gray neck as he spoke to him. Têtue's ears flicked back, evidently willing to be sweet-talked under the right circumstances. He felt Luc let a breath out beside him, and he turned his attention back to his tenant, squinting at him in the intense sunlight.

"Esme is wanting a babe of our own. Badly."

Gabriel quirked a brow at him.

Luc hunched his shoulders self-consciously.

"You've been ill Luc. Children will bless you and Esme when the time is right."

He wasn't expecting his friend's admission and didn't quite know what to make of it. *Le bon Dieu* knew his understanding of the mysteries of pregnancy and the subsequent birth didn't extend much beyond the calving and lambing that took place every spring on the farm.

"Right," muttered Luc. "She's mayhap getting. . . impatient."

"Well perhaps it will happen for the two of you when she returns, eh? You seem to be in better health lately." Gabriel offered. He looked down and noticed Luc's hands grasped the railing so tightly his knuckles were white.

When Luc didn't respond, Gabriel tried again. "Is there something more?"

Luc looked at Gabriel, piercing him with his gaze. "Esme is younger than me, by a few good years, aye?"

Gabriel nodded quietly.

"I've been thinking of late that it's wrong of me to tie a beautiful, young woman like her down to an older, wretched man who can't give her what she wants. She deserves happiness, Gabriel. What if it isn't meant to be with me?"

It felt like Luc had punched him in the solar plexus. He stared at his friend in mute disbelief for several long seconds as his mind scrambled for the words to soothe Luc. *How long had he been thinking along these lines?*

"Luc," he croaked. He cleared his throat. "There can be no question that Esme loves you. She never cared about the difference in your age before. I'm guessing you haven't spoken to her about this?"

Luc shifted his stance and shrugged a shoulder. "Nay, not yet."

"I thought not. If you had, you would know that she wouldn't want to be free to have a *bébé* with anyone else."

Luc narrowed his eyes. "You can't know that man."

"I *do* know that," insisted Gabriel. "She loves you. You need to speak to her, Luc."

Luc sighed.

Gabriel narrowed his dark gray eyes at him. "You *will* talk to her about this, aye?"

"Aye," muttered Luc.

"*Bon*," replied Gabriel succinctly. He clapped a hand on Luc's shoulder. "I'll see you on the morrow then."

Luc gave him a nod.

Fifteen
Le Jardin

I was micromanaging the packing for the trip. The tamped-down frustration as I hovered over Madame Devereux, trying to ensure that nothing Armand might need was inadvertently forgotten was palpable. You would think Versailles and Paris were the far ends of the earth, and I wouldn't be able to obtain whatever we might need if something were left behind. Was I being irrational? Absolutely. But the remnants of new mom anxiety were strong, and I couldn't seem to help myself.

"I'll just take Armand for a little walk through the gardens," I offered, ignoring the wet nurse's look of relief as I waltzed out of the nursery.

"*Merci*, my lady!" she called merrily behind me.

First, I'd take a quick peak at how Mademoiselles Adrienne and Noemi were managing the packing of my trunks, I told myself; the heels of my shoes tapping rhythmically on the wood floor as I made my way down the corridor to my chamber. Armand gurgled happily as I shifted him from one hip to the other. Under my breath, I hummed '*Au Clair de la Lune*'. Like most songs I knew, this one was written years in the future. It gave me a peculiar feeling in my wame every time I thought about it. Where I came from, how I got here. Would I ever become accustomed to it?

Armand reached for my earring, temptingly dangling at eye level. I hastily turned my attention back to his smiling aqua-green eyes, gently detaching his tiny fist before he could enthusiastically rip it from my ear.

"You're lucky you're such a handsome little stinker. God only knows what you'll get away with when you're older."

He shot me a disarmingly, mischievous smile as I brought his chubby, dimpled hand to my lips for a quick kiss.

Our chamber was chaotic. Three cavernous trunks stood open; my gowns, petticoats, stockings, and linens were in various piles; some folded, others tossed haphazardly across the bed or over the back of a chair. Mademoiselle Adrienne's plump face was flushed, strands of fine blonde hair stuck to her cheeks as her eyes met mine.

Armand waved his hands as I readjusted my hold on him. "Shall we stay and help?"

Her eyes widened comically. "*Non*, Madame la Vicomtesse! We have everything under control."

"*Oui*. Take that sweet *bébé* to the *jardin*. It's a beautiful day," added Mademoiselle Noemi firmly.

"I suppose we've been banished," I observed cheerfully. "To the gardens we go."

I made my way down the stairs, one hand carefully clutching the banister. Between my voluminous skirts, the freshly waxed floors, and the wiggling infant on my hip, a tumble seemed far too likely.

Monsieur Tremblay had thoughtfully placed Armand's pram at the beginning of the garden path and after tucking him in with a warm quilt and making sure his face was shaded from the brilliant, noonday sun, I began a leisurely stroll over the bumpy, cobbled path. Within a few minutes my arms were aching; pushing a stroller over stones was no picnic. But the exercise felt good, and I paused, tilting my face back to drink in the warmth on my skin.

Wisteria scrambled over a low stone wall, lavender clusters hanging low, swaying in the breeze, the fallen blossoms covering the walkway in a sea of violet. A bit further on there was a stunning flowering quince that Gabriel's mother had planted. The coral-colored blooms had become a favorite of mine and made the perfect backdrop for the bed of irises in front of it. Armand had gone quiet. A peek at his adorable face gone slack in slumber made a smile tug at the corners of my mouth.

Love for him had snuck up on me. Quietly filling the gaps and dark corners of my heart. A shadow stole over me, as I remembered his twin, my darling Aimée. How I wished they could have grown up together. Would he sense her absence as he grew? Did he perceive the loss of her now?

I sat on a marble bench in the shade of a massive willow, arranging the pram so I could watch Armand's expressions as they flitted across his face in sleep. This spot of the garden was my favorite; peace always found me here. I watched as a bumblebee perused the phlox and tea roses across the path when my ears picked up the familiar sound of Gabriel's footsteps.

"If that isn't the prettiest picture," he murmured, his voice gravelly as he walked around the bend.

I tilted my head back for his kiss and felt a jump in the pit of my stomach as he lingered over my lips. When he pulled away his eyes were dark with desire. My hand curled into the lapel of his coat, and I pulled him back for another.

"I may make it a habit to find you in *le jardin* if I'm going to get a greeting like that each time."

I poked him in the ribs, and he flashed me a wicked grin as he sat beside me, wrapping his arm around me and tucking me against his side. Content, I leaned my head on his shoulder and let the silence settle around us as a cool breeze played with fallen blossoms, whirling them in little eddies across the stones. Eventually, he stirred.

"How is the packing coming along?"

"Well, I think. It's a bit overwhelming, everything we need to bring."

"Mmph. Aye." He reached into his coat, rummaged around, and produced a letter with the Gardin crest stamped in red wax on it. "For you, from Amélie."

"Oh, thank you!"

"Best to read it now."

My brow creased in confusion at the somber tone in his deep voice.

Gently, I ran my finger under the flap, carefully loosening the wax to open the folded paper.

18th April, 1789
Madame Ava Cabot
Vicomtesse de Landévennec
Château Landévennec

My dear sister Ava,

How I wish we were traveling with you to Versailles! I envy you for your upcoming adventure. I've heard the Hall of Mirrors is simply divine. You'll have to write to me often to fill me in on the fashions. I hear that panniers are as wide as twelve pied. Can you imagine? How does one enter a room? I shudder to think.

How is my darling nephew Armand? Growing to be a charming little devil, I've no doubt. I do believe he has his entire entourage wrapped around his precious finger. His cousins are utterly smitten with him after our visit, and they ask after him daily. Étienne tells me he can't wait for Armand to be old enough to romp with him. Something tells me the two of them will get into quite a few escapades as they grow.

I hope this letter reaches you before you and Gabriel leave Landévennec. Jeanne's husband Corbin has returned from Carnac, and to be honest, I am fearful of what he will do next. He seems to have come completely unhinged since word arrived about Jeanne's untimely demise. He tore off to visit her mother, who tells me he did not seem satisfied with her explanation and was quite threatening, going so far as to suggest she might be to blame for her daughter's death. She was quite shaken by the exchange.

Although I do not see things as clearly as you do, I am filled with a sense of foreboding that in desperation he may consider searching for her there. 'Twould be best if Jeanne were not at Landévennec should he come looking for her. Is it within the realm of possibility that she accompanies you to Versailles? I wish you could see for yourself what his behavior has been like. I've spoken to Mathieu about asking him to leave, as I do not feel safe having him around. Mathieu feels we must tread carefully as expelling him outright may cause him to lose his sensibilities entirely and pose an even greater threat to us all. I've agreed to give it time, but I won't go so far as to walk the gardens alone knowing he is about.

Write to me as soon as you're able regarding your decision so I may rest easy that Jeanne, at least, is safe. Wishing you safe travels. I cannot wait to hear about court life!

Your loving sister,
Amélie Gardin
Baroness de Trégoudan

I sighed and pressed my fingers to my temples, massaging against the tension headache that crept up my neck.

Gabriel brushed his lips over my hair. "Is it Jeanne?"

"Yes. You knew?"

"Mathieu wrote to me as well. He thinks we should take her with us."

"Amélie says the same. Is it feasible?"

"She's taken a liking to Armand, has she not?" He nodded his head toward our sleeping babe, one chestnut eyebrow lifted in question.

"She has," I answered, thoughtfully playing with the bracelet on my wrist distractedly.

"Might she come along as help in the nursery? Madame Devereux will need help."

"How many attendants does one child require?" I teased.

"Two certainly isn't too many." His chiseled face was serious, and a wave of pure love washed over me.

"I think it's a lovely idea," I said truthfully. "It will keep her safe, and I do believe that if anyone can break down the walls that child has built around herself, it's another child."

"Aye. That's settled then. You'll let her know?"

"Of course."

"I need to see to the horses and carriage," Gabriel said, standing. He offered me a hand and I rose on my toes to steal one more kiss from him.

Sixteen
Poppy Fields

"I'm so glad you made it back from Madame Simon's before we left!" Ava wrapped her arms around her in a fierce hug.

Esme swiped a tear away and forced herself to embrace Ava in return. "I'm going to miss you this summer. When will you be back?"

Ava frowned as she stepped back, her eyes clouding. "I don't know," she admitted. "I think the meeting of the Estates-General should only last a few weeks, but I suspect we will be spending the summer in Paris."

Esme's eyes filled anew. She hated the idea of being apart for so long and blinked them rapidly away. She sat in her customary chair in the surgery and poured Ava and herself a cup of tea. "Why so long?"

"Gabriel will want to be in the thick of it for as long as he can stand it. He desperately wants to make a difference for the impoverished." She shrugged one shoulder and smoothed out her pale gray brocade skirt. "But I know he will be anxious about how things are progressing here as well. It's going to make him crazy that he can't be in two places at once."

She grinned. "Aye, he does prefer to oversee everything himself," she worded delicately.

Ava laughed. "You mean he has an overwhelming need to be in control."

"Basically," she agreed, smiling back. She raised her teacup to her lips and took a small sip, careful not to scald her mouth.

"So, tell me about Madame Simon. How was it? Did you feel it was worthwhile?" Ava picked up an almond biscuit and bit daintily catching the crumbs in her *serviette*.

Esme placed her cup back on the table. "It was better than I could have imagined. I learned so much; she has so much experience. I copied down as many of her recipes as I could. It was absolutely wonderful. I'll have to share what I can with you when you're back."

"I'm glad," she said simply. "Will you teach the girls while I'm gone?"

"Isabelle and Eloise?"

Ava nodded, her mouth full of cookie.

"Of course! The more knowledge we collectively have, the better. They're quick learners."

"I agree." Ava offered her a quick smile. "How is it being back? Luc missed you terribly."

Esme's stomach tightened at the mention of her husband. Their reunion the previous afternoon hadn't gone at all the way she'd envisioned it. "It's fine," she said softly. She picked up her cup and took a long sip to prevent any more questions.

Ava didn't get the hint. "He must be so happy to have you home."

She smiled tightly, the knot in her throat threatening to choke her.

Madame Devereux knocked on the door frame, holding Armand on her hip. Ava glanced over her shoulder toward the entrance and waved her forward. Esme watched in interest as Ava expertly took her son from the wet nurse's arms. At least her friend had turned a corner in her relationship with Madame Devereux.

"Did he have a good nap?" she asked.

The wet nurse softly rubbed Armand's back. "Aye, my lady. He slept well and ate heartily. He'll be happy to see Madame Esme I warrant," she said with a smile at Esme.

"As I am thrilled to see him again." Esme smiled. "Give me that sweet babe!" She held her arms out to receive him from Ava.

Armand burbled excitedly at her, filling her with a sense of joy at his innocent affection as well as a bittersweet ache that she didn't have this herself yet. Maybe she would never experience this with a *bébé* of her own, if Luc's reception of her was an indication of things to come. Her throat closed at the reminder of their argument this morning, and she found herself blinking hard against the prickle of tears. Not wanting her friend to see her expression, she hid her face against Armand's warm neck, tickling him with her hair and making him giggle. Her heart swelled at the sound. *Was she wrong to so desperately want this for herself?*

Gabriel blew out a long breath, trying in vain to expel his frustration with it. He had expressly asked Ava to come to the Estates-General meeting at Versailles with him. He had nearly lost her the last time he left her and didn't ever want to repeat the experience. A fist squeezed his heart at the reminder. His selfish desire to have her close to him wasn't the only reason though, her knowledge and insight would be invaluable to him over the coming months. He closed his eyes and let out another mighty breath, ruffling a stray strand of hair that had come loose during their travels.

He had expected their progress on the way to Versailles to be slow. Travel with an entourage of attendants, trunks, and his son, was turning out to be far more of a logistical nightmare than he'd prepared himself for though.

Auberges along their route had been surprisingly full, often only able to accommodate a portion of their group.

Thank the Lord he had the foresight to plan and write ahead, securing a house for them all just outside the Palais de Versailles, because he was beginning to doubt they would have been able to find even the meanest apartments to house them if he'd waited until their arrival.

They'd been on the road for twelve days, and by his calculations, it would be at least another two before they arrived. Or at least, it would have been another two if the damn carriage hadn't just lost a wheel.

Ava slipped her petite hand comfortingly into his and squeezed wordlessly. He looked down at his diminutive wife and his anger at another delay ebbed away like sand through an hourglass. Grateful, he squeezed back.

"Monsieur Le Gall," she called out authoritatively. "Have we a replacement?"

"*Oui*, my lady. Seznec, Hamon, and I will unload the carriage. Thankfully le Vicomte had the foresight to commission extra carriage wheels before our travels. It should only be a few hours delay."

She beamed at him. "*Merci*!" She turned her attention to the women clustered a few feet away. "Let's take advantage of the delay and have some *diner*. Mademoiselle Noemi, could you and Madame Jeanne set out the food? I believe we packed a basket. Madame Devereux, Armand looks like he may be due for a nap."

"*Oui*, Madame la Vicomtesse, I think so as well." She sat with her back against the trunk of a large willow, cuddling Armand on her lap.

"My lord and myself are going for a bit of a walk to stretch our legs," she announced, tucking her hand into the crook of Gabriel's arm.

He let her lead him down the dusty road quietly, feeling the knot of anxiety in his chest unravel as they strolled further from their entourage. A cool breeze sent the wild poppies in the field beside them dancing like so many crimson skirts swaying at a ball. It rustled through Ava's impeccable updo, teasing strands of hair free from its constraints.

"*Merci, mon amour,*" he said gruffly.

She eyed him. "Twas nothing, Gabriel. I could sense your frustration. It's taking quite a bit longer to arrive than you thought, isn't it?"

"*Oui.*" He ran a hand through his chestnut hair.

Ava stopped walking and gave him an impish grin. "You know, I've always wanted to run through a field of poppies."

Gabriel gazed down at her sparkling eyes, there was a light in them that he'd rarely seen over the last year. "I'll race you," he answered seriously.

"Wait." She held his arm while she balanced, removing first one shoe and stocking, and then the other. Enthusiastically, she tossed her garters on top, offered him a saucy smirk, and took off.

He stared after her for a second, the flash of bare legs flying beneath her skirts, her gorgeous, dark curls, tumbling in a cascade down her back, flying in the wind. *Dieu, how he loved her.*

Then he sprinted after her, his long legs eating up the distance between them easily. She was laughing breathlessly when he caught up to her beneath the shade of a massive oak tree. Ava tossed her head back, smiling brilliantly at him and his breath hitched as he placed his hands on her hips and walked her back against the trunk of the tree, pinning her with his body.

She didn't take her eyes off his as her amusement died in her throat. His dark gray gaze devoured her, slowly running down her exquisite face, lingering over her neck and decolletage. He watched her throat move as she swallowed convulsively, and he leisurely lifted his eyes to her lips, watching as her white teeth bit her lower lip.

It suddenly felt like there wasn't enough air to breathe.

"Gabriel." Her voice was thick, and his body tightened even further.

He brought her closer to him, until he felt every curve of her body against his, every breath she took. She rose on her toes, rubbing provocatively against him, twining her fingers through the hair at his nape, and lifted her mouth to his. Gabriel adjusted his grip, moving from her hips to the delicious curve of her buttocks, pulling her firmly against his aching need, but he held off kissing her. Instead, he reveled in her little gasp of breath, how her lids were heavy over eyes gone dark with yearning, the pressure on the back of his neck, as she begged him wordlessly to claim her.

Deliberately, he lifted his hands to cup her face gently. He rubbed his thumb over her bottom lip before finally kissing her soft mouth. He spent an eternity paying homage to her lips, ignoring his mounting desperation, determined not to give in and take her like a savage. He felt her legs give as a shudder wracked her lithe body and he lifted her, dropping to his knees as she wrapped her legs around his waist. He laid her back in the clover like she was made of glass and pressed his forehead against hers, vying for control over the fire raging in his blood.

Ava lifted her long lashes, unveiling jade eyes, hazy with longing.

"Please," she breathed against his mouth.

It undid him.

Seventeen
Boar's Head

There was a spring in my step as we strolled slowly back to our group along fields swaying in shades of lilac, rose, and butter yellow. Sweet wildflowers scented the balmy breeze tugging at my hair, and my limbs felt as deliciously limber as sun-warmed honey.

"You look like a maid who has been tumbled in the hayloft," observed Gabriel, a self-satisfied smirk on his handsome face. He reached out and picked a twig out of my hair.

I offered him a carefree smile. "You mean a proper lady taken in a field of clover by her very accomplished lover?"

I was delighted to see his cheeks flush. "Very accomplished husband," he corrected, but he was still smiling.

"Might my very accomplished husband help me pin my hair up so everyone doesn't immediately guess where we've been?"

He raised a sculpted eyebrow. "You do know that there will be no doubt in anyone's mind, aye?"

I lifted a brow haughtily at him in response.

"You look far too satiated *mon cœur*." His eyes twinkled mischievously.

"You look rather gratified yourself." I shot back saucily.

He lifted our linked hands and pressed a fervent kiss to the back of mine, his charcoal eyes serious. "I never seem to get enough of you. I want you again as soon as I've had you. My need for you is all-encompassing."

I stopped at the sober turn in our conversation and rose on my toes to capture his lips. He groaned against my mouth and my lips curved in a smile.

"*Dieu*, I love you, Ava."

"I love you too." I gathered my tresses over my shoulder and twisted my hair into a thick braid, curling it into a bun and tucking the ends under. I spun in a little pirouette. "How does it look?"

"Beautiful," Gabriel said softly.

I threaded my fingers through his. "I'm starving, let's go eat."

We arrived to find the carriage repacked, the wheel replaced, and Armand sprawled out on a blanket in the shade. If knowing looks were exchanged between Noemi and Jeanne, I blithely ignored them.

"Should I ride with you? We can eat on the way." I knew he was eager to get back on the road.

He squeezed my hand in thanks. "*Oui*."

"Le Gall, can you help my lady up?"

I smiled at Monsieur Le Gall as he handed me up onto Automne behind Gabriel. "*Merci*."

"There is a stream a little further on. We'll stop there to water the horses." Gabriel pulled his watch out of his waistcoat pocket. "I warrant we'll arrive in *Épernon*, well ahead of supper this evening. We'll stay the night, push on to *Le Perray-en-Yvelines* tomorrow, and if all goes well arrive at Versailles the following evening."

The men nodded; Gabriel clicked to Automne as he squeezed his sides, and we were on our way. Gabriel passed a piece of cheese back to me and I munched in thoughtful silence, remembering that the last time I'd spent any length of time riding astride behind Gabriel was when we'd gone to Nantes and back. I popped the last savory bite of cheese in my mouth and wrapped my arms affectionately around him, pressing a spontaneous kiss to his nape.

He turned his face, resting his cheek against my hair. "Once we arrive, you'll want to see about ordering some dresses made. *La Reine* is quite lavish."

"Mmm. I know," I said, resigned to several boring hours of sitting and standing while I was measured and fitted.

"Most women love shopping," he teased.

"I do love it, to a point. It just feels wasteful when I already have so many gowns and so many others can't even feed their children."

"Aye. We can afford it though, and without proper court attire we cannot hope to exert an influence and help the Third Estate."

"True. I hadn't thought of that," I conceded.

Gabriel offered me one of his lemon candies and I took it gratefully, letting its bright flavor flood my tastebuds.

We entered Épernon a few hours later through the Gate of Chartres and took the winding, cobbled road through the narrow, picturesque streets of the medieval walled town. Épernon was situated at the confluence of the Drouette and Guesle rivers which bisected the village. Gabriel pulled back on the reins, bringing Automne to a halt as he beckoned a young, dark-haired boy who looked to be about eight or nine over.

The lad approached with an eager smile, excited at the prospect of earning a coin for his assistance.

"*Oui*, my lord. How may I be of service?" he piped looking up at Gabriel and me.

"Could you point me in the direction of a large auberge situated near a carriage house and stables?" Gabriel gestured toward the array of people behind us with his hand. "We're traveling with several people and need a decent place to stay tonight."

"Of course!" he gushed. "Please, follow me." Barely waiting to see if we were behind him, he darted ahead, weaving expertly in and out of the bustling crowd. I crinkled my nose at the odor of several thousand villagers living in close proximity to each other, without a proper sewage system, and reached into the hidden pocket sewn in my dress, pulling out the linen handkerchief that I'd doused in lavender oil earlier this morning. The smell was overwhelming, and I held my breath until the little square of fabric was safely over my nose and mouth. I exhaled in relief, causing Gabriel to glance back at me.

"Alright *mon cœur*?"

"Yes," I replied with a grimace. It was impossible to fully disguise the mingled scent of horse and human dung with the sweetly cloying, metallic smell of blood from the butcher's market we were passing.

"*Oui.*" Distaste was etched on his chiseled face. "I do miss the clean smell of the country."

"Mmm." I muttered through my kerchief. "Me too."

We'd lost sight of our guide, but as we navigated through the throng and approached the next crossroad, I caught a glimpse of the lad waiting for us on the corner, leaning against the stone wall of a *boulangerie*, one knee bent, his foot propped against the wall behind him. I made eye contact with him, and he straightened, waving us on. We turned down a quieter street and followed him along the twists and turns of a charming neighborhood. He finally came to a stop before a neat stone carriage house with attached stables.

"The auberge is just across the street." He straightened his cap and pointed at a large, well-built house with a sign bearing the name *La Tete du Sanglier*.

The mullioned windows sparkled in the setting sun, offsetting the frisson of fear that skittered up my spine as I flashed back to the nightmare of a charging boar I had more than a year ago. I swallowed dryly, trying to ignore the tight, prickling of my scalp that heralded a tension headache.

"*Merci beaucoup.*" Gabriel flipped a coin at the boy who caught it easily, slipping it into his pocket in a smooth, practiced motion.

I smiled my thanks weakly, my stomach churning, as the lad gave a jaunty salute and disappeared around the corner.

Le Gall swiftly handed me down from Automne. "Seznec and I will handle getting the horses settled," he said to Gabriel. "We'll meet you when we're done."

Gabriel dismounted Automne and nodding his thanks at the men, offered me his arm, took one look at my pinched face, and pulled up short.

"What's wrong?" he asked under his breath, lifting a hand to my cheek gently.

I chewed on my lip. "It's silly. . . it's just, the name." I looked up at the boar's head painted on the large wood sign above the door.

Gabriel glanced over his shoulder at the sign, and returned his gaze to me, brows furrowed. "You're not thinking—"

"Of Denis? Yes. And the vision I had of it." I let out a shaky laugh.

"We'll find somewhere else to stay." He brushed a tendril of hair back over my shoulder.

"No!"

Gray eyes treated me to a quizzical look.

"It's fine. . . really. It just gave me a queer turn." My stomach was still twisted in knots, but I was definitely making a big deal out of nothing.

"Are you sure? I'm sure we can find something else, *mon cœur*."

My heart flipped and I nodded definitively. "Yes," I said softly.

"All right." He looked at me doubtfully, bent his head, and brushed his lips over mine. "Tell me if you change your mind, aye?"

Eighteen
Trust and Sinking Ships

I awoke with the dawn light, surprised that the night had passed uneventfully. Gabriel was likely the reason for that. Heat rose in my cheeks at the memory of the previous night. Where the man found the energy to love me into oblivion after the day we'd had. . . I shook my head.

The slight motion woke the reason for my movement. Warm, gray eyes with dark, sooty lashes stared back at me. His hand brushed my hair over my shoulder and cupped the back of my neck, pulling me in close for a sleepy, leisurely kiss. My heart stuttered, the blood pounding through my veins slow, hot and thick, like warm honey, as the moment stretched out.

He pulled away with an interrogative, "Mmph?"

"Mmm," I breathed, snuggling against the warmth of his chest.

Gabriel chuckled and the corners of my mouth tilted up as the sound waves traveled through our intertwined bodies.

"How did you sleep, *mon cœur*?"

"Dreamlessly, thank God."

"*Bon*," he murmured. "I was worried when we arrived last night."

"I was too," I admitted.

He shifted, tucking me against him firmly. "I know. Why didn't you tell me?"

"I didn't want to make a fuss."

He sighed. "Your feelings and thoughts are important. I don't ever want you to think they don't matter. I love you." Gabriel put two fingers under my chin and lifted, earnest, charcoal eyes pinning me to the spot, forcing me to acknowledge his words.

My lashes swept down, obscuring my inner turmoil.

"Ava," he murmured.

I lifted my gaze back to his. "It's weird knowing I can tell you anything. I'm still adjusting, I guess."

There was hurt in his steady, patient eyes. "Don't you trust me?"

"With my life," I answered passionately, fire in my belly.

He stared back at me, waiting for me to continue, knowing there was a qualification coming.

I shook my head, silently refusing to put my misgivings and fears into words. The last few years had taught me caution and I was convinced it had saved my life. There was little doubt in my mind that I would have been hung or burnt as a witch if people here knew about my time travel or visions. Deep down, I knew those rules didn't apply to my relationship with Gabriel. Obviously, I trusted him with both of those enormous truths, placing my life in his hands. He would never betray me, but I still struggled against the feeling of being a nuisance or a weight around his neck.

His eyes searched mine in silence. I was sure my every thought was reflected in my green gaze; I have ever been an open book. I watched his face, waiting for the change in his expression that would signal he'd read my mind. Somehow, he understood the twists and turns of my thoughts. I never imagined I would share such a connection with another human.

There it was. I watched as understanding dawned in his quicksilver gaze.

"Trust me."

It was a demand. Tempered with a deep guttural love. It lit an answering flame within me.

"Yes," I breathed. Doubt vanquished in an instant.

He yanked my hips against his, desperation warring with adoration.

We arrived in the village of Versailles well before the sunset the following evening. The streets were bathed in golden light as we found the handsome, well-appointed, stone house Gabriel rented for us. I tilted my face back to take in the pretty, carved facade that rose three stories into the azure sky.

We could have stayed in the château of course, but with the expected influx of people arriving in the village for the meeting of the Estates-General, in addition to the normal entourage of attendants, favorites, and hangers on, the apartments would have been limited, crowded, and likely not immensely comfortable. It was far costlier to rent a home outside of the castle walls, but Gabriel had an additional reason for preferring a degree of separation from the court.

'I have the feeling things may turn violent. I'd as soon not have you and Armand within the walls if my suspicion proves to be correct. It's imperative that we have the ability to leave quickly. I've no wish to be rats trapped in a sinking ship.'

His expression had been pained and serious as he explained his fear. Knowing how possible it was for events to go sideways when there was this much passion and fury simmering in the pot, I didn't attempt to change his mind. Honestly, I was glad to have our own space. Living in Versailles with hundreds, perhaps thousands of other people would likely leave a lot to be desired in terms of cleanliness and comfort.

That thought at the forefront of my mind, I turned and wrapped my arms around his waist. "This looks lovely. I'm glad you decided to stay here."

He dropped a kiss on my upturned nose and wove his fingers between mine. "Let's see the inside, shall we? I told the owner's staff when to expect us. Perhaps there will be food, I'm famished."

I laughed and shook my head. He was always hungry, though to be fair, I was starving myself. Gabriel raised his hand to the knocker, but the dark blue door swung open before he had a chance, revealing a neat line of staff in starched white aprons. I smiled to myself; it was like something out of a book.

"Monsieur et Madame la Vicomtesse! We're so pleased your journey has come to an end." A rosy cheeked, dark-haired woman dressed in a perfectly pressed, navy gown, bobbed a curtsey. "I will be your housekeeper during your stay, my name is Madame Eloise Blanchard."

Gabriel executed a perfect bow, and I beamed a smile in response. "We're happy to be here and eager to get settled in. The house looks lovely."

It was more than lovely, to be honest. The wood floor gleamed with polish, there wasn't a speck of dust as far as the eye could see, and vases of tulips and daffodils were set on nearly every surface. The wavy windows glittered in the late afternoon sun, letting streams of buttery light dance through the air.

I listened with half an ear as the rest of the household introduced themselves, the names spinning through my head in quick succession. Should I pay more attention? Absolutely. But I was itching to explore the rest of our accommodations for the foreseeable future. Seemingly reading my mind, Gabriel deftly maneuvered the introductions around to a quick tour.

"Of course, my lord. Madame Nicholas will show you the house and your rooms. If you need me, I'll be in the kitchen overseeing the preparation of supper." With a deep curtsey, she excused herself.

Madame Nicholas stepped forward with a kind smile. She had warm brown eyes, blonde hair streaked liberally with gray, and the cozy demeanor of a granny who would always have a hug, a wise word, and a sweet in her pocket for a mischievous child. I immediately took a liking to her.

She chattered merrily about the history of various pieces as she walked us through each room, sometimes lingering to fill in more information, sometimes merely nodding her head toward ornate doors that stood open to say, "the library is just through those doors," or "the household's quarters are up the back stairs there."

I smiled and nodded though it was all blurring into one dizzying maze, and I knew it would take me a week or more to really find my way around. All I needed to remember was where Gabriel and I slept, where the nursery was, where I could find sustenance for my starving stomach, and how to get the hell out should a quick escape prove necessary. Oh, and the library of course.

I snapped back to attention as we circled back to the corridor where Gabriel and I would be staying. Armand was just down the hall, getting settled in with Madame Devereux and Jeanne.

"I'll send up some water so you can wash the dust of the road off and some light refreshments for you," she murmured with a quick curtsey.

"Thank you so much, Madame Nicholas," I smiled back.

Gabriel quietly closed the door behind her and rolled his head from side to side.

"Sore?" I asked softly.

"*Oui*." He tried to smile, but it looked more like a grimace.

I wrapped my arms around his middle and leaned into him tiredly. His hands settled on my shoulders and kneaded gently before he pulled away, making me look up at him questioningly.

"Rest for a bit, aye? I'm going to check with the men that the horses have been settled in." He bent his head to mine and pressed a kiss to my forehead.

"All right." I squeezed him tightly one more time, absorbing comfort as much as I was offering it, and let go.

Nineteen
A Murder of Crows

The morning of May the fifth, I awoke with my stomach in knots. The Estates-General would officially convene today, setting the stage for what the rest of the year, and the coming years, would bring. I dismissed Monsieur Hamon, Gabriel's valet, preferring to administer to him myself. As I gently combed tangles out of his thick, chestnut strands, spreading them out over his shoulders to admire the gleam of fire and gold the light from the window picked up, I paused to massage his head and neck. I was drawing the preparations out, lingering over the morning out of nervousness.

Gabriel lifted his big hand, placing it over my petite one, halting my ministrations. "What's wrong, *mon cœur*?"

I swallowed hard, unsure why today of all days, I felt so wound up. "I don't know. What happens today is important. I suppose I'm wondering if history will play out as I learned it. If anything will change. If anything, even *can* change."

He turned sideways in his chair, tugged me down onto his lap, and pressed his forehead against mine for a long moment. "I'm playing my part in this charade, as is everyone else assembling today. We're all going into this meeting with the knowledge that things likely won't change in any meaningful way."

I blew out a frustrated breath. "Do you really believe that the majority of the country understands that?"

Gabriel frowned, the line between his brows more pronounced than usual. "They're excited, aye? The townspeople, the shop owners, they're all hoping that their voices and their complaints are finally going to be heard. Some of them may even hope that they're finally going to get a fair, representative piece of the vote. But I think most realize that the clergy and the nobility will never acquiesce to such demands."

My shoulders slumped in defeat. "Even with all the work that you, Phillipe, and the others have done to bring the aristocracy around, you don't think there is a chance?"

There was a long silence as Gabriel studied the silvery, gray fabric of my gown, plucking it absently between his fingers. When his eyes met mine, they were hard and flinty. *"Non."*

Gabriel shifted uncomfortably on the hard, wood bench beside Phillipe. It was outrageously hot in the overcrowded room. There were far too many bodies, all in full, court regalia. He was sweating profusely, the sweat trickling down his spine, and from the overwhelming odor, ostensibly being disguised by perfume, he wasn't the only one.

He felt a stab of guilt at his irritation with the proceedings. At least he had a drink in his hand to quench his thirst, and he hadn't had to wait with the Commons, as they were now referring to themselves, for over three hours in the unseasonable heat to even be presented to King Louis. For that matter, at least he had a seat, inhospitable as it was. Many of the men were relegated to standing and had been the entire day.

What followed the indignity of the initial isolation for the Third Estate, was an afternoon of interminably long speeches that thus far had barely touched on the societal reasons most were there to address. Even Necker, generally regarded as a champion of the impoverished had disappointed, his voice giving out only a few minutes into his speech. Someone else was now finishing Jacques' speech for him, droning on about the various financial issues the country was facing.

The longer the man spoke, the more Gabriel could sense the rage simmering beneath the surface. He couldn't blame them for their anger. Everyone in the country, regardless of social position had been affected by the consequences of the drought. Compounding the issue of widespread crop failure, the drought had been followed by the snowiest, most severe winter anyone could remember. North of Paris, the rivers had frozen deep, and snow had fallen nearly every day, far into April.

Gabriel and Phillipe had spent the morning speaking to parish priests who had painted a shocking description of the state of their parishioners. *Imagine spending nine-tenths of your income on bread?* He shook his head as he went over their conversation again. The starvation was real, it was extensive, and he didn't blame the commoners for their anger at the situation. He thought of little Armand and how he would feel if he couldn't afford to feed him. It made his gut clench and roil like he might vomit.

"... it's unfortunate that our beautiful country finds itself facing empty coffers, but this is the reality. We must all do our part to strengthen France's position—"

"If the queen wasn't such an utter disgrace, bedecking herself in gowns and jewels while her people starve!" called out someone in the back.

Gabriel straightened and craned his neck, searching for the source of the slur, while Necker's stand-in continued speaking as though nothing had happened.

"Can you see who it was?" muttered Phillipe, sounding annoyed that he didn't share the advantage of his friend's height.

"*Non*," he replied under his breath. "That part of the hall is far too crowded, and they insisted they all dress like crows, so it's impossible to tell them apart. It's a sea of black."

"*Merde*. Whose brilliant idea was that anyway? Just the ticket to rile them up more." Phillipe shook his head.

"No idea. It certainly wasn't well thought out," he admitted.

The crowd was getting restless. Over a thousand men had gathered in the hall for the formal commencement of the Estates-General. Since this morning, they'd waited through incessant and often inaudible speeches. Based on the angle of the late afternoon sun streaming through the windows, today's meeting would be ending shortly— with nothing accomplished.

"I was thinking about what the priest from Reims told us this morning. . . What was his name?"

"Père Lavigne?" suggested Gabriel.

"*Oui*, that was it. We knew about the price of bread of course— everyone knows. But what he told us about the number of parishioners they buried this winter. . . It's inconceivable."

"*Oui*," answered Gabriel softly. His stomach had been in knots over the priest's revelations all day.

"How is it that our king seems unaffected by the suffering we keep hearing about?" There was anger in his friend's voice.

Gabriel shook his head and hunched his shoulders as if he were trying to shield himself from a terrible reality he didn't want to face. "I can't fathom it. It makes me feel ill. And furious."

Suddenly everyone around them was standing up, jostling one another in their eagerness to escape the close confines of the meeting hall. Apparently, they were done for today and based on the undercurrent of dissatisfaction thrumming through the room, the closing remarks hadn't yielded an iota more than the previous hours had.

The tapestried and painted walls started closing in on Gabriel; feeling like he was suffocating, he jerked his emerald, silk cravat loose, desperate for a breath of crisp, clean air. Opulent as the palace was, it resembled more of a gilded prison.

Phillipe placed his hand on Gabriel's back, startling him. "Shall we go back to my place for a brandy?"

Gabriel managed a smile even though it felt like his head was in a vise. "Why don't you come to mine? I know Ava will be anxious to hear how we fared today."

"Aye, thanks. Did you ride or walk?"

"I walked. I thought the stables would be overwhelmed with the influx of people." He closed his eyes briefly, willing the pounding to cease.

"Mmm. I expect you were right. I walked as well." They were crossing the wide-open expanse in front of the palace, slowly making their way to the ornate, imposing gates. "I say, are you all right?" asked Phillipe, stopping suddenly, causing the gentleman behind him to bump into him.

"Aye. I've a nasty headache brewing." Gabriel winced despite himself as a sharp pain radiated up his neck, piercing his skull. It felt like his head was being split by an ax.

"You look like you've seen a ghost," Phillipe joked, his face concerned.

Gabriel tried to smirk, but it came out like a grimace.

"Why don't we have that brandy tomorrow instead?" suggested Phillipe. "Perhaps we'll have accomplished something and have a reason to celebrate."

Nausea rolled in his stomach at the thought of brandy. He managed a stiff nod. "*Oui. Merci* Phillipe," he answered as they came to the main cobbled road leading to Versailles. "I'll see you in the morning."

Twenty
Fever Dreams and Tea with the Queen

I'd been trying to lose myself in my sewing, albeit not doing a brilliant job of it, most of the afternoon. Truly, I'd simply been impatiently killing time until Gabriel returned from the first day of the Estates-General. I dropped my project— a hem that needed repairing, in my sewing basket the moment I heard him at the door and tried to walk demurely to the entry hall— instead of running like I wanted to. My heels tapped industriously as I came through the wide double doors, stopping short at the sight of Gabriel.

"My love! What's wrong?" My role as a proper lady of the house forgotten, I rushed to where he leaned against the wall. His skin had an unhealthy, waxy hue to it, and a fine sheen of perspiration stood out on his forehead and temples.

He shook his head and winced at the movement. With an efficient motion, I pressed the back of my hand against his neck, yanking it away at the heat that emanated from his skin.

"You've a fever," I said briskly. "Let's get you in bed."

I wrapped my arm around him, intending to shepherd him up the stairs when his valet, Monsieur Hamon entered the hall.

"My lord, I thought I heard you arrive, and I just wanted to go over your attire for tomorrow's meeting..." He stopped short. "Monsieur, Madame! What's the matter?" Without waiting for an answer, he strode over to us, helpfully taking Gabriel's weight off me, and tsked under his breath. "Into bed with you, my lord! Right away."

I was unwilling to admit that I probably couldn't have handled it by myself up the long winding stairs, but I was grateful the man showed up when he did. "Thank you, Monsieur Hamon. He seems to have a fever. Once we have him lying down, would you be so kind as to fetch Mademoiselle Noemi for me?"

"Of course, my lady. Please let me know how I may assist you."

Shockingly, Gabriel hadn't said a word of protest during this entire exchange, nor all the way up the stairs. Considering how stubborn the man could be, it was a clear indication that he wasn't well. With Monsieur Hamon's help, I managed to help him onto our bed, fluffing the pillows behind his head as I ran through his symptoms, considering and discarding possibilities.

"I feel nauseated," Gabriel muttered thickly.

Swiftly snatching the wash basin off the stand, I placed it on the floor beside our bed. Mademoiselle Noemi knocked on the door frame and anxiously curtseyed.

"You called for me?" She cut her eyes toward the bed.

"Yes, thank you, Noemi. Gabriel is feeling unwell. Could you ask the kitchen for another wash basin and fresh water?"

I rummaged through my box of supplies, peppermint for nausea I thought, setting it aside. I eyed the lemon oil we'd purchased from the apothecary in town. Hadn't my mother said lemon was good for fevers? What else could I give him?

"I'll be back directly, my lady."

"Mmm. Thank you," I murmured distractedly.

Gabriel moaned and my head popped up uneasily. Abandoning my box, I stood beside the bed and brushed his hair off his forehead.

"Can you tell me when this started? What other symptoms do you have?"

He licked his lips, his eyes glassy and unfocused. "I'm not sure. It began with the devil of a headache. I thought it was just the crowd and the heat. . ."

I nodded, silently urging him on.

"I'm so thirsty," he croaked.

I poured him a cup from the pitcher on the table and helped him sip, placing it back on the table when he lay back.

"So, thirsty, headache, nausea, fever. . . Is that everything?"

"Exhausted," he murmured. "But the headache, it was bearable, and then quite suddenly it was a monster. That's when I became nauseous. I wasn't sure I would make it back here without getting sick."

Noemi appeared with a second wash bowl, placing it quietly on the stand. "The cook said she'd send up some broth, Madame."

"Thank you. For now, out of an abundance of caution, those of us who have been with Gabriel today will not interact with Armand or his caretakers. I don't know if my lord ate something that has gone off, or if he's ill."

"*Oui*, Madame." Noemi nodded agreeably.

"Please let the others know. Hopefully, it will only be for a day or two."

I turned back to Gabriel, lying deathly still, eyes closed, breathing shallowly. "Try to sleep," I whispered tenderly.

"My lady?"

I looked up from the anthology of Shakespeare's work I was immersed in, identifying the hesitant, gentle voice as Noemi's, before I saw her. Carefully, I placed a scrap of parchment I used as a bookmark between the pages, closed my book, and waved her forward. Something in her expression raised the hairs on the back of my neck.

"Come sit, Noemi. It's been a long couple of days." Gabriel was finally feeling better, but he had spent the bulk of the last three days vomiting and sleeping.

She smiled tentatively and sat in the chair opposite mine. "Thank you, Madame."

"Of course. Now tell me, what's the matter?"

Soft, doe eyes looked at me startled.

I laughed. I couldn't help myself. "It's all right. It's just obvious that something is wrong."

"Ah, well." She twisted her fingers nervously in her lap. "I don't mean to worry you, Madame. It's only. . . I think something is wrong with Madame Jeanne."

My gut tightened uncomfortably. "Go on."

"Well, she's with child, aye?"

I cocked my head and nodded.

She stared studiously into her lap. "She barely eats, my lady. When she first came to us, she would smile or play occasionally with little Armand, but she never does anymore. I expected her to get better after being with us for a while, but she seems to be getting worse." She bit her lip.

"Has she spoken to you about her situation, Noemi? Have you become friendly with her since she arrived in Landévennec?"

"Not much. I tried a few times, but she keeps to herself. She cries at night." Quiet, brown eyes stared into mine.

That gave me a jolt. Was she crying because of what the bastard had done to her? Or did she miss him?

"You don't know why?" I guessed.

She shook her head quickly, blonde curls popping out of her starched cap. "I think it's something to do with her husband."

I frowned. The story we'd given out was that her husband had passed away. It made sense that Noemi would assume she cried over a broken heart, but something didn't feel right to me. I sighed, a headache edging in behind my eyes.

"All right, thank you for telling me. Please let me know if you notice it worsens."

"Aye, thank you, my lady." Her expression was a mixture of relief at having confided her thoughts and fear that she hadn't done enough.

Personally, I felt the same way.

I lifted a tiny forkful of apricot tart to my lips and bit daintily, while I tried not to stare at Marie-Antoinette languishing on a velvet, upholstered chaise lounge. Beside her, sharing her perch, was the endlessly fashionable and lively Madame de Polignac, who was regaling the small group of women with her latest encounter with her seamstress. The queen looked relaxed, her gray-blue eyes held a hint of laughter, and a half-smile played on her lips as she listened to her friend's story. She casually lifted her cup of wine, and her gaze met mine in her frank, self-assured manner. It sent a jolt of electricity through me.

I offered her a smile and lifted my glass to my lips. Jitters at my invitation to have tea with *la Reine* had stalked me since the royal letter had been received. The smooth, fruity, ruby-colored liquid slid down my throat as I remembered Gabriel's smirk when I professed my nervousness.

"Relax, *mon cœur*. She's a person, just like anyone else. Treat her kindly and be yourself. She'll be enchanted with you."

I'd rolled my eyes at him. The man simply didn't understand what it meant to meet royalty for the first time. Particularly when you knew the nasty little details of their lives. I'd racked my mind trying to come up with a reason to skip the meeting, but turning down Marie-Antoinette simply wasn't an option.

Sitting in this room was surreal, and the only thing that was going to get me through the experience was wine. Boatloads of it.

Madame de Polignac delivered the punch line to her drawn-out tale, and the gaggle of women tittered appreciatively. I followed suit, although I'd been completely lost in my thoughts and missed the majority of the story. Nervous sweat trickled uncomfortably down my ribs, and I sucked in a quiet, slow breath, holding it for as long as I dared before letting it out in a silent stream. My head swam dizzily, whether, from proximity to the queen, the wine, or the heat, I knew not.

One of the other ladies in a prettily patterned, rose sprigged, day gown started talking about her sister-in-law's apparent inability to carry a baby to term and how her brother was showing signs of frustration. I was unable to keep the names and faces of everyone I'd been introduced to straight, but one of the quieter women— Marie-something perhaps?— looked distressed with the turn the conversation had taken.

"I feel for her, of course. She's taking it quite hard, poor thing. . . and she doesn't want to disappoint my brother, but I'm certain there's something more she could be doing."

"Well, I suppose she's spoken to her midwife about it?" Madame de Polignac offered gently. Her unusual lilac eyes were full of sorrow for the rose-patterned lady's sister-in-law.

"Of course she has! She's been told that it simply might not have been the right time— why the fool even suggested she hasn't done anything wrong." She shook her head in bewilderment. "I told her to look for a new midwife. I even offered her mine, who has safely delivered three of my babes."

The quiet woman tutted under her breath.

My belly twisted. The idea that women believed they were to blame if they lost a child, curdled like sour milk. I knew I couldn't hide my expression, and I took another thoughtful bite of my tart; carefully chewing as I tried to school my discomfort into mild interest. My gaze met Marie-whatever her name was— I really must pay more attention when I was introduced— and I registered the anger simmering beneath the surface.

"Stephanie, I'm surprised that you would speak thus of your dear sister. You know that our own darling *Reine* has suffered two grievous losses through no fault of her own and went on to have healthy *bébés*!"

Rose lady— Stephanie— I corrected myself, looked taken aback. Before she could respond, the queen lifted an indifferent hand, waving away the apology before it materialized.

"It's fine— really. Though I do appreciate your words Marie-Thérèse. You are always so thoughtful and kind." She shot a look at Stephanie, who looked utterly abashed. "The truth my dear, is that most women lose a child. The fact that you haven't makes you very fortunate indeed." Her blue eyes skipped around the circle of women, resting on each of us for a moment before moving on. "I'll wager my new crimson ballgown that you're in the minority among us."

Poor Stephanie was now a dull red from the tips of her ears to her rose-sprigged decolletage. The rest of the women nodded to themselves and muttered agreement under their breaths.

"Madame de Landévennec— Ava, wasn't it? You don't mind if I call you Ava, do you?" Without waiting for my reply, Marie-Antoinette continued, her eyes looking thoughtfully into my uncomfortable ones. "You haven't been wed for long of course, but you have lost an e*nfant*, have you not?"

My apricot tart congealed in my stomach as all eyes turned to me. "*Oui*, my lady." I swallowed hard and blinked back the tears that the mention of Aimée automatically brought.

Her gaze softened. "I am sorry for your loss, Ava. It was a long time before I could speak of mine without being moved to tears." She cocked her head daintily as her eyes narrowed in on the woman to my left. "And you, Gabrielle?"

Gabrielle simply nodded. "You know I have lost two as well. We've spoken of it."

"We have," acknowledged the queen.

Shakily, I sipped from my wine as my dizziness intensified and I tuned out the rest of the conversation. How did she know about Aimée? I took another deep, silent breath, trying to regulate my heartbeat and calm my runaway anxiety. The palms of my hands were damp, and I clenched my *serviette*, ostensibly wiping crumbs from my lips while I dried them on the cloth. I straightened my back and turned my eyes back on the women, tuning in as the conversation took yet another turn.

"How is the dauphin feeling?" Madame de Polignac reached for a savory, cheese pastry.

A shadow crossed over *la Reine's* pretty features. "Much the same, I'm afraid. The physicians don't quite know what to make of his ailment, but I'm certain he will be better soon."

"I pray he will be healthy again soon," she replied, crossing herself dutifully.

Everyone in the room repeated the motion, faces serious at the mention of the prince's ill health. In the distance, the chapel bell chimed the hour and several women rose, murmuring their excuses and thanking the queen for her hospitality. Not wanting to overstay my welcome, and privately relieved that my ordeal was nearly complete, I stood as well.

"*Merci beaucoup* for the invitation my queen. It was an honor and a privilege." I smiled genuinely and executed a decent curtsey.

Marie-Antoinette took my hands in hers affectionately. "The pleasure was mine. I will see you soon."

Twenty-One
All that Glitters

"It's been an absolute pisser of a week." Phillipe raised his glass in a mock salute and drank deeply.

"What have I missed with the meetings? I've spent the last few days alone in bed. It's been absolute misery." Gabriel leaned forward, helping himself to one of the fresh pastries the maid set out.

"Better alone than in bad company," quipped Phillipe.

Gabriel raised an eyebrow. "That bad, hmm?"

"*Oui.*"

"All right then, I'm sorry to make you relive it. What do I need to know?" He took a healthy bite, the sweet, tanginess of apricot preserves filling his mouth.

Phillipe sighed and took a long sip of his ruby red wine. "Nothing."

"Nothing? It's been a week! Surely something has been accomplished." He wiped his mouth with his *serviette* and drank deeply of the crimson wine in his goblet.

"Honestly, Gabriel. Nothing. The Commons are demanding that votes be counted by head, instead of Estate."

He shook his head. "They must know they'll never get the aristocracy to agree to that."

"Exactly." Phillipe shrugged his shoulders and spread his hands out, palm up, as if to say there was nothing they could do.

"What of the clergy?" He reached out and put another pastry on his plate. They were delicious.

"Same as before. Divided as to what should be done. Some of them are sympathetic to the poor, some don't wish to empty their own fat purses to create a more balanced system." Phillipe held his goblet out as a maid refilled it.

"Mmm. And *le Roi*?"

"I hate to say it, but he's useless. He does nothing, he has no opinion, he prevaricates— half the time I don't think he's even listening to what's being discussed."

"The walls have ears," Gabriel warned.

"Aye," Phillipe acknowledged.

"So. We continue as we are. I suppose we will be here for longer than I initially planned." He finished his second pastry and leaned back in his chair, crossing his ankles.

"Seems like it," observed Phillipe as he stood. "I'm away. I'll see you at *le Palais* in the morning, aye?"

Esme was going to pace a well-worn path in her sitting room rug if she didn't stop. She paused, straightened her shoulders, and took a deep breath, filling her lungs with as much air as she could. Her eyes closed, she held it until she thought she'd burst, before letting it out in a steady, purposeful, stream; trying to let her worries go simultaneously.

She opened her eyes and peered out the window, trying and failing to take comfort in the soothing green landscape beyond her tidy home. It'd been a long month since Ava and Gabriel had left for Versailles and despite how busy she was tending to the tenants of Landévennec, she found herself at loose ends. She missed them and their sweet babe, Armand. Sometimes when she held his warm, comforting, solid weight in her arms, she would close her eyes, press her nose against the soft, swirl of hair on his head, breathe him in, and God forgive her— pretend he was hers.

Luc had been busier than ever, now that Gabriel was relying on him to keep the estate going in their absence. Correspondence was slow, but he'd dutifully sent a missive after the first shipment of smuggled goods arrived a fortnight ago. According to Luc, everything had gone smoothly, and she was hoping that the second shipment Luc had gone to meet would arrive without any problems as well.

She stepped closer to the window and blinked to make sure she wasn't imagining her husband's silhouette bent low over his dappled gray in the distance. She waited another moment; yes, it was definitely Luc. Without delaying any longer, she bustled to the door, panic unfurling in her stomach. Intuitively she knew something was wrong; if she was honest, she'd suspected it since late last night when she'd lain awake, tossing, and turning as the moon cast its glow across their quilts.

Esme threw the front door open and started down the cobbled path as Luc pulled up. Neige, Luc's horse, was lathered and mud-splattered from his hard ride and Luc appeared exhausted. She waited, impatiently shifting from one foot to the other as he dismounted and handed the reins to Georges Gustave. At twelve, Georges was another tenant Pierre's eldest son, and he had begun to help Luc and Esme out about three months prior. He was a good lad, and Esme had a soft spot for him since he'd lost his *maman* a few years ago.

"Thank you, Georges," she said with a smile. "When you've taken care of Neige, why don't you run in and ask Madame Allard for a slice of apple tart? If I'm not mistaken, she just pulled one out of the oven."

"*Oui*, Madame. *Merci*." He tipped his cap at Esme, ran the palm of his hand down Neige's muzzle, and led the horse away.

As soon as he was free, she raised her hand and laid it against the stubble of Luc's cheek, rose on her toes to brush her mouth over his, and rocked back on her heels to gaze into his warm, brown eyes.

"You're safe." It wasn't a question.

"*Oui*."

"*Dieu, merci*," she said fervently, sending up a silent prayer of thanks. "Who isn't?"

"The *poutain* Navy got Mathieu."

She recoiled, thinking of Amélie and the *bébés,* and closed her eyes momentarily, feeling like he'd punched her in the stomach.

"*Merde*."

"How am I supposed to enter the room with this ridiculous pannier?" I huffed, putting my hands on my hips and surveying the nearly ten-foot span of my crimson, ball gown. My seamstress wanted to go larger, but I refused, ensuing in a two-day battle of the wills, which I ultimately won. By a hairsbreadth.

Gabriel's lips twitched, but upon seeing the murderous look in my eyes, wisely composed his expression. "You are stunning, *mon cœur*. You'll be the envy of every woman there, and every single man will wish to be me."

Slightly mollified, even though my towering coiffure made me feel unbalanced and the hair pads Noemi used to build my updo into a monstrous masterpiece were hot and itchy, I offered him what I hoped resembled a smile and took his arm. "You look rather dapper yourself," I muttered.

He smothered a cackle. "*Merci, mon amour.*"

I side-eyed him as we passed under the towering gate adorned in gold leaf at the entrance and continued through the palace and into the immense, manicured gardens at the rear. "Let's get this over with. Remind me what I'm meant to accomplish tonight?"

"Just be yourself, Ava. The men will be falling over themselves to entertain you. Try to ingratiate yourself with some of the women, or *la Reine*, if possible. *Le Dauphin* is ill, so she may be preoccupied. I will try to stay close, though you know how intense these events can be."

"Mmm. And has there truly been no progress in the month that we've been here?" I walked purposefully toward a towering oak that promised shade on this hot afternoon. Between the hair and the monstrosity of a dress, I was sweating to death. Judging by the number of women clustered beneath other trees, resembling wilted flowers, I wasn't the only one.

"I never imagined that this entire endeavor would be a waste of time, but that's how it's beginning to feel." There was frustration in his voice and resentment at the utter lack of forward movement. "The king demanded we come to a swift solution a few days ago, but of course, nothing has happened since then.

"Give it another month. The Storming of the Bastille is only six weeks away."

He shook his head. "I still struggle with that," he murmured. A server passed and he took two glasses of champagne, handing me one.

"With what?" I took a sip, careful not to down the entire thing. Between the unseasonable heat and the alcohol, I was going to have to pace myself.

"Our future. Your knowledge of what's coming. The idea that our efforts are futile." His eyes were distant for a few beats before he brought them back to me. He smiled sadly.

I raised a gloved hand to his face, laying it gently against his smooth cheek. "Nothing is futile, my love. Somehow, I ended up here, in a time not my own, with you, and it's the best thing that has ever happened to me."

He laid his hand over mine and formally brought my knuckles to his mouth, the dark fire in his eyes branding me with its heat. "*Dieu, je t'aime—*"

"Gabriel! There you are! Did you just arrive?" Phillipe wrapped an arm companionably around Gabriel's shoulders. "You remember my sister Charlotte, of course?" He stepped back revealing the petite, buxom blonde behind him.

"Of course," Gabriel murmured with a bow. "You look lovely Charlotte. I didn't know you were going to join Phillipe." He stepped back, placing a gentle hand on the small of my back. "May I present my wife, Ava, la Vicomtesse de Landévennec? *Mon cœur*, this is Charlotte, Phillipe's sister."

I smiled gently at the younger woman. "It's a pleasure to meet you, Charlotte. I've heard all the young men are clamoring to claim you as their own. Now that I've met you in the flesh I understand why."

She cut her feline green eyes— remarkably like my own— at me and offered me a tight smile. "It's nice to make your acquaintance," she murmured.

"Why don't we leave you two to chat," suggested Phillipe. "There's someone I need to introduce Gabriel to."

"Gabriel!" Charlotte cut in, ignoring her brother, as she laid a playful hand on his forearm. "I didn't know you got married!"

Phillipe furrowed his brow. "I told you he wed over a year ago."

Gabriel cleared his throat and stiffly moved his arm away from her grasp. "*Oui*."

My eyes pinged back and forth as I tried to absorb the undercurrent. *Did Charlotte nurse a tendre for Gabriel?*

Phillipe tugged on Gabriel's arm. "We'll be back in a bit my ladies," he called over his shoulder as he forcefully dragged Gabriel away.

I turned my gaze back to Charlotte, silently absorbing the younger woman's shimmering, royal blue gown, dripping in expensive lace, the matching sapphire jewels adorning her decolletage and ears, and her towering blonde coiffure, powdered as fashion demanded. It was another point of contention that I'd drawn the line at.

"Well, this is a wonderful surprise. Phillipe didn't mention he was expecting you!"

She flicked an invisible piece of lint off her gown and gave me a bored look. "I needed a change of scenery. Paris has been dreadfully dull, what with everyone being here," she drawled.

"Mmm. I can imagine," I replied sympathetically. "This must not be all that exciting for you either though. I imagine you're quite accustomed to balls and such."

She tittered, but the laughter didn't reach her hard, glittering eyes.

I tried again. "Are any of your friends here?" I took a sip of my champagne, letting the bubbles sit on my tongue delightfully before I swallowed.

"There are a few," she replied noncommittally, snatching a glass of wine off a passing waiter's tray. "No one I particularly wish to see right now though."

"Mmm." I raised my glass to my lips again, realizing too late that it was already empty.

"You're quite a bit older than I expected. I wonder why Gabriel married you."

Shocked at her boldness, I met her jaded stare. I wanted to like Phillipe's sister, but she was making it impossible.

"I suppose he wasn't interested in a run-of-the-mill, spoiled, catty child," I answered sweetly.

Two could play this game. I'd gone through hell and back in the last five years of my life. I'd be damned if I let this rich, debutante steal my silver lining.

Her eyes narrowed thoughtfully. "*Touche.*" She raised her glass in a salute, drained the entire serving, daintily dropped the empty vessel on the grass, and sashayed away without a backward glance.

I stared after her, unsure whether I should snort in amusement or stomp my foot in frustration. A bead of sweat ran uncomfortably down my spine as I eyed the abandoned glass glittering on the ground. If I could have managed in this ridiculous getup, I would have picked it up, but intuitively I knew if I knelt down, I'd never make it back up again. I bet Charlotte would love to see that spectacle.

With the reminder that I was currently without a drink, and about to perish of thirst, I turned and scanned the gardens in search of a server. Perfectly manicured rows of trees lined the paths and long, narrow pools of water reflected the sun's glare. I caught a glimpse of Gabriel and Phillipe clustered in a small group, deep in conversation with the king.

"Mademoiselle Ava Martel, wasn't it? What a pleasure to see you again."

My heart stopped. Slowly, I turned to face the chilling voice I recognized from Nantes. Numbly, my lips curved into the facsimile of a smile. "Commandant des Rochefort." I inclined my head. "It's Madame Ava Chabot, la Vicomtesse de Landévennec now."

His thin lips stretched into a gruesome smile. "Ah *oui*. My apologies. I heard you wed. Is your husband, le Vicomte here as well? I wished to check on his health after his little injury last year."

"He's with *le Roi*," I said simply, wishing fervently for a damn drink. "It's so kind of you to ask after his wellbeing. I'll let him know you were inquiring, of course."

Des Rochefort casually pulled an engraved, silver case from his pocket, flipped it open, and let his fingers caress the finely rolled cigars within before choosing one. Unable to light it, he simply twirled it between his thumb and index finger, watching me from beneath his heavy-lidded eyes.

"Well, I won't keep you, Madame la Vicomtesse. It was lovely running into you. I'm happy to hear your husband recovered nicely. It's a shame he didn't know that someone within his group that evening was actually involved in the smuggling ring we were after." He sketched me a little bow and turned to go.

The blood roared in my ears and bile rose in my throat. Speaking through parched lips, I managed to ask, "Wait, what do you mean, Commandant?"

He looked back over his shoulder at me, obviously enjoying his little game of cat and mouse. "Oh, hadn't you heard? Your brother-in-law is being detained for smuggling. Quite a coincidence, isn't it?" He waited a moment for my response and then tipped his hat. "I'm sure I will see you again, Madame."

Twenty-Two
Three Times Three Strokes

The steady pounding of Automne's hooves kept time with the drumming in Gabriel's head. That *fils de pute* des Rochefort had gone out of his way to seek out Ava and taunt them with news of Mathieu's arrest and Gabriel swore if the Navy had harmed a hair on his head, he would hunt them to the ends of the earth to avenge his friend.

S'il vous plaît, Dieu. Don't let it be too late.

His innards were a mess of snakes, coiled in knots upon themselves, writhing constantly, sick with the certainty that Amélie was going to kill him for allowing Mathieu to continue their operation without him. Particularly after their run-in with the Navy last year, which resulted in a broken arm for Seznec, and Gabriel getting slashed in the ribs and smashed in the back of the head. In the absence of news from Luc and the others, he wondered if Mathieu had been the only one caught, or if Luc, Madec, Prigent, and Mathieu's men were ensnared as well.

His throat hurt from breathing in the dust of the road, and he slowed Automne down to a walk, drinking deeply from his wineskin in an attempt to quench his thirst. The countryside was bursting into bloom, a soothing sight to his farmer's soul, particularly after last year's crop failure. He tried to empty his mind and take in the splendor of rippling green fields, but it was futile.

He'd left Ava and their son in Versailles six days ago, reluctantly leaving his heart behind with that bastard des Rochefort lurking. It made his stomach curdle every time he thought about it. Ava swore they wouldn't leave the safety of the house, and Phillipe promised to look over them, but fear still stalked his every waking moment.

There had been no other option. It was imperative that he free Mathieu and any others who had been arrested with him immediately. Smuggling was a hanging offense and being a member of the aristocracy would not save Mathieu's neck.

S'il vous plaît, Dieu. Don't let it be too late.

I stared sightlessly at the missive that I'd written and rewritten countless times since Gabriel tore off in a frenzied attempt to save Mathieu's life. I'd thrown every other letter in the fire, the words I needed eluding me. *What could I say to Amelie? Did she know her husband's fate already? What if my letter ended up in the wrong hands? What if I further incriminated us all by writing the wrong thing?*

I sighed, tapping the quill thoughtfully against the desk. The last few days had dragged by in the worst way possible. Terrified that I'd run into des Rochefort again, I'd kept myself and Armand ensconced in the relative safety of the house we were renting. The endless loop of horrifying possibilities that ran through my mind every day, coupled with the boredom of being cooped up indoors in the glorious weather was beginning to make me a bit crazy.

The sudden clamor of church bells had me dropping my quill back in its stand and turning my head to glance at the clock above the mantle. *It must be supper time already.* I pushed my chair away from the sleek, mahogany desk and stood, automatically smoothing the skirt of my gray, day gown when I paused and tilted my head. It was half past four, nowhere near supper time yet, and the bells were not chiming the hour.

In the distance, I could hear additional cathedrals and chapels ringing their bells. Three times three strokes. The death knell.

A cacophony of noise began, distant first, but growing rapidly in proximity and intensity. The brisk tap of boots filled the hall, doors opened and closed loudly, and a buzzing filled my ears. In my hyperfocus about the Estates-General and the impending Revolution, I had completely forgotten this footnote in history. Overshadowed by everything that the summer of 1789 represented, the death of Louis-Joseph, the seven-year-old dauphin, and the king and queen's son had been entirely overlooked.

I sat down hard and closed my eyes, feeling vomit rise in my throat at the thought of what his parents must be feeling at this moment. To lose a child as we had, before we even got to know her, had been horrific. The thought of Aimée still made my throat ache, and my eyes burn with the tears I tried to keep at bay. To lose your future after seven years of growth, laughter, smiles, hugs, and kisses, was unthinkable.

I thought of Marie-Antoinette. The surprisingly sweet, fiercely intelligent, deeply devoted mother that I had become acquainted with over the last month. History treated her poorly, painting her as a flighty, careless spendthrift. This depiction would follow her through the centuries.

It was an indignity, though not one unfamiliar to her. The French did not hold her in high regard now, and likely never would. Far worse, however, was the heartache she was enduring now, and the loss the coming years promised her. The unfairness of the final years of her life hit me especially hard, in that moment.

Esme sat quietly as Luc ran his fingers through his thick, ash-blonde hair. The flickering candlelight highlighted the streaks of gray that hadn't been there when they met, or even when they wed. It was just as full and lustrous as it'd always been, but the stress and illness of the last year had left an indelible mark, not only on his hair but also on their relationship.

"After our near miss last year when Gabriel and Seznec were injured, we should have been more careful. We were too arrogant and now the *putain* Navy has Mathieu." His eyes were full of self-castigation.

"There's no way you could have known, Luc. You took precautions," soothed Esme. She twisted her hands in her lap, lacing her fingers tightly to stop herself from leaping up to try to physically calm him. Over the last two weeks, she'd tried, multiple times, to no effect. Or worse. Where she once wouldn't have hesitated to touch him, now there existed a gulf between them. One she couldn't figure out how to bridge.

He shook his head stubbornly. "Not enough. What will I tell Gabriel?"

"You know Gabriel will never blame you. You've changed your meeting locations, tightened your circle, and been more cautious than you've ever been. You've always known that this was a dangerous endeavor, and everyone took that risk willingly."

"But of all the men the Navy could have captured, why Mathieu? Many of us have no children."

She said nothing. This was not new territory, and she'd exhausted every rebuttal that came to mind.

"I wish they would've got me instead," he muttered sullenly.

Esme sprang to her feet. She was fed up with rehashing what went wrong, she was tired of Luc taking the blame onto himself, and she was absolutely infuriated with Luc for uttering similar sentiments ad nauseum.

"*I* don't wish they got you instead! I am thankful every day you were spared. I know you're thinking of his children, but what about me? Don't I matter too? Would you truly be all right with leaving me to fend for myself?" she exclaimed. She blinked hard, cursing the weakness of the tears that welled in her eyes and clung to her lashes.

Luc refused to make eye contact with her, resolutely gazing at the floorboards instead. "Of course not Esme. But I can't help but think that perhaps you would be better off without me."

"What is that supposed to mean, Luc?" There was a hard, painful knot that had lived in her heart for weeks, nay months, and it was expanding by the second. She suddenly felt cold, icy fingers of fear trailing down her arms, raising goosebumps on her skin in spite of the pleasant temperature, and she clasped her hands over her upper arms, chafing them in an attempt to warm up.

"Just what I said, Esme. I know you yearn for a child of your own, and it doesn't seem to be something I am capable of giving you. If I weren't around, you might find someone else. We could get an annulment," he offered quietly.

"Did you leave your mind on the beach along with Mathieu?" she shrieked. "I don't want to have a *bébé* with just anyone, Luc! I married *you*. I love *you*." She took a deep, shuddering breath. "I thought you loved me too," she whispered, shattered inside.

Unable to grapple with the repercussions of the words her husband had uttered, she turned away on shaky legs, nausea swirling in her stomach, and stared sightlessly out the window at the rapidly darkening, violet sky. *He regretted marrying her.* Bile rose in her throat. She braced her hands on the windowsill and leaned forward, pressing her flushed face against the cool glass. His words played over and over in her mind.

Dieu, what had she done? She'd been sure Luc was different, special. That he truly treasured her and wouldn't put her through the hell her father had put her through. *Was she wrong? Had Marguerite been right to call her a fool?*

She felt a sob work its way up from the depths of her gut, tearing its way through her chest. Esme swallowed hard, ruthlessly smothering the pain that felt like liquid fire, burning her heart to ash. Her shoulders shuddered as she thought of his words again. *'If I weren't around, you might find someone else.'* She shook her head in denial. Her grief was a wild thing, mixed with a rage she thought might swallow them both whole.

Other than the sound of their breaths, the room was silent. Filled with a thousand words unspoken. It stretched out infinitely until Esme felt herself slowly calming, her breath evening out, the roaring in her ears replaced by the song of crickets and cicadas. She opened her eyes and looked out at the velvety black beyond their window. It was a moonless night, with only the twinkling light of distant stars to comfort her. She straightened her shoulders. *Je l'emmerde* if he didn't want her.

His large, warm hand settled on her shoulder, hesitantly. "Esme."

Just the one word. Her name.

In it, she identified a broken longing. An apology, perhaps. Was she merely hearing what she wished to? A tsunami of heartbreak threatened to drown her on the spot. Should she turn to him? Indecision rooted her to the ground.

"Esme, I'm sorry. *Je t'aime tellement.* I'm an idiot. I just want you to have everything you want. You deserve to have a child of your own. I don't want to be the reason you don't have your heart's desire." He hadn't moved his hand from her shoulder, and he squeezed now. As if his touch might convey more than his words.

The tears she'd held at bay spilled over and ran silently down her cheeks, but she still didn't turn to him.

"You love me, but you'd be willing to let me go?" Her voice betrayed her, breaking on the last syllable.

"*Oui.* It would be the death of me. But if it meant you were safe and happy elsewhere, it would be worth it." His voice was soft.

Her heart shattered. "What if I said no?"

"No?"

"No. I would rather love you fully all my days and never have the joy of watching you hold a child of ours in your arms than live without you with a houseful of children." She turned to him then, blue eyes brilliant with tears, raising her chin fiercely, daring him to deny her again.

His arms went round her, roughly pulling her to him, and his mouth came down on hers in hopeful desperation. He pulled a fraction away. "Are you sure?" he asked gruffly, tears glistening on the stubble of his cheeks. "I need to know you're sure."

"I've never been more certain of anything in my life," she breathed against his mouth.

"I'm never going to be brave enough to ask you again," he muttered hoarsely.

"*Bonne.* I don't want you to." She grabbed either side of his face and kissed him hard.

Hoofbeats rang out on the cobblestones outside, followed by urgent pounding at the door. They sprang apart and Luc frowned.

"That must be Gabriel."

Annoyed, I set my teacup down on the prettily painted saucer with a clatter. What had possessed me to invite this petty, vixen of a child to tea was beyond me.

Charlotte raised a perfectly plucked brow at my display of temper. "Well, it's true," she pointed out reasonably.

"Which part? The part where the peasants are to blame for being unable to feed their families or the part where we should strongarm them into continuing their miserable, subservient lives to maintain the status quo?" I clasped my hands tightly in my lap to hide that they were trembling in my rage.

She eyed me over the rim of her cup as she sipped and daintily dabbed her pouting mouth with her *serviette*. "Does Gabriel know of your revolutionary sympathies? I imagine he would be utterly shocked to hear your thoughts." The look she shot me made me think of a cat with bird feathers sticking out of its mouth.

I smothered my laugh. She was convinced that all aristocrats believed as she did, and it honestly wasn't worth my time to argue with her. My idea of forming a connection with Gabriel's best friend's sister had quickly disappeared down the proverbial toilet. Wistfully, I thought of indoor plumbing. It topped the list of modern conveniences I missed.

I treated her to a sincere smile. "Of course, I understand, most men don't discuss politics with their wives, but Gabriel and I have no secrets between us."

Watching that little jibe hit its mark was nearly rewarding enough to make up for my irritation with her. Satisfied with myself, I unclenched my fingers, spreading them on the navy, silk gown I wore. Pleased that they were no longer shaking, I demurely reclaimed my teacup and sipped, letting the soothing steam warm my face.

Charlotte's feline eyes narrowed, and she sniffed. "Well, I certainly don't envy you that. It sounds an utter bore."

She reached up and adjusted the colorful flowers that adorned her hat. I eyed the monstrosity with an inner giggle. What would she think of a pair of jeans and a cozy sweater?

Stop that, I chided myself. I served myself an almond biscuit drizzled in dark chocolate and wondered why I was thinking so much of the future today. After nearly two years, I considered myself relatively well-adjusted, though I knew I would always pine for modern conveniences. I nibbled on my cookie and let her simmer while the sweet, grainy texture of the almond flour and the chocolate exploded in my mouth.

"Have you tried one of these yet?" I asked her finally, gesturing toward the biscuits. "They're quite good."

She eyed me suspiciously but placed one on her plate. "Thank you."

I nodded. "Are you planning on staying in Versailles for long?"

She rolled her eyes at my obvious change of subject. "I don't know. It's rather more boring here than I expected."

I raised my eyebrows. "What did you expect?"

Charlotte shrugged an elegant shoulder. "A bit more excitement? Perhaps some fighting?"

"But that would mean that Phillipe and Gabriel would have to fight. You can't really want that?" I blurted out in surprise.

Her green eyes glittered with indifference. "They would be fine," she asserted.

Taken aback, I let her words hang in the air. Dealing with her sarcasm and immaturity was one thing, but she possessed a shocking disregard for life, even the life of her brother, that I couldn't reconcile.

"There's no way we could possibly know that they would be fine. We would pray, but we couldn't know," I finally replied as gently as I could.

"Well, it doesn't matter, because there's been no fighting. The entire situation has been blown out of proportion. I've a mind to head back to Saint-Denis." She rose elegantly from her chair, leaving her biscuit untouched on her plate. "You'll have to excuse me. I have an appointment I can't miss. Thank you for the tea."

"I hope you're right, Charlotte. Thank you for coming. It was enlightening." I placed my cup back on the table and stood to walk her out.

Her silvery, blue dress brushed against mine as we made our way through the salon doors toward the entrance. I stopped abruptly, slumping against the door jamb as my gut tightened and my vision went dark.

I passed Charlotte a handkerchief and helplessly patted her back, battling back tears of my own as she sobbed on my shoulder. Her bright green eyes were red and swollen, her face blotchy from the force of her emotion. Over her shoulder I could see Gabriel standing stiffly and stoically in the hall, obviously bothered by something he couldn't vocalize. Based on the set of his shoulders, I imagined the politeness bred into true aristocrats was inhibiting him.

Charlotte's tears were slowly seeping through the fabric of my gown. I stared at Gabriel, willing him to turn and make eye contact, but he stubbornly kept his gaze trained on the wall.

"Shh..." I murmured. "It will be all right."

She pulled away abruptly. "How can you say that? It will never be all right!"

I gave her a little shake. "There's nothing you can do. It's terrible and unfair and you will live with it for the rest of your days. You've been coddled your entire life, Charlotte. It's time to wake up and come to terms with reality."

She collapsed against me, wailing anew. Helplessly, I gazed beyond her and wished myself away.

"Ava! Are you all right?"

I opened my eyes to see Charlotte peering at me grimly. "Whatever is the matter with you?" she demanded when my gaze met hers.

Weakly, I shook my head, dread churning in my stomach. "Nothing. I'm fine. Just a bit of a dizzy spell." I flapped my hand dismissively. "It happens sometimes."

She eyed me skeptically. "You don't seem the type to be prone to fainting."

It was a surprisingly astute observation for someone I was beginning to think was filled with fluff.

I forced a lighthearted smile. "You're right, usually. The last time I felt this way was in the early days of my pregnancy. Perhaps that's why."

She shot me a disgusted look. "Well, are you well enough for me to leave? Or shall I sit with you a moment more?"

Despite the dizziness still thrumming in my brain, I pushed myself away from the door. "Nonsense," I replied heartily. "I wouldn't want you to miss your appointment."

She hesitated— probably because it was a fabrication— and nodded. "All right, well, thank you again."

I held the ornate wood door open for her. "Thank you for coming."

I waited for her to walk away before I closed the door firmly and collapsed against it. I hated the visions. Who was Charlotte crying over? What was going to happen?

Twenty-Three
Amidst Rats and Refuse

"This here is the north facing side of the fort. Impregnable from this angle unless we want to attempt to climb the cliffs," said Prigent as he drew a rough outline of the fortress in the sand. He handed the broken branch they were using to Madec, who was crouched to his right.

"On the western side of the fort you've marsh. Boggy as all hell, particularly with all the rain we've had this spring. There are four sentries posted along the wall at the corners here, here, and here," Madec continued, marking where the lookouts were. "They're on a rotating watch, changing every two hours, and they pace. I imagine there are others posted within as well." He passed their writing implement to Luc.

"The south entrance is the most heavily guarded as it's the most accessible point of attack. We don't have enough men to consider entering here. The marsh on the west wraps around the southwestern corner, but on this side, we have triple the number of sentries stationed, with the same two-hour rotating watch schedule."

Gabriel nodded and frowned as he listened to the men and weighed their options. "The eastern side of the fort is not ideal either. The northeastern portion is built on the promontory. The cliffs here are inverse, making a climb even more dangerous than on the north side. Further down toward the southeastern end the land is more accessible, but of course it's much more heavily guarded."

Madec sat back on his haunches. "I explored down the coast a bit. There is a small inlet that winds inland through the marsh. It's quite shallow, but floods with the tide. If we could obtain a rowboat, we might be able to approach on the western end. Seems there are fewer sentries posted there and mayhap it's less treacherous than attempting the cliffs."

"The tide is out now." Prigent squinted at the azure sky, decorated with cottony clouds. "I reckon 'tis near seven now. High tide should be a bit past midnight."

Gabriel glanced out at the distant crashing waves thoughtfully. "Luc, can you get us a boat?"

"*Oui*," he answered without hesitation.

"There'll be a crescent moon tonight, mind. If we're lucky the clouds will offer some cover."

The men nodded.

"Madec, you and Prigent see if you can follow the course of the inlet as far as it goes and check if there's a path through the marsh beyond that. Don't let them see you," he warned.

"Aye, my lord," they gruffly replied.

The cheerful trill of birdsong dragged me out of dreams as peach hued fingers of light snuck through the cracks in my shutters. I groggily lay snuggled amongst the covers, stubbornly refusing to open my gritty eyes. It'd been a fitful night, sleep eluding me as I tossed and turned, my blankets twisting around my legs like shackles pinning me to the bed.

My head throbbed with congestion. The previous day had been spent in the perfectly maintained courtyard with Armand, and it was clear to me now that one of the gloriously, blooming plants did not agree with me. I wiggled my itchy nose in a vain attempt to forestall the imminent sneeze.

Grouchily, I stacked the pillows against the headboard and sat propped up against them, hoping a little elevation would alleviate the misery of my symptoms, while I mentally reviewed Phillipe's last visit. It was difficult to concentrate when my mind kept wandering to where Gabriel was and whether he was safe. He'd been gone for eleven excruciatingly long days, and I knew that even if everything went well with their rescue efforts, it would be at least another week before he returned.

On the bright side, I'd finally managed to send a very delicately written letter to Amelie. After thoughtful deliberation, I decided not to focus on Mathieu and what had occurred, instead concentrating on how she and the children were. I fervently hoped she could read between the lines and understand what I wished I could say. My heart ached for her and the overwhelming fear she must be feeling. Little Étienne and Thérèse couldn't possibly understand why their papa was away for such an extended period and having to navigate those feelings and explanations must be compounding her difficulties.

Reality made me acknowledge that even if they were able to break Mathieu out of whichever fort he was being held in, he would be a wanted man, unable to return home and forced to live in the shadows for the foreseeable future. Furthermore, that was the preferable outcome. I refused to ponder the very real possibility that their rescue effort would come too late, or fail, potentially resulting in Gabriel's arrest as well.

With a sigh, I kicked off the blankets and staggered to the shutters, throwing them wide to greet the dawn sky. The window overlooked the courtyard and faced east. Streaks of rose and magenta were splashed across the heavens. It was a lovely morning, still cool, though experience told me it would be an unbearably hot afternoon, likely ending in severe storms. A prickle of unease teased the hairs on my arms, tiptoeing up my back and making my scalp tighten. I no longer questioned my feelings or intuition. Something was brewing.

Clouds scudded across the moon, obscuring the meagre light it threw across the salt marsh as the men silently navigated through the narrow, winding inlet. A low, threatening rumble of thunder warned of the approaching storm. Prigent shifted nervously, one hand on his pistol belt as he kept watch over their rear.

"Stop here for a moment," instructed Gabriel.

Madec stopped rowing, resting the oars in the water to slow their momentum.

"They won't leave their watches in the storm, if that's what you're thinking," said Luc.

"Aye," agreed Prigent. "The weather may be in our favor though. The sound will muffle our approach, and the rain will reduce visibility."

"*Oui*. But it will make climbing slippery and treacherous, and it will make our descent with Mathieu more difficult as well," said Gabriel quietly.

"Do you still want me to stay with the *bateau*?" Madec adjusted his hold on the smooth, wooden handles.

Lightening briefly lit up the sky behind the fort, followed by a sharp, crack of thunder. The boat rocked slightly as a gust of wind rustled through the reeds and cattails.

"The plan remains the same. Let's go." Gabriel's voice was almost lost amidst the swishing vegetation.

Hoods were adjusted, daggers, swords, rapiers, and pistols checked as Madec steadily wended their vessel through the shallows, the hulking fort looming menacingly over them. He heard the steady, drumming of rain a moment before it reached them, sheer seconds before they came to a stop, the inlet allowing no further access. They were approximately twenty thousand *lignes* from the parapets.

Gabriel heard a muffled curse from far above as the naval officers on watch were inundated with pelting water. Taking care not to tip the boat, Gabriel, Prigent and Luc alighted, and soundlessly moved toward the roughhewn, stone wall ahead of them. As they approached, they split up, melting into the tall marsh grasses. Gabriel tested each footstep before committing, not wanting to find himself hip deep in sucking mud. He knew Prigent and Luc would be doing the same.

The rain splattered steadily onto the soft ground, dripping down his hood, the occasional gust blowing it directly into his face. He blinked against the water that ran into his eyes, trying to keep his gaze trained on his destination as lightning struck in jagged bolts of violet around them.

He reached the wall and plastered his body against it, letting out a slow breath as he untied the length of rope that was looped at his waist. His hand tented above his eyes to shield them from the driving rain, he tilted his head back, scanning the crenellations for the best place to throw his line. Decision made, he tossed the rope in a practiced gesture, smoothly letting it play out of his hand. The loop caught in the perfect place, and he pulled on the hempen line, putting his entire bodyweight on it to ensure it would hold. Satisfied, he began to climb, hand over hand, refusing to look down, trying to focus on his steady ascent, ignoring how the fibers dug into his palms.

Gabriel took a deep breath, wrapped his hands over the edge of the wall, and pulled himself up just enough to scan the top of the parapets. Two guards were huddled against the inner wall, seeking what little shelter they could obtain from the rain and appeared to be deep in conversation. To his left he could see only one of the sentries. No one was looking in his direction, so he hauled himself over the wall, landing light as a cat on his feet. Within seconds he had pressed himself into the shadows and watched, waiting for Prigent and Luc to arrive.

To his right a door swung open, spilling lantern light onto the wet stones. The missing guard sauntered out, reeking of sour, fermented grapes, a cup held loosely in his hand.

"Eh, Alexandre, the sky is pissing on you." He cackled at his joke as he slipped drunkenly in a puddle, catching himself at the last second.

Further down the wall, Luc landed gracefully and made eye contact with Gabriel. At his nod, they moved in unison through the pouring rain, Luc dispatching the sentry nearest him with a swift knock to the back of his head with the hilt of his dagger. Gabriel dragged the drunk major against the wall, one hand placed firmly over his lips. He stuffed a handkerchief in his mouth and efficiently tied his hands behind his back. Within seconds, the man was completely incapacitated. A glance to his right confirmed that Luc had the other guard well in hand. Prigent climbed over the wall on the far opposite end and was spotted immediately by the guards.

"Halt—" one of the sentries began to call out as Prigent clobbered him over the head with the flat of his sword.

He slumped onto the ground as his knees buckled. His friend was faster, slashing out with his dagger and catching Prigent in the arm. Gabriel sprinted over, nearly slipping on the wet stones, the heavily falling rain masking his approach, allowing him to catch the remaining guard unaware.

He grabbed him from behind, intending to pin his arms against him, but the man had a wiry strength that surprised Gabriel, twisting out of his grip with a spin and darting out with his dagger again, this time ripping through Gabriel's clothing, leaving a shallow cut across his abdomen. Gabriel grunted at the sharp, stinging sensation, but he didn't hesitate, letting the man's momentum turn him round.

Whipping his dagger out of its sheath, Gabriel grabbed a fistful of hair in his left hand, yanked back to expose his throat, and drew his knife across it. He shoved hard with both hands, pushing him over the crenellated edge into the marsh far below.

Breathing hard, Gabriel dragged the back of his sleeve across his eyes, wiping away the steady stream of rain that blurred his vision.

"Are you all right?" he whispered.

"*Oui*," replied Prigent. "It's not deep."

"*C'est bon*. Let's tie the other one up and move him out of sight."

Prigent pulled a length of rope from his pocket, swiftly cutting a piece with his dagger and handing it to Gabriel as he knelt to tie the other guard's feet together. They stood and Gabriel hooked his hands under the man's arms, pulling him back into the shadows.

"Ready?" Luc murmured.

Gabriel nodded, and the trio stealthily moved to the door. The handle gave easily under his hand and the carved, wood door swung out on well-oiled hinges. Luc and Prigent went in first, swords and daggers drawn. Gabriel watched their rear, pulling the door shut behind them.

Prigent had shared drinks and a few games of cards at the local *auberge* with some of the lieutenants and majors the night before. Most of them called it a night before getting too inebriated, but one sot had stayed, calling for drink after drink. Prigent, slowly sipping at a well-watered brandy, made sure to lose more hands than he won, genially paying for the man's cognac. As the hour grew late, his tongue loosened by alcohol, he divulged quite a bit of the fort's layout. As a result, they knew that prisoners were generally kept in the dungeons below, along the northern end, where the icy ocean beat against the cliff face, seeping in through cracks and chinks.

Gabriel made sure they timed their rescue effort shortly after the onset of a two-hour watch. He had lost all sense of time since they'd begun climbing the outer wall though, and as a result he wasn't sure how long they had left before the sentries due to relieve those they incapacitated would arrive. Thankfully, the hour was late, the corridors dark, and most of the fortress's occupants were abed.

They rapidly made their way to the north stairwell and began the climb down. At the first landing they encountered a heavyset guard whose comically open mouth made it clear he hadn't expected to see anyone. Luc knocked him out with a punch in the head and Prigent caught him as he fell backward. They made short work of trussing him up, and Luc and Gabriel dragged him into a dark corner where he hoped he wouldn't be found for hours.

Alert, they continued down the winding, shadowy stairs. The air was noticeably cooler, with a dank, musty aroma as they descended into the bowels of the fort. Lanterns cast feeble puddles of light against limestone walls that bore moldy, black streaks from the constant humidity. Gabriel wrinkled his nose as the smell of piss, rotting straw and despair wafted up from the dungeons.

Prigent came to a sudden halt, one fist raised— the signal to stop. He peered around the corner soundlessly and held up two fingers. Two guards then. The men waited, Gabriel barely daring to breathe until Prigent brought his hand down in a swift, slashing movement, their signal to move.

They burst into the room weapons drawn, but these guards were not so easily caught unaware. Gabriel swung his sword at one, aiming for his chest, but the man ducked and barreled toward his legs. He gave ground, dancing away, allowing his momentum to carry him into the wall. His opponent grunted in pain, but didn't slow as Gabriel hoped.

Sword drawn he charged at Gabriel, slashing viciously as he went. He was a large man, and what he lacked in finesse he made up in sheer brute strength. Gabriel stepped back, forced into a defensive stance as the lieutenant pressed his advantage ruthlessly. His foot came down on saturated, moldering hay, and slipped out from beneath him, twisting his ankle viciously. He gritted his teeth against the pain and stepped back, putting the dank wall solidly against his back.

There was no ground left to give; he was pinned and the gleam in the lieutenant's dark eyes showed he knew it. Gabriel held his breath, waiting for his next move. His opponent pulled his dagger out, it was the better weapon for close quarter fighting and Gabriel took the opportunity to spin neatly away, dodging his deadly jab by an inch. Undeterred, the lieutenant turned, mirroring Gabriel's graceful rotation and slashed at his abdomen. Gabriel caught the wide swing, easily deflecting it on the edge of his sword and forced him back a step. Their roles reversed as the officer mis-stepped, coming down hard on his knee.

Gabriel raised his sword over his head with both hands. It was a miscalculation; the man spotted an opening where Gabriel unintentionally left himself vulnerable and lunged with his dagger, sinking it into his side. Gabriel staggered, but the downward pull of gravity on his sword brought it down with fatal force on the lieutenant's head, splitting it like an overripe melon.

Gabriel limped to the limestone wall and leaned against it, ignoring the blood as it trickled from his wounds and soaked into his shirt. Luc and Prigent had the other guard on his knees in surrender, sword point at his neck, dark eyes bulging at the sight of his dead comrade.

"The keys. Where are they?" asked Prigent, his voice cutting harshly through the thick air.

The man spat at him. "*Va te faire foutre.*"

Luc pressed the edge of the sharp steel a little harder, drawing blood. "That was stupid. You want to join your friend here?" He jerked his head toward the fallen lieutenant.

The guard fell back, feinted to the left and then rolled toward Luc, taking him by surprise and knocking him off his feet. Prigent jumped on his back, aiming his dagger at his kidneys with a grunt and sank it deep, twisting it viciously before he yanked it out.

"You decided your own fate, *espèce d'idiot,*" Luc observed unemotionally.

Gabriel gingerly nudged the first guard with the toe of his boot, rolling him onto his back, trying to ignore the throbbing in his side. One hand against the wall to brace himself, he crouched down and began going through his pockets. Behind him, Prigent was similarly searching the second guard, while Luc walked down the dark corridor of shadowy cells looking for Mathieu.

Frustrated, he stood and hobbled toward Prigent when a muffled curse reverberated through the dungeon.

"Find the keys," he instructed Prigent as he took off as quickly as he could on his injured ankle in the direction of Luc's voice.

A few sorry looking men called out, reaching their hands through the bars beseechingly, but Gabriel didn't so much as glance at them. He was here for Mathieu and no one else. He came to a corner and turned to the right, spotting Luc standing outside the second to last cell. Gabriel sped up, eager to see his brother-in-law as Luc turned to him, fury writ on his face.

"We're going to have to carry him out of here."

Gabriel froze at the sight of his friend, rage igniting in his gut; Mathieu lay unconscious in the dirty straw amidst rats and refuse. His left leg was bent at an unnatural angle, his face bruised and bloody. One eye was swollen shut.

Boot heels rang on the stone floor and Gabriel turned, comforting weight of his sword in one hand, carved hilt of his dagger in the other.

Twenty-Four
Don't Rock the Boat

Brilliant aquamarine arched high above me as I held Armand up in the air. He giggled delightedly, kicking his chubby legs with glee. I brought him down to my upturned face and blew against his belly, making him shriek with laughter.

"I love you so much, do you know that?" I whispered against his warm hair, snuggling him against my side.

We were sprawled out in the most undignified manner on an old, quilted blanket Noemi had laid out on the grass, under a magnificent elm in the courtyard. Armand treated me to a drooling grin, showing off the two teeth he'd recently acquired and babbled something I was sure resembled *maman*.

I tiptoed my fingers across his belly, making him squirm and roll over, trapping my hand beneath him. He pressed his dimpled hands against the ground, pushing himself up on all fours, preparing to display how remarkably fast he could crawl away from me. The little monster had only become mobile in the last week, surprising the entire household, and had already mastered the skill, moving far too rapidly for my mama's heart. Keeping him out of trouble was proving to be a full-time job.

"*Pardon*, Madame."

I sat up and squinted at Mademoiselle Noemi, silhouetted against the blinding afternoon sun.

"Yes, Noemi. What's wrong?" Her anxious expression betrayed her.

"There's someone here to see you. He asked for my lord, but I gave out he was ill, as you instructed me. He's most adamant that he speak to you immediately."

A stray welcome breeze lifted a sticky tendril off my neck, and I frowned. I wasn't expecting anyone, but I pushed myself up, dusting my lavender sprigged, muslin gown off quickly.

"He's waiting in the *salon*, Madame. Shall I send for refreshments?" She twisted her hands together nervously.

"Yes please. Thank you, Noemi. Will you bring Armand to Madame Devereux, or shall I?"

"I will." She moved toward Armand, scooping him up as he tried to escape. "Come here you wee rascal," she said affectionately.

I dropped a kiss on the soft whorl of hair on his head and turned away, walking through the wide doors thrown open to receive the fresh air, toward the *salon* and my unexpected guest.

My hand on the knob, I opened the door, a welcoming smile pasted on my face and stiffened when I saw the Commandant in his smart naval uniform relaxing in my favorite chair.

I gritted my teeth. "To what do I owe the pleasure, Monsieur le Commandant?"

A lazy smirk spread across his swarthy face. "The pleasure is all mine," he assured me, his almond eyes glittering merrily.

I stalked over to the settee and sat stiffly, my back ramrod straight. "I'm told you were hoping to see my husband, le Vicomte. I regret to inform you that he's quite ill. Is there a message you wished to leave for him?" My hands clenched each other painfully as they lay still in my lap.

"Ah, Madame. I'm sorry to hear he's unwell." The gleam in his dark eyes gave away the lie. "I thought perhaps he left the Estates-General early. Mayhap he nursed the mad idea of attempting to extricate his brother-in-law from the difficulty he found himself in."

Sweat trickled down my spine as my stomach lurched. I forced a light-hearted smile to my lips and summoned a convincing chuckle from the depths of my petrified soul.

"I'm afraid not, Commandant. We were both shocked to hear of the accusations leveled against le Baron de Trégoudan." I smiled prettily. "Of course, we have wondered about the accuracy of your claims, but my husband has been far too ill to lead an investigation. Was that all you wished to inquire about?"

Noemi bustled into the room with a tray laden with pastries, a decanter and goblets.

"That won't be necessary, Mademoiselle Noemi. Le Commandant des Rochefort was just leaving."

She shot me a confused look, before rapidly lowering her eyes and beginning to back out. "My apologies, Madame la Vicomtesse."

Le Commandant rose languidly. "Nonsense, Madame la Vicomtesse. How could I refuse your wonderful hospitality? I'm sure I can steal a few more minutes from my duties to enjoy your lovely company, while I sample a glass of that port, of course. It does smell delightful."

Noemi glanced at me, and I gave her a gentle smile and a nod. "I'm so pleased you have a couple moments to spare, Commandant."

Carefully resting the tray on the sidebar, Noemi expertly filled two goblets, placing one before des Rochefort and the other on the carved side table beside the settee. She laid out several plates, temptingly piled with peach tarts, little cakes, candied almonds, and a bowlful of cherries on the table before le Commandant, and backed away, exiting the room quickly.

Des Rochefort lifted his cup to his nose, breathing deeply before he saluted me. I left my glass untouched on the table, refusing to drink or exchange further pleasantries with the man. He smiled before taking a long, slow sip, his eyes full of amusement.

"Was there something further you wished to discuss?" I asked frostily.

His Cheshire cat smile grew. "As a matter of fact, there is."

I waited, refusing to take his bait. After a few long minutes, the air heavy with expectation, he began.

"I found it enlightening to discover that your entire story about being a Martel of Roussillon was fabricated," he drawled. "Which begs the question. Who are you truly? Does your husband know?" He cocked his head, studying me, no doubt waiting for a reaction.

Ice froze in my veins, and I sat still as a hare, hoping to escape a predator's notice by emulating a statue. My face felt cold, then hot; heat and fury rising through my body, melting away my momentary inability to react. My lips stretched in a grimace that I hoped passed for a smile. Numbly, my fingers wrapped around the stem of my goblet, and I raised my glass to my mouth, hiding my false smile behind it. I lowered my lashes, studying the deep crimson contents within before taking a lengthy sip. My hand shook as I placed the port back on the table beside me and I hoped he didn't notice.

"You're misinformed," I said calmly.

He barked out a laugh. "Well, I must admit, I didn't expect you to deny it outright." Des Rochefort raised his cup in a mock salute and tossed back the remainder of his port. He stood and sketched me a little bow. "I won't keep you any longer, Madame. Something tells me we will see each other again soon."

Relief coursed through Gabriel as Prigent appeared at the end of the corridor, the dull iron of the keys glinting in his hand. He made quick work of the lock and swung the metal bars open. Gabriel strode into the cell, holding his breath against the overwhelming stench that assailed his senses. He whipped off his cloak, ignoring the sharp pain in his side and his protesting ankle, and knelt in the dirty, damp straw next to his friend. Painstakingly, he straightened Mathieu's broken leg, wincing as a shudder ran through his brother-in-law's prone body.

"Prigent, find me a board or something flat we can use as a splint," he instructed without looking up.

While Prigent was gone, Gabriel took stock of Mathieu's other injuries. He was bruised and battered, his face a swollen mess, his nose crooked. Two fingers on his right hand were broken.

"*Qu'ils aillent en enfer*," he cursed under his breath.

Prigent reappeared with a piece of wood that looked to have been pried off a bench. "This was all I could find," he said apologetically.

"It will serve." Gabriel took the board and placed it under Mathieu's leg.

With Luc's help, they wrapped his cloak around it as tightly as they dared, tying it with rope to hold it together. He rocked back on his haunches and frowned. It would have to do for now.

"I'll carry him," offered Luc.

"Alright. Prigent, you lead, I'll follow," said Gabriel.

The three of them draped Mathieu over Luc's shoulder and moved as quietly as they could out of the dungeons, leaving the metallic scent of blood and misery behind them as they climbed the spiral stair toward fresh air and freedom. Gabriel scarcely dared breathe as they retraced their steps. By some miracle they made it out the door and onto the parapets without encountering another soul. It was still raining, but it had slowed to a gentle, cleansing rain.

"How are we going to accomplish this?" asked Luc doubtfully, glancing from the wall to Mathieu's broken body.

Prigent cleared his throat. "One of the sentries we left tied up is gone. We best make haste."

Panic blossomed in Gabriel's stomach, acid burning unpleasantly into his chest. "Prigent, you go down now. Tug twice on the line to let us know you've reached the bottom. I'll tie Mathieu on, and Luc and I will lower him to you."

Prigent nodded and disappeared over the crenellations.

Gabriel turned to Luc. "Cut the other lines and stuff them in your bag, quickly."

One hand on the rope, he waited for his signal. As soon as he felt the tug, he hauled the line up, hand over hand and knelt, tying it carefully around Mathieu, trying to create a harness of sorts without causing him further injury. Mathieu groaned brokenly, but his lashes didn't so much as flutter. A blessing, no doubt.

Luc picked Mathieu up and slowly lowered him over the side. Gabriel wrapped the line around a parapet, so it wouldn't slip under his weight, and they painstakingly let him down, hand over hand. The wet rope burned his skin, tearing his palms, but he scarcely felt it. When they'd played all the line out, they waited, facing the door, praying for a few more precious minutes.

The rain was warm and gentle against his skin, and he felt it soaking through his shirt, mingling with his blood and trickling down his abdomen. Another tug on the rope.

"Go," he whispered to Luc. "I'm right behind you."

Luc clambered over the wall.

"*Un, deux, trois, quatre. . .*" Gabriel slowly counted to ten. He didn't want to crowd Luc.

He threw his leg over the edge and cautiously dropped down, wrapping his legs around the rope, his fingertips burning from gripping the top of the wall.

"Halt!" screamed a sentry peering down at him

"*Merde.*"

Gabriel let the rope run between his hands, ripping them to shreds as he flew down, the ground racing up at him with dizzying speed. He half jumped, half fell the last ten feet, grunting as he hit the marsh seconds after Luc, and rolled. Something splattered the muddy ground inches from his face, and he flinched away. The man was shooting down at them.

Luc fired his pistol at the sentry while Gabriel lurched to his feet, his bad ankle threatening to give out. He yanked his pistol out, praying the powder wasn't too wet to ignite.

"Run!" he hissed at Luc as he aimed and fired. The guard ducked behind the wall and Gabriel disappeared into the reeds, biding his time. The rain continued to fall, obscuring his vision. Luc should be back to the boat by now. A head popped up behind the parapets. It turned slowly, scanning the marsh below before leaning dangerously out over the wall. Gabriel took his time aiming, held his breath as he squeezed the trigger and hit his target. The man fell, much further than Gabriel, and hit the ground with a sickening thud.

Gabriel limped as he ran out of the vegetation, his body screaming with every step, and slashed the man's throat for good measure. Crouched over, hoping the tall grass and cattails would provide some cover, he moved in the direction of the *bateau*, praying no other guards were coming after them.

Breathing hard, he stumbled to the edge of the stream and collapsed into the boat, rocking it wildly. "Get us out of here," he managed.

Madec wasted no time, rowing smoothly and steadily. The tide had reached slack water while they were in the fortress, and had now turned, ebbing back out into the ocean, the current pushing them along.

"We can't travel far with Mathieu in this state, and the Navy will be scouring the countryside come morning, if not sooner." Luc broke the silence, grimly stating what they were all thinking.

"What are our options?" asked Prigent.

"He can't go home," said Luc.

"Landévennec?" suggested Madec.

Gabriel shook his head. "Des Rochefort knows of our connection. They will look there."

"Aye, but didn't you say le Commandant was in Versailles?" asked Luc.

"*Oui*, but that was neigh on a fortnight ago. He could be anywhere now." Each breath hurt. Ava was going to throttle him for getting injured again.

"Landévennec for now," offered Luc. "We'll obtain a carriage or a wagon. Esme will set his leg and fingers and tend to him for a few days at least. Surely, we can afford that much? When he's stable, we move him."

Gabriel absorbed the idea in silence. There could be no doubt that Mathieu needed a healer and at least Esme could be trusted. *What of the other tenants though?*

"We arrive under the cover of night," he ruled. "Two days at Landévennec, no more. After that, can the three of you bring him south? I must return to Versailles."

"Aye," agreed Prigent.

"Do you have a town in mind?" grunted Madec, rowing consistently. They were nearing the mouth of the inlet now and the current was stronger.

"Roussillon," decided Gabriel.

Twenty-Five
Midnight Visitors

I trailed des Rochefort out of the *salon*, my body so stiff it ached. The man was more than just a thorn in my side. He had unofficially declared war against Gabriel and me. Intuitively, I'd known we hadn't heard the last of him back in Nantes. He wasn't the sort of man to let petty grievances go. The question was, how dangerous was he? Had he really traveled or sent someone to Roussillon? Or had it been a lucky guess?

I watched him leave and leaned against the doorjamb, my neck and shoulders throbbing from tension.

"Commandant, what brings you here?" Phillipe's voice was smooth, but I detected the thread of hostility in it and wondered if des Rochefort heard it too.

"Ah, it's le Comte de Sainte-Denis, is it not? Well met, Monsieur," replied des Rochefort urbanely.

I straightened my shoulders, unease creeping into my neck and the base of my skull. A full-blown headache was imminent. As much as I enjoyed Phillipe and his updates, I could do without right now. At least he had witnessed des Rochefort leaving though.

"Likewise," replied Phillipe, not troubling to mask his impatience.

"I just had a bit of business to attend to with the lovely Vicomtesse de Landévennec. I'll see you around, Comte."

Phillipe's silhouette appeared at the door. He stepped over the threshold, letting the butler shut the door and stalked over to me scowling. "Did he threaten you?"

I lifted my shoulders and let them fall. "Yes and no. Come sit." I walked back into the bright *salon*.

Noemi poked her head in. "I've a clean cup for you," she offered with a curtsy, holding a full goblet out to Phillipe.

He took it with a smile of thanks and sat on the settee. Noemi topped mine off, and I walked with it to my preferred seat.

"What news?" I sipped delicately, letting the port sit on my tongue and fill my senses.

"Yesterday Sieyès put forth a motion inviting the first and second estates to join the Commons. They want an assembly, aye?" Phillipe chose a tart, placing it on his plate.

I furrowed my brow in confusion. "That's good, is it not?"

"It might have been, except no one responded and today the Commons moved forward with a roll call." He carefully took a bite of his tart, chewing thoughtfully before washing it down with a drink of his port.

"And that means what? They're gainsaying their fellow estates authority?" Unobtrusively I arched my back and rolled my shoulders back, trying to ease the strain.

"*Oui*. They've taken the power into their own hands without *le Roi's* consent. The man is grieving for the loss of his heir and they're moving forward as if their prince wasn't lying in his casket."

I closed my eyes against the prick of tears at the mention of the doomed dauphin. Since his passing, I'd been struggling; the event dredging up my grief over Aimée's death.

"I imagine the news will spread like a wildfire," I murmured.

"The Commons are the only estate to allow spectators. The Parisians will know tonight." He shook his head.

"This truly backs you into a corner," I observed, taking another sip of my port.

"There are many that will resent the Third taking power onto themselves," he said grimly.

"And quite a few more who will join within days."

He nodded in acknowledgement. "What of des Rochefort? What did he want?"

I sighed, mention of the Commandant making my belly feel hollow. "He claimed he wished to speak to Gabriel. I've been giving out he's ill, as we agreed, so there's no way for des Rochefort to know he's gone. . . unless someone in the household spoke."

Phillipe nodded and twirled his glass between his hands.

"I think he suspects he's away." I raised my right shoulder in a shrug. "Who knows, really?" I couldn't mention the business of Roussillon, I didn't think Gabriel had explained all that to Phillipe, and there was no point in further complicating affairs. "Overall, I believe he just hoped to intimidate us, maybe scare me into an admission he could utilize against Gabriel and me."

Phillipe swallowed the last bite of his peach tart and rose. "I'll keep a closer eye on him. I'm beginning to question whether he truly has business to attend here, or if he's simply lurking and hoping to rile you into providing him with something he can use against you."

I placed my cup on the table and stood. "He left emptyhanded today," I noted grimly.

"No word from Gabriel, eh?"

I shook my head as we walked to the door. "I'm praying he's back within the week."

Phillipe frowned. "I'm worried about Mathieu."

"Waiting for news is the hardest thing. I loathe being left behind," I said emphatically.

He observed me, face inscrutable. "We have to put our faith in *le bon Dieu* and Gabriel's abilities. I'm confident that if Mathieu can be found, he will be."

I crossed myself dutifully. "I pray you're right. By the way, what of your sister? Is she still here? Shall I have her for tea again?"

A look of discomfort flitted across his chiseled face. "Charlotte decided to go back to Saint-Denis."

"Oh?" I asked, carefully neutral.

He shifted from one foot to the other. "I happened across a letter she was writing to a friend of hers. Scheming to somehow insert herself between Gabriel and you." His face was turned to face the window, no doubt avoiding my eyes.

"Oh..." I said again, inanely.

"We had words," he said simply. "I love my sister dearly, but she is immature and spoiled. She thinks only of herself and her conquests and what it means for her vanity. Winning over Gabriel would be a game to her."

"I— thank you, I suppose. I assume that means you took up for me?" I asked awkwardly.

"Well..." his eyes met mine. "I think of it more as taking up for Gabriel and his happiness. You do that for him, and I know she would make him miserable. Charlotte needs someone like Gabriel, but she doesn't need Gabriel, if you get my meaning."

"Aye, I suppose I do," I murmured.

"*Bon*. Now that we've addressed that bit of awkwardness." He flashed me a smile. "I will see you on the morrow." He bowed over my hand and left.

Esme startled awake and lay in the dark listening for the noise that had torn her from her dreams. From the hall below, she heard the steady ticking of the clock, and the wind rustling the leaves of the oak outside her window. She lay in bed, ears straining, eyes wide, waiting. It didn't matter how she knew something was coming. . . she had always been highly in tune with her senses.

There! A knock so soft upon the front door, she barely heard it.

She threw the quilt off, swung her legs over the side of the bed and rested her feet on the bare ground for a moment, gaining her bearings. Her wrapper was laid on the chair in the corner, and she pulled it over her nightdress, tying the belt at her waist as she moved toward the door. She fumbled for a moment; her fingers clumsy with sleep as she tried to light the wick of her lantern.

At the front door, she placed the lantern on the hall table and threw the bolt, stepping back at the sight of the men in the shadows.

"Luc!" She threw her arms around his neck, reveling in the feel of his solid body against hers and his arms tight around her. He smelled of road, dirt, sweat, dried blood and something else she couldn't identify, but she didn't care. He was home.

She stepped back so he could enter and took stock of the others at her threshold. Gabriel stepped forward with a grimace, obviously in pain.

"We've Mathieu in the wagon. He's in a bad way. Can you tend him?" he asked softly.

"Of course," she murmured. "Bring him upstairs into the guest room." Esme lifted the lantern off the table and led the way. "You're injured as well," she stated, once they were upstairs and she saw how gingerly Gabriel moved.

"Maurice Prigent too," he replied. "But we'll keep. Mathieu needs you first."

Luc and Madec carried Mathieu up the stairs while Esme waited on the landing. She lay her lantern on the washstand beside the guest room bed and grimaced at the sight before her. Mathieu's face was unrecognizable, one soft brown eye open and unfocused, the other swollen shut. His face turned to her and recognition shone in his eye. That was good then, at least he wasn't insensible.

"What do you need?" asked Gabriel simply.

"Someone lay a fire. Luc, get more lanterns please, I'll need light," she directed, her training taking over. "Gabriel, please rouse Madame Allard and tell her we need water boiled quickly." Without turning around, she knew her directions were being followed to the letter.

"What more?" asked Madec. "Where's your box of tinctures and such?"

"In the surgery. Down the stairs, second door on the left." Her hands were busy sawing through the rope around Mathieu's broken leg. Boots clattered down the stairs, no doubt leaving caked mud and dirt in their wake, but there was time enough for that later.

Gabriel reappeared by her side. "Cut the cloak. I've no need of it, and I prefer not to jostle him more than necessary."

She nodded, cutting the cloak without hesitation, pushing it away from his leg. "Can you remove his boots?"

She slit the leg of Mathieu's breeches to see the extent of his injury while Gabriel and Prigent unlaced his boots. Footfalls on the wooden stairs heralded Madec's return. He laid the heavy box on the floor, carefully opening the lid to reveal its contents.

Esme remembered Prigent's inability to handle blood when she caught a glimpse of his face. "Maurice, can you run down to the kitchen and see if Madame Allard has the water ready?"

Relief swept across his features. "*Oui,* Madame." He practically ran from the room.

"Georges, Gabriel, can the two of you carefully lift Mathieu's leg?" She pointed. "Here and here, so I can remove all this." Esme waved her hand at the pile of discarded wool, rope and wood.

Mathieu grunted in pain as they lifted him and Esme's heart squeezed. They laid him back down gently and she grabbed a cloth, soaked it in her wash basin, and went to work gently rinsing away the blood and dirt crusted on his leg, mentally running through her options.

"Gabriel, can you find me the bottle of Helichrysum?" She swiped a second cloth, dunked it, wrung it out and handed it to Madec. "Clean his face a bit for me, aye?"

"This one?" Gabriel squinted at the small bottle doubtfully as he held it up to show Esme.

"*Oui.*" She held out her hand and he reverently placed it in her palm. She'd obtained the rare oil from the apothecary near Madame Simon, where she'd trained, after learning that it reduced swelling and bruising.

"Luc, can you please find the cognac and bring it here? Mathieu should have some before I begin." They had tried to straighten his leg; she could tell as she gently ran her fingers down his femur and tibia. *Le bon Dieu* only knew how long ago it'd been broken, it was swollen grotesquely and mottled shades of violet, and a blue so dark it appeared black in the flickering light. She probed as softly as she could, knowing she was causing him more pain by his ragged breath and the sheen of perspiration that had broken out on his face.

"I'm sorry," she murmured. She could feel the bone had splintered in at least two places, pulling it correctly back into place was going to hurt immensely.

Twenty-Six
Inherited

The sun was high overhead when Esme pressed her hands to the small of her back and stretched, trying to work the kinks out. Her muscles screamed in protest, but she was satisfied that she'd done everything she could. Mathieu was thankfully asleep, his leg straight, splinted and wrapped in clean bandages, a makeshift crutch waiting for him by the bed, though it would be at least a day or two before she would allow him to attempt using it. His hand had been mangled badly, but she'd managed to straighten the smashed fingers. She wondered how well they would heal.

His nose would likely be crooked forever, unless it were broken again in some future mishap. Madame Allard had proved her mettle, successfully getting some broth and soft, freshly baked bread in his belly while Esme tended to the other men. Maurice had a long, shallow cut along his forearm, already scabbed over by the time she looked at it. It hadn't required much more than a thorough rinse, some ointment applied and a clean bandage. She sent him home to sleep with strict instructions to keep it clean and return to her immediately if it began to show signs of infection.

Gabriel was in somewhat worse condition. The cut on his abdomen was fairly shallow, similar to Prigent's, though the skin hadn't fully knit itself back together, still oozing blood in some places where the blade cut deep. The injury in his side was a deal worse, requiring several stitches. She was annoyed at his insistence that he depart tonight, as soon as it was full dark.

"You should wait at least a day or two. Give your body a chance to begin healing," she argued.

"It's not possible." He refused to look her in the eye as he pulled a clean shirt out of his saddle bag. Gabriel pulled the linen over his head and winced. "Ava will be out of her mind with worry and *le bon Dieu* only knows what is happening with the Estates-General."

The man was as stubborn and implacable as a boulder. She sighed. "Rest today at least. And tell me what the plan is. Mathieu cannot stay here for long." She sat down tiredly, her entire body aching.

He frowned. "You look like you need to rest as well, Esme. You've been on your feet for hours."

She waved him off. "I'll be fine. I'm not going on a ten-day journey with fresh stitches."

Gabriel grinned at her disarmingly. "I've asked Luc, Madec and Prigent to move Mathieu as soon as possible. They're to leave under cover of night. Expect them to be gone for three weeks at least. While they're away, you'll give out that they're doing a job for me."

"Aye, all right. Does anyone know you're here now? How will you provision for Mathieu?"

He frowned, fine lines appearing between his brows. "I've been thinking about that. I think it's best if we keep our presence here as quiet as possible. I know we can trust many of the tenants, but I cannot vouch for them all." He pinched the bridge of his nose.

"I agree." Esme flexed her fingers, trying to ease the cramps.

"I intend to write a letter to you giving you leave to collect certain items from the château. You're to go later this afternoon and pretend you received it from Versailles and that you're to send a package to me. Mathieu will need clothing. I'm larger than him, but we will make do. I'll need another cloak. I've coin for you to get as well, he'll need money to survive until he can find work, and they'll need it for the trip as well."

"Best write that letter then. I'm off for a quick nap. I'll go to the château after *diner*." She yawned.

The days melded one into the next, warm and sunny, the breeze chasing clouds across the azure sky, with little to mark the passing of time other than Phillipe's faithful visits. Long days were spent lolling in the courtyard with Armand or chasing him about while he shrieked with joy. The occasional summer rain shower found me curled up with a book borrowed from the well-stocked library.

I tried not to think about Gabriel, Mathieu and Amelie, but it was an exercise in futility. During the days, I generally managed to occupy myself, but the nights were spent staring wide-eyed at the canopy above our bed while I considered the many ways the rescue effort might have gone awry. Amélie was often on my mind. I couldn't imagine how worried she must be.

Phillipe, true to his promise, came nearly daily, inquiring after des Rochefort, who thankfully hadn't put in another surprise appearance, and filling me in on the excitement at the Estates-General. As we expected, a few parish priests left their order a few days after the roll call. This was all it took for the floodgates to open. Nearly twenty priests had joined the Third by yesterday's end.

This evening, Phillipe came with the news that the title of National Assembly had been adopted, with a unanimous agreement that all current taxation was illegal, but that it would be temporarily permitted until a new system was agreed upon. Additionally, they had officially elected a president to represent them. It was a direct challenge to the king's authority and wouldn't go unanswered. Despite knowing how this would all end, I found my anxiety building ever higher as we moved inexorably toward war.

I was lying in bed mulling over the latest changes and trying not to let my mind wander to Gabriel when I heard a bloodcurdling scream. The hair on my arms stood up as I leapt up and ran for the door. The sound came from the servant's quarters and went on and on without pause, new voices joining in the cacophony. Without waiting, I sprinted to the back stairs at the end of the corridor and took them two at a time. Doors opened and slammed, and feet pounded on the wood floor, vibrating above my head. The door at the top of the stairs opened and I nearly ran into Noemi as she raced down the stairs.

Her face was streaked with tears. "Oh, my lady, thank the Lord. Please hurry. Monsieur Meyer is cutting her down now!" She turned and ran back up the stairs.

I followed her, not comprehending what she meant. "Who is he cutting down? What do you mean?" In my haste I tripped on my long nightdress and threw my hand against the wall to catch myself.

The hallway in the servant's quarters was narrower than below and not as well lit. Noemi disappeared into the second door on the right, and I traipsed in after her. The room was in disarray. Two twin beds were pushed against the walls, each with a small armoire against the wall opposite the head of the beds. It was clearly meant to be shared amongst the female staff. It was a cramped room, but it was clean, warm and serviceable.

Crammed into the room were the butler, housekeeper, and maids clustered around the bed to the left. They blocked my view, but my eyes traveled up to the exposed wood beams where a sturdy rope hung swaying from one. My stomach churning and my heart in my throat, I pushed my way through the throng to the bed where Jeanne lay motionless. The noose was still wrapped around her pale neck, though someone had loosened it.

"Cut it off," I ordered through the lump in my throat. "Is she—" I couldn't bring myself to say the words.

"*Non*," said the butler. "By some miracle she didn't break her neck."

He crossed himself before pulling a knife out of his pocket and gently sawing away at the hempen rope, pulling it away from her neck to expose the ring of rope-burnt skin and the dark bruises that had already begun to form.

"I think I walked in immediately after she did it." Noemi's voice shook.

"*Dieu merci*," murmured the housekeeper solemnly, crossing herself.

I gently reached out and laid my hand on Jeanne's white cheek. A tiny breath escaped through her parted, colorless lips.

"Do you share this room with her?" I looked at Noemi.

"*Oui*." Her soft brown eyes were rimmed in red and swollen from crying.

"All right." I turned to face the crowd. "Thank you all for your quick actions tonight. Without it, Jeanne likely wouldn't be with us. For now, I'd like to ask everyone to return to their duties or chambers." I met Noemi's gaze. "Could you please stay?"

She nodded wordlessly while everyone else murmured amongst themselves and filed out of the room. When it was just the three of us, I quietly shut the door.

"Will the babe be all right, Madame?"

I blew out a breath. "Truly, I don't know Noemi. With all my heart, I hope so. But time will tell the truth of it. Does she know her letters? Did she leave a note?"

She held out a crumpled bit of parchment in her trembling hand. I took it, scanning the words swiftly before lifting my eyes to her steady gaze.

"Did you read it?" I blinked hard against the prickle of tears.

"Aye, my lady."

"Do you know what Jeanne's husband did to her?" Rage bubbled within me. Although we had successfully extricated her from the monster she married, she carried the unimaginable trauma of his abuse buried within her. I hadn't pushed her to speak about her experience, hoping that trust would come with time, and I was furious with myself for not realizing how deep her scars ran.

"No, although I think I am beginning to understand," she said softly.

I nodded and clenched my fists, fighting the urge to hit something.

"Is it possible? What she wrote?"

"It's possible. Children take other traits from their parents, don't they? Eye color, the shape of their face, their height. . . Why shouldn't they also inherit a kind spirit, a sense of humor or a love of animals?" I shrugged my shoulders.

"Or. . . an evil heart?" she suggested.

"*Oui*. Or an evil heart," I agreed. "Mind, I don't think it's probable. More than likely the child would be a wonderful person, particularly since Jeanne herself is. But it's impossible to say."

Noemi was looking at the ground, her blonde curls falling out of her cap and straggling over her shoulders after the chaos of the evening. When her sad eyes met mine, I was struck by how young she was. Not much older than Jeanne if I were to guess.

"I suppose I can understand why she feels as she does."

My heart ached. "She needs a good friend. I'm relieving you of your other duties for the time being, Noemi. Please just stay close to her. I'm going to get a few items from my medicine box for her."

"*Oui*, Madame."

Twenty-Seven
Blades of Grass

Esme was right, of course. He was in no condition to be riding through the rough terrain of the countryside and sleeping on the rocky, unyielding ground. He was reminded of this fact with every bone jarring, tooth-gritting step. Still, he pushed on; determined to get back to Ava as quickly as he could. The stitches in his side held up relatively well for the first three days of his journey, but he'd reopened his wound two days past, and it now steadily oozed a questionable looking mixture of blood and pus.

She'd insisted he pack spare bandages and a foul-smelling ointment in his saddle bags, taking up precious space for provisions. At this point in his travels, however, he was actually grateful. His head throbbed in time with his heartbeat and there was a strange whooshing sound in his ears, rather like being underwater. He was parched and he'd finished the last precious drops of water in his wineskin hours ago. At the time, he'd been confident that he'd come across a stream soon, but he was beginning to question every choice he'd made since leaving Landévennec.

The sun was setting behind the verdant hills to the west, throwing streaks of crimson and tangerine into the darkening violet sky. From the top of a hill, he glimpsed a small village in the valley below, nestled like a jewel glinting in the last golden rays of light, and prayed it was large enough to boast an *auberge*. He needed a bed tonight.

Automne plodded onwards valiantly, his ears turning and twitching, picking up the rustle of leaves in the breeze, the twitters and songs of birds as they called to each other, settling in for the night. The first stars were twinkling to life in the east as Gabriel and Automne approached the outskirts of the sleepy town. Gabriel's head pounded so loudly he cringed at the sound it made as it echoed between his ears.

They made their way down the main thoroughfare, past shop windows that reflected light dancing from the lanterns hung on the rough stone walls. There were a few villagers still out, but they all appeared to be in a hurry, rushing home before night fell. Luckily, Gabriel spotted a neatly lettered hanging sign advertising an *auberge* bearing the name *Le duel de châtaignier*, likely named for the abundance of chestnuts in the area, about halfway down the street.

Dizzy with relief, he reined Automne in, dismounted unsteadily and hitched him to the post. The world swayed under his feet, and he leaned against Automne's solid, comforting bulk, trying to get his bearings. *I just need to make it through the next few minutes.*

A chilling wave of ice water in his veins, followed the sweating spell he'd just endured, making him shiver uncontrollably. *Just long enough to make it up the stairs and into bed.*

First, the saddle bags needed to be unstrapped. He fumbled with the buckle, the edges of his eyesight turning black, as the boat he was on heeled precipitously to one side. He felt like a drunk stumbling down an alley, bouncing back and forth between narrow walls to his right and left. He shook his head to clear it, and the ground rushed up to meet him as his vision went dark.

I was to blame, I knew. Jeanne had been to the fiery shores of hell and back in the last year. Her innocent life had been upended and shifted around enough to make anyone's head spin. I couldn't imagine getting married at fifteen, only to discover that my husband was a real-life monster, having to fake my death, and uproot my life to escape his abuse, only to realize that I was pregnant, and have to move yet again because the lunatic I married was searching for me.

The signs she was struggling had been there though. Noemi had approached me about it, but I had been too wrapped up in my issues to focus my attention on her the way I should have. I'd been plagued with fear during my pregnancy with Aimée and Armand and I should have realized Jeanne would have trepidations as well. What was more, her anxiety that the infant might inherit its father's evil proclivities was not without merit.

I sighed and rested my cheek against Armand's soft hair, his boneless weight comforting and warm, his head heavy as he slept on my chest. The tree trunk at my back was wide and solid, the generous boughs above sheltering us from the intense, noonday sun. These moments were fleeting; already he was showing his preference for mobility, enjoying the freedom of crawling at a mad pace across the courtyard, picking up sticks to wave them exuberantly aloft, trying to taste the acorns he discovered, before we wrestled them from his shockingly strong grasp, and terrorizing the tiny creatures that shared the garden with us.

I inhaled the sweet scent of him and tried to imagine the terror Jeanne must have felt— perhaps still felt— to feel that taking her life and that of her child's was the best course of action open to her. My chest felt tight as sadness swelled within me, constricting my heart and lungs painfully. I shut my eyes against the tears that were gathering and tried to direct my thoughts toward finding solutions.

"My lady?" A soft, melodic voice interrupted my musings.

My lashes lifted and I tilted my head back to see Jeanne's slight frame standing before me, her belly gently curving out in her dove gray dress, her light blonde hair and pale skin a startling contrast to the livid bruising and raw skin around her neck.

"Jeanne." I patted the grass beside me. "Please, sit."

She sat, biting her lip and staring at her slender hands clasped on her lap. Her fine, delicate features were shadowed, violet rings beneath her warm, brown eyes, her lips red and chapped, likely from constant nervous chewing. She'd obviously come to say something but couldn't gather the confidence to begin.

"What can I do for you, Jeanne?" I asked as gently as I could. Armand's breath puffed against my chest and his heartbeat was a tiny, steady drum, comforting me with its regularity.

She lifted haunted eyes to my face, resembling a frightened rabbit, frozen with indecision. "I apologize for the trouble I caused the household, Madame." Her voice wavered.

"Oh Jeanne." It was hard to get a breath in. "It was no trouble. I am grateful you're still here with us. I wish you would have come to me, or Noemi, or... someone... *anyone*— and trusted us with your thoughts and fears. Would that we could have allayed them or helped you in some way. I hate that you felt there were no other options open to you."

"It was very kind of you and the Gardins to help me," she whispered. "I feared. . ."

"What did you fear?"

"I feared he would kill me," she finished. "Indeed, there were days I wished he would just end my misery," she admitted, looking down as she plucked blades of grass.

My heart shattered. Marriage should be a safe place, where you could rest when you were weary, where you were cherished, and lifted when you felt you couldn't continue. It had been the opposite for the child that sat miserably before me.

"Jeanne," I began, unsure of how to continue. "What you endured. . . It's something no one should ever experience. It infuriates me that this happened to you, and I wish, more than anything, that I could somehow erase your past. But I can't do that. You will live with the trauma of how he treated you for the rest of your life."

She lifted eyes shiny with unshed tears, and I felt tears smart in my own eyes. "I want to forget it."

"I know. I want you to forget it as well. But we both know you never will."

Jeanne swallowed hard and nodded.

"But it doesn't have to dictate your whole life. You can move forward from this and have a gorgeous babe who will bring joy, wonder and love into your life. We have pledged to keep you safe. You need never worry while you are with us. And I hope, very much, that one day you meet someone who cherishes you and shows you what marriage is truly meant to be."

Jeanne frowned. "I don't think—"

"I know, you cannot imagine such a thing right now, and I don't blame you. I just want you to know, marriage can be a wonderous, beautiful experience and I hope one day you see it for yourself."

The small pile of desiccated grass beside Jeanne's skirt continued to grow as she studiously shredded each blade she picked. I shifted against the tree trunk, easing the itch between my shoulder blades. Armand's head lolled and I cupped the back of his neck, feeling his soft curls between my fingers as I adjusted him against my bosom.

"What if my *bébé* is like its father?" Her hand rested protectively on the small mound of her belly, but her eyes were dark with fear.

I let her question hang in the sultry summer air for a moment. "What if your *bébé* is absolutely nothing like its father?"

"They may not be," she conceded, frown lines between her brows. "But don't you think it's possible?"

"No," I answered, sudden certainty sweeping through me. "No, I think you will have a daughter. A lovely, gentle, gorgeous girl like yourself, without an ounce of your husband's sinister proclivities."

The tears Jeanne had been harboring, spilled over silently, leaving silvery tracks on her pale, delicate cheeks.

"Come here," I said softly, my voice thick. I patted the space beside me and wrapped my arm around her as she wept soundlessly against my shoulder, her tears soaking through my gown, while I stared over her head unseeing. How I knew Jeanne would have a girl, I couldn't say. I hadn't touched her, which had generally been the trigger for my visions in the past. Yet somehow, I knew. *What did it mean?*

Twenty-Eight

"We are here by the will of the people and can only be made to leave by the force of bayonets."

Le Comte de Mirabeau

I was falling.

Spinning, falling, and spinning through the air weightlessly on my back.

My eyes were wide open, taking in the dark around me; not a pinprick of light to be found, no matter how my eyes searched and strained. As I spun, my arms and legs splayed wide, like a parody of a snow angel, the skirt of my gown belled out, held aloft by the air beneath me.

Still, I fell.

My stomach lurched unpleasantly, lodging in my throat, reminding me of an elevator in free fall. I opened my fingers, spreading each digit out, feeling blindly in the absolute black surrounding me for something to hold on to. The air whistled as it rushed past my empty hands.

It was a dream.

I knew it the way one always knows... particularly when it's one that's been repeated throughout the course of your life.

I knew, but I couldn't wake myself from it.

I had to hit the bottom first.

I waited, my heart thumping uncomfortably in my chest, my hands splayed out helplessly— praying to catch myself on something— knowing that I wouldn't.

My body thudded sickeningly as I hit the ground.

But I didn't wake up.

An agony of pain bloomed, beginning at my core and radiating to the tips of my fingers, before starting the return journey, throbbing through my arteries and veins. Every inch was fire racing through my bloodstream back to my heart, where the torment traveled back to my extremities again. I didn't know how long I lay there, every breath ripped from my lungs, the world beyond my anguish nonexistent, but after an interminable time I became aware of the beginnings of light around the edges, resembling the lightening of the sky before dawn, heralding the sun's inevitable appearance.

I opened my eyes and a weathered face with kind, blue eyes framed by abundant crow's feet swam into view. The room beyond my immediate focus was hazy and indistinct, the pain that anchored my limbs to the soft linens beneath me made it impossible to absorb anything beyond the man that hovered over me. I wet my lips, but my voice was naught more than a hoarse croak.

I awoke in a cold sweat; my damp shift clinging to me uncomfortably, my eyes open wide, straining to see into the dark, shadowy recesses of the room. I shivered as I pushed my crumpled blankets aside and swung my legs off the bed, the feel of solid wood beneath my feet grounding me. The night loomed threateningly, and I fumbled blindly, using the lit taper on the table to light additional candles, spilling hot wax on my hand as I did so. The flickering, yellow light held back the gloom, as I sucked on my injured skin, trying to take the sting out of the burn. I dragged the softest blanket off the bed and wrapped myself in it, the end trailing behind me as I walked to the window embrasure and opened the shutters, letting the cool night air wash over me.

A shaky breath escaped my lips as I stared into the inky night. The moon had already set, leaving behind nothing but heavy clouds and the occasional star twinkling valiantly where the clouds broke. Rain was coming; I could smell the moisture in the pregnant air, heavy with the expectation of the approaching storm. I sat in the window seat, pulled the blanket more firmly around me, and leaned my head against the wood frame.

Gabriel was ill or injured. . . perhaps both. I closed my eyes, trying to recall the details, summoning the sensations that had felt so intensely real during my dream. *Had the pain been localized to a specific area?*

No. It had been an all-consuming, fiery pain that engulfed my body. *His body*, I corrected myself. *Where is Gabriel?*

I squinted against the swirling wind into the gathering storm as if I might pluck the answer from the clouds. Lightning flashed, outlining the silhouette of the buildings and trees in ultraviolet light. The hairs on my arms prickled in response, goosebumps rising on my skin, my entire body attuned to the electricity in the air as I shivered. *I hate lightning.*

There was a time when I loved it; fed on the adrenaline that coursed through my body and pumped in my veins with every storm, but that was before I lost Carri, and our boat, and found myself in a time not my own. I swallowed down the aching lump in my throat at the memory of Carri, blinked back the sting of tears, forced my thoughts back to Gabriel as I burrowed deeper into the cocoon of my quilt.

He'd been gone for nearly three weeks, but he could be anywhere between Trégoudan and Versailles. I bit my lip and tasted metallic blood. It would be impossible for me to search for him without more information. As much as I wanted to order the horses saddled and ride south out of Versailles, I knew it was better to stay put. Either for someone to send word to me, or for Gabriel himself to find me. Not to mention, with des Rochefort lurking around, it was best not to draw any attention to our household or to the fact that Gabriel was not in residence.

A jagged bolt zigzagged across the sky, running like a current through my body, making my hair stand on end. Unnerved, I leapt away from the window. The howling wind tugged strands of hair from my braid, whipping it about my face as it tore into the room, followed by a torrential downpour. The rain beat so hard against the windowsill it pinged and bounced onto the wood floor.

I carefully navigated back to the window, closing the heavy shutters against the storm. The floor was slick and slippery, the mist carried in on the wind leaving a fine layer on the wood. I latched them, enclosing myself in the pretend sanctuary of my bedchamber, safe from the lightning that made my heart thud uncomfortably.

My breath came in short gasps as I huddled on the bed, hugging my knees to my chest and listened to the deluge. Thunder clapped and rumbled, furiously close, shaking the house down to the foundations. Electricity crackled in the air, but at least I couldn't see it anymore. I pressed my forehead against my legs and closed my eyes. *Breathe in. Breathe out. Slower next time. Breathe in, hold it, let it out.*

Over minute increments my breath slowed. I kept going, willing my shoulders to relax, pushing the tension and anxiety out with each exhalation, emptying my mind of everything except Gabriel. My limbs heavy,

I lay down, curled in the fetal position, and clutched a pillow to my chest. *Where is Gabriel?*

"I'm sorry I haven't stopped by the last few days," Phillipe apologized over his tea.

I smothered a yawn. Last night I'd managed to fall back asleep, but it'd been fitful and chock full of nightmares. I waved off his explanation. "It's fine. I'm sure you've been busy. I hear things came to a head?"

"*Oui...*"

Worry over Gabriel had been gnawing at me all day. I'd chewed my bottom lip raw and was running on the fumes of adrenaline from the storm. I fiddled with the tasseled end of a cushion, looking up just in time to hear the end of Phillipe's tirade.

"... Of course, the First Estate was left with no choice but to formally vote to join them, and then the debacle with *le Roi* and the deputies and the damned tennis court oath, as they're now calling it." He shook his head, annoyance plain in his eyes. "It's an absolute disaster."

"Mmm," I murmured noncommittally, lifting my teacup and inhaling the fragrant steam before I took a careful sip. "I did hear about that. But what happened after?"

Phillipe rolled his eyes. "Louis agreed not to increase taxes in the future without the Estates-General's agreement. Necker convinced him to grant an end to frivolous imprisonments and to eradicate serfdom. Then he had the gall to advise the aristocracy to give up our privileges."

This was a turning point. I had long wondered how many members of the Second Estate had been willing to do so, but it was the sort of detail that was lost to the annals of history; the more significant events relegating the minor moments to the shadows. I knew it had been too little too late to placate the Third Estate, but I asked anyway.

I raised a brow. "So?"

"The Third was unimpressed, as I'm sure you surmised. *Le Roi* tried to exert his authority and remind everyone of his power by ordering us all to return to our Estate's quarters. The Third refused. Le Comte de Mirabeau issued a proclamation that has them all up in arms."

A chill ran down my spine. "We are here by the will of the people and can only be made to leave by the force of bayonets," I quoted softly.

Phillipe looked surprised. "Oh, you heard already?"

I smiled sadly. "Something like that."

He drained his cup and set it gently on the side table. "Well, I best be going. There's talk of action this evening. The people seem restless." He stood, waiting for me. "I thought perhaps Gabriel would be back by now."

"I'm praying it will be soon," I answered, the pit in my stomach growing at the thought of Gabriel lying in a strange bed, God only knew where.

Phillipe crossed himself. "It will be. Don't fret."

Twenty-Nine
Corrosion and Clock Gears

That night I watched from the relative safety of my window, standing well back in the shadows to avoid notice, as crowds burst into the palace. They carried torches, shouting in excitement, tasting victory in the air. It was electrifying and emotional, and although I didn't expect the knot of foreboding in my stomach to intensify, that was exactly what happened.

Events had been set in motion that I could never hope to control, or even to sway. Truth be told, the historical clock gears that moved relentlessly in the direction of the revolution had begun far before I had even arrived in the eighteenth century. It was the grossest form of egotism to believe that I could alter the course of history; that I could slow the inevitable ticking of the hands of the clock as they made their way ever closer to the fourteenth of July.

It left a sour, unsettled feeling in my gut. Although no one would lose their lives tonight, two archbishops would come close to being lynched, saved only by a last-minute intervention from soldiers. In the morning, the aristocracy would begin formally joining the National Assembly. It was a strange thing to witness. *I wish Gabriel was here.*

The sense that Gabriel was in danger hadn't left me the entire day. It corroded my insides, leaving me faint and nauseated, making it impossible to eat more than a few bites of the cook's stewed mutton. I closed my eyes firmly and crossed myself. *Please God, let him be okay.* Maybe tomorrow

I could have Le Gall or Seznec escort me to the cathedral so I could pray properly for his safe return.

In the meantime, there was nothing I could do but wait. Resigned, I picked up the book of Shakespeare's sonnets I found in the library and settled into bed to read.

Esme merrily swung her basket back and forth in her hand as she walked the flower-strewn path to the *château*. A finch startled out of a nearby beech tree and wheeled into the cerulean sky, scolding her furiously for the interruption. Esme threw her head back and laughed, drinking in the glorious warmth of the sun on her face as her hat tumbled from its perch atop her head.

Luc had been loving and attentive since that awful night, and the newfound tenderness between them colored her entire world rosy. She strolled down the hill, verdant from the recent rains, and around the bend as she thought ahead to the list Eloise, Isabelle, and she needed to complete—preferably by the week's end. The kitchen garden needed tending. Weeds threatened to choke their thyme patch, and the rosemary needed attention as well. In the stillroom there was early lavender to hang and distill into oil, and balms to replenish their stores of. Monsieur Tremblay and Mademoiselle Adrienne had promised to accompany her into town next week so she could pick up some items from the apothecary.

As the *château* came into view, limestone glinting in the bright, summer sun, she came to an abrupt stop, intuitively stepping into the shadow of a large chestnut. One hand pressed against the rough bark, she listened carefully, straining to pick up the conversation that carried fitfully on the breeze. A large contingent of naval officers milled around the grounds, metal buttons and braid reflecting the sunlight. Monsieur Dubois stood stiffly on the steps, straight backed as any soldier, as he spoke calmly to what appeared to be the officer in command. The warm breeze shifted away from Esme, stealing the conversation from her ears.

Stealthily, she crept forward, meticulously keeping to the tree line, her eyes warily watching the confrontation taking place before the *château*. Monsieur Dubois was vastly outnumbered, she counted at least a dozen men on horseback, Prigent and Madec were away, carrying Mathieu to safety, and Gabriel had left Seznec and Le Gall in Versailles with Ava. Esme crouched by the base of an oak and deftly cut several mushrooms, placing them in her foraging basket. If anyone noticed her loitering within earshot, she'd best play dumb.

There was a sudden shout, and she glanced up, just in time to see Monsieur Dubois fall heavily on the stairs. The commanding officer swept by him carelessly, walking authoritatively into Landévennec. Several other officers dismounted, tossing reins at the remaining officers as they followed him into the *chateau's* hall. Esme sat back on her haunches, mentally reviewing her options. Luc was in the fields, *le bon Dieu* knew where. He hadn't mentioned which field he would be checking today, and it could take her hours to find him, particularly on foot. Instinct warned her to keep her distance from the *château* and its current egotistical inhabitants.

Lithely, she retraced her footsteps away from the *château* and back onto the main path. Her long skirts held in one hand to avoid tripping; she broke into an unladylike run. Stray branches reached out, snagging her gown and apron as she stumbled up the hill, loose pebbles skittering beneath her feet and roots protruding from the sandy soil, all attempting to slow her. She careened around a bend in the path, nearly losing her footing as dry leaves slid underfoot.

Stays pinching uncomfortably, breath shuddering, she broke into the clearing that led to her house, tossed her basket haphazardly at the path, and continued running toward Monsieur Marec's hut, which sat several hundred yards further down the path. Heart pounding, she scanned the area around his home, hoping to spot the head gardener working in his small, fenced garden or chopping wood in the back, but it was eerily quiet. Esme ran onto the small porch and pounded on the door.

"Monsieur Marec? Are you at home, Monsieur?" She listened for a moment while she panted, trying to catch her breath, but it was clear no one was there. Esme squeezed her eyes shut in frustration, blinking back tears and determinedly stepped off the steps.

Skirts kirtled up, gripped tightly between both fists, she started running again, heading toward the next cottage. She and Luc relied on Georges Gustave's help around their home, and she prayed between the short breaths that were ripped from her lungs that he or his father Pierre would be home. Blackberry brambles lined the path, bees drowsing amidst the light, rose-tinted flowers as she rushed past.

Esme burst through the break in the bushes and skidded into the Gustave's yard. A small gate kept the twins corralled within the garden and they dropped their matching stuffed dolls to stare at Esme in surprise. She pressed her hand to the cramp in her side and tried to smile cheerily at the six-year-old girls.

"*Bonjour* Helene, *Bonjour* Josephine! Is your papa home?"

Helene, identifiable from her sister only by her longer hair, pointed at the cottage mutely.

She lifted the latch on the gate and let herself in, consciously ensuring that it clicked properly into place behind her.

"Monsieur Gustave! Are you home?" she called as she walked past the girls in their summer frocks and aprons toward the open front door.

Pierre Gustave, a spare man with graying hair, shirt sleeves rolled up to expose wiry forearms, came around the small house with his ax in his hand.

"Madame Morvan, well met! Are you looking for Georges?"

"*Non, merci,* Monsieur Gustave. I came because there are naval officers at the *château*. They pushed Monsieur Dubois to gain entrance, and I am worried about what will happen since le Vicomte and la Vicomtesse are away. I came for help. You are the first person I have seen."

Pierre shifted the ax back and forth between his hands, frown lines drawn between his brows while he absorbed her news.

"I will gather some of the men and head to the *château*," he said finally. He met her gaze frankly. "You'll stay with the girls until I return?"

"*Oui, bien sûr. Merci!*" she gushed gratefully.

He shook his head as he started down the path, ax still firmly in his grasp. "Don't thank me yet, Madame."

The recesses of the Cathedral Saint-Louis were dim and shadowy, the cool air a welcome respite to the hot sun outside. I breathed deeply, inhaling the comforting aroma of incense, wood, and the particular scent of stone. If one closed their eyes, you might imagine you were in a cavernous, limestone cave. Slightly damp, mayhap, but protected. Hundreds of lit candles lent the unmistakable, slightly sweet smell of warm beeswax.

I slid forward off my perch onto my knees, clasped my hands on the smooth wood of the pew ahead of mine, and lowered my head. My lashes veiled my eyes, and I absorbed the silence around me, letting it soothe the tangled knot of disquiet that had preoccupied me since Gabriel left. My lips moved silently as I mentally replayed the last month.

I finished as I always did, with prayers for my parents, Carri and my beloved Aimée. I squeezed my eyes shut against the stab of pain and let the bittersweet memories flow through me like a tidal current. My greatest regret in moments like this, was that I had no memories of my daughter. There was no shared laughter, secrets or joy to look back on fondly and clutch like a warm wrap around my shoulders to ward off the bitter, cold reality of her death.

I crossed myself and sat back down, tilting my head back and watching as dust motes danced in the light streaming through the stained-glass windows arching high above me. It transformed the tiny swaying specs into sparkles painted crimson, emerald, cobalt and gold. Mesmerized, I let peace flood me, filling every inch of my body with wonder as they floated above me.

A throat cleared beside me, interrupting my quasi-catatonic state. Embarrassed that I didn't notice his approach, I met the bishop's kind, brown eyes apologetically.

"Pardon me, your excellency. I seem to have been lost in my thoughts."

"Don't apologize my child." He gestured to the empty pew beside me. "May I?"

"Yes, of course." Nervously, I looked down at the flagstone floor and intertwined my fingers on my lap.

He sat, his robe spreading around him, and gazed thoughtfully toward the altar. After a moment that stretched an eternity, I began to think he just wanted company while he pondered the scene of the crucifixion. When I was on the verge of excusing myself, he began.

"It's Madame la Vicomtesse de Landévennec, *oui*?" His lined face smiled kindly.

"Yes, your Excellency." I unobtrusively smoothed the skirt of my lilac gown with my palms.

"Ah, I imagine you and your husband are here for the Estates-General," he stated simply.

"We are. I suppose there are quite a few new faces in recent weeks?" My sense of peace was beginning to evaporate as I wondered whether the man had a point or if he was simply making conversation.

"Indeed, there are. Our proximity to the seat of the monarchy means we get more traffic than most village cathedrals, but there's been an increase for us nonetheless."

I looked around the still, serene church. "It's quite tranquil at the moment."

He let out a sad sigh. "Aye, it is. Most of the people that walk through those doors," he nodded at the massive, wood doors that stood welcomingly ajar, "They've got an agenda. They're here for any variety of reasons, and it rarely has to do with their souls, or the souls of the people they love."

I nodded in agreement. He wasn't wrong, after all.

"Why are you here?" he asked.

"To think. To pray and ask for guidance. To remember those I've lost," I answered honestly.

"Admirable reasons, all." He fell silent for a time and then roused himself. "I don't think I would have gone out of my way to find you, but as it happens, you found your way to me, in a sense."

I frowned and wondered if the old man had all his marbles.

"I overheard a conversation between two gentlemen, as one often does in my profession." He gave me a conspiratorial wink. "People have a tendency not to notice us or realize that we can hear them... or perhaps, they simply don't care." He ruminated on this for a minute before shrugging to himself as though he answered some internal debate.

I felt my brows draw together in confusion.

"I apologize, my child. You must be wondering what I'm blathering on about. The gentlemen in question... well one questions if one can really call one of them a gentleman... Well, my dear, you were their topic of conversation. I thought you might like to know."

"M—Me?" I squeaked in surprise.

"*Oui*."

"These... gentlemen, what did they look like?"

"Ah, well. One of them was that Commandant des Rochefort. Nasty sort, that one." He shook his head. "The other, I can't say. I've never seen him before. Dark, mustache." His hands spread out palm up as if to say he knew it wasn't much to go on.

My heart thudded sickly in my ears. "Tha—Thank you, your Excellency. I appreciate you telling me."

He squinted at me in the dim light. "Are you acquainted with le Commandant?"

"Unfortunately."

He nodded sagely. "I thought you might be. I didn't quite hear everything that was said, but I do know money exchanged hands." He placed his hands on the pew and pushed himself up to rise. "Look after yourself, my child. Le Commandant is not someone I would cross." He waved his hand solemnly in the air above me. "May God bless you and keep you."

"*Merci*, your Excellency. May God bless you as well." I rose and stumbled out into the sunshine as if demons were on my heels.

Thirty
Strawberries and Cream

I stared out the window, watching the patterns the rain made as it clung and ran in rivulets down the glass. The world outside was blurry, the colors fractured by the waves and dimples created by the storm. *Where is Gabriel?*

He'd been gone for a month. Each additional day of his absence grew the festering knot in my gut further. There'd been no word from Landévennec nor Trégoudan, and I had no idea if the lack of correspondence was cause for celebration or not. Idly, I picked up my cup of wine and lost myself in the swirling, garnet depths, pondering how to move forward if Gabriel didn't return soon.

Phillipe paused his pacing directly in front of me, forcing me to take a sip of wine and return my attention to him.

"You haven't heard a word I said." His tone wasn't accusatory, merely observant.

"I'm sorry," I acknowledged, gripping my cup tightly, feeling the sharp edges of the crystal dig into my fingers.

"It's Gabriel, isn't it?" He sat in the chair opposite mine.

"It's been a month," I said simply.

He sighed and picked up his goblet, turning it between his hands. "I would tell you not to worry, but that would be futile, wouldn't it be?"

I met his gaze over the rim of my glass as I drank deeply of the sweet, smooth wine.

"I've wondered what is taking him so long myself," he admitted. "But des Rochefort is still lurking about, and I imagine if he had word that Gabriel was in trouble, he wouldn't waste a moment in sharing it with you. He's the type that relishes that sort of thing."

"I agree, but what if Gabriel hasn't been detained by the Navy? What if instead he is hurt or ill somewhere and unable to notify me?" I shook my head angrily. "It was the height of stupidity to let him travel alone. At a minimum he should have brought Le Gall or Seznec with him."

"You know he was trying to avoid notice, Ava—"

"It doesn't matter what his intentions were! What matters is the outcome!"

Phillipe raised a brow at me and said nothing. I'd been rude, interrupting him, and I'd been careful not to let my anger or apprehension at the situation show. Until now. The silence stretched out between us while the rain continued to pour down the windows unabated. My hand shook as I carefully placed my wine on the carved, cherry table beside me. I let out a shuddering breath as I concentrated on regaining control and centering my emotions.

"Phillipe, I—"

"I apologize for the interruption, Madame la Vicomtesse, le Commandant des Rochefort is here to see you." Madame Blanchard's calm voice cut through the tension in the salon effortlessly.

My spine straightened and my gaze cut across the table to meet Phillipe's grim, determined eyes.

"Please show him in Madame Blanchard. And send in some refreshments." Calmly, I poured myself another serving of wine and lifted the liquid courage to my lips. "Can I offer you more, Phillipe?"

"*Merci*, Ava." He held his cup out.

"Now, what were you telling me about the National Assembly?" I asked, tacitly changing the conversation.

He shook his head. "The members of the aristocracy and clergy who didn't join of their own accord were commanded to by *le Roi* a few days ago. I submitted Gabriel's pledge for him," he added, straight faced.

"*Merci*, Phillipe. I know he would prefer to have done it himself; he's just been so ill." I lied smoothly, surprising myself by how easy it was to fib when des Rochefort might be listening. "I hear work has already begun on a new constitution?"

"*Oui*, we began laying out the foundations this morning. Once Gabriel is well enough, you should consider moving to Paris. Things are heating up. There's been an immense build-up of the military over the last few days. *Le Roi* mentioned over thirty thousand troops have been garrisoned in the region."

I raised my eyebrows. "Thirty thousand—"

The painted wood doors to the *salon* swung open and des Rochefort sauntered in, sweeping his hat off his head and placing it over his heart with a flourish.

"Vicomtesse de Landévennec et le Comte de Saint-Denis, thank you for seeing me. I didn't intend to interrupt your *tête à tête*." His dark, almond eyes glittered with malice.

"Not at all, it's a pleasure to see you again, Commandant," drawled Phillipe, lazily sipping from his wine.

I smiled, my clenched jaw aching. "Please, have a seat. Madame Blanchard should be right in with *petite déjeuner*. To what do I owe the honor, Commandant des Rochefort?"

Des Rochefort settled himself on the brocade settee, taking the proffered cup of wine from Madame Blanchard with a murmured word of thanks, letting anticipation marinate in the silence that followed while he took a leisurely drink. He fastidiously wiped his mouth with his linen *serviette*, arranging it meticulously on his lap, before treating me to a wide smile.

"Madame Chabot, pray tell, how is your husband le Vicomte faring? I did so hope to see him around *le Palais* by now."

"Unfortunately, his malaise appears to be of the lingering variety, Commandant. He is slightly improved and eager to get back to work for *le Roi*. Perhaps in a few more days he will feel well enough to return to the National Assembly."

He pulled his silver cigar case from his breast pocket and opened it, glancing at me as he did so. "You don't mind?" He gestured with the case in his hand toward the lit taper beside him.

"Not at all," I replied airily.

Des Rochefort took his time selecting a cigar, closing the metal case with a snap, before leaning into the flickering flame to light it. He breathed the smoke in deeply, holding it in his barrel chest for a long moment, before letting it escape in a slow, sinuous curve toward the paneled ceiling.

With a glance at Phillipe, he murmured, "It's quite kind of you, Comte, to spend so much of your time here with your convalescing friend and his wife."

"A great deal has occurred over the last month, Commandant. I merely seek to ensure that le Vicomte de Landévennec is kept abreast of the changes in *ma belle* France," he demurred.

"The safety of our nation forces me to ask if you have seen le Vicomte in the last month, or if you've been whiling away your time with his lovely wife instead?" Des Rochefort lifted a dark, smooth brow in question.

I sat up straighter. *Why the little weasel...*

"I sincerely hope you aren't suggesting I am having an affair with the la Vicomtesse?" Phillipe sounded utterly affronted. "She is undeniably stunning, but if I may be honest, I prefer to indulge my fantasies in blonde haired vixens."

Des Rochefort barked out a laugh. "Don't blame you a bit, Girard— I may call you Girard, eh? I'm partial to redheads myself." He waved expansively, outlining a buxom figure in the air, spilling cigar ash indiscriminately across the Turkish rug at his feet.

"Ahhh, I was with a gorgeous redhead once," Phillipe reminisced. "Strawberry curls down to the most delicious *derriere* you've ever seen." He waggled his brows and cupped his hands as though he had a woman's bottom in them for emphasis as des Rochefort sipped appreciatively from his glass.

I stifled a giggle at how thoroughly Phillipe had distracted him. My stomach was still clenched in a tangled mess of concern for Gabriel, but the way Phillipe was playing le Commandant was an impressive event to witness.

Des Rochefort leaned forward and placed several pastries on a plate while Phillipe regaled him with a story about the strawberry blonde. I relaxed slightly in my chair while I drank my wine, wondering idly if the story Phillipe was weaving was real or imaginary. This was my third glass on a fairly empty stomach, and I was beginning to feel pleasantly tipsy. *I should eat something to soak up the booze before I inadvertently say something I shouldn't in front of the eagle-eyed commander.*

My mind wandered while I served myself an apricot tart and took a bite of flaky crust, tuning out the sound of the men's conversation.

"— I do so hope to see le Vicomte the next time I visit," said le Commandant, bringing me back to the present.

A throat cleared behind me. "I apologize for keeping you waiting, Commandant. I didn't realize you were here," said Gabriel.

Des Rochefort's face froze, but he recovered without missing a beat, smoothly standing and bowing. "I heard you've been ill, Monsieur Chabot. I hope this means your convalescence is nearly over?"

I hurried over to Gabriel, clasping my hands together tightly, fighting the urge to physically check him over. His face was pale and there were lines of pain bracketing his mouth, but he was standing before me, finally.

"Unfortunately, I have been unwell for some time. I was just in the stables checking on the horses." Gabriel smiled, though it didn't reach his eyes. "It's not easy to stay indoors for so long, though my wife reprimands me for overextending myself." He wrapped his arm around my waist and gazed down at me.

His ribs protruded through his coat when I leaned against him, and I had to school my expression to look unconcerned. "I keep telling him to stay in bed so he can regain his strength, but he's stubborn!" I chided teasingly.

A fine tremor ran through Gabriel's body, the shaking so slight and controlled you wouldn't notice it looking at him. The vibration passed through us both, making me tighten my hold on him.

"Ah, well. I'm delighted to see you, Vicomte. I rather thought you might have had the questionable idea of getting involved in your brother-in-law's troubles." Des Rochefort flashed a toothy grin at his joke.

"I wouldn't dream of it, Commandant. He made his bed, eh?" Gabriel flipped back.

"He did indeed." Des Rochefort shook his head ruefully. "I hope you recover fully soon, Monsieur Chabot. Thank you for your hospitality, Madame Chabot." He bowed over my hand. "It was a pleasure seeing you again, Girard! You'll have to tell me more about Mademoiselle Strawberry next time." With a wink at Phillipe and a final bow, des Rochefort sailed blithely through the *salon* doors.

Gabriel swayed on his feet and leaned heavily against me as soon as we heard the front door close. I let out a slow, controlled breath.

"You're not well," I observed, supporting most of his weight.

"*Non*. I need to lie down. I'll tell you all of it later, *mon cœur*."

"I can't tell you how glad Ava and I are to see you back," said Phillipe heartily. "Mathieu?" he trailed off uncertainly.

"Safe. Or as safe as he can be," murmured Gabriel wearily.

"*Merci, Dieu*." Phillipe crossed himself.

"Come tomorrow, eh? I'll tell you the whole of it then."

"I will. Rest *mon ami*." Phillipe hugged Gabriel, bowed to me with a flourish and made a hasty exit.

Thirty-One
Copper and Crockery

Esme stood amidst shards of ceramic and glass as she listened, barely registering the destruction, the months of careful, meticulous hard work that lay strewn across the surgery floor. Her face was frozen, she hoped in a soothing expression. Within her veins flowed pure, molten rage. Deliberately, she flexed her hands, forcing each metacarpal out of its clenched position.

The desecration and the wanton destruction the Navy had committed to draperies, tapestries, and furniture could be repaired or replaced. But this, this was something else entirely. Finally, she approached Isabelle, noting how the girl flinched from her outstretched hand. Madame and Eloise Bleuzen, Mademoiselle Adrienne and her aunt Mademoiselle Ollivier were clustered protectively around her, their faces displaying emotions ranging from bewilderment to anger.

"Isabelle..." Esme paused, weighing her words. "I can never tell you how sorry I am this happened."

The girl didn't raise her green eyes to acknowledge her, keeping her gaze trained on the flagstone floor. Ash blonde hair straggled around her young, bruised face. Someone had wrapped a blanket around her thin shoulders, covering her torn clothing. She sat hunched on a stool, curling her body around herself, hiding her injuries and emotions.

Esme hesitated and then gently placed her hand on her shoulder.

"I'll need to examine you," she added softly.

A fine tremor shook the girl's body. "Can you ask them to leave?" Her voice was a thread of sound.

"Of course," murmured Esme. "Mademoiselle Eloise, could you and your *maman* see to Monsieur DuBois and any others with minor injuries?"

Eloise curtseyed. "*Oui*, Madame Esme."

"*Merci*, Madame Bleuzen, could you send the broom in for me as well? Someone is going to cut their foot on all this ceramic."

"Aye, Madame Morvan." She wrapped her arm around her daughter's shoulders, firmly herding her to the door. "Come with me."

Eloise threw one last anguished look over her shoulder at her friend, before being led away by her mother.

Esme knelt in front of Isabelle, taking her fine boned hands between hers comfortingly. "Your aunt, would you like her to stay?" she asked in an undertone.

Isabelle's eyes were closed, but tears soundlessly squeezed from beneath her lashes, slowly tracking over the cut on her cheek, dripping off her bruised chin, onto the blanket she kept gathered firmly on her lap. She shook her head minutely and Esme glanced up, catching Mademoiselle Ollivier's eyes.

"I will stand by you, Isabelle, no matter what happens," her aunt swore vehemently. She squeezed her niece's shoulder tenderly before following the others out.

Esme nodded at her, gratitude rushing through her. Isabelle didn't have much of a family life, and unfair as it was, the taint of rape would likely only strain her relationship with most of them. At least she would have her aunt, and Esme herself to stand beside her. Eloise too, if the look on the girl's face was anything to go by. The unjustness of it curdled like sour milk in her belly.

Mademoiselle Adrienne stood by the door uncertainly. "Can I get you anything, Esme?"

"A tea for Mademoiselle Isabelle, and a bucket of clean water, s*'il vous plaît*." She kept her eyes on Isabelle as she instructed Adrienne. "Come," she murmured to the girl, gently tugging her hands. "Mind you don't cut your feet on the mess."

Isabelle followed her across the surgery to the small bed Ava insisted they keep for examinations, without a word of dissent. She sat on the edge and grimaced in discomfort, clutching the blanket about herself like a shield.

"May I?" Esme held the edge of the quilt between her fingers, dropping it as Isabelle vigorously shook her head. "Right, then. . . Can you tell me what happened?"

Madame Bleuzen poked her head in, broom in hand. "I'll take that, *merci*, Silouane," she said.

Esme began to sweep the mess, giving Isabelle space. She knew the feelings that accompanied abuse all too well. Shame, embarrassment, anger. Physical and emotional pain. The questions that raced through your mind: Why me? What now? The memory of her own experience made her stomach clench with nausea. Other than tending to Isabelle's exterior wounds, shallow scrapes and bruises, and offering her a judgement-free ear, she knew there was little she could do for the girl. As her thoughts swirled in a tornado of fury and remembrance, she found herself nearly flinging the shattered crockery across the floor.

Esme bit her bottom lip hard and forced herself to slow down. What her father had done to her was long in the past. He couldn't hurt her anymore. What mattered now, was helping Isabelle. She diligently swept the mess into a tidy pile by the door, propped the broom against the wall and retrieved two remaining cups from the shelf. On her toes, she reached and opened the furthest cupboard, taking down Ava's best cognac. *Merci, Dieu,* the swine Navy didn't open that particular cabinet.

With a thoughtful glance in Isabelle's direction, she tipped a healthy measure of the golden liquid into each mug and carried them to the bed. Isabelle hadn't stirred from her perch and Esme sat beside her, taking the girl's hand and wrapping it around one of the cups.

"Drink," she urged. "It will help with the shock." She took a long sip, reveling in the burn as it slid down her throat.

Esme cut her eyes toward Isabelle and noticed the girl was trembling. "I was a deal younger than you, when my father used me the first time," she said, conversationally. She watched her words sink in and waited for Isabelle to turn her green eyes on her, surprise penetrating through the haze.

"Your father?" she whispered.

"*Oui.* I'm not telling you for sympathy, Isabelle. I've come to terms with it and separated it from my life, as best I can. I'm telling you because I want you to know that I understand, as much as someone can. And I want you to know that this is not the death knell of your dreams. It does not signify the loss of the life you imagined for yourself. Do not let one man's dishonorable act become what defines you."

Isabelle's eyes overflowed as she shakily raised her cup to her split lips and drank. "*Merci,* Esme," she said hoarsely.

A timid knock sounded at the door and Mademoiselle Adrienne hesitantly pushed it open. "All right if I come in for a moment?"

"*Bien sûr,* thank you, Adrienne." Esme waited while she placed the bucket of water on the worktable, carried over the ceramic teapot and cups and left again.

Esme deftly poured the rest of Isabelle's cognac into her tea and handed her the cup. "Finish that," she said briskly. "I'll tend those cuts, and we'll talk more afterwards."

Grimly, I took Gabriel's boots and breeches off and tucked him into bed like a child. There were a million questions to be answered, but his eyes were cloudy with pain, and he was finally back. Nearly everything else could wait.

"Everyone is safe?" I asked, pulling the soft, quilted blanket up to his chin.

"As much as the circumstances allow," he murmured.

I poured water into a cup from the carafe, held it to his lips, then rearranged the pillows and quilt.

"*Merci, mon cœur.* You're an angel."

"Not even close," I laughed. "You must be truly addled if you can say that."

"Mayhap I am. . . a bit. . ." His eyes were heavy, nearly closed, when they sprang back open. "Armand? He's well?"

"He's a perfect terror." He smiled at the affection in my voice. "You'll see him when you wake," I added tenderly. His eyes were already closed.

I leaned over and pressed my lips to his forehead. *Thank you, God, for returning him safe.*

Esme paced the length of Luc's small study while she chewed her lip and thought about what she should do. She'd made up her mind to write her mother. It was the perfect cover and excuse for finding out how Amélie and the babes were faring without Mathieu, and to find out the status of Jeanne's husband— maybe— she amended. She would still have to be careful about what she wrote, but no one could fault her for sending a letter to her *maman*, right? Luc had actually been the one to suggest it. She'd given it careful thought for several days, trying to consider every angle and every possible repercussion before finally deciding to go for it.

With a sigh she sat at the small desk. There was no point in putting it off any further. She lifted the top, revealing several sheets of parchment beneath. Selecting the piece on top, she closed the desk and laid it, and her other writing implements out. Her fingers drummed nervously on the wood while she stared out the window. Finally, she picked up her quill and began.

8th July, 1789
Château de Trégoudan

Madame Margaret Blanchard

My dearest Maman,

I hope this letter finds you well. I miss you, Amélie and the children terribly, but other than these inconveniences, I am well. Luc continues to heal, and I am beginning to hope that he may eventually make a full recovery. It has been a long, arduous road, not only for him, but for our relationship as well. I can see the sunshine breaking through the clouds at long last and it is a delightful feeling to bask in its warmth.

Here at Landévennec we have heard the most distressing news regarding le Baron. I had hoped it was merely scurrilous lies, but we had a visit from the Navy that has sadly put paid to those hopes. They aggressively searched for Amelie's husband while here, refusing to take our word that he hasn't been here, though of course, their search turned up nothing. While here, they caused quite a bit of damage, not only to the château and its furnishings, but also to some of its inhabitants. Sadly, I know you will understand my meaning.

How does Amélie fare without le Baron? Regardless of his illegal activities, she must be finding her adjustment to life without him, difficult, though if I know la Baroness, I know she will handle it with grace and aplomb. I know it is not easy to live as a woman alone, even for someone in her position, or perhaps, especially for someone in her position. Many might try to take advantage of her, and I hope the household is doing everything they can to protect her from such a fate. I think of her and les enfants often and I hope I will be able to see all of you soon.

Gabriel and Ava are still in Versailles, or perhaps they are in Paris by now. It's been quite dull here at Landévennec without them and their little darling, Armand. It's my fondest hope that they will return before the winter season, although there's been no indication of when we might expect them as of yet.

Please give the children a kiss from me and save one for yourself. Until I see you again, stay well maman.

All my love,
Your daughter,
Madame Esme Morvan

I buttered my bread— the bread that was becoming increasingly harder to purchase flour for, even for the affluent— and took a dainty bite as I stared across the table at Gabriel. His eyes were shadowed, full of pain and self-castigation as he told me about Mathieu.

"I do not know how to get word to Amélie about the situation. I know she must be mad with worry. I can't imagine how she'll handle the estate on her own... and she has that loose cannon, Jeanne's husband to contend with as well..." He ran his hand through his hair in agitation. "The risks were too great. We should have stopped after the debacle with that *foiré* des Rochefort at the beach last spring."

My hand covered his, feeling the strength of muscles and bones beneath the soft skin. The wiry hairs under my fingertips were familiar; rough and soothing. I squeezed hard, interrupting the flow of regret spilling from his lips.

"You did what you thought you should, what you *all* thought you should— at the time. This is no time for recriminations. Mathieu and Amélie would be horrified to hear you talk."

He shook his head. "You didn't see what *ces enfoirés de mères* did to him," he growled. He picked up his teacup and put it down again angrily, without taking a sip.

"You got him out. You got him help. That's all you can do now, other than make sure that Amélie and *les enfants* have everything they need and are safe," I interjected firmly.

"We should leave here. Return home."

I met his bleak gaze. "Is that what you want to do? There's much to consider. I haven't even filled you in on what's happened while you were away. And you're in no condition to travel further."

A muscle twitched in his jaw. "What have I missed?"

"Quite a lot. I'm sure you've heard bits of it, and Phillipe will tell you all of it as regards the National Assembly. . . But des Rochefort came a few times while you were gone. I don't think he believed you were ill. I wonder what will happen when he hears that Mathieu is no longer in custody—"

"Well, he saw me yesterday," he interrupted.

"Thank God for that. But it may not be enough to save you." I grimaced, imagining the commandant's fury at the news. "But also, Jeanne hung herself— don't worry, she was found immediately, and didn't break her neck by some divine miracle, but it was quite a shock."

"*Merde.*" He swallowed hard. "How is she? Did she say why?" His hand was trembling as he lifted his cup to his lips.

I closed my eyes and took a long breath in through my nose. "She's not well. She's haunted by what that sorry excuse for a husband did to her. She's terrified that her *bébé* is going to inherit his monstrous qualities. . ." I shook my head as I trailed off.

"To commit a mortal sin though—"

"She wasn't successful, that's all that matters. That and ensuring that she never feels that is the only recourse open to her again. We must make her feel safe and wanted. And her baby too, when she arrives," I said emphatically.

"She? You know the child will be a girl?"

"Aye." I buttered another piece of bread and chewed, letting the admission hang in the air between us.

Finally, he broke the silence. "So, you don't think we should return to Landévennec yet."

"I don't think it would be the wisest thing for Jeanne, although she isn't the only one to consider. Events are rapidly coming to a head. The coming month is going to be crucial."

"Ava. . ." Gabriel reached across the table, palm up, and waited for me. I placed my hand in his and sensed his hesitation. "Do you believe that we are going to change the outcome of this war?"

Goosebumps rippled across my arms and my stomach twisted. "No."

A spasm flashed across Gabriel's face, but he didn't let go of my hand. "I thought not. So, we go to Paris?"

"For now."

Thirty-Two
Skip a Stone

The sun beat down on our party of weary travelers as we wound our way through the heavy throngs of people crowding the cobblestone path that bordered the Seine. Paris was a nervous hive of activity. A sense of expectation hung ominously in the air, like natural gas, sinuously penetrating every molecule of oxygen, patiently awaiting a single spark to burst into flame.

Once the decision to move to Paris was made, we didn't tarry longer than it took to pack our belongings. It was a sedate three hour walk from Versailles, the only reason I'd agreed to leave immediately when Gabriel had insisted. I eyed him surreptitiously. His face was pale in the bright, afternoon sun and I suspected he remained upright on Automne solely out of sheer stubbornness. Sweat trickled down my spine and my skin crawled, itchy against the damp cotton of my gown. I wiggled my shoulders, trying to ease the tension from my neck and back as I rode beside Gabriel.

"We'll turn right at the next street, then it's a left on la Rue de Lille," directed Gabriel.

The carriage obediently turned right before us, leaving Gabriel and me to follow behind as we left the river and jolted down the bumpy road. A quick left at the next cross street and we pulled to a stop before a handsome, limestone house. Gabriel dismounted Automne, his face contorting with pain.

"Although I sent Timothée Seznec and Jean-Paul Le Gall ahead of us to alert the staff of our impending arrival, I don't know what condition the house will be in," he said softly. "I haven't been here in years."

"When were you here last?" I asked, sliding off my mount in a graceless heap.

Gabriel's lips twitched. "Before my papa married that murderess."

I smirked at him. "Don't you dare laugh at my horsewoman skills, Chabot."

"I wouldn't dream of it, *mon cœur*." He smoothly lifted my hand and kissed my knuckles, turning my knees to butter.

"Hmph. "Why didn't you stay here when you came last summer?"

He shrugged, shadows lurking in his gray eyes. "It made me think of her," he said, referring to his stepmother. "And Phillipe invited me. But you deserve to stay here. Change what you want; make it ours. It will be Armand's one day, and I won't let that woman take anything else from my family."

I looped my arms around his waist, mindful of his healing wounds and tilted my head back. "Kiss me," I demanded.

"In the street?" he queried, in mock surprise. He lifted a dark brow at my daring, but the glint in his eyes matched mine as he lowered his lips to my mouth.

When he pulled away amidst catcalls from Le Gall, I shot him a saucy grin and put my hand on his arm. "Now show Armand and me our new home."

"When you're done at the milliners, meet me here," I instructed Noemi as she walked away.

I pushed open the heavy door of the apothecary shop and inhaled the comforting aroma of herbs, spices and old, lovingly oiled wood. Monsieur Abadie, the proprietor, was busy with a gentleman at the counter; so, I slowly perused the shelves, taking the opportunity to browse. I peered at dried mushrooms I couldn't identify, each piece resembling a desiccated ear, and raised an eyebrow at the collection of bones, teeth and tusks displayed beneath the glass counter. Familiar, round seeds displayed in a round bowl on a shelf behind the counter caught my eye. I had promised Gabriel my rendition of Mexican food. Perhaps if I managed to grow cilantro, I could deliver on that.

"Ah, it's Madame la Vicomtesse de Landévennec!" exclaimed the small apothecary. "It's a pleasure to see you. What can I get for you today?"

I smiled at his enthusiasm. "How are you, Monsieur?"

"Better now that you've returned to visit me." He offered me a wink and a toothy grin.

His audacity made me laugh. "Is that coriander?" I asked, pointing at the bowl behind him.

He raised a sandy brow. "It is, Madame. You're familiar with it?"

"Yes, though mainly for seasoning food. What do you use it for?"

"It has a calming effect on those suffering a nervous disposition. Would you like to take some?"

"Yes please, I'll take fifty *drachme*[1] of the coriander." While he weighed and bagged the seeds, I walked slowly along the counter, squinting to read the labeled, amber colored jars neatly lining the shelves.

"Were you wanting something else, Madame?" He placed the small linen bag on the counter.

"A bottle of laudanum, quite a lot of rosemary. . . how much can you spare?" I tapped my fingers on the counter while I thought. I should have written my list down.

"I have a decent store of the rosemary. One hundred *drachme*?"

"Yes please. What about helichrysum?" Esme's most recent letter had talked about the merits of the herb, but it was difficult to source.

He hesitated. "I have some bottles of essential oil."

"I'll take one," I said decisively as he measured the rosemary on the scale. "You have clove?" My nose picked up the familiar scent.

"*Oui, bien sûr*. It's rather dear though," he replied apologetically.

I flapped my hand at him. "How do you have it? Dried cloves? Or oil?"

"Both, Madame." He put the bag of rosemary beside my coriander and placed a small bottle of laudanum on the counter.

I thought for a moment, tapping my fingers on the glass. "I'll take a bottle of the oil as well, s'*il vous plaît*."

"Of course, just one moment." He disappeared into a small room, and I continued to meander toward the end of the shelves.

"*Pardon*," he murmured, reappearing, bottles in hand. "I keep some of my more unique finds in the back." He carefully placed two more bottles beside my growing pile.

"Mmm. I'd do the same." I wondered what else he kept hidden away.

---

1. Drachme: In apothecary measurement, drachme is a unit of weight that is 1/8 of an ounce.

"Will there be anything else today?" The bell above the door tinkled and he glanced up with a nod and a smile.

"Yes, I'll take three of the large bottles of sweet almond oil, a small bottle of the rose, and a hundred *drachmes* of dried lavender. I think that will be it."

"Wonderful, Madame." He efficiently added the rest of my items to the pile on the counter as I pulled out some francs to pay him.

I began carefully laying my purchases in my basket as he counted out my change.

"Ah, Madame. . ."

He sounded unsure, and I looked at him questioningly. His eyes followed the two women who had entered behind me hesitantly and then he leaned over the counter, dropping his voice.

"I debated whether I should tell you, but after your visit last week, a gentleman came in and inquired about you."

A chill ran down my spine and my smile froze on my face. "Oh?" I asked carefully, trying not to betray my unease.

"*Oui*. I thought it rather odd. He was. . . far beneath you in class," he answered, choosing his words with care. He said he was supposed to meet you here and missed your rendezvous. Then he asked for your address. I didn't give it to him, of course."

"Hmm," I answered noncommittally. "This gentleman— what did he look like?"

He shrugged. "I don't usually pay much attention, Madame. Tall, dark. Mustache." He waved a hand, indicating height.

"I'm afraid I'm not sure who it might have been. Do let me know if you see him again?"

His brow cleared and he straightened back up to his full height. "Yes, of course. Here's your change Madame."

"*Merci*," I said cheerily, packing the last of my items and spotting Noemi by the door. "I'll see you soon!"

"Did you get everything you wanted?" asked Noemi, her warm, brown eyes wide.

"*Oui*, and then some," I replied in satisfaction. As we walked quickly down the street, I firmly put the apothecary's message out of my mind. My basket was heavy, and I moved it from one arm to the other.

"Excellent," she said.

"And you? Did you find what you wanted at the milliners?"

"Yes, thanks. I found a nice pattern for a new dress as well."

"Good for you!" I answered heartily. The back of my neck prickled, and I glanced over my shoulder.

"Did you forget something, Madame?"

"Hmm?" I craned my neck, trying to see. "Oh, no. . ." I said, realizing what she asked and looking back at her. "You know when it feels like someone is watching you?"

She gave me a queer look. "Do you think someone is watching you, Madame?"

My stomach coiled apprehensively. "Perhaps," I murmured.

"Well, let's get back home, aye?" She cast a nervous glance over her shoulder and shifted her basket.

"Yes, let's," I agreed.

I picked up the pace as we wound our way down the main thoroughfare. Suddenly hyperaware of what was around me, my scalp tight with tension, I focused on weaving around the fruit stalls as quickly as I could. The feeling of being followed intensified, but I refused to give in and look behind me.

We turned down a smaller thoroughfare, side-stepping carts, carriages, and throngs of people. Ahead of us, the crowd thickened. A woman hurried past, bumping into me. She continued down the street without looking back. I stopped in my tracks and turned to Noemi with a frown.

"Is there another way?"

Lines marred the smooth skin of her forehead. "I'm not sure, Madame. Mayhap we could turn back and ask someone."

A mother with two children firmly in her grasp scurried around us, jostling Noemi's basket. I looked back the way we came, but we were firmly in the crowd now and being pushed down the street toward the square ahead.

"Forget it. We'll just continue this way. I'm sure it's fine." After all, it wasn't July fourteenth yet.

We continued walking with the flow, but I linked my arm through Noemi's so we wouldn't get separated. My stomach churned nervously as we were pressed into more of a crush. Her elbow jammed into my side as a tall man stumbled into her.

"Oh Madame! I'm sorry!" she exclaimed.

"It's alright Noemi," I murmured, though my eyes stung with sudden tears at the pain. "Let's get through here and over the river as quickly as possible."

The crowd funneled us down the rest of the street and into the square as it opened up.

"They are killing the prisoners!" someone shouted.

My head swiveled to the right as I searched for the source of the accusation. I gripped Noemi's arm as panic surged through my body.

"Get out of the way!" yelled a red-faced driver as he maneuvered his horse and wagon around us.

I jumped back, dragging Noemi with me and bumping into two teenaged boys.

"Excuse me, I'm sorry," I said hastily.

"They are killing the prisoners!"

I stood on my toes, trying to see what was happening as the blood coursed through my veins.

"Can you see anything?" I asked Noemi.

She shook her head, sending blonde curls flying. "I'm just as short as you are. But it's coming from the prison."

"Are you sure?"

"*Oui*. Let's go," she added as a break in the crowd opened up before us.

Her hand grasped mine as she pulled me along. I tripped over my dress and hitched my basket higher on my arm, holding my skirt out of my way as we began to run through the people milling around outside the Bastille.

"The wardens are killing the prisoners! You must get us out!"

People were beginning to push angrily toward the prison. I glanced back and saw an aristocratic face at a window through a crack in the horde. We were bumped and shoved as we fought to make our way out of the square. Sweat streamed down my sides and tendrils of hair stuck damply to my face as my heart galloped. The mob was now surging toward the Bastille from every side street, pushing us closer to the small prison with every step.

"They are murdering us!"

It felt like we were drowning in a sea of people, fighting to keep our heads above water. My head swam with dizziness, and I shook it, trying to clear it and focus on escaping.

"Madame!"

The sheer panic in Noemi's voice snapped me out of it. I narrowed in on her wide, doe eyes and pushed with all my strength to get out of the square. When we broke through, people were still streaming toward the mayhem, eager not to miss the excitement. The street ahead of us lay quiet, a few shoppers and families hurrying along. The air sizzled with enthusiasm and something else. I swallowed hard, trying to calm my breathing. It tasted like fear.

"I don't know who could have been asking for me," she said, her brow furrowed as she absently handed the wooden train back to Armand.

"You had Noemi with you?"

"Yes. Well, we split up. She left me at the apothecary and went two doors down to the milliners." Armand sent the train rolling back to her and she smiled at him before sending it back.

"I know it takes longer, but next time don't split up. Anyone who knows you would have approached you directly." He deftly caught the train Armand lobbed at him before it connected with his face. The movement made his wound twinge, and he flinched before he could stop himself.

Ava sprang up from where she sat on the nursery room floor and moved toward him. "Are you all right?"

"*Oui*, thanks. It's just a bit tender still." It was, in fact, quite sore. But if he ever admitted it, she would lovingly hover over him until he lost his mind.

"You're still healing. All the riding back and forth to Versailles is aggravating it." Her clear, green eyes were full of concern.

He shrugged. "I'm fine." Gabriel flashed her a wicked smile and wrapped his arm around her waist, pulling her against his side. "Although if you've a yearning to tend to me, there are parts of me that've been lacking attention recently."

She snorted and her eyes danced with laughter. "I had your health in mind," she scolded teasingly.

"Mmm, why don't you give your invalid a kiss?" His eyes dropped to her mouth, parted and waiting for him.

He brushed his lips over hers and felt the lurch deep within him at her response; the way she always responded. He turned and brought his hands up to cup her face, pinning her in place while his world spun out in lazy, golden lust.

Her arms wrapped around his neck, and he shifted, intensifying the kiss, letting hunger edge into the embrace. Armand's warm, solid bulk crawled onto his lap, interrupting them. She started to pull away, going into maternal mode, making room for their son. He growled playfully and pulled her back in for another fierce, brief kiss.

"Later," she promised, her eyes hazy with longing.

"*Oui*," he agreed. "Come here you wee rascal," he added, scooping Armand up and holding him upside down by his chubby legs.

Armand squealed with glee and Gabriel felt something move inside him when his eyes met Ava's smiling ones over their son's feet.

"So, tell me the latest with the Assembly," said Ava, as Gabriel gently lowered Armand back to the green and gold Turkish rug and handed him his train.

Gabriel sighed. "You know the Assembly passed that motion asking *le Roi* to withdraw his soldiers last week?"

She leaned against him, resting her head on his shoulder. "Yes. And Louis refused."

He wrapped his arm around her and inhaled the intoxicating scent of roses on her. "Correct. He's spent the last few days replacing half his ministers, and of course, he included Necker."

She shook her head sadly. "I knew he would, but I hoped he might have been swayed not to."

Gabriel shifted. "The people are furious."

"You can't blame them."

"I don't. I'm none too pleased with him myself. I hoped he would be more open to reason. If he kept Necker it might not be so bad."

"He didn't just dismiss him, Gabriel. He ordered him to leave the country. There's no coming back from that." She pulled away slightly to look at him. Her eyes were rife with frustration, and he realized how upset she was.

"There were riots last night. The city isn't safe. I'm not sure you and Armand should be here."

"We aren't going anywhere without you."

"Ava, I can concentrate on *le Roi* and trying to sway him much more effectively if I'm not worried about you and Armand."

"Over my dead body," she answered heatedly.

"What? What is that— one of your modern sayings?"

A small smile played at the corners of her luscious mouth.

"Yes," she conceded. "It means—"

"Nevermind, I can figure out what you meant. We'll talk about it more later, aye?" He took her hands in his and lifted them to his lips. "*Je t'aime, mon cœur.* I need you to be safe,"

She deflated slightly. "I love you too, you know?"

"I know." He shot her a crooked smile. "Did you hear what that nonsense you and Noemi got caught in was all about?"

"No, tell me."

He shook his head. "That lunatic, le Marquis de Sade... He incited a riot claiming the wardens were killing the prisoners."

Understanding dawned on her face. "What happened then?"

"He was moved to an asylum that night. Luckily, no one was hurt." He squeezed her hand meaningfully.

She ignored his innuendo. "Speaking of the Marquis... His existence will spawn a whole new word based on his sick proclivities."

He raised a chestnut brow. "Oh?"

"Sadism."

"I haven't heard it."

"Well of course not." She bumped her shoulder affectionately against his. "It doesn't exist yet."

"I'll never get over that."

"What?"

"You. Knowing things that haven't happened yet. It's bizarre, aye?"

"Mmm. I suppose it must be. It's odd for me too. Particularly when I meet someone and know exactly when, where, and how they will die."

He shuddered. "How do you live with it?" He ran a finger lightly over the back of her hand.

"I hope that somehow what I know will happen, doesn't come to pass. That the future can still be changed."

"Can it?"

"I don't know. Am I changing the future simply by being here? Where I'm not supposed to be? Or was I meant to end up here all along? And if it can be changed, I question at what cost. Is it worth it?"

"I'd like to believe you were always meant to be here. With me," he murmured, his chest tight at the idea of her being elsewhere. "But wouldn't any life saved be worth it?"

"What if that life translated to two lost because history was altered? Or ten? A hundred? Who knows how many ripples there would be, reverberating from a single changed event?"

"Cast a stone into the water..."

"Exactly," she answered heavily.

They both fell silent, contemplating what was, should be, could be, and would be. Where would this road lead them?

Thirty-Three
Street Walking

Esme sat down heavily and stared at the blank parchment before her. Her stomach churned at the thought of writing this letter, but it had to be done. With a sigh, she plucked the quill from its pot, dipped it in the ink and bent her head to the task.

12th July, 1789
 La Vicomtesse de Landévennec
 Madame Ava Chabot
 14 Rue de Lille
 Paris, France

My dearest Ava,
I hope this letter finds you well. I wish I could write that everything is wonderful here at Landévennec, but unfortunately that wouldn't be true. I'm sure Gabriel will be receiving a letter from Luc, but I imagine ours will concentrate on vastly different news. You'll be glad to hear the crop is coming in nicely during your absence, and the kitchen and herb garden are as well.

As long as we continue with regular rain through the autumn months, this year will be vastly more productive than the last, Dieu merci. Luc's health continues to improve, a fact for which we are both thankful. It's difficult to believe that over a year has now passed since Marguerite's death, and he is still recovering. There are so many things I wish I would have done differently, but I digress.

The true reason for my letter is because we received an unexpected visit from the Navy. They forced their way into the château, even though Monsieur DuBois tried valiantly to bar their access. He was rewarded for his efforts by being pushed down the stairs and suffered a broken arm. Some of the officers then gained entrance to the château and destroyed many pieces of furniture, draperies and even some paintings.

The worst by far, however, is what happened when they came across Mademoiselle Eloise and Mademoiselle Isabelle in the surgery. In addition to wantonly ruining many of our medicines, one of them cruelly abused young Isabelle. The entire household is extremely shaken by the experience, and we have (largely) rallied around her. It is too soon to know what consequences there may yet be for the day's misadventure, but I pray fervently that Isabelle does not suffer further.

The Navy claims they were searching for your brother-in-law, le Baron de Trégoudan, though why they were looking for him at Landévennec is a mystery. Presumably they had cause to believe he would be here, though of course, he was not. Le bon Dieu only knows where the man might be hiding, and good riddance to him. I can only imagine the shock le Vicomte must have experienced upon learning about le Baron's illegal activities. I do worry, however, for la Baroness and the children and how they may be faring. Please ask Gabriel if he has heard from his sister and if there is anything we might do to help.

May God watch over and protect you in your travels.

Your loving friend,
Madame Esme Morvan

Esme placed her quill in the pot and re-read her letter with a critical eye. It was important to be factual concerning the Navy's visit and the state of life at Landévennec. Ava and Gabriel had to know about what happened to Isabelle. She had no idea if restitution of some sort was a possibility, but if it was, Gabriel needed to know as soon as possible.

She chewed her lip as her eyes scanned her final paragraph. Esme hated writing poorly of Mathieu, but if the rest of them were to escape unscathed, it was of the utmost importance that they pretend he'd been operating on his own. She knew he would be devastated if the monarchy's blade fell on anyone else's neck during his absence. It was bad enough that he was exiled from his family. Who knew how long he would have to remain in hiding for?

Satisfied, she meticulously folded her letter, picked up the candle nearest her, dripped wax into a small puddle and pressed her thumb against it to seal it, wincing only slightly at the minor burn. Odds were high that someone would lift the seal somewhere between her hands and Ava's, hopefully they would believe her line about Mathieu.

"You're not going out today." Gabriel's eyes were steel gray in the early morning light.

"Of course, I am." My voice was calm and measured as I twisted my hair up, securing it with pins.

"Ava..." Exasperated, he ran his hand through his hair, dislodging the carefully tied ribbon that held it back.

"You are going to Versailles, are you not?"

"*Oui, le Roi* invited Phillipe and me to hunt."

I inserted the final pin into my hair and pushed him firmly into a chair.

"Sit." Annoyed, I swiped the brush off the table and moved behind him. "I have a list as long as my arm that I need to do and I'm not going to sit inside all day when I could be accomplishing something." I tugged the brush through his chestnut strands.

"Ava... I understand. But it's not worth the risk." He winced as I pulled at a knot, and I gentled my angry strokes.

"Gabriel, no one is going to get hurt today. I already told you that." The weak, gray light highlighted the array of colors in his hair as I deftly retied the ribbon.

He waited patiently until I finished and then turned sideways in the chair, taking my hand in his. "We know nothing for certain. And you told me the commander will be beheaded," he reminded me.

I sighed and turned my hand over in his, meeting palm against palm and lacing my fingers through his. His hand was strong and comforting, calluses roughening the warm skin against mine.

"Aye," I admitted.

"Tis just one day," he pleaded.

"Hmph," I grunted.

He tugged my hand, pulling me down on his lap and wrapped his arms around me. I leaned my forehead against his and closed my eyes. Lately, it felt like we were both constantly coming and going, him more than me; although I'd attended a few gatherings with the queen over the last month. I missed just being with him.

His hand tilted my face up and his mouth came down on mine, warm, hungry, impatient. Blood thrummed in my veins and roared in my ears as I gave myself to his kiss, letting the stress that held my shoulders taut go. His hands tangled in the hair at my nape, dislodging the pins I'd just put in, tugging gently as he changed the angle. I lifted my chin and parted my lips, letting him deepen the kiss. Desire blossomed to life within me, unfurling tendrils of warmth that spread through my limbs like a drug.

My hands roamed up his back, beneath his coat as he shrugged out of the garment, carelessly letting it fall onto the chair. Gabriel hooked an arm under my knees and another behind me, lifting and carrying me easily to the bed, where he dropped me unceremoniously.

"I don't remember having such a hard time carrying you before," he said teasingly, as he pinned me down onto the soft mattress.

"You're still recovering," I pointed out. "You weren't so weak before—"

"I'll show you weak," he threatened against my mouth.

I wove my fingers in his hair and smirked against his lips. "Please do."

"Are you sure you need to go today, Madame?" Noemi looked at me anxiously.

"Yes, why? Are you unable to come with me? I can find someone else," I offered. "Maybe Jeanne would like to get out of the house?"

"Oh no, it's not that." She hesitated and twisted her hands in her apron. "It's just that le Vicomte mentioned you were indisposed before he left and said you would be staying home today."

Drat that man!

Outwardly, I smiled. "I'm feeling much better now. I'm quite sure I feel well enough to go out."

"If you're sure, Madame. I'll have them ready the carriage." She looked at me doubtfully.

"Thank you, Noemi. Was there something else?"

She twisted her hands together. "The city seems restless today."

"Oh?" I looked at her in interest, surprised that she picked up on the undercurrent.

Encouraged by my response, she nodded. "You know the feeling in the air when something bad is about to happen?"

"Yes."

"Maybe it would be safer to stay in. There's plenty we could do here," she offered hopefully.

I looked at her speculatively. Did Gabriel put her up to it? She seemed genuinely distressed, and it wasn't improbable to believe that someone without foreknowledge would pick up on the wave of revolutionary fever in the air.

"All right," I capitulated. Safety won out over the temptation to witness history by walking the streets of Paris during the Storming of the Bastille. Gabriel would be pleased.

The air was dry and hot on my face without a breath of wind to cool it, as I stood by the window and looked out over the city. In the distance, the orange glow of fires dotted the Parisian landscape. The lack of breeze was a blessing, even though the sun had set, and I was sweating. I crossed myself and breathed deeply, catching a whiff of smoke. The fires would spread out of control if the wind picked up in the slightest.

I picked up my fan, spread it open and rhythmically moved my wrist. The breeze I created blew my damp curls away from my face. Gabriel hadn't returned from Versailles yet and my unease about where he could be was making me hotter. As long as he'd decided to stay for the night, he would be safe. My concern stemmed from the thought that he might attempt the return trip. Now that Bastille Day had finally arrived, revolutionary sentiment was at a fever pitch. They had murdered the poor commander, impaling his head on a pike. Reports from those who braved the streets today had varied wildly, but according to the housekeeper, dozens of people had been killed in the mêlée when the fortress was stormed.

Since then, the poor had gone on a rampage, setting fires and attacking noblemen and women, landlords, business owners, and tax collectors.

Anyone perceived to be remotely affluent was a target. I had not fully understood or appreciated the hysteria that would accompany today's events, and I was secretly glad that I'd been convinced not to go out. Depending on the night's events, I might not leave the house tomorrow either.

I snapped my fan shut and placed it on the table wearily, swapping it out for the glass of wine that sat waiting for me. I took a slow, thoughtful sip. A letter had arrived today from Esme and my stomach had been in knots since.

I had hired Isabelle. If not for me, she wouldn't have been at the château when the Navy arrived. She wouldn't have been raped.

My hands shook as I took another drink of wine, holding the liquid in my mouth as I closed my eyes. I thought of Cifarelli, the way his big hands had held me down effortlessly, the drip of his saliva on my neck, the casual violence he'd treated me, and probably other women with, and swallowed the mouthful convulsively.

Heavily, I sat and propped my chin on one hand while I tipped the glass back for another sip. The wine roiled sickly in my gut while I thought about Isabelle and how she must have felt. How she must still feel.

Thank God Esme was there. She would take care of Isabelle in every way I wish I could. I closed my eyes and clenched my hands tightly on my lap before deliberately straightening each finger. I felt the soft, silky fabric of my wrapper beneath my hands, cool to the touch, flowing like a waterfall over my lap, down to the carpeted floor, puddling around my feet.

With trembling fingers, I poured myself another glass. If I had to sit alone on the night of the Storming of the damn Bastille, while Paris burned around me, wondering where my husband was, maybe I'd get a bit tipsy. I stared into my cup, remembering how hard I had tried to fight him off. I'd kicked, thrown punches and bit, I recalled, hastily drinking more wine to wash the taste of his blood out of my mouth. I shuddered. If it hadn't been for Esme and Gabriel, that night would have ended very differently.

Jeanne's bruised, rope-burned neck and haunted eyes swam into view, and I tilted my cup back, drinking deeply. I wanted desperately to believe that her life would only improve now that she was with us, but her actions in Versailles made me wonder if she was too damaged. I rolled the cup between my hands and tried to ignore the building headache behind my eyes.

Was there anything Gabriel could do about the Navy's visit and their actions?

He had the ear of the king, inasmuch as such a thing was possible. God knew Louis did what he wanted, regardless of his advisors, and damn the consequences. But the actions of the commander, whoever he was— attacking an aristocrat's home and being violent with his staff— surely there would be some repercussions for this? I lifted a hand to my temple and pressed hard, hoping to ease the pressure.

Annoyed at the way my pulse beat against my fingertips, I drained my cup, placed it unsteadily on the cherry wood table, and walked to the bed. I curled on my side atop the blankets and closed my burning eyes.

Thirty-Four
Trampled

Gabriel clicked under his breath as he reined in Automne, pulling up beside Phillipe. Behind them, Seznec and Phillipe's valet, Lacoste came to a stop. In silence, they looked over the meandering, moonlit ribbon of the Seine as it wound through the landscape toward Paris. Even from this distance, the various fires glowed like beacons scattered across the city.

"Perhaps we should have stayed behind the safety of Versailles' gates," observed Phillipe.

"It's too late for that." Gabriel's gut clenched. "And besides, Ava and Armand are in the city. I cannot leave them."

Phillipe shot him a knowing smirk. "It does warm my heart to see you so happy in marriage, *mon ami*, but it's bizarre to see how your priorities have shifted."

He rolled his shoulders, unease making them tight. "I'll not apologize for that. You'll see for yourself when you find a woman that warms more than your bed," he retorted.

His friend chortled heartily. "*Touché, mon ami. Touché.*"

"My place is closer. You and Lacoste will stay the night," he ruled. Over his shoulder, he added, "We'll stay close together going through the city, gentlemen. Move as quickly and efficiently as possible. Phillipe and I will take the lead. We'll be avoiding the area around les Tuileries. You saw how it was at Versailles. I imagine it will be worse here. Especially since they have gunpowder now."

Phillipe nodded and kicked his stallion into a canter. Gabriel squeezed his legs and gave Automne his head, leaning low over his neck as they picked up the pace. Behind him, he could hear the steady, galloping hoofbeats of Seznec's and Lacoste's mounts. The orange dots on the horizon grew brighter as they followed the path of the Seine into Paris. Smoke hung low, suspended in the sultry, summer night air, burning his lungs and throat with every breath.

The hour was late, and they were able to thunder down the largely empty Champs-Élysées undisturbed. They were forced to slow as they entered the heart of the city, and the streets grew narrow and more congested. Gabriel eyed a burning *palais* and his eyes clashed with Phillipe's grimly. His throat, already raw from the ash falling like snow flurries, tightened with fear as they trotted down the cobbled roads. To their left lay the smoldering ruins of a tax collector's home. He'd passed it every time he'd entered Paris, for as far back as he could remember. He wondered if the man would rebuild.

"Halt!"

A band of ruffians materialized from a side street, their short, skinny leader brandishing a rifle threateningly. He reached out, and boldly grabbed Automne's bridle, making the horse sidestep and whinny.

"Well, what have we got here?" One of his sidekicks grinned widely, showcasing several missing teeth in the flickering, glow of a nearby fire. He spat out a glob of saliva, and Gabriel's gaze followed its trajectory to its resting place, glistening on the smooth stones beneath him.

Gabriel calmly rested one hand in his horse's mane, feeling the taut, bunched muscles in his neck, and the other on the hilt of his sword. Two more scrawny men were ranged in front of Phillipe's horse, and he sensed another three behind them, neatly surrounding their group. Seven against their four. They were outnumbered, but their attackers were not mounted, and seemed inexperienced, riding high on bravado and their success earlier today.

"Looks like a couple of silver spooned members of the Second Estate to me," laughed one.

"Aye, with a few lucky bastards that got to tag along with their majesties," observed their leader. "You get to eat their scraps, eh?"

Out of his periphery, Gabriel saw the metallic gleam of Seznec's dagger as it slashed down onto one man's unprotected arm. His sword unsheathed in one fluid motion as he tightened his knees around Automne's sides and wheeled him around in a tight circle, chopping indiscriminately left and right, focusing on the ruffians closest to him. He knew without looking, that his men were quickly dispatching their would-be attackers.

The leader of the gang let go of Automne's bridle and stumbled back, avoiding the horse's hooves. His eyes gleamed with malice as he used the butt of his weapon as a baton, smashing against both men and horses. Gabriel felt Automne stumble beneath him as the iron came down hard on his flank.

"Easy," he murmured soothingly.

Lacoste grunted in satisfaction as he smacked the broad side of his sword against the leader's back, making him yelp and flee. Gabriel pulled back on Automne's reins as he turned in the tight confines of the narrow street and thrust his sword at the last man in the group, trying to grab the bridle of Phillipe's horse.

"Good riddance," he muttered as the undernourished youth ran down the street.

A shot rang out, breaking the silence. Gabriel's stomach tightened with dread. It was too loud, too close. Before he turned in his saddle, he knew.

Seznec sat slumped sideways in his. A dark stain unfolded, spreading rapidly across Timothée's chest and abdomen.

The leader stood twenty [1] *pied* away, smoking rifle in his hands with a look of startlement on his grimy face. Spurred by a wave of fury, Gabriel urged Automne into a gallop. A guttural scream ripped from his throat as he raised his sword high above his head. The man dropped the rifle and ran in panic. He didn't make it more than a few feet before Automne rode him down and he fell on the street, trampled beneath the stallion's hooves. Gabriel dismounted and pulled his dagger out, holding its lethal point to the injured man's neck.

"In your ignorance, you've killed one of my most loyal men." He ground the words out between clenched teeth. "What you did not realize in your quest for justice, is that you chose two aristocrats that are sympathetic to the Third Estate's hardships."

"P—Please, Milord." Sweat shone on his forehead as understanding dawned in his expression.

"I could have overlooked the fact that you waylaid us with ill intent, but I cannot let my friend's murder go unavenged."

A haze of grief clouding his eyes; Gabriel slit the man's throat in one decisive movement; letting the warm blood gush over his hands. He rocked back on his haunches as his life's blood pooled beneath him, spreading across the cobbles and soaking into the dirt between the stones. Smoke from a nearby blaze wafted before his eyes, blurring his vision further as he stared unseeingly at the dead man sprawled on the street.

Phillipe's hand settled on his shoulder.

"We have to go," he said gently, snapping him back to the present.

---

1. Pied: A measurement for length. Pied literally translates to foot, and was traditionally based off the length of the king's foot.

Absently, Gabriel wiped his bloodied hands on his breeches and stood. He didn't look back at the dead man as he mounted Automne.

"Hand Timothée up to me, Phillipe. You guide the horse back," he instructed hoarsely.

They worked in grim silence as the ash continued to fall around them, dusting their hair, clothing, and mounts in a fine, gray layer. Shellshocked, their group quietly wound their way down the Parisian streets, arriving at Gabriel's without further incident.

Voices drifted into my subconscious, melding sinuously into dreams of Cifarelli, Isabelle and Jeanne. With effort, I wrenched myself awake. My eyes burned and my throat was hoarse from the smoke that drifted in from the open windows. I lifted a leaden arm and rubbed my eyes as I lay in the dark and listened with half an ear for the sounds that woke me. My head throbbed to the beat of my heart and my eyes felt heavy from the lack of sleep. With a yawn, I pulled the coverlet over myself, chilled despite the warmth of the summer night and let myself drift, halfway between wakefulness and dreams.

A door slammed somewhere below, and I startled awake. Alert this time, I strained my aching eyes, searching the dark corners of my bedchamber for shadows lurking where they ought not. My heart thudded painfully in my chest and my muscles contracted as I huddled beneath the blanket, listening.

The sound of boots floated up the stairs, accompanied by voices I could now identify. Relief crashed over me like a tidal wave. Gabriel was home safe, and had brought Phillipe with him, from the sounds of it. I pushed the blanket away as I sat up, tightening the sash of the wrapper I still wore around my waist. Passing a hand over my hair, I pattered, my bare feet soundless against the rugs that lay scattered over the wood floor, to the door. I was annoyed that Gabriel had left me alone today, but gratitude that he was home safe, warred against my irritation, ultimately winning.

The metal knob was cool in my hand as I prepared to open the door, but it softly swung open before I could. Gabriel stood before me, dark eyes haunted, mouth set in a grim line, with what appeared to be blood, splattered across his face.

I gasped and took an involuntary step back. "Gabriel!"

"Ava," he sighed.

The grief in his voice hit me squarely in the solar plexus and I moved forward to embrace him.

"Don't," he warned. "I'm covered in blood and ash. Let me wash first."

I shook my head, sending my curls flying. "Don't be an idiot." I pressed the palm of my hand against his face, feeling the smoothness of warm skin and the stubble of his beard against my fingertips.

His lashes swept down, veiling his eyes, and his Adam's apple bobbed as he swallowed hard. One filthy hand lifted, cradling mine against his cheek.

"What happened?" I whispered.

"Timothée—" he croaked. His tongue darted out to lick his lips. "He's gone."

Tears sprang to my eyes. "What— how?" I managed around the lump in my throat. I thought of his young wife, Charlotte, pregnant with their first child and waiting for him at Landévennec. He would never get to meet or hold his first born. Charlotte would raise their child alone. It was so damn unfair.

Gabriel's shoulders slumped as he dropped my hand and his hair, usually meticulously clubbed back, fell over his face. "We were attacked by ruffians. La putain d'idiot of a leader— he's probably never held a rifle in his hands before— shot him."

My heart constricted as my tears spilled over. "I'm sorry." My words felt painfully inadequate. "I know how important he was to you."

My hand found his and I squeezed hard. Gabriel hadn't just relied on Seznec as one of his right-hand men, I knew he had considered him a friend and that he would hold himself personally responsible for his death, even though he couldn't have prevented it. I tugged gently, leading him into the room.

"Come."

He followed me without a word of protest as we crossed the room. In the meagre light of the moon, I gently stripped his stiff, blood-soaked clothes from his body, dropping them in a heap on the floor. I dipped a cloth into the tepid water in the wash basin and wrung it out before carefully washing the dried blood from his face and neck. I moved painstakingly down his body, taking special care between his fingers and around the bed of his nails.

Satisfied, I tenderly dried him with a soft, clean cloth and dressed him like a child before I led him to bed. He didn't utter a word during my ministrations. His eyes held a faraway, vacant expression that made me think he was dissociating his emotions from the night's events. I crawled under the sheets beside him and was startled when his arms came around me fiercely. I pressed myself against him as if I could rip open my chest and cradle him within the safety of my body, tucking his face firmly in the crook of my neck and held him in the quiet, dark of the night.

A shudder wracked his body. It moved from his skin through mine, and I realized my hair and neck were wet with tears as mine ran down my face and mingled with his. I tightened my hold on him, wishing desperately I could tell him it would be all right. But of course, it wouldn't be. Not for Seznec's family. Not for his friends. Not for Gabriel. Not, for a long time.

Thirty-Five
Two Birds, One Stone

The rain fell softly and quietly, clinging like glistening diamonds to the leaves of nearby oaks and seeping into the freshly turned earth. Gabriel paid handsomely for a gravesite beneath a towering willow in the new *Cimetière de Vaugirard*, located not far outside Paris. Our small group of mourners stood clustered together, enveloped in numb disbelief as Seznec's casket was lowered into the ground.

I side-eyed Gabriel's smooth, stoic expression and slid my hand into his large, warm grasp wordlessly. His fingers interlaced with mine and he squeezed my hand gratefully. Regardless of his statue-like demeanor, I knew he was a raging tornado of sorrow and fury inside.

When we returned to the house, dodging ruined homes and shops, I would send the letters Gabriel, and I had written earlier this morning to Timothée's widow informing her of her loss. It was one thing to be the bearer of bad news, but to live in a time when you couldn't tell someone of the loss of their loved one promptly was infinitely worse. At least in the future— I gave myself a mental shake— you could pick up the phone and drive or fly to the funeral. By the time Charlotte Seznec would receive the news, her husband would be buried leagues away, days, or possibly weeks before she was even aware. It robbed people of the closure of saying goodbye.

I realized the service was over and everyone was walking away, back toward the relative shelter of their carriages. Gabriel and I were the only ones remaining, standing beside the grave now industriously getting filled in. With a glance up at Gabriel, I noticed his eyes were wet.

"One day, I would like to bring Charlotte here, to see where he was laid to rest," I said quietly.

Gray eyes swimming with sadness met mine. He forced a smile, the corners of his mouth tilting, though it wasn't echoed in his gaze.

"I would like that," he answered softly. Turning toward me, he raised our linked hands to his lips, pressing a gentle kiss to my knuckles. "Come, let's get out of this weather."

We walked back to the carriage, mud squelching beneath our feet as the rain fell in a mist around us, shrouding the world in a fine, gauzy veil.

"Mind you don't slip," he murmured as he handed me up and settled in beside me.

With the curtains drawn tight against the weather, the light within was dim and gray. I leaned back against the cushions, the cool, damp air penetrating my bones and making me feel cold in spite of the fact it was summer. Gabriel took my hand in his, idly tracing little patterns of vines and flowers along the back.

I broke the silence. "I've been thinking about the letter I received from Esme."

"Mmm. About Isabelle? Tis a nasty business." He shook his head, a dull flush creeping up his neck.

"Yes, and I got to wondering if it wasn't a matter that could be brought up to the king?"

Gabriel shot me an incredulous look. "*Mon cœur*, you don't think *le Roi* cares a fig about what happens to some peasant girl in my employ, do you?"

"Well... no," I admitted. "But I do think it's all about how you present it. You're an aristocrat, Gabriel. You're affronted because the king's royal Navy has grossly overstepped and destroyed your property and defiled this young lady. Surely, this was not the king's intention and surely, he would be appalled to hear that his commanders have violated your estate in such a way. It reflects poorly on him."

His gray eyes were skeptical, but he nodded thoughtfully.

Encouraged, I continued. "Approach it as if you know the king would wish to know about this. Turn it into an opportunity for the king to rectify. And maybe you can plant the seed that des Rochefort has been unfairly targeting your family and raise questions or doubts about the veracity of the accusations against Mathieu."

Gabriel's eyes lit, as I knew they would, at the idea of possibly helping Mathieu. "Aye, Ava. Perhaps you're right. I will ask Phillipe to accompany me. I know he would welcome the chance to help Mathieu. And if I can cast doubt on that *fils de pute* Rochefort with the same stone, all the better."

Esme latched the kitchen garden gate behind her and chose a circuitous path through the growing plants on her way to the surgery that morning. A few bees drowsed in a cluster amidst the scrambling vines and shrubs, and lavender scented the balmy breeze. In the bright sunshine, one could almost forget the remnants of destruction that awaited within.

She lingered by the patch of oregano that tumbled over the path, tiny white flowers rioting over their neighbors in messy profusion, knowing she was putting off the inevitable, but unable to force herself inside. The rosemary grew in a sunny patch, well protected against the wall of the garden and she rubbed the spiky leaves between her fingers and breathed deeply as they released their sharp, resinous aroma. Her hand trailed over the trellised aubergine and staked peppers as she slowly walked to the door.

With a hefty shove, she let herself into the dim, warm recess of the kitchen, letting the door swing shut behind her.

"*Bonjour*!" she sang out, trying for cheer, even as her spirits sank.

"Good morning, Madame Esme." Madame Bleuzen threw a smile over her shoulder before she turned back to the bubbling pot she was stirring.

Aware she was procrastinating; Esme sniffed the air appreciatively. "What have you got there?"

Madame Bleuzen held up a finger as she carefully tasted the contents of the cauldron. Esme leaned her hip against the huge, wooden work surface that dominated one wall of the kitchen while she waited. She could idle the entire day away here, without having to look into Isabelle's haunted eyes. She passed her hand over her face tiredly. Since the Navy's unannounced visit, she'd awoken in tears with Luc's arms tight around her nearly every night. Dreams of her father that she'd buried years ago had resurfaced, making her relive her worst childhood moments every time she closed her eyes. After several weeks, it was beginning to take its toll on her.

"Today is for marmalade. The raspberries have all come in, so I'll be preserving as quickly as I can. We should have a good store this winter." Madame Bleuzen moved the pot onto a higher hook so the contents would simmer and walked to the worktable beside Esme. She immediately began to sort through the berries heaped in baskets along the counter.

"That sounds lovely," said Esme wistfully.

"Lovely isn't the word for it, my dear. I'm as hot as a whore in church."

A little snort of laughter escaped.

"The girls are waiting for you in the surgery," observed Madame Bleuzen.

"Aye, I best get to it." Esme pushed herself off and resolutely crossed the room.

"One more thing," called Madame.

Esme paused with her hand on the door and looked over her shoulder. "*Oui*?"

"We all appreciate everything you've done for Isabelle." Her face tightened, rage showing briefly in her gentle, blue eyes. "I know she's not in a position to acknowledge it at the moment, but she will remember your kindness for the rest of her days. You've given her something to cling to."

She swallowed hard and managed a nod. "*Merci*, Madame."

Madame Bleuzen nodded back. "Now, off you go," she said briskly.

Gabriel leaned forward and steepled his fingers together, trying to prepare himself for what he'd come to say today. Phillipe shifted in his chair and crossed his legs negligently. His relaxed attitude seemed to urge Gabriel to take a breath before he began. The king was often a reasonable man, generally kindhearted, if an ineffective ruler. Still, he was the king, and as such wielded incredible power— should he choose to use it.

"You look like you have something on your mind, Gabriel," observed *le Roi*, as he selected a pastry from the platters spread before them.

Gabriel sighed. "Indeed, I do, your Majesty. It pains me to bring this matter to your attention. . . In fact, I considered not bothering you with such a trivial matter, sire— but unfortunately I feel it's something you should be aware of."

The king nodded, his eyes alert, but kind. "Is this anything to do with your brother-in-law?" he asked shrewdly.

Of course he would know about the arrest. Gabriel should have expected as much. "Yes and no," he began. "I'm sure you're aware that *mon beau frere* was arrested and accused of smuggling?"

Louis raised an imperious brow. "*Oui.*"

Gabriel nodded. "Just so. I'm not here to argue in his defense, your Majesty, but I am here to raise concerns I have about Commandant des Rochefort and his command."

There was a slight thinning of the king's lips at the mention of his commander. "Go on."

"It seems that shortly after my brother-in-law's arrest, he was able to escape wherever he was being held. For some reason unbeknownst to me, the Navy thought le Baron might be hiding in my *château* at Landévennec." He paused and licked his lips. "While they were searching my estate, a great deal of my possessions were destroyed, my butler was accosted and suffered a broken arm, and one of the young ladies in my employ was used in a most grievously."

The king's eyebrows both rose in surprise. "I was not aware so many liberties were taken with your estate, Gabriel. I do apologize."

Gabriel forced a smile. "It's quite all right, sire," actually, it was not all right, but he couldn't say so, "but of course, I feel I must raise the question of restitution, particularly for the young lady's maidenhead. One cannot in good conscience expect our Navy to act in such a manner, particularly considering that my family and I are innocent of wrongdoing. Our Navy represents you, my king, and I feel they have done you a grave injustice by acting the way they have." A trickle of sweat ran uncomfortably down his spine.

Louis nodded, his round face serious in thought. He took a bite of bread and meat and chewed slowly.

Gabriel lifted his glass and took a long sip to fill the silence.

The king finished and swallowed, brushing the crumbs off his waistcoat with a distracted hand. "You're quite right, Gabriel. They represent the queen and me, and we must hold them to the highest standards of behavior and excellence."

"Just so, your Majesty. Those were my thoughts precisely." Gabriel felt a prickle of hope at the king's response.

"I will look into the matter, Gabriel. You may rest assured. And I will also settle a sum on your young lady in restitution for the abuse she withstood. Use it as you wish."

"Thank you, your Majesty. You are too kind."

The king inclined his head magnanimously. "Was there anything else?"

"Simply that I wondered if there have been other complaints lodged against Commandant des Rochefort? My family has had a few run-ins with the man— of the unpleasant variety. He visited my wife on several occasions with vague threats during my convalescence. I'm beginning to think he has an ulterior motive against my family. . . Perhaps even against my brother-in-law as well," he submitted delicately.

Louis' brows drew together. "Are you suggesting that the charges against le Baron were fabricated? The Navy is under my royal command, and you know our stance on smuggling Gabriel. Tis not a light matter."

Phillipe leaned forward. "If I may, your Majesty," he raised an eyebrow in question, waiting for the king to nod. "Gabriel and myself have known Mathieu for more than half our lives. We both are having a difficult time reconciling the man we know, with what he's been accused of. I've had a few interactions with le Commandant, and I can't help but wonder if the man is the most honest sort."

"But smuggling, Phillipe! It cannot be borne. Anyone caught smuggling must face the full weight of the law. If they are of a noble family, or peasants or of the clergy, the punishment must be the same!" Louis' face was turning red.

"Of course, your Majesty. Please believe me, Gabriel and myself are fully aware of the seriousness of the situation. We would never suggest you look the other way merely because Mathieu is an aristocrat. We are simply asking you to consider the possibility that the man was set up." Phillipe paused, letting the suggestion sink in. When the king nodded, the crimson color fading from his cheeks, Phillipe continued. "Smuggling is entirely out of character for Mathieu, and I cannot imagine he would ever put his family at risk by doing so. He stands to gain nothing and lose everything." He sat back.

"Being that le Commandant has shown questionable morals in other areas, is it possible that Mathieu was wrongly accused?" submitted Gabriel delicately.

Silence settled over the threesome while the king waved a servant over, gesturing for a refill. His goblet topped off; he took a lengthy drink before setting it down on the table. "I will take your suggestions under consideration," he answered finally. "Commandant des Rochefort has had complaints lodged against him in the past for his... unorthodox ideas. I'll have someone look into the matter."

Gabriel knew not to push further and bowed his head in gratitude. "*Merci beaucoup, mon Roi.*"

Louis waved his thanks away. "Now, what of the National Assembly? What foolery are they up to now?"

He leaned in, "Well, sire..."

The rain earlier in the evening had been a blessing, cooling the air to a comfortable temperature. For the first night in over a week, I was able to snuggle against Gabriel and not feel like I was melting. Idly, I ran the tip of my index finger along his forearm, up to the tender crease of his elbow and down to his wrist, back and forth. I loved the difference in texture between the soft, smooth skin on the inside of his wrist and the wiry hairs on the back.

He shifted and pulled me closer with his other arm. "A lot of families are leaving," he observed quietly.

"Mmm. Where are they going?"

"*Le Roi* ordered the Polignacs to leave, for their safety, of course."

"Of course. They're not exactly popular with the Third," I murmured.

"*Oui*, for many reasons. They've gone to Switzerland. I believe she has family there." With one hand he played with a curly tendril of hair, rubbing the ends between his fingers thoughtfully.

"The queen will miss her dearly."

"Speaking of *la Reine*, that reminds me. Louis mentioned that she was asking after you. I imagine she must be feeling out of sorts without her regular entourage. I would expect another invitation from her soon."

I adjusted my position, trailing my hand up and letting it tangle in his chestnut hair. "I like her," I started hesitantly. "But I wonder if it's wise for me to be seen with her often. The enmity she garners from the revolutionaries will spill over onto anyone close to her." I tilted my head back to see his expression and was rewarded with a frown.

"Will they truly murder la Princesse de Lamballe for standing her friend?"

"Yes," I whispered. Goosebumps rippled across my arms as I thought of the quiet, gentle woman I had met in Versailles on a few occasions. "There's some disagreement about exactly what will happen, but it's generally agreed that she will be stabbed to death during the September Massacres after her appearance before the tribunal." I shuddered. "Then they'll mount her head on a pike and parade it around Paris."

"*Merde.*" He wrapped both arms around me suddenly in a suffocating embrace.

"Mmph," I said, my voice muffled against his chest.

"Sorry." His voice sounded strangled, as he loosened his hold on me slightly.

"I don't mind."

"Perhaps you shouldn't see her anymore," he conceded.

"Aye, but what about you and *le Roi*? They don't look kindly upon his courtiers either." I pointed out.

"True, but I have no intention of staying here much longer *mon cœur*. I'd like to be back at Landévennec before the winter." He ran his hand down my spine and let it settle on my hip.

"Alright, what about the others that are leaving Versailles? They're not all fleeing the country?"

"*Non*. Some are, but most are going to their country estates and laying low. No doubt hoping the storm will pass them over without causing too much damage."

"There's plenty of damage already." I was thinking of the fires that had decimated many homes, and in some cases, entire blocks of palatial residences.

"*Oui*, and I've heard talk of some *châteaux* away from the cities sustaining damage as well," he murmured. "Phillipe is concerned about his sister, staying at the château in Saint-Denis without him."

"He thinks she's at risk?" I asked in surprise.

"Well, we all are, aye? He was telling me yesterday that he's considering going back to help keep her safe."

His admission hung in the air between us for several long moments.

"What will you do if he leaves?" I yawned.

His hand traveled up my back and settled in my hair. "I don't know yet," he admitted. "You're tired, sleep *mon amour*."

"Mmm." My eyes were already closed. "We'll talk more in the morning, aye?"

"Of course."

I felt his lips move in my hair reassuringly and smiled sleepily.

My hand was tucked securely in Gabriel's arm as he led me away from the apothecary. He placed my parcel in the carriage and handed me up, waiting patiently for me to arrange my skirts around myself on the plush seat before joining me and shutting the door smartly behind him. I leaned back against the seat and closed my eyes briefly as the carriage began moving, willing away the headache I could feel forming.

We'd been making the rounds today. Social calls and errands were both on the agenda, and at this point in the day I felt hot, sticky, irritable and ready to be home. As we rumbled and jolted over the uneven road, his hand plucked mine off my lap. He tenderly peeled my glove off, gently placing it back on the seat beside me, before doing the same to my other hand. The air that flowed over my skin was not refreshing in the least, but it was a welcome improvement regardless.

"Where's your fan?" he asked, as we hit a particularly bad bump.

I lifted my lashes tiredly and rummaged in the hidden pocket of my dress, locating it and presenting it with a flourish. He plucked it out of my grasp, opened it with an expert flick of his wrist, making my brows rise in surprise, and started waving it about, creating a small windstorm inside our carriage. Loose tendrils of hair flew about my face, tickling my cheeks and neck.

"Mmm. Thank you, my love," I murmured.

"I think we should call it a day, *oui*?"

"Yes. We did most of what we wanted to accomplish anyway."

He rapped on the carriage roof, popped his head out the window, and said, "*à la maison, s'il vous plaît.*"

"*Bien sûr*," came the driver's response.

Gabriel drew the curtains closed and I sighed. The brightness of the light combined with the heat was beginning to make me feel slightly nauseous, though how he seemed to divine that fact was a mystery. He slid closer to me and his hands settled on my shoulders, turning me away from him with a gentle push before he started kneading the sore muscles in my back and neck.

I moaned in appreciation as his fingers found and worked on knots and danced up the sides of my neck which were tender with stress. I let my head flop forward as his hands tunneled into the hair at my nape and firmly pressed where it hurt, releasing the tension in the tendons and muscles. The cushion behind me dipped as he shifted closer to me, and I felt his breath warm on the back of my neck a moment before he kissed me. Desire moved through me, golden and sweet as his lips traced the same path his hands had taken.

"Gabriel..." I managed thickly.

"*Oui, mon cœur?*" He barely paused, lifting his busy mouth from my skin only long enough to reply before reapplying himself.

The carriage jolted to a sudden stop, and I lifted my head in confusion. My neck was cold where Gabriel had been plying me with desire mere seconds prior. I turned my head and met his sharp, gray gaze, suddenly registering the change in volume and the strange element of excitement threading the air outside.

Gabriel pulled the curtain away, allowing the sunshine to flood the carriage, temporarily blinding me with its brightness, and looked outside. Scooting closer, I peered around him, realizing that we had stopped moving because our carriage appeared to be completely hemmed in by a restive crowd. Nervously remembering the last time Noemi and I got caught in a crowd, my hand crept across the seat and found his. He gave me a comforting squeeze and shot me a soothing smile.

"I'm sure everything is fine, *mon cœur*. They don't seem to be particularly upset."

Outside, I could hear the driver urging the horses to continue moving, though from my vantage point I couldn't see that there was anywhere for them to go. Miraculously though, the carriage began to slowly and painstakingly move down the street again. There were a multitude of stops and starts. Sometimes I didn't think we budged more than a few feet before coming to a halt, but at least we were making forward progress.

We rumbled approximately halfway down the street before hitting another roadblock.

Frustrated, I looked toward the window to see what it might be this time, and bit back a gasp as Gabriel tried to block the view with his body. I only managed to catch a glimpse, but it was unmistakable. A man's body dangled limply from the lamp post, as a crowd looked on quietly. Gabriel quickly pulled the curtain shut, but it was too late. The image was burned in my brain.

When he turned back to me, his face was a careful mask.

"Do you know who that was?" I asked, speaking slowly in my shock. I didn't recognize the face, but the man was well dressed.

"*Oui*," he answered shortly. "*Le Roi* is going to be most displeased."

I swallowed hard. "Who was it?"

He glanced at me, and I saw in his eyes he wasn't nearly as calm as he was trying to be. "Joseph Foullon de Doué."

"Necker's replacement," I murmured.

"*Exactment.*"

Our eyes met grimly, mine likely reflecting my horror, Gabriel's showing resignation.

Thirty-Six
Charmed

I sat on the bench beneath a large ash in the courtyard as Armand explored on his hands and knees. Although my mind wandered to the scene of the hanging— *à la lanterne*— as they were now calling it, I kept a sharp eye on my son. He had a gift for rooting out anything that might prove dangerous to him and launching himself at it enthusiastically. The acorns and twigs that found themselves in his chubby fists, inevitably made their way toward his mouth unless I intervened.

He tried to grab a wooden ball, but it rolled away, bumping over the uneven grass, across the small garden and out of sight beneath a bush. Perplexed, he stared after it for a long moment, his dimpled, round, face scrunched in consternation. A wren trilled nearby, its cheerful song drawing his attention away from the missing toy. He cocked his head to the side, listening attentively as his blue-green eyes searched for the source of the music.

I watched as a squirrel crept across the grass, one wary, beady eye on Armand. He turned his head, seemingly making eye contact with the furry creature before lunging at it with a gleeful shriek. The squirrel leapt onto the tree and ran up onto a high branch, castigating him in a loud chatter all the way. I smothered a laugh at Armand's crestfallen expression.

"*Pardon*, Madame la Vicomtesse."

I looked up, squinting against the sun at Madame Devereaux, neat in her apron and cap with her hands clasped before her.

"*Oui?*" I offered her a self-conscious smile.

"It's the little master's nap time," she answered with a curtsey.

"Of course," I murmured as I stood in a swirl of royal blue skirts.

I took a few steps across the path and scooped Armand up, giving his warm, flushed cheek a smacking kiss. He giggled delightedly and grabbed my nose. I lifted him high in the air, his arms and legs waving wildly, before I lowered him for one last kiss and handed him off to the waiting wet nurse.

"He's a bit dirty," I said apologetically.

She smoothed his chestnut hair back affectionately. It was lighter than his father's but would darken with age. "No matter. Little boys are meant to get dirty."

What about little girls?

But I crushed that thought ruthlessly before it could lead where I knew it would. Instead, I forced a carefree smile and waved as she carried Armand into the house for his nap. Once they were gone, I flopped back down onto the bench. Without Armand distracting me from my thoughts, they circled to the revolution, Jeanne and her evil spouse, Isabelle, and my desire to go home, to Landévennec. It was odd to realize that over the last two years, Landévennec had become home. The particular scent of mingled resin from the pines and the salt of the crashing ocean; the sprawling fields and patches of forest; and the tenants, many of whom I now considered friends. It all came together to fill an empty, aching space inside me.

I stretched my head to the left and then the right, closed my eyes and rolled my shoulders, listening to the sound of tiny vertebrae popping in relief, and took a deep breath.

The familiar sound of Gabriel's footsteps crunched on the path behind me, but I kept my eyes closed for an extra moment. I never knew anymore if he brought news or was just seeking out my company, but the news was never good. I felt him settle himself on the bench beside me and I peeped up at his face. For once, he looked relaxed, so I leaned my head against his shoulder and let my eyes close again. His arm came around my waist, pulling me closer to him and I let the solid, warmth of his body comfort me. A breeze rustled through the leaves, stirring the hairs on my neck delightfully. A little sigh of contentment burbled up from somewhere deep inside me and escaped through my lips.

"Wouldn't it be lovely if we could sit here forever?" I asked, my voice wistful.

"Mmm. Perhaps our bed would be a better choice." There was a hint of laughter in his suggestion.

"It's delightful outside though," I persisted. "Perhaps a nice, soft bed out here?"

"As long as you're in it, *mon cœur*, I don't much care where the bed is."

I opened my eyes and tilted my head back to meet his serious, gray gaze. "Gabriel..." I began.

"*Oui, mon amour?*" His hands came up to frame my face.

I shook my head, overwhelmed. "I love you."

The corners of his eyes crinkled and he brushed his lips over mine. "*Je t'aime*. And," he added, pulling away and reaching into his pocket, "I have something for you."

My eyes fell on a small, drawstring, velvet bag and I took it from his hand. "What is this for?" I asked, as I loosened the string and reached in.

"It's quite small," he murmured when I couldn't find the item inside. "Here," he said as he gently upended the bag into my open palm, dislodging a little piece of metal.

I bit my lip as my eyes filled. Nestled in my hand was a beautifully worked charm in the shape of a poppy.

When I didn't say anything, he gently picked it up, letting the sunlight fall on it. "I got the idea when you told me the chrysanthemum was to remember your sister by." His voice was gruff. "The best jewelry makers are here, of course, and it took a while to find someone who seemed to understand my vision. I wanted you to have something to remember our Aimée by. I thought you could wear it on the same bracelet." His fingers were warm on my wrist.

"It's gorgeous." I managed around the ache in my throat. "Thank you." I wrapped my arms around his neck and kissed him hard. When I pulled away breathlessly a long moment later, I saw his eyes were bright with unshed tears. I held my arm out. "Will you do the honors?"

His hands trembled and fumbled with the clasp on the bracelet until I leaned forward and pressed my mouth against his. I felt his lips curve in a smile, and pulled away slightly. The bracelet came off easily, for the first time in years, and he slipped the new, bright charm that represented Aimée, beside the older charm that represented her aunt before putting it back on my wrist. We both stared down at the two charms in silence before I grabbed his face with both hands and kissed him.

Esme lowered the parchment she held in trembling hands and picked up the folded letter that lay on the table beside her. Both had arrived this afternoon, the folded one tucked within the one she'd just read, one addressed to her, the other made out to Charlotte Seznec. She licked her lips and pressed them together tightly.

There was no point in delaying the inevitable. Ava had instructed Esme to deliver the missive to Charlotte and to stay with her. If Charlotte couldn't read, then Esme was to read Gabriel's note to her. She passed a hand over her face and stood up, refolding the letter from Ava and tucking them both in her pocket. She already knew Charlotte had never learned to read. Breaking the news to the young mother to be, was going to fall on her shoulders.

She walked to the door, cramming her hat onto her head with one hand as she yanked the door open with the other. She hated giving bad news. It ruined her day— no, her week— although she knew it would wreck Charlotte's entire year. A wave of sympathy rushed through her as her steps slowed. She had no right to complain when she was about to turn this young woman's life upside down. She hesitated at her gate. Turn to the right and see if she could find Luc and convince him to accompany her, or turn to the left and head straight toward the Seznec's place?

Her teeth worried at her lower lip as she lifted the latch and let herself out onto the path. With a pause to make sure it clicked shut behind her, she looked down the path toward the château, hoping she might spot Luc heading home. No such luck. Decision made, she turned to the left and walked up the hill, letting her mind skip around from topic to topic as she tried to distract herself from the job at hand. The forest darkened around her as the clouds moved across the sky, obscuring the sun's rays. She shivered in the shade as the temperature dropped, pulling her shawl tightly around her shoulders.

She crested the hill, and began the walk down toward the Seznec's small, neat cottage. Timothée had built the house himself, carefully fitting the timbers together and even whitewashing them. The love and pride he'd put into the work was obvious when the sun peeked out from behind the clouds, letting the house shine prettily in a ray of light. Esme walked up to the door which stood ajar, and Charlotte met her at the threshold.

"It's my favorite midwife!" she exclaimed with pleasure, her cheeks pink with exertion as she wiped her hands on her apron. "To what do I owe the pleasure?"

Esme hesitated. Charlotte was one of her favorite people at Landévennec. She always had a ready smile on her lips and a twinkle in her merry, brown eyes for whoever she came across. She dreaded being the one to extinguish the light in her eyes. Charlotte sensed her discomfort, grabbing the door frame blindly with one hand.

"What is it? What's happened?"

Esme put her hand out to soften the blow, but Charlotte's expression made it clear she already knew. She managed to catch the young woman under the arms as her knees gave way. Staggering under the combined weight of mother and child, she straightened her shoulders.

"Come," she managed through gritted teeth. "Let's get you in a chair."

With the brunt of Charlotte's weight on Esme, she managed to half walk, half drag the young woman into a wooden rocking chair. Esme pulled a stool up beside the chair and sat, panting and sweating for a moment, then she took Charlotte's limp hand in hers.

"Charlotte—"

"What will I do without him?" she asked in a broken voice. Tears streamed down her pale cheeks and dripped off her chin onto her lap.

"I'm so sorry," she said helplessly, feeling the uselessness of her words twist in her gut. Empty, meaningless words that would never bring Timothée back. Charlotte would have to bring their baby into the world without his father and raise it alone. Nothing she said could improve her reality.

"What—" Charlotte's voice cracked, and she licked her lips and tried again. "What happened to him?"

Esme didn't bother asking how she knew Timothée had passed. She believed that if something happened to Luc, she would know. Why wouldn't the same be true of Charlotte? Instead, she reached into her pocket and pulled forth the crumpled papers.

"I've a letter here for you, from le Vicomte. Would you like me to read it to you?"

"Aye." Her voice was a thread of sound.

Esme patted her hand and unfolded the letter from Gabriel. Her eyes scanned the first few lines, and her lips compressed, holding back the tears that Gabriel's words stirred. She took a deep breath and began.

"Madame Seznec,

It is with the heaviest heart, that I write to inform you of your husband, Timothée, and one of my greatest friends' passing. It pains me tremendously to burden you with this, the saddest of news.

Please know that your husband passed from this earth into the arms of Our Father, swiftly, and I think— painlessly. We were set upon by rogues late on the evening of the fourteenth of July as we reentered Paris from Versailles. One of these ruffians was possessed of a rifle and he availed himself of its use against your honorable husband. Though I know it's a minor balm, rest assured, I avenged Timothée, and the man paid for his crime with his life.

My lady, Ava and I buried him in the new Cimetière de Vaugirard beneath a beautiful willow tree. Tis a peaceful spot and I believe he will rest easy there. I have promised my lady that when the opportunity arises, we will escort you and your child to Paris to see where we have laid him to rest."

Esme paused, clearing her throat and rubbed a hand over her wet eyes.

"I know your finances will be the furthest thing from your mind in this moment, but I pledge to you, that you and your child will want for nothing as long as you live at Landévennec. Please take care of yourself and your unborn infant. If you have any need that should arise, please instruct Madame or Monsieur Morvan to write me post haste.

Gabriel Chabot, le Vicomte de Landévennec."

Esme sat quietly while Charlotte wept. She couldn't leave her in this state, and she was beginning to realize she should have left a note for Luc. No one knew where she was, and Charlotte would need someone to stay with her. She stood stiffly from her perch and stretched her back. The light was a soft golden color, apricot, with smudges of gray-violet clouds low on the horizon. She'd been here for hours and Charlotte and her *bébé* needed sustenance.

She crossed the cabin and filled the kettle with water from the bucket in the kitchen, stoked the fire, adding a log from the pile, and hung the kettle over the hearth to heat. A quick search through the larder and cabinets uncovered a quick, cold meal she could serve the grieving mother. Efficiently, she sliced a few pieces of roasted lamb, a chunk of hard cheese, leftover bread from the morning meal— it hadn't gone stale yet— and a handful of olives and almonds. She placed it on the table and plucked the piping kettle from the hearth before it began to sing, expertly filling the pot she found on the shelf with leaves and hot water.

She crossed back to the rocking chair that Charlotte hadn't stirred from and knelt before her. "Come," she coaxed, as if she were a child. "You need to eat, for your babe's sake."

Charlotte allowed her to lead her to the table and sat meekly before the plate of food but made no effort to eat. Her gaze had turned inward, showing no sign of hearing Esme when she pleaded with her to take a bite. A knock sounded on the door frame, and Esme looked up to find Madame and Eloise Bleuzen hovering at the threshold. She waved them in tiredly.

"What's amiss?" asked Madame Bleuzen briskly.

Esme shook her head. "I'm glad to see you. What are you doing here?"

"We always stop by on our walk home in the evenings, being that she's alone here and expecting any day," answered Eloise.

She closed her eyes. "I'm happy to hear it. I didn't realize."

Madame Bleuzen shrugged. "So?"

Esme pulled her toward the door and filled her in quickly. She knew it would hit close to home for Silouane and Eloise, dredging up memories of their loss. Madame Bleuzen's blue eyes filled with tears of sympathy.

"You need to get home to Luc, aye?"

"*Oui*, but I can't leave her here alone."

She tutted. "Of course not. Eloise and I will bring her back with us. She'll come to the château with us during the day and stay with us in the evenings. We'll get her packed up."

Her eyes filled with tears of relief. "Of course, why didn't I think of bringing her home with me?"

"You can't think of everything," scolded Madame Bleuzen kindly. "She can stay with us until she's ready to be alone again."

Impulsively, she threw her arms around Madame. "*Merci*."

"*Bien sûr.*"

Thirty-Seven
Hairpins and Daggers

Gabriel rode Automne wearily through Paris' desecrated streets and took in the destruction. Over the three weeks since the Storming of the Bastille, there had been riots, fires, and hangings nearly every day. Many of the city's wealthier citizens had fled, either because they'd already been targeted by the revolutionaries, or because they feared they were next. Even though he knew he was working on their side, in concert with *le Roi*, he worried he or Ava would meet with a violent end. After all, most of the city's occupants didn't know who he was, all they saw when they looked at him was power and privilege. Exactly what they were fighting against.

Although it was late in the day, the sun beat down on his head and shoulders mercilessly. Even the breeze was as hot and dry as tinder, offering little in the way of relief from the late summer temperature. Uncertainty and fear crackled in the air, evident in the hurried walks and pinched faces of Parisians. A living, breathing beast that stalked the city's streets by day and terrorized its citizens by night. Gabriel clicked to Automne and guided him to the right, past another burnt building, this one belonging to the king's brother. The slight wind stirred the ashes, whirling them in little vortexes across the cobbles beneath Automne's hooves. He watched it with a sense of detachment. *Was this all really happening? Or was he stuck in a dream?*

The hairs on Gabriel's neck prickled as his horse sidestepped fallen timbers that hadn't yet been moved off the road. He glanced over his shoulder as Automne's years of training took him effortlessly around the obstacles in his path. Gabriel couldn't see anything of note behind him, but the spot between his shoulder blades twitched, a sure sign someone had their eyes on him. As he allowed the horse to weave his way through the crowd, he mused about the state of the country and shook his head at himself. The stress of the last months was beginning to wear on him.

The king seemed to live in a state of denial. He, Phillipe and others had initiated countless conversations with their monarch by now, and little that they discussed seemed to make its way into actual policy. Gabriel suspected there were other people within the king's and queen's circle who counseled against their suggestions; downplaying the seriousness of the situation, insisting that as the divine rulers of the country, they had the right to ride roughshod over the peasantry. Gabriel grimaced. It was like playing chess without knowing who all the players were. Casually, he glanced over his shoulder again, certain he was being followed. He scanned the faces of the crowd, looking for familiar features, but no one appeared out of place.

Despite the tightening in his gut, he kept his hand on the reins light as Automne picked his way around an overturned cart and turned his mind back to the matter at hand. Over the last week, the National Assembly had voted to abolish feudal rights and privileges. At the same time, they'd decreed that the future constitution would be preceded by a declaration of rights. As Ava had said they were taking a page out of the Americans' book.

Jefferson— damn the man for his meddling— was filling the revolutionary's minds with all sorts of ideas. Many, he would grudgingly admit, were fine, but some he feared were taking them further down a road they couldn't return from. It all felt like it was spinning out of Gabriel's control. How could he hope to slow the wheels of this runaway carriage? Was he mad to convince himself he could make a difference?

He shook his head as Automne found his way onto their street. The National Assembly's latest vote hadn't been signed into law yet. But it would be before the month was through. In the meantime, the queen had asked about Ava again, and Gabriel had been forced to lie and say she was feeling unwell. His stomach tightened at the reminder. He hated being deceitful, especially to his king and queen, but Ava and Armand's safety had to come first. A relationship with a doomed queen wouldn't serve them.

Automne stopped dutifully in front of the stables conveniently located next to their house and Gabriel dismounted. With a gentle hand on the bridle, he led Automne into the dim, cool stables. He breathed deeply of the comforting aroma of hay, animals and manure as he walked his horse to his stall. Efficiently, he uncinched the buckles of his saddle, and removed his tack, hanging everything on the hook outside. Fetching his brush, he slowly went over the horse's glossy coat while he thought of Ava. All the warning signs suggested that their time in Paris would be coming to an end soon.

I sat at the table, smoothing the creases out of my latest letter. I had finally received something from Amélie, and I was anxious to read it. My sister-in-law, niece and nephew had weighed heavily on my mind ever since the news of Mathieu's arrest had arrived at the end of May. It'd been two excruciatingly long months of waiting to hear how they fared. Eyes closed,

I crossed myself and sent up a silent prayer that at least some of the news would be good and settled down to begin reading.

20th July, 1789
   Madame Ava Chabot
   Vicomtesse de Landévennec
   14 Rue de Lille
   Paris, France

   My dear sister,
   I hope you, my brother, and my darling nephew are all in good health and staying safe in these uncertain times. I remain shocked by the rapid turn of events the last months have brought. You'll be relieved to hear that Thérèse and Étienne are well. It seems to me that they grow as quickly as flowers in the warm, summer months, and their presence is a joy to me, especially with their father so far from us.
   Of Mathieu, I have heard not a word. I keep the hope that he is safe, and that our divine king realizes he has been wrongly accused close to my heart, as one might guard a candle flame from a wicked, winter wind, lest it snuff it out. I am sure you and Gabriel are aware of what has transpired and were as shocked as I was to hear the news. The children ask for their father often and are baffled by his long absence. Margaret and I do what we can to reassure them, and keep them occupied, but there is a secret fear that lives deep within

me that they will forget their papa if he is forced to stay away from us much longer.

I know you will be worried for our safety without Mathieu here. You may recall that we have had problems with a gentleman in our employ named Corbin. He is an exquisitely talented stonemason, but he tends to drink, and violence, and the recent months since his wife's death have been no exception. Indeed, I do believe he has become less stable and more prone to outbursts since her untimely demise.

The men have been asked to keep a wary eye out for him as I have no doubt he could cause a great deal of damage should he choose to. I mention this because he has recently begun to make very strange proclamations and accusations suggesting that he questions whether or not his wife has truly passed. He has been heard making claims that she has been stolen from him and that he means to find her. I cannot begin to understand where he thinks she might have gone, but I wish you to be aware that he may materialize at Landévennec one of these days in a mad search for the poor woman.

Finally, I leave you with a bit of cheerful news in these uncertain times that I hope will put a smile on your beautiful face. Although Mathieu is not able to be with his family, he has left me with a new blessing to welcome into the world. I'm expecting the arrival of a new niece or nephew for you and Gabriel— likely in January. It's my dearest hope that I will see you both (and that sweet nephew of mine) soon— Perhaps for the Christmas season? Please write soon, I miss you dearly.

Your loving sister,
Madame Amélie Gardin
La Baroness de Trégoudan

I sat back and huffed out a breath, blowing loose tendrils of hair out of my face with the exhalation. Amelie's letter was chock full of news, and she'd managed to word the information in such a way that it left no room for interpretation. With one hand I rubbed the back of my neck where tension had settled and with the other, I picked up the letter and scanned the contents again.

Corbin was a threat, that much was clear. Whether because the man was mad, or because he somehow intuited that Jeanne was still alive, who could say? It didn't really matter. He was convinced she was somewhere, and he was determined to find her. With any luck he would visit Landévennec before our return and find that Jeanne was not there. Perhaps he would give up the search. Perhaps he would fall off a cliff and meet an untimely end. Perhaps pigs would fly.

I sighed, poured myself a glass of wine, raised it in a silent salute to Amélie and drank deeply. She was pregnant, and as lovely and wonderful as the news was, I knew she must be filled with anxiety and trepidation about Mathieu. In addition to dealing with his long, forced absence and keeping a cheerful demeanor in her children's presence, she also had to bring another child into the world— likely before her husband returned. For that matter, who knew if or when Mathieu would be able to return. Perhaps Gabriel's talk with the king would yield some fruit, but it was far too soon to hope for that.

Gabriel walked into our bedchamber, letting the door swing shut behind him. His gaze locked on me as he ran a hand through his hair in frustration. "I'm glad you're here, *mon cœur*," he leaned down and gave me a lingering kiss, his gray eyes landing on the letter.

"I'm glad you're here too," I murmured, letting myself sink into him. "I've had news from your sister."

He pulled out the chair opposite mine, poured wine into his cup and sat. "What did Amélie have to say?"

I lifted my cup. "We should begin with a toast, to her health and to your next niece or nephew." I smiled, determined not to show my sadness at the situation.

A broad smile spread across Gabriel's face, chasing away the weariness and stress that had settled onto it of late. "That's wonderful news. To Amélie and the *bebe's* health!" He clinked his goblet against mine and drank deeply.

I took a small sip and set my cup back down. "There's more, of course."

"Aye, I suppose it isn't all good either."

"The main thing, other than the fact that they are all missing Mathieu, is that Jeanne's husband is convinced she is alive somewhere and determined to uncover her whereabouts. Amélie says he is increasingly unstable, and that she is worried about what he will do next." My stomach churned at the possibilities as I remembered Jeanne's bruised neck.

Gabriel frowned. "That man is not going to stop looking for her until he's been taken care of. He's like a sick animal."

Startled, I looked at him. "Taken care of? You don't mean—"

"I do," he interjected firmly. "He's a danger to Jeanne and frankly, he's a danger to my sister and *les enfants* as well. Mathieu and I should have done something about him sooner."

I stared, shocked. "But Gabriel—"

He shook his head. "I'm sorry *mon cœur*. I would prefer not to speak of such things with you, but we are living in an increasingly dangerous time. In fact. . ." Gabriel stood up, walked to a small chest by the window where he kept his letters, weapons and other valuables and began to rummage around. "Here." He placed a small, wrapped object on the table before me. "Open it," he urged.

Hesitantly, disturbed by his strange behavior, I unwrapped the small bundle. Nestled inside was a thin, wickedly sharp dagger. The silver glinted in the candlelight, reflecting the fine sheen of the metal back at me. I looked up and met his serious, gray eyes.

"Gabriel. . ." I began.

"Please listen, Ava. Recently, I thought I was being followed. I know I didn't mention it to you. . . I didn't want you to worry but coupled with your visits from des Rochefort and what happened to Timothée—" A shadow crossed over his face. "It made me realize that we are not safe, neither of us. But at least I know how to defend myself, *mon cœur*. You are utterly helpless and it's my fault. I intend to rectify that." He nodded his head at the dagger. "Beginning tomorrow, you're going to learn how to use that."

My finger traced the pattern etched on the hilt slowly. The metal was cold against my skin. After several long seconds, I picked it up, my fingers wrapping around the hilt automatically. It was made for a small hand, it's weight comforting, but not taxing. I turned the weapon over, admiring the workmanship. It was strangely beautiful, though it didn't detract from its lethal, razor-sharp edge.

Gabriel plucked it out of my hand. "Tis a well-balanced weapon," he murmured. He extended two of my fingers out and laid the dagger across them, the juncture of the hilt and blade resting on my fingers. "See?"

I nodded and turned to look up at him. "Thank you, Gabriel. Though I dislike the idea of one day possibly using this, I recognize the importance of it."

He gave me a crooked smile, placed the dagger on the table and offered me his hand. I placed my fingers in his and stood to face him, tilting my head back to meet his gaze. His hands settled on my waist as he drew me closer, sliding around to cup my bottom as he lifted me against him. My hands ran up his chest to loop around his neck as I pulled him down for a kiss.

He tasted of wine, frustration and fear. His lips were rough against mine as he poured his swirling emotions into me. I met him beat for beat, offering my uncertainties and confusion. I was afraid. It wasn't something we usually spoke about, but it was obvious to me now that Gabriel was too. I ran my hands up his nape into his hair, wrapping my fingers tightly in the slightly rough strands, anchoring myself to him as my mouth opened under his. His breath was hot and ragged against my neck as he pulled away, dropping open mouthed kisses down my neck to my collarbone.

I turned my head to give him better access, my limbs turning to butter as my knees buckled. He adjusted his hold on me, scooping me up and depositing me on our wide bed as he trailed kisses along my gown's neckline. I grabbed his face between my hands and tugged him up to me, desperation making me impatient. His lips met mine, but they were softer now, as one hand trailed down the bodice of my dress, loosening the stays single handed and the other came up to fist in my hair, scattering pins across the blanket.

Desire coiled in my belly, tendrils reaching into my limbs as I roughly pulled his garments off, delighting in the feel of his skin against mine. I ran my fingertips down his ribs, gently across his scars, down to the waistband of his breeches where I lingered for a few minutes before I continued my journey further, pushing his clothing down as I went. He yanked my skirts off with a growl and I wrapped my fingers around him possessively, making him groan against my mouth.

"*Mon Dieu*, Ava—"

I captured his mouth with mine and lifted my hips in a frenzy of need, cutting him off.

"Now," I demanded, taking him into me.

He matched my urgency, slamming against me as I dug my fingers into his hips, until I felt myself coming apart. My body rippled in goosebumps as he shuddered against me. Gabriel pushed himself up and rolled onto his back, taking me with him and pulling the blanket over our tangled limbs. I lay with my head against his chest and my body blissfully tucked against his as I lazily ran my hand over his skin. Gently, I traced the scar on his ribs where he'd been stabbed on the beach the previous year, an ugly reminder that I'd nearly lost him, twice. My cheek pressed against his skin, I turned my head slightly, impulsively pressing a kiss over his heart.

His hand rested gently on my hair, his fingers slowly separating the tangled strands as he stroked. "You're the beat of my heart, *mon cœur*."

There was a raw poignancy in his voice that made my throat catch with unexpected tears. "I'm scared," I admitted in a small voice.

His hand tightened briefly before it resumed its careful, lazy caress. "I am too. That's why we arm ourselves as best we can."

"You'll teach me?"

"Of course," he said softly. "You only need the element of surprise, my love. No man will expect you to know how to defend yourself."

"All right," I acquiesced, lulled into sleepiness by his warmth. "I love you," I murmured.

His lips brushed over my hair. "I love you more."

The first fingers of pearly, gray light reached through the chinks in the shutters and teased his eyelids open. He generally woke with the dawn, the habits of country life too deeply ingrained, even when he was in the city. Ava lay sprawled across the bed, one arm thrown with abandon over her head, the warm, bare skin of her leg against his. His wife did not share his affinity with the early morn, and he generally didn't fault her for it, but this morning he had promised to begin teaching her how to use her dagger.

The rest of his day would be taken up by meetings, errands and balancing on a tightrope between the revolutionary's demands and the king's expectations. It was wearisome work, and he was beginning to think it was futile, but he had committed himself, hopeful that they would find a path forward even though no agreeable compromise had shown itself thus far.

He leaned over and pressed his mouth to Ava's bare shoulder, drawn in by the smooth, soft skin. Unable to stop himself, he trailed kisses to the sharp edge of her collarbone and buried his face against the curve of her neck, breathing in the warmth of her body and the scent of roses in her hair.

"Mmm," she murmured sleepily, stretching against him.

"Mmm— ouch!" He reached behind him, searching for the culprit. Something sharp had just poked him in the back.

Long eyelashes lifted, revealing sea green eyes. "What's wrong?"

"There's something here, ah!" Triumphantly, he held the offending object aloft.

She giggled. "My hairpin."

"No doubt one of many lurking around here waiting for the opportunity to stab me," he muttered darkly.

Ava pressed the length of her body against his. "As I recall, you were the one to destroy my coiffure last night." Her voice held a hint of promise.

He tossed the pin onto the table and ran his hands down her back, pulling her closer to him. "As I recall, you asked for it." He shot her a wicked smile. Maybe there was time for—

A knock sounded at the door. He bit back a groan.

"*Oui?*"

His valet poked his head in. "I apologize for disturbing you, my lord, but you've an invitation from *le Roi*. He wishes you to accompany him on a hunt this afternoon."

"Yes, of course, thank you Hamon."

"You're welcome, my lord." The door clicked shut behind him.

He sighed. "Will you have breakfast with me, *mon cœur*? I reckon I'll have a couple minutes to go over a few things with you before I have to leave."

She reached up and pressed a kiss to his mouth. "Yes." She rolled to her side of the bed and slid out of the sheets, slipping into her wrapper and belting it in one smooth motion. "What shall I wear?"

He frowned, feeling a headache form between his eyes. "A gown. You need to know how to move in one, aye?"

"Mmm. I suppose so," she replied as she rummaged through the armoire.

He watched her for a minute in silence, the way her lithe body moved gracefully around the room, how her hair tumbled in mad waves and curls down her back, picking up hints of light from the rays of sunlight that struggled through the shutters. His heart squeezed painfully, and he crossed himself. *Dieu, keep her safe.*

Thirty-Eight
Wedding Cake Hair

Sweat trickled down my ribs as I thrust my dagger up through the air into a clothed bale of hay. My wrist turned savagely as I twisted the knife into my pretend opponent and yanked it back again. Tendrils of hair stuck to my damp neck and cheeks, annoying me, and I pushed them back with my free hand.

"Not bad." Le Gall handed me a cup of watered wine— the water in Paris was foul— and I drained the glass in a single swallow.

I passed the empty goblet back to him. "Thank you."

Sticking the dagger back into my straw friend, I flexed the fingers of my hand gingerly. The muscles throughout my arm and shoulder throbbed from the repeated stabbing motions I'd spent the morning practicing.

Thrust from below... I didn't have the leverage to stab from above. Plus, I was more likely to do damage if I hit the soft unprotected organs beneath the ribs. Twist the dagger to optimize each thrust and pull it back quickly, in case I needed to use it again. Words of advice scrolled through my foggy brain.

"Gabriel wants you to start practicing against me tomorrow. The first thing we will go over is how to disarm me and avoid being disarmed yourself." Le Gall casually twirled his dagger between his fingers, frowning against the bright, overhead sun. "Your biggest advantage as a woman is the element of surprise, but any worthy opponent will recover quickly. You likely won't get more than one chance, so you must make your first move count."

I pulled my dagger out of the hay and carefully sheathed it, slipping it into the wide, hidden slit in my skirt. "Gabriel said the same."

He nodded toward my dress. "That's a neat trick, being able to hide your weapon in your gown."

My hands spread out before me. "I can't take credit for the idea. That was Gabriel's thought." I wiped my sweaty hands on my dress and retreated to my favorite bench in the courtyard. "Thank you for working with me, Jean-Paul."

La Gall's face turned red up to his sandy hairline and he scuffed his feet. "It's an honor," he muttered. "I'll see you in the morning." With a quick bow, he escaped in the direction of the house.

A warm breeze rippled through the grass and trees, lifting the hair off my neck in a soothing caress. My eyes closed as I mentally reviewed what I had learned over the last week. Gabriel had taken my first few sessions, and Le Gall had been instructed to take over on the mornings when he couldn't. I knew I was making progress; my thrusts had become smooth and quick compared to my first clumsy attempts, but I knew I lacked any real strength or skill. Still, I found myself flushing with pride when Gabriel nodded approvingly at my improvement. Perhaps with enough practice I would actually feel confident wielding the wickedly sharp weapon.

A shadow fell over me and I lifted my hand, tenting it above my eyes as I squinted at my intruder. Madame Devereux held Armand firmly in her arms as he wiggled, holding chubby arms out to me.

"This little imp was asking for you, Madame."

I held my arms out to receive his writhing body. "*Merci*, Madame. I'll keep him with me for a while. He can play in the grass."

"Are you certain?" She looked at Armand as he struggled to escape doubtfully.

I squeezed him and pressed my lips to his soft cheek before releasing him onto the ground. He immediately began to crawl toward a stray branch a few feet away.

"I'm sure. I enjoy watching him explore."

Her face softened, affording me a rare glimpse at her affection for him. "He's a good lad, Madame. Just energetic."

Armand rocked back onto his bottom, picked up the fallen branch and casting an eye toward his wet nurse and myself, made to taste it.

I jumped up and gently wrestled it away from him while Madame Devereux walked away laughing.

Esme followed the path to the Bleuzen's cottage, the moon lighting her way as Luc strode along beside her carrying her box of supplies. Word that Charlotte's birth pangs had begun arrived shortly after sundown and she quickly sprang into action, grabbing her bag and organizing supplies for the young mother to be.

Luc had insisted on accompanying her. Although Esme frequently traveled the large estate solo during the daylight hours, he refused to allow her to answer calls after dark alone. Since the incident with the Navy and Isabelle inside the relative safety of the château, he had become even more protective. She sometimes chafed with impatience at the new directives, but she knew he was merely worried about her and protecting her as best he could. She also knew his precautions were being mirrored all over Landévennec. Women and girls were being urged to stick together wherever they went.

Disturbing news about the revolutionaries was trickling into the countryside. Stories of peasants, half crazed with the taste of victory after looting the Bastille; made their way to Landévennec, where most of the tenants listened in shock to the tales of violence, burned homes, murder committed *à la lantern*, heads placed on pikes and paraded about, and the odd mention of rape.

Generally, people reacted by shaking their heads sadly at the state of the country and crossing themselves. Thank goodness things were not so bad here, they said amongst themselves. Le Vicomte and la Vicomtesse had done everything they could to lessen the burden on their tenants and make sure they had what they needed to survive. They were lucky.

Still, some whispered that they could have done more; that they were to blame for the rampant malnutrition and sky high death rates that affected the young and the elderly; that they sat in their high, stone châteaux with ample firewood for warmth during the bitterly, cold winter months, while the poor froze and huddled together in their pitiful huts.

There was anger at the unequal division of resources, and it spread like poison in the small towns and bars that surrounded Landévennec. Esme and Luc's evenings had been spent discussing the disturbing instances they heard in the safety of their bedchamber of late, and as a result they both went about their daily tasks with an increased sense of impending danger.

The path broke through the trees, revealing the Bleuzen's neat half stone and half-timbered house sitting in the middle of a tidy, fenced garden. Esme unlatched the gate, letting Luc and herself in before she strode up to the door. She shifted her bag to her other shoulder, reached out and rapped her knuckles on the sturdy, wood door.

Eloise must have been waiting for them, because the door swung open almost immediately, spilling candlelight onto the threshold. Her cerulean eyes looked relieved to see her as the worry on her young face faded.

"Madame Morvan, Monsieur Morvan." She opened the door wider with a smile. "Please come in."

Luc waited while Esme went before him into the small house. She quickly scanned the interior, nodding in satisfaction as she noted the pot of boiling water, bubbling above the hearth, and the herbs laid out on the neat, work counter. Madame Bleuzen had already begun to prepare for the labor.

"*Merci*, Eloise. Where is she?"

"We've given her my bed," murmured Eloise, as she led the way to the back of the house.

They passed a closed door where Monsieur and Madame Bleuzen had shared a room, and Eloise pulled aside a curtain, revealing a decently sized alcove, which housed a single bed, a small wardrobe, and a carved oak chest at the foot of the bed. It was a neat, cozy space, brightly lit by two lanterns. Charlotte paced the width of the small space while Madame Bleuzen stood calmly speaking to her. Eloise was apparently sharing her mother's room while Charlotte stayed with them. A wooden cradle had been brought into the space and stood waiting in the corner.

Charlotte saw them first, stopping in her tracks and flashing the facsimile of a smile at Esme. "I'm glad you're here," she murmured.

Madame Bleuzen turned to Esme in relief. "Oh, good. Did Luc come with you?"

"Yes, though I imagine he will return home, now that I'm here." She shot an assessing glance at Madame Seznec, her experienced eyes taking the measure of the situation. Considering that it was Charlotte's first birth, it would likely be hours before the *bébé* arrived. "I'll walk back home tomorrow."

Madame Bleuzen nodded. "I'll just give him a glass of ale before he leaves then." She patted Esme's shoulder as she pulled the curtain aside to leave. "Send Eloise if you need anything."

"*Merci*, Madame." She approached Charlotte calmly, placing her bag of supplies on the floor by the wall, hopefully out of the way. "How often are the pains coming?"

Charlotte stood doubled over by the bed, her long hair straggling loose from the plait that hung down her back. She straightened as the contraction passed. "I'm not sure, there's a few minutes in between them, though they've been more frequent the last hour or so." She pushed her hair back off her face.

Esme nodded. "Alright, let's get you settled, it'll likely be hours yet. You might as well be comfortable."

She quickly unpacked linens and rags from her bag, setting them on the chest as she spoke and then pulled the curtain aside. Her eyes settled on the chairs by the table. Luc sat comfortably in one, her box of medicines and a tankard of ale on the table before him.

"I'll be right back," she assured Charlotte as she walked purposefully into the kitchen.

"What can I help with?" asked Eloise eagerly.

The child looked at loose ends and desperate for a task. Madame Bleuzen had mentioned that this would be Eloise's first birth, having finally been deemed old enough to attend one, and she was beside herself with excitement. Apparently, she had doted on Madame Seznec in the month since word had arrived of Monsieur Seznec's death, and she was thrilled at the idea of hosting the young mother and infant in their home. Eloise had shown herself to be possessed of a calm demeanor in emergencies, and she had a remarkably good memory for various herbs' uses. She'd been a real asset in the surgery and Esme had been pleased with the girl's progress.

"I'm going to bring this chair into the room. Could you brush and braid Madame Seznec's hair so she's more comfortable?"

Esme hefted the solid wood chair up, preparing to carry it away. Luc stood up and drained his cup.

"I'll carry the chair for you, *mon chou*," he said gruffly. He gently pulled it out of her hands.

She looked at him gratefully and rose on her toes to peck his cheek. "Thank you, my love."

"*Oui*, Madame," murmured Eloise.

"Thank you, Eloise. "Esme smiled at her. "There should be a bottle of lavender oil in my box. Use some in her hair to help relax her."

She waited while Luc walked away, and Eloise disappeared with the bottle of lavender.

"She's a good girl," she said quietly to Madame Bleuzen, rummaging through her box. She found the salve she had prepared with sage— excellent for laboring mothers and set it aside.

"Aye," agreed Silouane. "Her father was so proud of her. I wish he could see how she's grown in the last year." Her voice was wistful, and her blue eyes were shiny with unshed tears that she quickly blinked away.

Esme felt her own eyes fill and she awkwardly hugged Madame. "I've no doubt he's looking down on you both from heaven. He sees the beautiful, hardworking, young woman she is becoming."

Madame Bleuzen's arms came around Esme in a surprisingly strong embrace. "Thank you," she said, her voice thick. "You've helped our *petite fée* tremendously over the last year. You and la Vicomtesse have been like aunts to my girl. I'll never be able to thank you for what you've done for her."

Esme stepped back and shook her head to clear the emotion she felt rising like a tide within her. "Nonsense. It's been an honor."

Luc cleared his throat, and the women smiled at each other. "I'm going back, Esme, unless there is anything else you need?"

"*Non, merci, mon amour.*" She lifted her mouth to his for a kiss. "Get home safely, I'll see you tomorrow."

He gave her a quick, chaste kiss that managed to make her toes curl inside her boots and nodded his head to Madame Bleuzen. "I hope she is safely delivered of a healthy babe."

"God willing." Esme crossed herself and carefully shut the door, latching it behind him. She turned to Madame Bleuzen. "Let's get that *bébé* birthed."

I shifted unobtrusively and flicked my fan open, trying my hardest not to wave it around with gusto. It was outrageously hot beneath the hundreds of lit tapers, and I felt faint from the lack of air flow in the ballroom. My hair towered above me, making my headache beat in time with the music as overdressed aristocrats whirled about the room. With a sigh that I barely managed to suppress, I turned my attention back to the cluster of women who tittered and gabbled like a muster of peacocks about their dresses, the difficulty of sourcing flour for their pastries and the arrogance of the peasants' demands.

Gabrielle's grating voice broke through my internal dialogue. "Would you believe they had the audacity to set fire to our house in Paris? It's utterly ruined. I had to order a whole new wardrobe of gowns. Thank goodness my seamstress was available to make a few items for me immediately." She preened in an extravagant, emerald confection as the other women murmured sympathetic platitudes and admired her gown.

"It truly is shocking," agreed the queen. "I've heard the city resembles a war zone. Burnt buildings everywhere and utterly unsafe with bands of ruffians roaming about." She shuddered delicately. "I'm so grateful we are safely ensconced here in Versailles."

I hadn't seen her since the death of the dauphin, and she was resplendent in a decadent, black mourning gown. Her ash blonde hair, adorned with a cockade of red and blue to symbolize her support of the revolution, and her white, unlined skin contrasted prettily against the dark color. Her large eyes glittered with false gaiety, cloaking her inner anguish; although I knew most people in attendance tonight would not look far enough beneath the royal surface to notice.

I smiled, nodded and tuned them out, letting my gaze roam the room in search of a particularly tall, broad-shouldered man. I spotted Gabriel across the room, deep in conversation with Phillipe, le Comte de Mirabeau and another gentleman I didn't recognize. His gray eyes met mine, he said something to the men, and smiled before starting toward me. A mixture of relief and guilt at pulling him away from his business swirled through me as I watched him steadily weave through the crowded dance floor.

The woman next to me sighed theatrically and tapped my forearm with her closed fan. "The way he looks at you, my dear. You're so lucky."

Marie-Antoinette nodded. "I've heard he's quite in love with you. And if my eyes don't deceive me, you're rather in love with him yourself, aren't you?"

I glanced at her to assess her words, but her expression appeared earnest. "I consider myself very lucky in my marriage," I demurred, "Although I hear that *le Roi* is quite devoted to you, your Majesty."

She smiled coquettishly and cast her eyes down. "We fumbled in the early days of our marriage, but we eventually found our way to each other. A fact for which I am eternally grateful."

My eyes found Gabriel's as he closed the last few feet between us. "Good evening your Majesty, ladies." He bowed deferentially to the queen before kissing my gloved knuckles. "If I may deprive you of my lovely wife's company for a few moments." He smiled charmingly and tugged me onto the dance floor, pulling me close for a waltz.

"You look miserable," he said under his breath. "What's wrong?" His arm was firm around my waist, the heat of him searing through our clothing.

"Was it that obvious?" I asked, abashed. My eyes smarted as I tilted my head back to meet his gaze.

His expression softened when he saw the threat of tears. "*Mon cœur*, what's the matter?"

"I don't know." I felt overwhelmed, the proximity to too many people and the noise overstimulating me. "I think I need some air. Aren't you hot?"

"*Oui*, the sweat is running down to my *derriere*," he replied, with a smirk. "Let's take a turn around the garden."

With his hand firm at my waist, he guided me through the double doors into the slightly cooler evening air. I sighed as the fresh breeze caressed my damp skin.

"Thank you, my love. My head felt like it was going to burst in there."

He led me to a bench and sat beside me quietly as I filled my lungs with air heady with the scent of roses.

"Do you sense the change in temperature? The seasons are changing," he said softly.

I closed my eyes and rested my head against his shoulder, listening to the sounds of the night insects, the musical tinkle of a nearby fountain, the rustle of the breeze through the trees that arched above us, blocking out the light of the stars. My head pounded sickly, and I squeezed my eyes shut against the pain.

"Mmm. You're right. The nights are cooler. I can't believe it's already September."

"Armand will be a year old in another month." He shrugged out of his coat and draped it over my shoulders. The comforting, familiar scent of lemon and rosemary enveloped me.

Our son was on the cusp of walking, and I suspected, on the verge of terrorizing the entire household with his mobility. The simple joy and zest he had for life made the corners of my mouth lift in a smile. I didn't answer Gabriel, and a comfortable silence settled around us. The incessant throbbing in my head had me shutting my eyes as I concentrated on my breaths. *In. . . and out. In. . . and out.* Darkness swooped in like a curtain closing, luring me into a kind of half slumber.

He shifted, bringing me back to the present and I opened my eyes, bringing on a wave of dizziness that had the garden spinning around me. My stomach roiled in protest and a shudder ran through my body as I closed my eyes again in a bid to calm my nausea.

"Are you thinking of her?" he asked, in a sad voice.

My hand automatically went to my bracelet, finding the charm he'd given me and rubbing it like a talisman. "I wasn't, though she's never far from my thoughts."

"You seemed far away."

"Mmm. I feel terrible. Tired and achy, like my head is in a vise." My voice could barely be heard above the crickets' song

"Let's go," he said decisively. "You need to rest. Come." With his arm sturdy around my waist, he practically carried me up the walk toward the doors.

"No, it's all right," I protested feebly as he guided me into the hall and aimed for the entrance, skirting clusters of aristocrats and diplomats with aplomb.

"It's not," he asserted simply. Gabriel paused and nodded amiably to le Duc d'Orléans, before steering me out the grand entrance doors onto the steps. He accessed me in the pool of light cast by the lamps. "You're quite pale, *mon cœur*. Perhaps you're getting ill." Supporting me with one arm, he raised the fingers of one hand, flagging down a porter with ease.

Resplendent, in a smart waistcoat and coat, piped in the royal colors, the porter bowed. "Your carriage, Monsieur?"

"*S'il vous plaît*. My lady is feeling unwell, if you could make our excuses to *le Roi et la Reine*."

"Of course, Monsieur."

He turned away, murmuring directions to another porter who stood like a statue a few feet away. I watched through half-lidded eyes as he sprang into action while the first man disappeared into the *palais*, presumably to carry our regrets to the king and queen. The edges of my vision darkened as I swayed on my feet.

"*Merde*."

Gabriel's voice was far away, like I was floating beneath the placid surface of the ocean, watching the interaction of mesmerizing, colorful sea life in the miniature world of a reef. Tiny bubbles rose, popping at the top. The water faded from a crystalline aqua into dull gray as clouds rolled across the sun, obscuring the light and throwing shadows.

My lashes lifted to a jarring, rolling motion. The air surrounding me was black and I turned my head weakly, flinching at the starburst of pain that radiated behind my eyes. I licked my lips, unsticking my tongue from the roof of my mouth to do so. Gabriel ran his hand over my hair soothingly, wafting the scent of his soap over me.

A sigh escaped my lips, as my body melted once more into the carriage cushions. My head rested on Gabriel's lap, his fingertips massaging tiny circles on my scalp and pressing into the tender muscles and tendons of my neck. I turned my head back and the weight of my hair slid off his lap. As he gathered the mass of waves in his hands, twisting and coiling it across the seat I realized he must have painstakingly removed the pins, braids and hair pads from my monstrous, wedding cake hair in an attempt to relieve my pain.

"*Merci, mon amour.*"

His fingers stilled for a moment before resuming his ministrations. "How do you feel?"

I started to shake my head and stopped abruptly as jagged bolts of light careened in my brain. "Not great. I don't remember leaving."

"Aye, well you wouldn't, being that you fainted in my arms." There was a hint of amusement in his voice, overlaying the tension I could feel coiled in his body.

"I'm sorry—"

"Nay my love. Don't apologize for being ill," he inserted, seriously. "Besides," he added in a lighter tone, "this affords me the rare opportunity to tend to you. Our roles are usually reversed."

"Mmm." The dark was creeping back into my hazy vision.

His hands resumed their gentle stroking and detangling. "Close your eyes, *mon cœur*. You're safe."

Thirty-Nine
Smoke and Pearls on the Breeze

I winced against the bright light as I opened my eyes. My mouth tasted like I'd eaten chalk for supper the previous night, my tongue felt thick and unwieldy, and my head was strangely heavy. Bit by agonizing bit, I managed to turn my face. Gabriel had one foot crossed negligently over the other as he sat reading by the fire. As though he sensed my gaze, he glanced over the book at me, his gray eyes widening with relief when he saw me. He placed a scrap of parchment between the pages to mark his place and set it down on the table.

"How do you feel?" He pressed the back of his hand against my cheek, and forehead, and frowned worriedly. "You're still burning hot."

I licked my lips. "Water, please."

He poured me a cup from the carafe and helped me sit up, propping the pillows behind me. His smoky gaze dark with concern, he watched me drink thirstily, taking the empty cup from my hand when I finished.

"What can I get you? Noemi wants to know how she can help."

The room spun like a carousel around me, and I closed my eyes, attempting to slow the dizziness. "Right now, I just want to rest. I'm so tired. Can you hand me the little jar of lavender salve on the vanity?"

Gabriel looked at the small glass jar doubtfully, but dutifully he swiped it off the vanity and deposited it in my palm. "This one?"

"Yes, thank you." I applied a generous amount to my cracked, dry lips, screwed the lid back on and handed it back to him.

My eyes were burning, and I let them drift closed.

"Wait, let me help you lie down, *mon cœur*." Gabriel fluffed my pillows, expertly flipping them to the cool side and eased me back.

I sighed; the coolness of the pillow was soothing against my cheek. His fingers trailed through my hair, lulling me back to sleep.

Gabriel rode companionably beside Phillipe through the fiery woods. Autumn had arrived, painting the leaves in flagrant shades of crimson and gold. They drifted down, floating in the breeze, until they came to rest on the forest floor, where they were crunched underfoot by trotting horses and hound dogs.

In the week since the ball, Ava had improved dramatically, thank God. Today she had actually been up and about, dressed and practicing her moves with the dagger and Le Gall. When the missive from the king arrived, asking him to join him for the hunt, she'd essentially thrown him out of the house.

"Go!" she said, laughing. "I'm fine."

Reluctantly, he'd framed her face in his hands and kissed her solemnly, gratitude that she was better swelling within him. Now that he was out in the crisp air, breathing in the comforting aroma of earth and growing things, he realized he'd needed to get out of the house.

Phillipe brought his horse closer to Automne. "Ava is feeling better, I gather?"

"*Oui*, finally. She gave me a bit of a scare."

"That's good. I was wanting to ask you—"

"Philippe! Gabriel! Come join me," invited the king.

Gabriel glanced at Phillipe who mouthed, "later," and they both spurred their horses onward.

Le Duc d'Orléans fell back, making room for them near Louis. They fell into step beside the king's mount, flanking him while they continued to meander.

"My king," murmured Gabriel with a short bow in the saddle.

Phillipe mirrored his move as *le Roi* flapped a hand at them.

"It's a quiet day for a hunt," Louis observed.

Phillipe nodded in agreement, but Gabriel remained quiet. There was a sudden tightening in his gut that usually precluded bad news.

"I've had news about your friend." The king glanced over his shoulder at Gabriel. "And your brother-in-law."

"Thank you, your majesty, for looking into the matter," said Gabriel quietly, warning bells chiming in his head.

"Mmm. It appears that there can be no doubt that le Baron was involved in some sort of smuggling. I'm sorry to be the bearer of bad news, but of course you know, the crown cannot stand for such a thing."

Gabriel hoped he looked properly horrified. "It's such a shock to think he could have been a part of that..."

Phillipe and Gabriel exchanged grim glances behind the king's back.

"Aye, well. Sadly, people can't always be trusted. I'll have you know I looked into le Commandant as well, Rochefort." He let the sentence hang in the crisp autumn air, likely content to leave the matter at that if Gabriel or Phillipe didn't pursue it.

Luckily, Phillipe nudged him along. "Were you able to uncover anything of interest, your majesty?"

"Ah, *oui*, perhaps. It seems that rumors abound about des Rochefort. He seems to leave the stench of distrust behind him, wherever he goes. But—" He shrugged his shoulders. "He is either exceptionally talented at covering his tracks, or his former colleagues simply mislike him." He looked over his shoulder at Gabriel. "There are people that can't seem to get on with others. Might he be one of those?"

Gabriel hesitated. "I have encountered such persons in the past, my king. But, no, I don't believe des Rochefort falls into that category. There is something sinister about the man." He rolled his shoulders uncomfortably. "I wish I had evidence I could present you with, regarding the commander."

"Well, if you ever uncover something concrete, please let me know. In the meantime, there's really nothing further I can do."

"*Merci, mon Roi.*" Understanding they were dismissed; Gabriel and Phillipe fell back toward the end of the hunting party in tandem.

"Now what?" muttered Phillipe angrily.

Gabriel cut his stormy eyes at his friend. "Now we wait. And hope that asshole des Rochefort fucks up."

I ran my fingers through Gabriel's chestnut strands, candlelight glinting off the bits of red and gold in his hair. The tension came off him in waves as I rubbed little circles on his scalp, trying to soothe him. Inside, I felt sick. He would only be this upset if something terrible had happened, and he'd barely said a word since he stormed in from Versailles. My mind was conjuring up dozens of scenarios as I tried to imagine what might have occurred.

He'd walked into our bedchamber, shucked off his clothing and thoroughly ravished me in silence. I shifted and he lifted his head off my stomach to look at me.

"Am I too heavy?"

In response I pressed his head back down and resumed my ministrations. I ran my fingers down his neck, pressing, and kneading, hoping to ease his stress. He would tell me what was going on soon.

Eventually he moved with a small groan. He plumped the pillows beside mine and sat against the headboard beside me. Chilled without the warmth of his body, I pulled the blankets up higher.

"You went hunting with the king today." I prompted him.

A sigh whooshed out of him, like a deflating balloon. Irreverently, I wondered when balloons were invented and shook my head at my wayward thoughts.

"He invited Phillipe and me. Others as well of course," he began.

Of course. The king wouldn't go anywhere without a sizeable entourage.

"Was everyone wearing the appropriate colors?" I asked flippantly.

Gabriel shook his head, the ghost of a smile hovering on his lips. "*Le Roi* was dressed in purple. Most shocking, although he had an armband in the blue and red."

I raised an eyebrow, surprised that he wasn't taking the matter more seriously. "And everyone else?"

"I think most everyone else did. My mind was elsewhere for the majority of the hunt," he admitted.

"So, what happened?" I shimmied closer to him until my shoulder bumped comfortably against his.

"Louis says the evidence pointing to Mathieu's involvement is irrefutable."

His words settled in the air between us. My stomach dropped and I let out a slow, shaky breath.

"Nothing can be done then."

"No," he agreed.

"Shit."

"*Oui*. He also said he inquired about des Rochefort. Apparently, the man is not well liked, but there's never been anything concrete against him."

"I expected as much. But the news about Mathieu is worse."

"Aye," he said gruffly.

"Have you heard anything from him? Do we know how he is?"

Gabriel shook his head slowly. "*Non*. I gave him instructions to write me when he felt it safe. We agreed on an alias of course. But I've heard nothing since I left him at Landévennec. I know they got him to Rousillion, but otherwise that's it."

"What about Amelie?"

"Too risky," he said simply.

I laced my fingers through his and squeezed his hand. "She must be so worried."

"Aye. She's stronger than she looks though," he said confidently.

"Mmm. Even the strong can waver. We need to get news to her." I remembered how sick I'd been with worry when Gabriel had been gone for a month in Versailles. How much worse would it be after several months?

"I don't imagine we'll be staying in Paris for too much longer. We'll visit her when we head home."

"What will we do about Jeanne?" I chewed my bottom lip as worry corroded my innards.

"She'll come with us, of course. She's due any day, no?"

"Yes. But what about her husband? Amélie seemed very concerned about him in her last letter," I reminded him.

"We can offer to leave her here, although I think she would be safer with us. We could teach her some defensive skills. You've taken pretty well to your dagger... Perhaps we should teach her as well?"

"That's actually a good idea. I wish I had thought of it sooner," I mused. "It would give her some confidence if she could fight back. I'll speak to her about it."

"*Bonne*. It's settled. I think we should plan to leave a few weeks after she has *le bébé*. She'll need a little time to recover from the birth."

I yawned. "Alright then. I have an early morning practice session with Le Gall. We should get some sleep." I pulled the pillows down and burrowed beneath the blankets. "Come keep me warm," I invited.

I swiped a sweaty strand of hair back absently and smiled at the sweet bundle in my arms. Jeanne labored for a surprisingly short time before delivering the little miracle I held. A downy swatch of platinum blonde hair adorned her head, and her eyes had been a shockingly dark, deep blue when she'd opened them, screaming angrily at birth.

"She's a beauty, Jeanne. You should be so very proud."

Jeanne smiled shyly, though her eyes drooped in exhaustion. "Thank you, my lady."

"Would you like to hold her? Or shall I put her in the cradle?"

"In the cradle, please. I'm right tired." She covered a mighty yawn with her hand.

Gently, I lowered the infant into the bed beside her mother. "You should sleep while she's sleeping."

"Aye, so I've heard," she answered wryly. "Though I hear that's easier said than done."

"Mmm," I replied noncommittally.

Unfairly, perhaps, I hadn't experienced that part of motherhood. Maybe if we ever had another child I would. Wistfully, I thought about all the things I missed with Armand in his first weeks and stubbornly pushed it aside. His first birthday was coming up, and I realized I'd been avoiding it because it reminded me of Aimee. Would his birth ever cease to be tainted by her loss? Sadness swept through me and tears pricked my eyes. With the tip of my index finger, I caressed the baby's cheek.

"Have you chosen a name for her?" I withdrew my hand from the cradle, lacing my fingers together before me.

"Margaux. She reminds me of a perfect pearl," she said fancifully.

"It's a beautiful name. Get some rest." On quiet feet, I retreated, closing the door with a nearly soundless snick.

Esme walked slowly back home, her lower back aching in the pleasant sort of way that indicated she'd had a productive day. She'd visited Charlotte and her babe Timothée after putting in a few hours in the surgery, and now she followed the winding path through the sunset hued forest toward her house. The seasons had changed, seemingly overnight, and the air now carried a perpetual chill, even on the sunniest days.

Today had been a stunner. The sky was the deep, bluebird blue that heralded crisp autumn days, the sun shone brightly, and the final harvests were being brought in as the nights grew colder, dipping ever closer to frost. Colorful leaves floated down, swooping and swaying on the breeze. Esme reached out her hand, catching one in her palm. She held it close to her heart for a moment.

"I wish for a child," she whispered into the empty air around her.

She thought of Timothee's sweet coos and rosy cheeks. Of the comforting baby scent of him, and extending her hand, let the leaf drift away on the next breeze. It was colder beneath the towering canopy of trees, and she shivered, pulling her shawl tighter around her shoulders as she resumed her walk. Her hand crept to her abdomen and rested there for a few seconds. Perhaps by this time next year they would have their own child.

Esme crested the summit of the hill and began her descent. The last letter she'd received from Ava had hinted at the possibility of their return from Paris, hopefully before winter set in. She gazed in the direction of the chateau, thinking about how nice it would be to have her friend back.

From here, she couldn't make out the building, the trees still sported far too many leaves for that, although when they were bare, you might catch a glimpse through the trunks.

Shades of cherry, apricot and orange glowed in the distance, painting the sky gloriously as the sun sank behind the horizon. She admired the flamboyant colors as she walked peacefully. With this temperature it would be perfect to snuggle in bed with Luc, spinning dreams and plans. She would have to lure him into an early bedtime tonight. Her lips curved in a wicked smile.

Suddenly she halted in her tracks and glanced to her left. The château was situated north of her— not where the sun would set. Over her shoulder, she could see the beginnings of the real sunset. She glanced back toward the chateau, noting the intensity of the glow. The breeze stirred, carrying with it the faintest whiff of smoke.

Before she knew it, she had her skirts kirtled up and she was speeding down the hill as quickly as her legs would carry her.

Forty
"I'm Just a Girl, in the World."
-No Doubt

The bell tinkled merrily, heralding our arrival, as Noemi and I walked into the warm, bright apothecary. I inhaled the jumble of aromas that vied for attention in my favorite Parisian shop. Monsieur Abadie beamed at us, as he totaled another customer's order. I gave him a nod and ducked into one of the small aisles, running my gloved fingers down the polished wooden shelves. Some of the more common herbs and spices were cleverly displayed in small, prepackaged quantities, making it simple for someone in a hurry to get what they needed. Larger orders and rare items required the apothecary's assistance.

Generally speaking, I only purchased large quantities and unique finds, stockpiling my purchases for when we eventually returned to Landévennec. But, I never knew what I might find on his scrupulously organized shelves, which made my hunting expedition interesting every time. On this trip, I had tasked myself with purchasing some items to send to Amélie.

Without Mathieu around, the winter approaching, and another infant on the way, I knew she would have limited time to prepare for the illnesses that cold weather typically brought. I eyed a jar of salve; its neat label claiming to reduce and soothe coughs. Intrigued, I slipped it into the wicker basket over my arm. I would have to question Monsieur Abadie about its contents.

A musical tinkle from behind me indicated that Monsieur's customer had left, or perhaps another had arrived. A glance over my shoulder suggested Noemi and I were the only patrons left in the shop. I placed the jar of ointment I'd been considering back on the shelf and walked toward the long counter that dominated the room.

Monsieur wiped his hands on a rag and stood up straighter when he saw me approach. "*Bonjour* Madame! I have the order you placed ready for you. If you'll give me just a moment..." He disappeared into his mysterious back room, reappearing a moment later with a large, wrapped package. "Would you like to look at the list of contents I have here?" He slid a piece of paper across the counter to me, waiting patiently while I ran my eyes over his neat script.

"This all appears to be in order, Monsieur. Thank you for taking care of this while we ran our other errands." I pushed the list back across the glass surface and hefted my basket onto the counter beside me. "There was something else I found that I wanted to ask you about..." I rummaged around until my fingers closed over the cool, glass jar and I pulled it out.

"Ah yes, this is actually one of my favorite remedies." He plucked the jar off the counter and turned it in his hand thoughtfully.

"What's in it?"

"Oh," he waved his other hand in the air and gave me a wink. "I can't give away all my secrets, Madame. But the main ingredients are eucalyptus, which is quite difficult to source, as you may know, peppermint, myrrh and lavender."

"Hmm. May I smell it?"

Monsieur unscrewed the lid, offering the open jar to me with a flourish. "*Bien sûr*, Madame."

The unmistakable scents of eucalyptus and menthol assailed my senses, taking me back to my mother rubbing Vicks on my chest when I was sick.

"Lovely," I murmured in surprise. "Do you have this in larger quantities? And do you sell the eucalyptus separately as well?" My mind raced with the possibilities. I hadn't seen eucalyptus sold in any of the other apothecaries I had patronized in the last two years.

"Yes, to both, though the eucalyptus is quite dear. How much of each would you like? I can have them both ready for you the next time you come."

I frowned thoughtfully. "Can I get ten times this amount of the prepared salve? I'll take this small jar with me today and—" My fingers drummed on the counter. "Does the eucalyptus come as an oil? Or just the leaves?"

"I have both, Madame. The oil will travel easier, though it's more expensive of course."

"Yes, I'll take the oil." Gabriel would be annoyed at the sizeable bill, perhaps, but it would be worth it. "Two bottles, if possible."

"*Bien sûr*. Was there anything else for today?" He added the jar of salve to the list he had prepared for today, glancing up at me before he totaled it.

"Noemi, did you want to add anything?" I turned to look at her.

"*Non*, Madame, not for me. *Merci*." She came to stand beside me, sniffing the minty air appreciatively.

I pivoted back to the apothecary. "That will be all for today. I'll be back next week for the salve and eucalyptus." I reached for my small purse, snapping it open to pay him.

"It will be ready for you," he assured me as he counted the francs and placed them in his strong box. "*Merci*, Madame!"

"*Merci*, Monsieur." Noemi and I split the hefty bundle in two, stowing our purchases in our baskets, and made for the door.

"Where are we off to next, Madame?" she inquired, switching arms and pushing the heavy door open.

I sighed. The small of my back ached, my arms throbbed, and my feet were sore. "I don't want to go anywhere else," I admitted, dodging an apple cart. The donkey hitched to the wagon appeared to have given up, its owner alternatively pleading with and prodding the recalcitrant animal. I shot him a sympathetic look; I didn't want to walk any further myself. "Was there something else we needed to do today? Or can we go home?"

She frowned thoughtfully and sidestepped a pile of horse manure. "I think we can go home. Everything else can wait, Madame." Her eyes cut across to me as we wove through the crowded street. "You look a bit tired," she offered.

I paused, a cluster of people standing outside the butcher shop blocking our way. "I'm still not fully recovered from my illness."

Impatiently, I stood on my toes trying to see if there was a way around the crowd. *What was the hold up?*

Beside me, Noemi craned her neck. "Can you see anything?"

"No, maybe we should—"

Someone bumped into me from behind, hard. Knocked off balance and annoyed, I turned my head, ready to snap at the culprit when my vision went dark. Startled, I lashed out, my hands automatically trying to pull the hood or whatever had been thrown over me, off. Rough hands grabbed me from behind, pinning my arms to my sides.

The wicker basket slid off my hand, falling to the ground with a clatter. My feet scrabbled for purchase, slipping on the dirty, refuse-strewn street as I was dragged backwards. Panicked, I thrashed trying to connect with something, anything. Then, I locked my knees, forcing them to pull me. I kicked hard behind me, my boot making contact with my assailant's leg. I heard a grunt, and a flash of satisfaction coursed through me, though it was short lived.

"You'll regret that *petite pute*."

My breath hitched as he threw me over his shoulder and tossed me onto a hard surface. I landed on my back and immediately rolled onto my side, my hands reaching for whatever obscured my vision when my head snapped savagely to one side. I tasted blood and gagged on the metallic taste. It smelled like onions, the pungent scent further disorienting me. My head throbbed dizzily, and I closed my eyes, trying to concentrate. *Don't fight back until you know what's happening.*

Roughly, I was turned onto my stomach, one knee pressing down on my back as my hands were bound behind me. Don't struggle, don't struggle. I repeated it like a mantra as my head spun sickly, clinging to the words like a lifeline. Each breath a struggle, I turned my head, attempting to get a clear lungful of air. The sharp aroma of onions was overpowering, the urge to retch climbing from the depths of my stomach until I tasted it in the back of my throat. Please don't vomit. Knowing him, he would leave me in a puke-filled bag.

The pressure on my back eased, but I didn't dare move without knowing where he was. Goosebumps rippled across my arms and torso. It was a fairly warm autumn day, but fear skittered up my spine, chilling me to the bone.

Where was Noemi? Had she gotten away? Had she realized what happened? I had to believe that she had, and that she was going for help. My mouth went dry, Gabriel wasn't even in Paris. . . who knew what time he would return from Versailles. No, no. Don't think like that, I lectured myself.

There was a jolt and then bumpy, forward motion. I was in a cart or wagon then. . . Where was he taking me? I opened my eyes and strained to see. Some cloth or burlap sack had been pulled over my head. Whatever it was, it had housed root vegetables before me. I could see shadowy shapes through the uneven, thick weave, but I was too disoriented to puzzle anything out.

If Cifarelli was driving the cart, then I could probably move into a more comfortable position, I thought as we continued to rumble down the street. I shifted, tucking my knees up toward my chest and trying to roll onto my side. It was difficult without my hands to leverage myself, but maybe I could get into a seated position. I was swinging my bent legs around, tangled in my skirts when something collided violently with my head and the world went black.

The first thing I noticed was the smell. Damp and sour. It smelled of desperation and fear. My own, most likely. Wincing, every follicle on my head aching, I lifted my lashes a fraction. I could feel that the onion bag was gone, but I didn't want to advertise that I was conscious yet. My surroundings were dark, though there appeared to be a small light source somewhere to my left. What lay to my right, I couldn't say. That eye was glued shut. The agony was concentrated on the right side of my head and face, my hair stiff and sticky. My lip was tender and swollen. Eyes shut; I tried to take stock of my situation.

Somehow, Cifarelli had found me. Whether by accident or design, it didn't matter. A tiny voice in my head asked if perhaps he had been following me or asking for me... dark and mustached fit the description... but truthfully, that didn't matter right now either. Had he been working in concert with des Rochefort? I had to suppress the shudder that ripped through me at the thought.

By some miracle, I was still dressed. I was surprised, but perhaps Cifarelli wanted me awake and aware when he violently raped me? My stomach lurched and I clenched my teeth until my jaw ached. I was in a seated position, my head slumped forward, and I could feel bindings around my legs and torso. I'd been tied to a chair. The now familiar, comforting weight of my sheathed dagger rested against my thigh, but it was useless to me right now.

A scraping sound to my left, followed by a maniacal chuckle. "I know you're awake, you dirty slut. No need to pretend for me."

I suppressed the urge to move, though the feeling of thousands of ants crawling over my body was overwhelming.

Think!

The voice in my head screamed, but the dizziness swimming in my brain suggested it would be easier to slip back into the blessed relief of unconsciousness. I fluttered my lashes, letting them lift briefly over my left eye and began to raise my head before letting it fall forward again and feigning a faint. I forced my limbs to go limp. *Please God, let him believe it.*

I concentrated on my breath, trying to keep it deep and regular. If I was right, and he wanted me awake, this would possibly buy me time. How long had it been since I'd been knocked out? It was damp, chilly and dark, underground perhaps. I couldn't expect Gabriel to find me unless there was a trail of some sort to follow.

He was closer to me now, I could smell him, rank and unwashed. The particular scent of an alcoholic's dried sweat, ripe on his clothing. Breathe in, breathe out. Don't gag on his scent. Don't tense your muscles.

The sense of Cifarelli slowly circling me like a shark closing in on its prey was suffocating.

He leaned in, his breath hot on my skin. "Wake up, *petite pute*. Your husband will be here soon. I can't wait for him to watch all the things I'm going to do to you." His tongue rasped up my cheek, slimy, fetid.

I tensed. *Dammit*!

He laughed inches from my ear. "I knew you were pretending. You're not very good at it."

Wearily, I opened my good eye and jutted my chin in defiance. If he released me, and he would have to at some point, I would go for the dagger. It was my only shot.

Cifarelli pressed his thumb against my bruised, swollen cheekbone, a smile stretching across his face as I flinched and then resumed his circular pacing. "As I was saying, I expect the Vicomte will be joining us shortly. I can't wait to see his face when he sees what I've done to yours."

In dawning horror, his words penetrated through the fog in my brain. He had laid a trap for Gabriel. Or... if he was working with des Rochefort, perhaps he was being brought here by force. I shook my head, trying to think and grimaced as nausea rose and my thoughts rattled and pinged around my brain. Eyes closed, I clamped my jaw and battled for control.

I steeled my spine and forced my left eye open, meeting his delighted gaze. The man was certifiable. The realization was like a splash of icy water.

"Could I possibly have a drink? I'm parched." I tried to pull my swollen lips into something resembling a smile.

His jack-o-lantern grin wavered in confusion. I hadn't reacted as expected. He narrowed his eyes at me, trying to puzzle out the trick, no doubt, and then shrugged one shoulder.

"One moment." He walked away and returned quickly with a metal cup. "Not the finest vintage, eh? But I expect you'll take what you can get."

"Thank you," I murmured. "Could you..." I let my voice trail off, lifting a shoulder awkwardly. "Do you mind helping me?"

Blurrily, I watched the thoughts race after one another as he considered the possibilities. Finally, he pulled a knife out of his boot, walked behind me and sliced through the rope that bound my hands free. In shock at his stupidity, I made a big show of rubbing my wrists and flexing my fingers as blood flowed painfully back into my extremities.

"I expect you can help yourself, now." He thrust the cup at me.

I fumbled, wine spilling onto me. My reaction was sluggish, my aching muscles and joints struggling to keep up with my brain's commands. Through my good eye, I could see him watching me, obviously enjoying my difficulty. Trembling, I took a small sip. It tasted of vinegar, but I forced it down my dry throat.

"Thank you," I said, as graciously as I could muster.

He nodded at me jerkily. "Don't get any grand ideas," he warned, tossing his knife back and forth between his hands.

I opened one eye wide, trying to appear innocent. "What do you think I could do? I'm just a girl tied to a chair."

"Just so." He flashed me a nasty smile. "Don't forget I'm armed and twice your size, eh?" He paced back and forth impatiently.

I took a deep breath, trying to ignore the panic, rising like bubbles underwater. My eye followed him around the room, back and forth, while I swallowed another tiny mouthful of wine. It churned like acid in my belly, while I wiggled my fingers, pushing the numb, pins and needles away by sheer force of will.

He was obviously agitated as he walked the length of the room. Perhaps there was a delay, or maybe he couldn't handle the anticipation of whatever sick fantasy he had planned. I forced myself to focus on his pacing, ignoring the nausea that his pendulum-like movements dislodged in my gut.

"What exactly is the plan?" My voice squeaked in fear as I forced the words out around the lump in my throat.

He stopped in his tracks and turned to stare at me, disbelief written on his face. My speaking to him or questioning him clearly wasn't part of the plan. His eyes narrowed as he debated whether or not to reply. I held my breath as his expression wavered in indecision. If I could get him to talk, maybe he would relax.

Finally, he answered. "Once the Vicomte arrives, the fun will begin." He smiled like the Cheshire cat and licked his lips. "There's a bed behind you. I'll tie you up there, while your husband watches from here." He gestured with one hand toward the chair as his other hand crept to the front of his breeches.

I stared at him, trying not to shudder as he rubbed himself slowly, his eyes half closed. "Perhaps the *petite pute* would like to sample what's in store for her now? I'll show you what a real man is like." He grinned, obviously delighted with himself for the idea.

He started toward me and knelt by my feet, fumbling with the ropes that tied them to the chair legs. My right hand buried itself in my skirt, creeping toward my hidden dagger. This would be my only opportunity. Once tied to the bed, I couldn't hope for another chance to present itself. I gritted my teeth as my fingers closed around the hilt.

One foot was free. He paused to look at me, "Don't try anything stupid, eh?"

Mutely, I shook my head, hoping he could see my terror in my left eye. He returned his attention to the hempen rope binding my right foot, muttering under his breath about how it was so tight it wouldn't come loose. Inch by inch, I slid my right hand out, keeping it well hidden amongst my skirts, grateful for once, for the ridiculous fashions of the era.

My foot was free, and he stood, not a moment too soon, and leaned over me menacingly. His hands came down on my shoulders as he crushed his mouth to mine, pressing my lips so hard against my teeth that I tasted blood. Now! My brain screamed as I tried not to buck against the bruising kiss.

He sensed the movement of my hand and pulled back a fraction as I stabbed into his abdomen with all the strength I could muster. The metal cup clattered to the ground. I registered the surprise on his face as I twisted savagely, just as I'd been taught, and pulled back. He stumbled back and reached for the dagger I knew he had in his boot. I lurched upward, taking the chair still tied to my torso with me as I stabbed upward again, trying with all my strength to rip through the thick muscles that protected his internal organs.

I saw his knife coming in a swift downward arc and I threw my left hand up to block him as I ducked to the right. He missed, his arm connecting with mine. The momentum behind his body coupled with the chair brought me to the ground. Thrown to the floor on my right side, with the chair tied to me, I knew I couldn't possibly move fast enough.

As he advanced on me, bleeding profusely, the gleam in his eyes told me he knew it. I breathed deeply through my nose and lurched onto my hands and knees, intending to throw myself at him. He sidestepped swiftly, avoiding my clumsy movement and slipped on the spilt wine, going down hard on one knee. It was a lucky break, but even with his injuries, he still had the upper hand.

The comforting hilt of my dagger firmly in my hand, I leaped off my knees, aiming directly for him, hoping by some miracle I could knock him down. Miraculously, I landed on him in an awkward crouch. He tried to fend me off, screaming gutturally at me as I pressed the point of my knife into his left eye. I felt his weapon connect with my side and it pulsed in an agony of throbbing heat. Blood sprayed, obscuring my vision further as he fumbled, and I continued to push.

The full length of the metal was buried to the hilt in his eye, and all movements had ceased for some time before I realized he was dead. Adrenaline slowed and every inch of me returned to a kind of excruciating ache. In a daze, I pushed myself off his prone body. I stared at the dagger protruding from his skull in horror, feeling the bile rise swiftly through me. On my hands and knees, I retched onto the moldy, bloody stones beneath me until there was nothing left.

Dry heaving and shuddering, I managed to pull the knife out of his face, wiped the blade on his shirt and sawed through the ropes that still bound me to the chair. I stood and pressed my hand to my side, feeling the stickiness of blood as it seeped through my gown. Swaying on my feet, I sat, hauled up my skirts and used my knife to cut away a strip off the bottom of my petticoat. I gritted my teeth as I awkwardly wrapped it around my torso, tying the ends sloppily to keep them in place.

I stood and unsteadily walked to the wall nearest me. The sticky hilt of my dagger in one hand and the other against the slimy wall for support, I hobbled forward, searching for a way out. If Cifarelli hadn't lied, Gabriel was on his way here now. The idea of having to potentially fight someone else off, made me sick with dizziness and terror.

Ahead, I spotted a rough opening in the stone. I kept my gaze on it as I began to shiver uncontrollably. My teeth chattered, echoing loudly in my head as I made a beeline for it. Please God, please God, please God. Let it be the exit. I swayed against the wall and braced myself against it.

Forty-One
The Gate of Hell

The sense of desperation lay heavy and thick in the air as she adjusted the handkerchief tied over her nose and mouth. The clouds hung low, angry and foreboding, warning of an imminent storm. Esme glanced up at the sky furiously. Why couldn't it have unleashed its fury when they needed it?

The wind and the men's shovels stirred the ash, blowing it about and settling like a fine layer of snow on her hair and shoulders. There was a shout from Madec, and the women surged forward as one, eager to see what, if anything, had survived the blaze. Esme stepped gingerly through the wreckage of the former kitchen and watched as they lifted the hatch that led to the cellar. Miraculously, the wood appeared to be intact, unlike the roof beams and wooden floor joists of the entire second and third stories of the château.

She crossed her fingers superstitiously, hiding the furtive movement beneath her thick, woolen skirts. Holding her basket in one hand and her dress in the other, she carefully made her way down the stone stairs. Madame Bleuzen, Eloise and Mademoiselle Ollivier had arrived before her and set out lanterns they'd brought from their homes to illuminate the dark cellar.

Today's mission was simple. Evaluate what, if anything, had survived the inferno and begin the process of moving whatever they could to a new location for the winter. As Esme scanned the organized shelves lining the large, underground room, relief swept through her. If nothing else, at least they wouldn't starve this year. Neat rows of jars, crates of root vegetables and apples packed in straw, barrels of wine and ale, and large wheels of cheese filled the room.

Isabelle was the next to make her way down the stairs and she let out a little sigh when she saw the stores. The women exchanged glances of relief.

"*Dieu, merci.*" Mademoiselle Ollivier crossed herself.

Esme followed suit automatically. Within a few minutes, they had created a system of which items to prioritize moving first, and they began handing them down the line, and up the stairs, where they were passed off into wagons to be brought to various locations. Esme and Luc's cellar and larder would fill, as would the Bleuzens. Although it had gone undiscussed, Esme knew the assumption was that if Gabriel and Ava returned before the winter, they would stay with Esme and Luc. Their home was the largest and had the most space.

Charlotte and baby Timothée were still with the Bleuzens, and she had offered Mademoiselle Ollivier and Isabelle her home for the winter. By some miracle, no one had been severely injured in the fire, and Landévennec's usual occupants were scattered throughout the property, bunking with tenants that had room to spare.

A flash of the rage that simmered in her gut flared to life as she remembered everyone's terror on the day of the fire. It had been set deliberately, by a group of wild, angry, men and boys from the neighboring town. People who didn't know Ava and Gabriel and had no idea what wonderful landlords they were compared to most. The injustice of it, and the number of lives it affected, other than le Vicomte et la Vicomtesse infuriated her to no end.

Still, she would take this small miracle, this bounty of food to carry them all through the coming winter, as the balm it was. At least no one would starve. The entire surgery, all the tools, medicines, and herbs there, whatever had survived the Navy's visit, and what they had hustled to make and store since— it was all gone. She had a small quantity of tinctures and salves at her house, but it wasn't nearly enough. It was something she would have to focus on in the coming month before the snow set in and made travel hazardous.

A visit to the apothecary in town had moved to the top of her list of things to do. She'd sent a letter to Ava and Gabriel in Paris, hoping they would be able to purchase certain items while there. But, without knowing when they planned to leave, there was no telling if they would receive it. She heaved a crate of apples and passed it down the line, bending and reaching for the next one automatically, as she began to create a mental list for the apothecary.

Gabriel's footsteps echoed eerily as he hurried through the twists and turns of the limestone tunnel. His breath came in short, tortured pants and he swore his heart was going to beat out of his chest. His lantern spilled precious little light, the walls seemingly closing in on him. He cast a wary eye at the disorganized piles of bones, barely managing to push his superstitious fear of the dead aside. His terror for Ava was the only thing that kept him going.

How much time had elapsed since he'd arrived home to find the entire household frantic? How long before that had Ava been snatched off the street in broad daylight? Noemi had been hysterical, barely managing to get the story out in a coherent manner. In the end, he'd convinced her to show him where she'd disappeared from. They'd been walking out the door when a note had arrived for Gabriel, delivered by a young lad who was unable to give any identifying information about where the missive had originated from.

On a dirty scrap of paper in a barely legible scrawl, there'd been a taunting message.

You'll find your whore in the ossuary.

It was a gamble, but it was Gabriel's best guess. If he were wrong, he'd be wasting precious time. He'd dashed a message off to Phillipe, asked Le Gall to follow him with the carriage, and arming himself with a lantern and his pistol, rode Automne as fast as he dared through the crowded streets toward the outskirts of the city. He'd arrived at the [1] *Barrière d'Enfer* in a cold sweat, tied Automne to a nearby tree, crossed himself, and entered the old quarry.

Gabriel had heard that Paris' cemeteries were being emptied, but only in the most abstract sort of way. For years there'd been stories of basement walls collapsing around the city's cemeteries and even of entire buildings built above the vast network of old quarries caving in. This, combined with the appallingly unsanitary conditions where the main market at *Les Halles* abutted Paris's largest cemetery *les Innocents*, had finally precipitated the current solution. For the last two years they'd been exhuming and transferring bodies into the old limestone tunnels.

Now he found himself navigating the damp, dark labyrinth, his gut a writhing mess of snakes.

---

1. Barrière d'Enfer: Literally, the Gate of Hell, was a pair of tollhouses that served as a gate in the old city walls. The tollhouses, which still exist, were designed to collect taxes on goods entering Paris, and are located near the entrance of the catacombs.

"*S'il vous plaît à Dieu. S'il vous plaît à Dieu.*" He chanted under his breath, the sound of his own voice strangely calming.

He came to a fork in the tunnels and paused, lifting his lantern to illuminate first one and then the other. Had he already been at this juncture? The pile of skeletons to his right looked familiar. Was he going in circles? He felt hopelessly lost, churning acid rising and threatening to choke him. He looked down each tunnel again, hoping something would decide for him. Every second he hesitated, his sense of despair mounted.

"*Au diable,*" he swore, as he turned left.

He moved swiftly down the tunnel as the floor sloped away from him. As he traveled deeper underground, the cold and damp penetrated his clothes, leaving him chilled to the bone. Gabriel slogged through puddles of standing water— the tunnels were prone to flooding— trying to ignore the shuffling, scurrying sounds that echoed throughout the catacombs. He disliked rats under the best circumstances. The idea of Ava being trapped down here made the hairs on his arms and neck prickle with unease.

A different sound reverberated through the stone corridors, and he halted. Were those footsteps? He cocked his head and held his breath, waiting. After a moment, he heard it again. Warily, he tightened his hold on his dagger and lantern and advanced cautiously, trying to step soundlessly. *Le bon Dieu* only knew who might be lurking around the next corner. Each breath was a quiet exhalation. His heart pounded so hard he felt sure someone else would hear it.

Ahead, there was an opening to his left and he sidled up to it, his back against the dank wall. There was someone on the other side, he could hear a strange, uneven, shuffling step and labored breathing. He took a deep breath, carefully lowered his lantern to the ground and stepped rapidly into the rough opening, his dagger poised to strike.

A muffled scream greeted him, and Ava fell forward into him in a faint. He barely managed to catch her, staggering under her unexpected dead weight. The metallic smell of blood clung to her, along with the sour aroma of spoilt milk. His stomach turned at the combination, but he sheathed his dagger after completing a quick scan of the room.

Gabriel shifted intending to pick Ava up, but she came to suddenly, screaming like a feral, cornered animal, her hands outstretched like claws. Intuitively he held her tightly.

"Shh, *mon cœur*. You're all right. I've got you."

Her struggles died down and her screeches turned into shuddering sobs as he held her. Eventually, she lifted her face to his. As the light of the lantern fell on it, he recoiled. The right side of her face was swollen, cut, and bruised monstrously. Only her left eye remained open. The rest of her face was covered in blood. It was in her hair and appeared to cover most of her body.

The breath left his lungs. "*Je jure devant Dieu que celui qui vous a fait cela est mort.*"

She hiccoughed and smiled grotesquely. "He's already dead."

"Who?" he managed, through the knot engulfing his chest.

"Cifarelli," she managed. "I'm so. . . dizzy." Her lashes fluttered and she slumped in his arms again.

He grunted and scooped her up properly in his arms. Determined to ascertain that Cifarelli had been disposed of, he knelt to grab his lantern and walked through the opening Ava had come out of. The tunnel system here opened into a large cavern; his light didn't penetrate the darkest corners of the cave. The area was largely empty, though there was an overturned chair, several lengths of rope, a crude bed and the prone body of a man.

The contents of the room made his stomach tighten. Blood pumped through his veins as hot and thick as lava. Not one to leave anything to chance, he carried Ava to the body and looked dispassionately down at the ruined face. Urine and blood were puddled around the body, and there was the metallic gleam of a sharp, bloody knife in his right hand. With the toe of his boot, he nudged the dead man. Satisfied, he walked away. It didn't matter if they found the body soon, or years from now.

Forty-Two
Resurrection

I wandered the damp tunnels of the catacombs, piles of skeletons lining the walls and filling the dark cavities. The light of my lantern illuminated rows of skulls, arranged atop one another, grinning hideously back at me. My wrists burned; the skin worn raw from the hemp rope with which I'd been restrained. Dizzy and disoriented, I stopped and turned in a slow circle, my lantern spilling light around me. Had I come this way before?

I'd been searching for a way out for hours and I was beginning to think I was caught in a labyrinth. Fear coated my mouth, the taste coppery, and tiptoed up my spine. Every minute sound, the scurrying feet of mice, the echoes of my shuffling, stumbling steps; it all stirred up the acerbic, liquid sloshing within me, threatening to come barreling up from the depths of my stomach any minute. My breathing was loud and harsh in the stone confines of this maze.

A sound behind me. I knew I wasn't imagining it. My scalp tightened and I turned to face my attacker.

I came to with a scream upon my lips. My eyes opened and I gritted my teeth. Every inch of my body wept in agony. It took all my strength not to cry out loud. A whimper escaped. Immediately, I felt the bed dip behind me as Gabriel came awake and shifted closer. His arm wrapped around me, and I had to fight myself not to stiffen in his embrace.

"*Mon cœur*. I'm here. You're safe," he whispered. His breath stirred my hair, tickling my nape.

I lay on my left side. It was painful, but I knew it would feel like I was on the surface of the sun if I turned. Incrementally, my body relaxed, recognizing the safety of Gabriel's arms even though my mind was in fight or flight mode. Realistically, I didn't think I could accomplish either option anyway. My breath shuddered out while I fixed my one-eyed gaze on the flickering, yellow light of the lit taper beside the bed.

"Is there anything I can do to help the pain?"

In Gabriel's voice I could hear the intense need to do something constructive. His helplessness in the face of my injuries was eating him alive. Love for him swamped me, temporarily obliterating the overwhelming torment.

"I don't know. The laudanum gives me nightmares. Could you put some of the lavender salve on my wrists and ankles? It helps reduce the burning."

He fairly sprang out of bed in his eagerness. I bit my lip to hold back the whimper as it jostled me violently. He must have noticed my reaction, because he winced.

"I'm sorry," he said gruffly. "I'm an idiot." He shot me a crooked smile.

"It's all right," I murmured.

He brought the candle closer and carefully pulled the blanket away. Gentle fingers applied the salve to my rope burnt skin as lightly as the brush of a butterfly's wings.

"Anything else?" he asked, settling the coverlet back over me.

"Just stay with me," I whispered through cracked, swollen lips. "Waking up without you is terrifying."

"Always, *mon cœur*. I wish I could resurrect that *fils de pute* just so I could kill him again."

Something resembling a half-strangled laugh bubbled out of me.

With a rueful smile, Gabriel tenderly brushed my hair away from my swollen, bruised face. "I'm serious, aye?"

"I know you are."

He replaced the candle and salve and climbed back into bed behind me, carefully this time. His hand rested lightly on my hip, and I felt his lips move in my hair.

"Sleep *mon amour*."

Gabriel reclined comfortably on the settee, Ava's hand firmly in his. She sat with her spine ramrod straight, even though he knew she was still hurting. The knife wound in her ribs was slow to heal, and though the bruises had faded, there were still hints of green and yellow around her eye and temple.

She had headaches nearly every day, and he felt her awaken with nightmares every night.

Still, here she sat. More concerned about someone else, than herself. His heart felt like it was being squeezed every time he remembered the state he found her in, and he gently squeezed her hand. He knew she was more nervous about this conversation with Jeanne than she let on.

Jeanne sat in the chair across from them, her infant snug in her arms. Motherhood had lent a glow to the girl, making her pretty in a bland sort of way.

"I'm glad you're looking so much better, Madame," she offered, in a soft voice. "I hope you're feeling well?"

"Thank you, Jeanne. I'm feeling much improved," replied Ava. She cut her soft, green eyes at Gabriel, silently begging him to begin the conversation.

"We asked you here today, because we've decided it's time for us to go back to Landévennec." Gabriel paused and cleared his throat, watching the girl's reaction.

She seemed nonplussed.

"We've heard from Amélie. Corbin seems to believe you are still alive, Jeanne," added Ava softly.

Doe brown eyes widened at this news, but she still didn't say a word.

"We are worried about your safety," said Gabriel simply. "It's a possibility that he will come looking for you at Landévennec. We thought you would be safer here in Paris, and you're welcome to stay here if you wish, or you can come back to *Bretagne* with us if you prefer."

After a long pregnant silence, Jeanne spoke. "I would prefer to stay with you and Madame, if that's all right."

Beside him, Ava tensed. "Of course it's all right. We've given it a lot of thought and wanted to propose an idea we had to you."

Jeanne looked back at them both blankly.

"I'm sure you know that Ava has been learning knife skills these past months," he began.

Jeanne nodded quietly, fine blonde hairs escaping from her kerchief. With the light streaming in through the window behind her, she almost looked like she had a halo.

"I believe those skills saved my life last week," asserted Ava.

"There's no doubt in my mind," he added. The thought of what would have happened to Ava if he hadn't given her the dagger kept him up at night.

"We thought you might like to learn as well. Another line of defense," offered Ava.

Jeanne looked like she'd been hit over the head with the blunt end of an ax. "Oh no! I couldn't possibly."

"Why not?" asked Ava bluntly.

"I. . . Well, I don't know the first thing about weapons, and it's just not a very lady like thing— no offense to you, Madame," she added hastily. "It's only I can't imagine myself ever doing such a thing." She bit her lip.

"Even if it saves your life? Or little Margaux's life?" Ava looked surprised at her refusal.

Jeanne shook her head. "I'm sure there won't be any need for such drastic measures. He would never go to Landévennec."

"I don't believe he's in his right mind," warned Gabriel. He was perplexed at her disconnection from reality.

"I'm quite certain we will be fine," she insisted, an earnest expression on her face.

"All right then. We hope to leave in a week."

"I'll be ready," she promised. "It will be nice to get away from the stink of the city and get back to the country."

"That's something I think we can all agree on."

The journey back to Landévennec, though welcome, was tedious, uncomfortable and slow. For the most part, the weather was sunny and relatively warm during the days, provided one had sufficient layers, but as soon as the sun dropped behind the verdant hills, a chill penetrated my clothes, enveloping my heart in a fist of ice.

We traveled back to *Bretagne* the way we came, though a great deal wearier. The last six months had taken a tremendous toll on our hopes for the future. On our way to Versailles, we'd been hale and hearty, excited at the prospect of shaping the early events of the revolution and filled with lofty aspirations. We returned injured both in body and spirit. We had the joy of another healthy baby in Jeanne's sweet Margaux, though I was filled with trepidation at her refusal to learn self-defense.

We left Seznec buried beneath a lonely willow, leagues from his home, his wife, and his newborn son. I knew his loss still weighed heavily on Gabriel's shoulders, though he rarely spoke of it. My body was still unhealed from my brush with Cifarelli, but I made it a point to spend time each morning and evening in the various *auberges* we stopped at, stretching and practicing my lunges. I never went anywhere without my dagger strapped to my thigh. Though the bruises were gone, and most of my cuts had healed, I found myself skittish and quick to startle. Nightmares haunted my sleep, a mingled mess of Cifarelli, Carri, the shipwreck and my parents. If it weren't for Gabriel's steady, comforting presence, I doubted I would get any rest at all.

The valet Gabriel had acquired in Versailles, Monsieur Hamon, had permanently joined our entourage, taking Seznec's place as outrider. I knew Gabriel was relieved to have another healthy man along, though he didn't verbalize it. His gray gaze constantly searched the hills, valleys and forests we traveled through for signs of danger. Although we all dressed in our plainest attire, and proudly displayed our revolutionary cockades, there was no disguising our wealth. As our carriage rumbled past the burnt, looted homes of the affluent in every town we passed through, I sensed Gabriel's growing hyperawareness of the precariousness of our situation.

For my part, I just wanted the whole miserable trip to be over. Although winter was edging ever closer, and I dreaded the long nights and bitter temperatures, I couldn't wait to see the proud, limestone chateau, buttery in the bright sunlight. When I closed my eyes, I could nearly smell the sharp mingled aroma of pine resin and sea salt. I would hug Esme and tell her how much I had missed her, and I would do everything I could to nurture sweet Isabelle.

The carriage slowed to a stop, interrupting my thoughts, and I peeked out the window. Gabriel dismounted Automne, and holding the reins firmly in one hand, he approached. With my hand on the latch, I opened the door and stepped out, taking Gabriel's hand gratefully. After hours in the carriage, my muscles had tightened and stiffened. Today the sky was a moody gray that matched Gabriel's stormy eyes. The low-hanging clouds made the hill we had stopped on feel strangely claustrophobic.

I slowly scanned the horizon. There was a small town we'd already passed through to our north, and a patch of woodland to our west. The summit of the hill and the approach was clear in every direction, making it easy to spot anyone in the vicinity. Instinctively I knew Gabriel had chosen this spot deliberately.

With a firm grip on my elbow, he guided me away from the carriage. "I thought you might want to stretch your legs a bit. We can have lunch here before we continue."

"I think everyone has had enough of being cooped up in the carriage. Armand is ready to terrorize this hill."

A smile touched his eyes at my mention of Armand. He had turned one during our voyage back home and had begun to walk two weeks ago. His eagerness to explore and wriggle away from the adults was constant and exhausting. Keeping him entertained during the long journey had been wearisome to say the least. The only times he wasn't actively attempting to escape the confines of the carriage were when he was napping or eating. He was most content when Gabriel took him up in front of him on Automne and he could babble excitedly about everything he saw through the passing countryside.

"We're getting closer. I reckon we should arrive home the afternoon after tomorrow."

I turned and stepped into his ready embrace, pressing my cheek against the warmth of his cloak. "I can't wait."

"Me either," he answered huskily.

I tightened my arms around him. "I won't break, you know."

"I don't want to hurt you."

Since I'd been kidnapped by Cifarelli, Gabriel had treated me like spun glass. As endearing as it was, I needed to feel his strength when he held me. My head tilted back, taking in his chiseled jaw, the sharp lines of his cheekbones, and the ever-present pain in his eyes. This year had taken its toll on us in so many ways. He looked as haunted as I felt.

I looped my arms around his neck, tangling my fingers in his windblown hair and coaxed his mouth down to mine. Against my lips, I felt his lift in a smile.

"Kiss me," I demanded, feeling his breath fan against me.

"In front of all these bystanders?" he asked in mock astonishment. "For shame, Madame Chabot!"

"It's nothing they haven't seen before," I whispered against his mouth, hoping I was tantalizing him.

His arms tightened around my waist, lifting me against him, and his lips closed the distance between us. Finally. The world tilted beneath my feet and then righted. When he stepped away, the shadows had lifted from his mercurial eyes.

"We'll have to finish this later," he growled against my ear.

Freshly fallen leaves crunched underfoot as we broke through the trees that skirted the property. The aroma of earth and leaf mold was overlaid with the faint scent of salt marsh. The air that caressed my skin was crisp and though the sun hung low in the azure sky, I felt confident we would arrive at Landévennec with the light.

I hugged Gabriel around the middle and kissed his back spontaneously. The wool of his cloak tickled my nose. I could hear the smile in his voice when he spoke.

"What are you looking forward to the most?"

"Everything!" I laughed.

"Tell me one thing," he urged, his hands light on Automne's reins, as he guided us through the meadow of heather and gorse.

"Being back in our bed," I whispered intimately.

He turned slightly in the saddle and dropped a kiss on my head. "Mmm. Me too."

"What else?" I asked excitedly. Now that we were close, I could hardly wait.

"Seeing everyone, I suppose. Seeing for myself how the harvest has come in. Smelling the salt and pine and walking down to the beach to watch the waves crash ashore. I haven't seen the ocean in too long."

Tears pricked my eyes. His love for his home was palpable in his wistful voice. I knew, without seeing his face, that his silver eyes were alight with emotion.

"All of that," I managed, trying not to give the lump in my throat away.

One of his warm hands covered mine and he squeezed comfortingly. "Don't cry, *mon cœur*. We are almost there."

We rode through a small copse of trees, the carriage and riders rumbling and trotting behind us, an excited buzz at our proximity discernable in the air. Automne strained at his bridle, sensing where we were and eager to return.

With a laugh, Gabriel turned his face toward me. "Hold on!"

My arms tightened around his waist, and I leaned forward against him as he gave Automne his head, letting the horse fly up the hill toward the château. Too soon, Gabriel pulled back, forcing Automne to slow before we'd crested the summit. I peeked over his shoulder, expecting to see a tenant he'd halted to greet, and my mouth went dry. In a terrible kind of silence, we slowly trotted toward Landévennec's ruined entrance and came to a halt.

In a trance, eyes blurry with tears, I slowly dismounted Automne and walked toward the wide, stone steps. Most of the stone structure stood amidst charred beams, the creamy limestone blackened with soot. The grand entrance gaped open, the handsome carved doors gone, the inner walls, floors, and roof— all built of wood— burnt to cinders. Some of the chimneys were still in place, but several had crumbled into towering piles of stone.

Shocked, I turned to face Gabriel as he came to stand beside me beneath the lintel. My hand groped for his, gripping tightly when I found it. His eyes reflected shock, sadness, and a grim determination. Behind us, I could hear the arrival of the carriage, and other riders, but neither of us turned to face them.

"I was naive to believe that we were well liked here," murmured Gabriel wearily, his fingers sadly brushing over the sooty, limestone.

"You are well liked," I said fiercely, furious at the resignation in his voice. "Ask around, all your tenants feel you're far fairer than most landlords."

"Then why all this?" He waved his hand at the destruction around us.

"These weren't your tenants, Gabriel. These were revolutionaries who don't know you and saw an opportunity to loot and burn." Fury twisted in my gut.

He looked at me, eyes the color of the ash surrounding us, as everyone formed a semi-circle behind us. They murmured, creating a low hum in the background, but they didn't inch closer, respecting our grief as we stood on the threshold of the wreckage of our home.

Gabriel reached up, stretching on his toes to reach the lintel over the entrance. He brushed the soot away, revealing the date carved in the stone. His index finger shook as he traced the date his family had built the château in the ash.

"The year of our Lord, fifteen forty-two," he breathed. "We will rebuild."

Forty-Three
The Song of the Sea

Esme briskly led the way from her house to the remains of the château. Ava and Jeanne, with baby Margaux wrapped snuggly against her chest, and Isabelle and Eloise, arm in arm, whispering amongst themselves, followed at a more sedate pace. The trees had shed most of their leaves; only a few stubborn, crinkly gold and withered brown ones remained. They rustled and crunched beneath her feet. This time of year, always filled her with a wistful yearning and nostalgia, though she couldn't pinpoint why. Perhaps it was the shorter days, the knowledge that winter with all its hardships was on its way. This year especially.

She'd been thrilled to fill all the unused rooms in her and Luc's house. Ava and Gabriel in one room, Madame Devereux and Armand in the next, Jeanne and her sweet babe Margaux in one attic room, and Gabriel's valet Monsieur Hamon in the other. The house felt full of bustling life, and she cherished every moment she got to share with Ava— and took every opportunity to cuddle the babies, though Armand was less enthused with the idea of being held and coddled then he'd been just six months ago. It hurt her heart to think of the time she'd missed with him. He hadn't even recognized her when they returned; but she'd gone out of her way to get reacquainted with him in the week since, and just this morning he'd raised his chubby arms to her.

Ava had arrived with a veritable bounty of herbs, spices, oils and salves from Paris— bless her heart. They were still frighteningly short on several important ointments and medicines, but they were in a far better position now. With all the girls pitching in and concentrating on their stores, they had a chance at rectifying the situation before the roads became impassable.

For today, their mission was simple— feed the men, who had gathered at the blackened shell of the château. They'd been at it since early the morning after they arrived at Landévennec, gathering the soot and ash covered stones from the various collapsed chimneys, clearing away the rubble, picking through what was salvageable, and making plans to rebuild. It was hard, back-breaking work. Luc had nearly fallen asleep at the supper table the previous evening.

The women had focused on organizing their food stores and preserving, and each afternoon, they brought lunch to the men. They were always grateful to see them, and Esme loved the break she shared with Luc in the middle of the day. It was a nice excuse to escape the house and enjoy the sunshine while it lasted.

As they began their final ascent toward the château, Ava caught up to Esme and bumped her shoulder against hers companionably.

"I don't think I've properly thanked you for taking us all in. You must be going mad with so many extra bodies in your house."

Esme cut her eyes at Ava. Her cheeks were flushed with exertion and her green eyes were bright.

"I love it," she admitted. "The house can feel a bit empty when it's just Luc and I. You know I've always wanted a home full of kids." She smiled self-consciously. "This kind of achieves the same end."

"You must miss the solitude, though? It's so loud." Ava laughed nervously.

"Not yet. Maybe after being stuck in the house all winter with all of you I'll feel differently," she said flippantly. In her gut, she knew she wouldn't though.

As they approached the château, she snuck a glance at Ava, who'd gone quiet. The bright laughter had left her face, leaving behind a pensive sadness. Ava glanced back at her.

"This year hasn't been what I expected," she said softly.

"Life is never what we expect," pointed out Esme. But she felt a pang of sympathy for her friend. Life hadn't gone the way Esme envisioned it either.

"Gabriel. . . He never lets on how upset he is. I know he's not dealing with it well, but I don't know how to help him." She bit her bottom lip.

Esme sighed. "It's something to do with being male. Their heads are as hard as those burnt stones there." She gestured up the hill at the piles that had been cleared away. "I'll never understand it."

"I don't either," she mumbled.

"You just have to chip away at them. Usually in bed," she offered with a smirk.

Ava laughed, a pretty blush staining her cheeks.

"Anyway, put a smile on that gorgeous face. Here come the men."

My hand tucked snuggly on Gabriel's arm, we picked our way down the cliffs to the roaring ocean below. The cerulean sky was peppered with horse tails; long wisps of gossamer white, chasing each other across the sun, promising a change in the weather. The wind kicked up the surf, white caps riding the choppy tips of each wave, and blowing a fine layer of sand over the beach.

I leaned my head against Gabriel's shoulder as I thought about the sermon during the morning mass. We had so much to be grateful for. Each other and Armand at the top of the list, followed by an army of loyal friends and tenants. Gabriel led me to an outcropping in the cliff face that sheltered us from the blustery wind and sat, beckoning me to sit beside him.

With his arm wrapped around me, we stared at the boiling sea. I closed my eyes and breathed deeply, inhaling the salty mist from the waves that crashed ashore. As sad as the ocean sometimes made me— I rarely gazed upon it without being reminded of Carri— it also cleansed my spirit in a way nothing else seemed to accomplish. The rhythm of the tides was as steady as a heartbeat, the sound that drowned out your inner voice, forcing you to let go of the things you couldn't control.

I opened my eyes and peeped at Gabriel. His shoulders looked more relaxed than I'd seen in months. His gray eyes, so often filled with storm clouds of late, studied the ocean. When they met mine, they were clear as a silver pool. He pressed his lips to my hair and inhaled.

"Have I told you how much I love the smell of you?" he asked huskily.

I giggled. "That's such an odd thing to say."

The corners of his mouth tilted up. "Aye," he acknowledged. "But it's true nonetheless."

I lifted my lips to his, intending a quick kiss, but the moment spun out as his lips fused to mine and his arms tightened around me. My body melted against his. God, I had missed this raw, honest emotion these last months. A whimper escaped as he dragged his lips and teeth down my throat to the edge of my cloak.

"Gabriel," I murmured, as he pressed me back into the soft sand, kissed his way up my neck, along my jaw, and found my mouth again.

The blood sang in my veins as I fisted one hand in his hair and settled the other on his hip, pulling him against me. I was filled with a primal need as the song of the sea filled my ears, obliterating everything but the heat that pumped off his body and the feel of his skin against mine. My hand fumbled with the laces of his breeches, need making me clumsy.

His fingers trailed up my stockings slowly, pausing to caress the tender skin at the top tantalizingly. Goosebumps rippled across my body and heat shot through me, pooling low in my belly. I arched my hips up, silently begging for more as he rucked my gown out of the way. His charcoal eyes were dark and intense on mine as he watched my reaction, his fingers inching ever higher.

His touch was light as a feather, driving me to the brink and his teeth grazed my lower lip making heat coil and spiral lazily within me. Dizzily, I closed my eyes and gave myself to him, digging my fingers into his hips in desperation and rising to meet him as he sank into me.

Warmth spread throughout me, rising to a fever pitch as his tempo increased. Every nerve in my body tingled as I reached my crescendo. His groan mingled with my cry as he collapsed above me.

Spent, we lay pleasantly tangled together, his flesh damp and warm against mine, cocooned in our cloaks. I closed my eyes, tracing little spirals and patterns on his chest as I listened to the muffled thump of his heart.

"When will we visit Amélie?" I asked.

We had decided not to travel out of our way to Trégoudan as we'd initially planned. The anticipation of going home again had been too strong. Of course, we hadn't imagined what awaited us at Landévennec, or we might have traveled on. It was now the beginning of the second week of November, and we would have to make the trek soon. His hand traveled up and down my back soothingly.

"I was thinking about that earlier." His chest rumbled beneath my ear. "I'm torn. I would like to have at least another week to work on clearing the rubble away and to mark some of the trees I want felled for timber. But, I can't help but think how unfair it would be to Amélie to wait any longer." His hand trailed up into my hair.

"Waiting months for word of your safety would be excruciating," I said honestly.

"Twould be the same for me. I cannot stand being apart from you, *mon cœur*."

"It will take at least a couple days to prepare for travel," I pointed out reasonably. "Instead of focusing on the rubble, why don't you take the next two days to mark out the trees you want, and to give instructions? You know you can rely on Luc to follow them to the letter."

"Aye," he agreed reluctantly. "So, we'll leave Wednesday?"

"And we'll travel as light as we can. We won't stay long."

Gabriel frowned, his stomach tight with foreboding, and picked up the latest letter from Phillipe. His eyes flicked over the parchment as he reread it a second time.

16th December, 1789

Monsieur Gabriel Chabot
Le Vicomte de Landévennec
Château de Landévennec

My dear Gabriel,

I hope this letter finds you and your family well. You'll be relieved (I hope) to hear that I have retired to my château at Saint Denis for the upcoming season. The situation in Paris has become untenable. Since our king and queen have been forced out of Versailles and into les Tuileries, tempers have been at a fever pitch. Sadly, la Reine seems indisposed to changing her alliances or allegiance. The common folk are furious, and now that winter is once again upon us, it is only a matter of time before things come to a head. It has made being an aristocrat rather uncomfortable as one never knows when someone will take afront to your presence.

Charlotte has become a force unto herself over this last year, and it has become a source of concern for me. Rest assured, my friend, it's nothing so sordid as a lack of morals (I can visualize you with an eyebrow cocked, shaking your head as you read this). Instead, she has taken to verbalizing her thoughts and feelings regarding the state of our belle France. Loudly.

As you might imagine, her political opinions are not of the popular variety, and she has found herself in a spot of trouble on more than one occasion in our current incendiary environment. I am utterly flummoxed by her behavior, as she has never shown an interest in politics before, but alas, since I seem unable to stop her from making proclamations she shouldn't, I have decided that my presence in Saint-Denis is necessary. I was making little headway with Louis anyway, so I do not imagine I will be missed from the court. All things being equal, perhaps it's for the best if there's a bit of distance perceived between myself and the royals.

I was greatly saddened to receive the news about the calamity that has befallen Landévennec, though I am certain that you will build her back to stand proudly and beautifully on those blasted cliffs you call home. I hope to see you soon my friend. Give your lovely Ava a kiss from me. God keep you until we meet again.

Yours,
Phillipe Girard
Le Comte de Saint-Denis

Gabriel put the letter down and rubbed his forehead tiredly. Charlotte had long been a source of frustration for Phillipe, though he loved his sister dearly and would never castigate her for making his life difficult. His friend was downplaying the situation, he was certain. He would only abandon his efforts with Louis if he felt that his sister was in danger and in need of his protection. While he did not doubt that the situation in Paris was precarious, Gabriel knew that Phillipe had no real concern for himself.

He sighed deeply. There was nothing he could do, least of all from here. He would find a way to cheerfully write him back later, but he couldn't summon the energy for it at the moment. He folded the letter and placed it on top of the pile that required his response. His stomach rumbled as he caught a whiff of the stew Luc's housekeeper was preparing. His mouth watering, he pushed away from the desk and stood, stretching his back. Perhaps after supper he would reply to Phillipe. He would talk it over with Ava. She generally found a way to cast a positive light on the things that worried him.

Forty-Four
Tryst

I handed the glass jars I'd cleaned and sterilized to Esme as she lined them up on one end of the wooden work surface in rows as strict as an army sergeant. The warmth of the roaring fire and the bubbling cauldron was suffocating, even with the bitter temperatures outside, and I lifted the back of my hand to my forehead, wiping away the beads of perspiration. Tendrils of hair had escaped my pins and stuck to my damp neck, further irritating me.

I wandered away to the window and pressed my hot cheek to the freezing glass as I watched the snow gently drift down, covering everything in a downy blanket. It had snowed consistently since before Christmas, and the world outside Esme and Luc's house lay deep beneath drifts taller than me. I had only left the house once a week for the last three weeks to make the freezing trek to the chapel for mass.

The men went out every day, regardless of the weather. There were animals to tend to, firewood to bring in, and tenants to check on. Whenever Gabriel had spare time, he generally snuck off to the barn, a portion of which he'd dedicated to woodworking where he was slowly and painstakingly carving furniture. So far, he'd proudly showed off a beautifully carved table, sans chairs, and a small bed frame for Armand. His next project, he'd informed me with a glint in his eyes, was a bed for us.

"Will you help me with this?" asked Esme as she stirred almond oil into the melted beeswax. She nodded her head toward the metal bowl. "That one there is ready to pour."

I pulled myself away from the window, slipped my hands in the protective mitts and picked up the bowl. The hot liquid poured easily into the waiting jars where it began to form a skin and harden almost immediately. I set the bowl back down and went to work scraping the cooled salve off the inner edges. Every little bit counted, especially since we were low on supplies this winter.

Esme blew her hair away from her forehead and I glanced at her. She was flushed from the heat and her blue eyes looked glassy.

"Why don't you let me finish that? Stand by the window for a moment and cool off. It's so hot in here."

She shot me a grateful look and dropped her mitts onto the counter.

"The two of you have no idea what it's like to be working here all the time," muttered Madame Allard. "And now I'm sharing my space with your lot, constantly underfoot you are."

My eyes widened and I ducked my head, concentrating on counting drops of oil as they went into the mixture to hide my expression. Madame Allard had always been lovely, but since the château had burned, her kitchen had been taken over as partial surgery, and it was beginning to wear on her. I couldn't imagine how much worse it would become as the months dragged by.

"We're so grateful to you, Madame. I know it hasn't been easy. You've become responsible for feeding four times as many people overnight, your work and living space has become cramped—"

"You don't know the half of it, Madame," she interrupted.

Esme raised her eyebrows and shot me an apologetic look from the window.

"Madame Allard," she said firmly. "Madame la Vicomtesse is our guest. I know being cooped up in here with us all day is wearisome, but we are all in the same position. I assure you, Ava would far prefer to be in her comfortable château than here, if she had the option."

Madame Allard's lips thinned as she pressed them together and she turned away, busying herself with removing a loaf of bread from the oven cut into the side of the hearth.

Determined to resist the urge to argue, I was feeling prickly, dammit—I focused on adding the final ingredients to the bowl that was suspended over the small brazier. With slow, smooth strokes, I thoroughly mixed the balm, carefully scraping the sides to ensure even mixing.

Esme returned from the window, and I gave her a measured look. Her color was less hectic, and her eyes were more focused, but she still looked overtired.

"Why don't you go rest? I'm almost done in here and I think that's it for today," I offered, trying to ignore the sweat trickling down my spine.

I desperately wanted a proper bath after this, but Madame Allard would have a conniption if I asked her to boil kettles of water now. I could almost imagine the way her eyes would bug out and I tamped down the rising burble of laughter. Regretfully, I would have to settle for a quick sponge bath at the washstand.

Esme hesitated. "Are you sure? I don't mind staying."

"Go!" I said with a laugh. "I'm about to pour this and then it's just cleaning up."

"All right." Impulsively she hugged me. "Thank you. I don't know why I feel so tired today."

"It happens to everyone," I soothed.

The mixture was ready, and I poured it into the waiting jars as she left the kitchen. I shot an assessing glance at the housekeeper, but decided I didn't want to poke the bear any further. Humming '*Imagine*' to myself, I began to screw on the lids to the salve that had already hardened.

"What's that you're always humming?" she demanded testily. "I've never heard that song before."

Startled, I looked at her guiltily. Of course you haven't heard it. It's not been written yet; I wanted to scream. Instead, I bit my tongue.

"You haven't? My mother used to sing it to me when I was a child. It must be from the south."

I offered her a pert smile and quickly finished closing the jars. Next, I extinguished the flame on the brazier and cleaned out the bowls we'd used. Finally, I stacked everything neatly on the end of the counter.

"Well, I suppose I will see you later. Supper smells delicious," I added appreciatively.

"You're leaving that mess there?" she asked testily, waving her hand at our supplies.

I raised an eyebrow at her. "Where do you propose I put it?"

Seeming to realize she'd pushed me too far, she turned crimson up to her hairline. "I suppose where you left it is fine."

"Thanks," I said, and left the kitchen without a backwards glance.

Gabriel walked with his head down against the bitter wind. Winter had set in early and cruelly this year, storms rolling in off the ocean from the north every few days, bringing heavy snow and freezing temperatures. The gusts that whipped across the cliffs had been incessant for weeks. It whistled constantly around the eaves, rattling and banging loose shutters, and ripping vulnerable branches and roof shingles, turning them into projectiles that threatened people and livestock.

Quarters were cramped in Luc and Esme's house, though there was no point in complaining. At least they had a roof over their heads. Come spring, they would begin working on restoring the château. He hoped fervently that they could enclose a portion of it before the next winter arrived. Tempers had begun to fray since the weather had forced everyone indoors, prompting his solitary walk to the chapel. He desperately needed a little time alone with the Lord.

Someone else must have had the same thought, he mused. A set of footprints— no, two— led the way past the stone shell of the château toward the cliffs and the chapel. He followed along, idly inspecting the evidence and making up stories in his head about who he might encounter. One set was obviously larger than the other, was it a couple? A tryst perhaps? He smiled at the romantic bent of his thoughts and shook his head at himself. What had Ava done to him?

The wind carried a shrill scream, making his head snap up, like a wolf scenting danger. He froze where he stood, trying to locate the sound as the air rushed across the land, buffeting him about. Slowly, alert to possible danger, he turned in a circle, scanning his surroundings for a clue. Nothing. There was no one else out there. Incrementally, his shoulders relaxed. Mayhap the sound hadn't been human. The wind was capable of creating terrifying sounds when it had a mind to.

Gabriel began walking again, setting his gaze on the chapel that stood like a beacon in a sea of glittering white. A movement caught his eye, near or perhaps in the small graveyard to the left. He squinted, his eyes watering from the cold, and began to move more purposefully, burying his hands deep in his pockets and hunching his shoulders against the cruel wind. He followed the footprints around the left side of the chapel, curiosity forcing him to continue past the arched doors, when all he wanted to do was get out of the wind.

He spotted two dark figures behind the church, standing perilously close to the cliffs. They were too deep in their argument to notice his approach, a gust snatching the words they were heatedly exchanging away. It was definitely a couple. The man grabbed the woman roughly, his hands wrapping around her neck, making the hood of her cloak fall away to reveal her terrified face. The blood in Gabriel's veins froze. His hand automatically went to the dagger at his waist, his fingers curling around the hilt as he unsheathed it in one smooth motion. He crept forward, the immense snow drifts and buffeting gale muffling his advance.

Just as he was within reach, her brown gaze slid over the man's shoulder, recognition and a wild kind of hope in her eyes as she noticed Gabriel. Her assailant must have sensed his presence a moment before Gabriel reached them, because he shoved her hard over the cliff as he whirled to face Gabriel. The suddenness of his action startled Gabriel, who reached out a desperate hand, knowing he was too far away, and seconds too late. Her mouth opened in a soundless scream as she fell onto the rocks far below. Gabriel reacted with feral rage, thrusting the dagger hidden beneath his flapping coat hard into the larger man's belly. There was such force in the blow that the other man stumbled backward, losing his footing on the slippery, snow-covered rocks, and fell over the edge after his wife.

Gabriel backed away from the precipice, nausea rolling up from his gut like a wild animal, clawing up from the bowels of his stomach to get free. He doubled over, panting in disbelief. The entire altercation had lasted mere seconds. Two lives lost in the time it took to blink.

Forty-Five
Comeuppance

I stood and stared down at the pale, young face laid on the table before me. Her light, blonde hair, neatly brushed back, warm, brown eyes closed peacefully, forever. No blemishes marred the smooth skin. To look at her, you might imagine she was merely asleep. Her broken body had already been wrapped in her shroud, only her face remained uncovered. But, as the bile rose into my throat, I couldn't bring myself to do it.

It was so fucking wrong. I swallowed hard, bitterness thrumming through my veins. I had assured her we would keep her safe. Blindly, stupidly, I had believed my own words. *'We have pledged to keep you safe. You need never worry while you are with us.'*

I was an idiot. We knew Corbin was unhinged and a threat to Jeanne, but we had come back to Landévennec anyway, trading our safety and comfort for hers. I reached out a trembling hand and gently ran my finger down her cheek.

"I'm sorry for failing you." A tear dripped off my cheek onto hers. "Your daughter will want for nothing in this life. She will be loved and treasured, and we will tell her all about her wonderful, kind, brave lioness of a mother."

I picked up the edge of her shroud and gently pulled it like a veil over her face. My tears blinding me, I stumbled out of the smokehouse, refusing to glance at the wrapped body of her husband and terrorizer. Jeanne and Corbin would stay here until the ground thawed sufficiently in the spring to bury them. A familiar arm came around me as I tripped over the hem of my gown, and I leaned into Gabriel's warmth, desperately needing his stability as we walked in a stunned silence through snow drifts and towering, snow covered pines, back to Esme and Luc's.

I swiped at my runny nose angrily with my handkerchief, my eyes filling and overflowing in a constant stream of sadness and disbelief. The fire crackled merrily in the hearth, casting a warm glow throughout the small sitting room. The metal edges of the cup I held dug into my fingers punishingly. It shook, the garnet-colored liquid sloshing and threatening to spill as I lifted it to my lips and sipped.

Esme sat across from Gabriel and I, Luc at her side, holding little Margaux protectively against her chest. The infant slept peacefully, unaware that her life had changed forever.

"We'll keep her," she said decisively, pressing a proprietary kiss to the soft, blonde hair on the baby's head. She glanced at Luc, who sat unobtrusively beside her. "Won't we, *mon amour?*"

"Of course," he murmured, adoration shining in his patient, brown gaze as he looked at his diminutive wife.

I thought in grudging admiration that he was wise enough to see that Esme was already in love with the infant.

Sky blue eyes looked apprehensively at me. "You don't mind, do you, Ava?"

I shook my head, dislodging another cascade of tears and pressed my cheek to Gabriel's shoulder. "I know you'll love her like your own. We'll have to find a wet nurse for her though. I imagine Madame Devereux will do for now?"

"Aye." Gabriel's deep voice rumbled through his chest.

"What will we tell the little mite about her parents?" Luc looked at us doubtfully.

"You are her parents now," pointed out Gabriel, shifting and pulling me closer to him on the settee. "You'll tell her of her mother, of course, when she is older. But there is time enough to sort out the details later."

I sat with my legs tucked beneath me, curled up in a chair by the hearth in our bedroom. The coverlet from our bed was draped over my huddled body as I tried to get warm. My book sat unopened on the cherry wood table before me. Every time I had a few spare minutes to myself, Jeanne's face flashed before my eyes. Tears burned my eyes as I thought of how we'd failed her. We should have insisted she learn to defend herself. We'd both known it was a mistake to let her refuse, yet we'd allowed it anyway.

My throat bobbed convulsively as I tried to ignore the tight feeling of suffocation. What had she thought when she'd seen that Corbin had come for her? Had she regretted her decision? What about when he pushed her? Had she seen her daughter's face in her mind's eye as she fell to her death?

Stop.

I had to stop thinking like this. I knew I was spiraling, but I seemed unable to pull myself away from the brink. I caught myself staring out the window at the frosted, snow globe world outside, thinking about Jeanne and Margaux all the time. I laced my trembling fingers together tightly and tried to distract myself.

A wave of dizziness swept over me and I closed my eyes, fighting the nausea. I let a slow breath out through my nose. I had an inkling this time around what the overwhelming exhaustion and unsettled stomach pointed to, but I wasn't ready to come to terms with it. I was too wrapped up in the events of the last weeks to tackle more.

I glanced over my shoulder at the sound of the door opening and smiled in anticipation. Although I knew that Gabriel was equally bothered by Jeanne's death, his presence never ceased to calm me. My smile froze on my face at his ashen expression. I threw off the blanket and leapt to my feet in alarm.

"Gabriel? What's wrong?" My stomach tightened unpleasantly as I hurried to him.

His charcoal eyes were dark with shock as the door swung shut behind him. Clenched in his hand was a crumpled sheet of parchment. Wordlessly, he handed it to me, his gaze begging me to read it. I felt sick as I reached out to take the letter. With my other hand, I grabbed his tightly.

My eyes scanned over the sloppy penmanship; my brow furrowed as I tried to decipher the words through the tear splotches marring the ink.

14th January, 1790
   Monsieur Gabriel Chabot
   Le Vicomte de Landévennec
   Landévennec Château

Gabriel,

Please forgive me for writing you. I didn't know where else to turn, and I knew you would want to know.

God forgive me, Phillipe has been arrested and is being held for trial, for treason. I'm sure it is entirely my fault. I should have listened to him.

He's being held at the local prison in Saint-Denis. Please come with all haste. I do not know whether they will release him or execute him.

Yours,
Charlotte Girard
Château Saint-Denis

The letter escaped my limp fingers, floating down, and coming to a rest on the floor. My eyes searched his out as my arms wrapped around him, offering comfort the only way I knew. Gabriel rested his forehead against mine.

"I'll come with you." The words tumbled out of my mouth. I couldn't let him go alone.

"Are you sure? The weather is terrible for travel." He was being gallant, as always, but I could see the pleading need in his gaze.

"Absolutely. Just the two of us. We'll leave first thing in the morning." In my mind I was already planning what to bring, and what to leave behind.

"It's going to be uncomfortable, *mon cœur.*"

I grimaced. "Aye. I know it will be. But if you think I'm going to send you into the fray alone, you don't know me."

A rueful smile touched the corners of his mouth. "Thank you, *mon amour*. It will be easier to bear with you there."

I hesitated. "Do you think you'll be able to speak to anyone? *Le Roi*?"

He shook his head. "If the situation is what I believe it is, involving the king would only be more detrimental to Phillipe's case. But I will try to talk some sense into them."

I frowned in confusion. "But Phillipe is with the revolutionaries— they don't believe he's with the monarchy?"

"I should have told you, but I didn't want to worry you. I received a letter from him last month. Charlotte has been vocal about supporting the king and queen. She has no concept of repercussions. I suspect that Phillipe has been caught up in her mess somehow."

"Dammit."

"*Oui*. We'll leave at first light. Best get packing." He pressed a light kiss to my lips. "I'll go let everyone know."

I pressed my numb face against Gabriel's back and thanked God that his body gave off so much heat. Without him, I was certain I would have frozen on this hellish trip north. The terrain was unforgiving; roots, stones and holes disguised beneath a thick layer of ice and snow. I knew Gabriel chafed at the slow pace, but he would never trade Automne's safety for a quicker arrival. When the conditions allowed, we galloped, flying over meadows that slumbered beneath the brittle, winter burnt stems and wild grasses.

The decision to leave Armand behind was a difficult one, but I knew we couldn't afford to go in a carriage. It would slow us tremendously, and though it remained unspoken between us, I knew Gabriel was worried we wouldn't arrive in time to speak on Phillipe's behalf. Time was against us on this voyage. We both felt it.

Packing had been rather less of a challenge than I'd imagined. A spare wool gown, shift and stockings for me, along with a handful of toiletries packed in a saddlebag with Gabriel's clothes. Everything else was worn in layers, in a futile attempt to stay warm. Even with our cloaks and furs, the inhospitable temperatures made every hour in the saddle torturous. Still, I refused to complain. I'd demanded to come along, and I'd be damned if I pulled Gabriel's attention away from Phillipe.

We passed through a small town, slowing to a trot to avoid splashing through the mud splattered, icy puddles in the streets. Gabriel looked at me over his shoulder.

"Are you alright, *mon cœur*?"

My grip around his middle tightened. "Fine, my love." I pressed my lips to the rough stubble on his cheek.

"Hungry?" He rummaged in the bag closest to him and produced an apple.

My stomach lurched at the thought of food, but an apple might settle it somewhat. "Thank you."

I plucked it from his palm and forced myself to take a bite as he pulled another out for himself. It crunched as my teeth bit into it, and juice dripped out. I wet my lips, licking the sweet juice off, surprised by the pleasant rush the natural sugar gave me. I'd been feeling out of it and unable to focus since we'd left the *auberge* this morning, and the fruit gave me unexpected energy.

I finished the apple thoughtfully, feeling a renewed sense of purpose as we left the village behind us.

"Have you any of your lemon candies?" I'd found that the citrus calmed my nausea.

Gabriel reached into his pocket and produced two, handing one back to me. "Did you doubt I would?" he asked teasingly.

"No," I admitted. "But I couldn't very well go reaching in your pocket and helping myself."

He cocked an eyebrow at me, as I popped the tangy candy in my mouth. "Oh, I assure you, I wouldn't protest if you did."

I grinned at him, relieved to see him a bit more lighthearted, and spontaneously leaned in to kiss the soft spot under his jaw, beneath his ear.

"I love you," I whispered.

His mouth found mine for a lingering, lemony kiss that left me dizzy again. *"Je t'aime, mon cœur."*

We trudged through the village of Saint-Denis, literally. A blizzard had howled through the region overnight, making the roads impassable. The storm had been chased by a blast of warmer air, making the snow melt rapidly throughout the day. Since night had fallen, the temperature dropped, freezing the slushy puddles into slippery hazards. We were far too close to stop now though, and so, we put our heads down, pulled our hoods and scarves up, and pressed on.

Not too far distant, Phillipe's château loomed over the moonlit, snowy landscape. My shoulders relaxed as we drew steadily closer. We'd spent well over a week on the road. The unceasing travel, poor eating and sleeping, and concern over what we would find when we arrived, had me on the brink of a breakdown. The only thing that kept me together was Gabriel and the knowledge that whatever I was feeling, it was undeniably worse for him.

The château was impressively large, turrets reaching high into the sky, scraping the gray clouds that scuttled across the navy backdrop of the heavens. To see its imposing size, was to understand the scale of Phillipe's family's wealth compared to ours. The high iron gates barred our entrance, shut firmly against visitors or looters. Gabriel pulled back on Automne's reins, halting beneath the stone entrance.

"Chabot for Girard!" he called out loudly.

"Do you suppose anyone is awake?" I asked nervously. It was neigh on midnight and the windows were all dark.

"If not, someone will be momentarily," he replied grimly.

He stood in his stirrups, cupped his hands around his mouth and called again. "Le Vicomte de Landévennec here for le Comte de Saint-Denis!"

He sat and we watched, waiting for the telltale flicker of a candle. Finally, it came, like a firefly winking in the dark. We waited, shivering in the cold, until one of the tall doors opened and a figure holding a lantern hurried down the path toward us.

"Monsieur le Vicomte! We are so glad to see you."

The man fumbled with the keys, eventually finding and inserting the correct one. He pulled one of the gates open, holding the lantern high and letting us pass. Gabriel paused, allowing the man to shut and lock the gates behind us. We came to a stop at the grand stone entrance, and I slid off the horse wearily. My legs were rubbery from fatigue and disuse.

"I'll take your horse to the stables, Monsieur. I've got one of the lads up already. You and your lady go right in."

"Thank you, Tomas." Gabriel removed the saddle bags from Automne and gave me his arm. "Careful on the steps," he murmured to me. "They're treacherous with the ice."

We walked into a gorgeous hall, lit cheerfully with a dozen tapers, banishing the shadows to the corners of the room. The ceiling soared far above us and the walls were hung with warm tapestries depicting hunting scenes. I raised my brows and shot a glance at Gabriel. As welcoming as it was, there was no one in the hall.

Suddenly, a rapid tattoo of footsteps skittered above us, culminating in Charlotte fairly flying down the stairs to launch herself at Gabriel.

"You came!" she screeched, "Oh, *Dieu, merci*, I was worried you wouldn't arrive in time."

Her long hair hung down her back and she was dressed only in her nightgown. My eyebrows shot all the way up to my hairline as I watched Gabriel attempt to extricate himself from her embrace. His gray eyes met mine in helpless discomfort and I had to bite back a chuckle.

Gabriel cleared his throat and gently set her back away from him. "I apologize for the late arrival, Charlotte. We came with all haste. What happened?"

She glanced at me, seemingly just becoming aware of my presence and composed herself, smoothing her hair away from her face and visibly gathering her thoughts.

"Why don't the two of you come into the salon?"

Gabriel sighed. "Charlotte, we appreciate the invitation, but we have traveled ten days to be here. We are filthy, sore and exhausted. Please, just tell us what we are up against, so that I may go to whoever passes for the authorities in these parts first thing tomorrow."

Her lower lip pouted, but the look on Gabriel's face brooked no argument. "I'm sorry. I wasn't thinking. The short version of the story is that I said a lot of things that Phillipe thinks I shouldn't have said. They came for me. Phillipe offered to go in my stead." She closed her eyes, obviously feeling guilty about the turn of events. "He's been in prison ever since. They won't let me see him or buy food or blankets for him." When she lifted her lashes, her eyes glittered with tears. "They already tried him. The execution is set for the day after tomorrow."

Her words hung in air that suddenly seemed too poisonous to breathe.

"*Qu'ils soient tous condamnés à l'enfer,*" muttered Gabriel under his breath. "You're responsible, Charlotte," he said harshly. "You and your hardheaded, petty ways, that Phillipe foolishly allowed. Your brother's blood is on your hands."

She stepped back, shock plain on her face. "How could you—"

"How could you?" He cut her off, scathingly. "I will do everything I can, Charlotte, but you must understand how dire the situation is. I love Phillipe like a brother, but you— all you've done is take advantage of how he dotes on you."

I put my hand on Gabriel's arm tentatively, trying to pull him away from the precipice. I'd known he was upset, but I hadn't realized he was simmering like a volcano on the verge of exploding. Judging from Charlotte's expression, she hadn't anticipated this reaction. In all likelihood, she'd never been spoken to in such a way in her pampered life.

Gabriel took a deep breath. "We'll stay tonight, if we may. I'll go to the prison tomorrow."

Charlotte nodded, looking stunned. "I'll show you to your room." Stiffly, she turned away and led us up the stairs, pausing at the second door on the left. "Please ring if you need anything."

"We will, thank you." I offered her a smile, but she walked away without another word.

I closed the door and pressed my forehead against the smooth wood tiredly. Gabriel's hands settled on my hips, spinning me to face him. My arms slipped around his waist as I stepped into his embrace.

"I shouldn't have lost my temper," he admitted, holding me against his chest.

"No," I agreed. "But she needs a reality check."

"Aye. But it doesn't matter anymore. The damage is done," he said sadly. "Someone should have talked sense into her years ago."

"Perhaps. But that wasn't your place," I pointed out, my voice muffled against him.

His chest rose and fell in a drawn-out breath. "Come to bed, *mon cœur*. I need you."

Forty-Six
Reverberations

We pushed our way to the front of the crowd, Gabriel easily shouldering the jeering townspeople aside as I slipped into the space he created. More than a few dirty looks were leveled at us, but Gabriel was too focused to notice, and the handful of people that spoke up in protest had the sense to shut their mouths after a single glance at his flinty expression. I managed to stay with him only because he held my hand firmly in his.

We arrived as close to the hastily built barricades as possible, pressing forward against the gendarmes that stoically held the mob back. We found ourselves caught between the open space before us that housed the hastily erected platform, and the press of the crowd at our back, eager to catch a glimpse of an aristocrat paying the price of years of inequality with his life. The sick irony was that they had no idea how hard Phillipe had fought for them.

I wanted to shout, *'You are making a mistake! This man is innocent. He fought for you! He believes in your cause.'* But that would be the height of folly. It would do nothing to save Phillipe's life and judging by the mood of the crowd, these people wouldn't hesitate to haul me up to the platform next.

I stole a glance at Gabriel standing beside me. His countenance was the picture of desperation; his face was white, lips pressed together in a thin line, and despite the frigid temperature, a fine sheen of perspiration stood out on his forehead. His steely eyes missed nothing as Phillipe was marched out of the prison flanked on either side by guards.

The mob surged forward, craning their necks and lifting children onto their shoulders to watch as he was marched toward the platform. Phillipe shrugged off the guard's hands on his arms, voluntarily stepping up, and a hush fell over the crowd. I was as silent as the rest while his eyes swept over the motley jumble of people assembled to witness his death, and I caught the moment when his gaze locked on Gabriel's.

A thousand words were exchanged in that moment. Memories, acknowledgment of what might have been and would never be; apologies, regret, grief, forgiveness, and absolution. It was wrenching to witness.

Whatever Phillipe was searching for, he found reassurance in Gabriel's unfaltering gaze. He nodded once, waited for the executioner to tie his blindfold, crossed himself, and knelt before the block. Gabriel squeezed my hand hard as a spasm of agony crossed his face.

I squeezed back, trying to convey all my feelings in that single touch.

"You don't have to watch." My voice was a whisper, lost in the excited hum of the crowd, but somehow, he heard me.

"I cannot prevent this travesty of justice, and I will carry it with me for the rest of my days." His eyes were wide and unflinching as the blade came down. "I'll not have him look death in the eye alone."

It was over in a moment, but I knew in my bones that we would live with the reverberations of today for the rest of our lives.

Also by Veronique Wallrapp

The Rise of the Guillotine Saga

Etched in Stone
Traced in Ash

Thank you, dear reader, for coming along on this ride. I hope you laughed and cried as much as I did.
If so, please take a moment to post a review and tell a friend.

Follow along on Instagram for more from Veronique Wallrapp
@VeroniqueWallrappAuthor

Acknowledgements

With immense appreciation,
 Thank you to...

...Sienna, Logan, Ethan, and Emmeline, my personal little book dragons. Watching you all learn to love reading is the greatest gift.

...My parents and siblings, Clarisa, Albert, Jean-Paul and Noelle: For the unswerving love and support. I can never tell you all how much it means to have you in my corner.

...My amazing in-laws. You all sure know how to make a girl feel special. Thank you all for the endless support.

...My incredible husband Stephen, who surely didn't understand what he was signing up for when he suggested I begin writing again, but has supported me wholeheartedly, nonetheless. With every beat of my heart, I love you.

Made in the USA
Middletown, DE
24 May 2025